SHERRYL WOODS

Driftwood Cottage

Recycling programs for this product may not exist in your area.

ISBN-13: 978-0-7783-2947-3

DRIFTWOOD COTTAGE

For questions and comments about the quality of this book please contact us at Customer_eCare@Harlequin.ca.

www.MIRABooks.com

Printed in U.S.A.

Dear Reader,

Welcome back to Chesapeake Shores!

Connor O'Brien, who's been living in Baltimore, is probably the least well-known of the siblings in this large, dysfunctional family. In some ways, though, he's the son who's most embittered by his parents' divorce and the least likely to walk willingly into marriage. And yet Connor's love for Heather Donovan and the son they share runs deep. He's devastated when she calls off their relationship, no longer able to pretend that their halfhearted arrangement is enough. Heather wants it all—the vows, the ring, the piece of paper legally binding them together.

Only when an accident nearly claims her life does Connor realize that a future that doesn't include Heather is no future at all. But ironically, after all the years of declaring his distrust of marriage, Heather doesn't believe his sudden turnaround. Or does she have issues of her own, after all?

I hope you'll enjoy the ride as these two struggle to find their way toward happiness—of course with all those meddling O'Briens around to nudge them determinedly in the right direction.

And next month, at last, not only Jess but Uncle Thomas will each find the love of their life. There are hints about that in this book, but, as always, it will take some serious prodding for true love to triumph. What's the fun of a happy ending if there haven't been a few roadblocks along the way? Enjoy!

All best,

Sherryl

1

Heather Donovan propped open the front door and stood just inside the brightly lit storefront in Chesapeake Shores so she could inhale the scent of sea air from the bay across Shore Road. Turning slowly, she studied the stacks of colorful fabric bolts that had to be sorted and displayed, the unopened boxes of quilting supplies and the quilt racks that still required assembly. Her pride and joy, the carefully crafted shelving units, had been built to her specifications by her son's grandfather, famed architect Mick O'Brien, for whom her son, little Mick, was named.

Seeing it all coming together was a little overwhelming. Not just opening a business, but all of it—moving to this quaint town, deciding to raise her son on her own, giving up on a future with Connor O'Brien—these were all huge steps. Her mind still reeled when she thought about the recent changes in her life. She might embrace the changes, but that didn't mean she wasn't scared to death.

If anyone had told her a few months ago that she would leave the man she loved more than anything, that she would take their son and move from Baltimore to a small seaside town and embark on a whole new career, Heather would have laughed at the absurdity of the predictions. Even though Connor stubbornly had refused to consider marriage, she'd thought they had a good life, that they were committed to one another. She'd believed that so strongly that she'd ignored her parents'—actually it had been mostly her mother's—warnings about the mistake she was making by having a child with Connor without a ring on her finger.

But, in fact, they—she, Connor and their son—might have gone on exactly like that for years if she hadn't seen how Connor's career as a divorce lawyer was chipping away at their relationship, how his anger at his parents was corrupting their day-to-day lives. She didn't like the embittered man she'd seen him becoming, and he seemed to have no desire to change.

It wasn't as if she'd made her decision to break up lightly. She'd gone away for several weeks, leaving their son with Connor's family while she'd pondered what was best for her future and for her child's. She hadn't been happy about the conclusion she'd reached, that she needed to start a new life on her own, but she'd made peace with it. And, in time, she knew she'd find the fulfillment that had eluded her with Connor.

Not that she could envision a day when she'd stop loving him, she thought even now, months after making the decision. She sighed at how difficult it sometimes was to reconcile emotions with common sense and facing reality, especially with a precious little boy as a constant reminder of what she'd given up.

A bell over the shop's front door tinkled merrily, interrupting her thoughts. Megan O'Brien stepped inside, carrying her grandson who beamed at the sight of Heather.

"Mama!" he cried, holding out his chubby little arms. Just over a year old now, he was the joy of Heather's life.

"He was missing you," Megan explained, then gave her a commiserating look. "And I thought you might be needing a glimpse of him about now. I know you're still not over all those weeks the two of you spent apart."

"Thank you," Heather said, reaching for her son.

"Feeling overwhelmed?" Megan asked with the kind of insight that Heather had come to treasure.

So many times in the past few months she'd regretted that Megan wouldn't be her mother-in-law. In many ways Heather felt closer to Connor's mother than she did to her own mother back in Ohio. A wonderful salt-of-the-earth woman who went to church on Sundays, volunteered at a homeless shelter and in a children's hospital, Bridget Donovan had an endless store of compassion for everyone except her own daughter. She flatly refused to accept that any daughter of hers would willingly choose not to marry the father of her child.

Heather sighed. As if marriage to Connor had ever been an option, no matter how desperately she might have hoped for it.

Heather bounced baby Mick in her arms as she nodded in response to Megan's question. "You're right about feeling overwhelmed," she said, gesturing around the store. "I have no idea where to start. What if opening a shop, especially here, is a huge mistake? I don't know anything about running a business. And being here, in this town, surrounded by O'Briens, what was I thinking? Why on earth did I let you talk me into this?"

"Because you knew it was a brilliant idea," Megan said at once, obviously still pleased with herself for coming up with this solution for Heather's future.

"Still, doubts are understandable," she consoled Heather. "You've made a lot of changes recently. All good ones, I think. As for starting your own business, this is a natural fit for you. The minute I saw those handmade quilts of yours, I knew it. You do absolutely beautiful work. Everyone in town is going to want to own one of your quilts or have you teach them how to make their own."

Megan fingered a small folk art quilt of a bay scene as she spoke. "This one, for instance, is a treasure. How can you bear to part with it? And at this price? It needs to cost twice as much."

"The price is fine. I was just experimenting," Heather said modestly, still astonished that anyone thought her hobby could turn into a thriving business. She had always enjoyed quilting, and it had filled the quiet evenings while Connor studied. She'd never envisioned it as anything more than a hobby.

In fact, her college degree had been in literature. She'd never quite figured out what to do with that besides teach. After two years in an out-of-control Baltimore high school classroom, she'd gratefully quit when she'd become pregnant with Connor's baby.

She gestured to the quilt Megan was admiring. "If you aren't just saying that to calm me down, if you really like it, I'll make one for you."

Megan's eyes brightened. "I'd love it, but I will pay you

for it, and I swear I'm going to talk you into doubling the price."

"Absolutely not."

"Well, that's what I'm paying," Megan countered just as stubbornly. "You've a business to run, after all."

Heather sighed. "Starting a business is just one of my concerns these days," she admitted. "What about moving out on Connor? Was that the right decision, Megan?" She couldn't seem to keep a wistful note out of her voice.

"Even that," Megan assured her. "My son is stubborn, and you've given him exactly the wake-up call he needed." She patted Heather's hand. "He loves you. Just tuck that knowledge away. He'll come around if you're patient."

"For how long?" Heather asked. "We met our freshman year in college, dated for four years, moved in together when he was in law school. When I found out I was pregnant, I was so sure we'd get married, especially when he encouraged me to quit my job to be a full-time mom. I was certain we were finally going to be a real family, the kind I'd always wanted. He even said that's what he wanted, too, just without a marriage license."

She waved off her regrets. "I should have known better than to expect him to change his mind. Connor always told me he had no intention of ever marrying, that he didn't believe in marriage. It's not as if I didn't understand the rules from the very beginning."

"People don't make rules about things like that," Megan said dismissively. "They just let the past control the future. In Connor's case, his attitude is all because of what happened between his father and me. Now that Mick and I have remarried and started over, I'm convinced

Connor will see that love can endure all kinds of trials, including divorce."

Heather smiled at her optimism. "Have you met Connor? He's stubborn as a mule. Once he gets an idea into his head, he won't let go of it. And look how long it's been since I moved out. It was last Thanksgiving when I left to think things over, January when I officially left him. It'll be Easter soon, and he still hasn't shown any signs of changing his mind. He may not be entirely happy that I'm gone, but he's not doing anything at all to change the situation."

Megan grinned. "I'm married to a man just like that, his father. Believe me, there are ways of getting through to their hard heads." She glanced pointedly at the boy in Heather's arms. "And you've your ace in the hole right there. Connor adores his son."

Heather shook her head. "A couple can't build a future around a child. It's not fair. My parents did that. They stayed in a miserable marriage because of me. They thought it would be best, but it wasn't. The tension was unbearable. I won't have that for my son."

"I'm not suggesting that you be together for your child, only that he'll keep you in Connor's orbit while he gets his feet back under him and realizes how much he loves you both. Having you with him was entirely too comfortable. He had it all his own way. The stance you've taken is the smart one. Eventually he'll realize what he needs to do to have the two of you back again."

"I hope you're right," Heather admitted, though she wasn't counting on it. In fact, if things didn't work out with Connor, it could make her decision to move to Chesapeake Shores where she'd be surrounded by his family the worst one she'd made in years. The O'Briens might provide an enviable support system, but she'd be reminded of what could have been every minute of every day.

"Of course I'm right," Megan said confidently. "Now tell me what I can do to help you get organized in here. Do you have a system?"

Even to her own ears, Heather's laugh had an edge of hysteria about it. "If only," she said, glancing around at the chaos. She regarded Megan hopefully. "Are you sure you have some time to spare?"

"Of course I do. At Mick's insistence, I've hired a very competent assistant at the gallery, and things are under control. In the meantime, I'll let her know I'll be right next door if she needs me," she said, flipping open her cell phone. When she'd made the call, she told Heather, "Now, just put me to work."

Heather didn't hesitate. "If you could start opening those boxes, I could begin sorting the fabric for the displays," she suggested, settling Mick into the playpen she'd already set up in a corner. He uttered an immediate howl of protest, then spotted one of his favorite toys and was quickly absorbed with that.

Heather and Megan worked in companionable silence for a while before Megan inquired, "Have you told Connor about the shop yet? He didn't mention it last time we spoke and I certainly didn't want to be the one to fill him in."

Heather stiffened. "It hasn't come up. Truthfully, we barely exchange a dozen words when I drop Mick off to spend the day with him. I haven't even told him I've moved here. He reaches me on my cell phone when he needs to, so it's not as if it really matters where I've settled. I suppose if I'd run off to California, he might have a legitimate complaint, but I'm barely an hour away. Nothing's changed in terms of his schedule to see little Mick."

Megan looked distressed by her response. "Oh, Heather, you need to tell him," she said. "And you need to do it before he comes home for a visit and discovers it for himself or before someone else in the family blabs. He'll be furious that you've kept it from him."

Heather shrugged. "It'll just be one more thing to add to the list. He's already angry that I refused to move back in. To be honest, he wasn't all that happy when I insisted on keeping little Mick with me after I'd left him here with you while I was trying to sort through things and get my head on straight. He apparently thought the arrangement was going to be permanent."

"There's no question that he liked having the baby here with him and the rest of the family," Megan acknowledged. "We all did. But I think everyone except Connor understood it was only temporary."

Heather regarded her with sorrow. "Sometimes I think I'm destined to keep making things worse between Connor and me. If we talk at all, we're at odds over everything."

Megan smiled at that. "It's only awkward right now because you won't give him what he wants—an unconditional commitment that doesn't include marriage. He has to learn that he can't always have things on his own terms."

"But aren't I doing the same thing, expecting to have things on *my* terms?" Heather asked.

Megan regarded her thoughtfully. "I suppose that's

true. Maybe it's just because I think you're the one who's right that I'm not blaming any of this standoff on you. I think two people who love each other and have a child together ought to at least try marriage, that they ought to be fighting to make it work."

She sighed. "Goodness knows, I spent years trying to make things work with Mick before I took the drastic step of leaving. Even in hindsight, I don't think I had a choice by then, though I know I should have handled things differently and much better where all of our children were concerned. I still regret that, and I'd never have forgiven myself if I'd simply run at the first sign of trouble, rather than leaving as a last resort."

Heather grinned at her. "But here you are, together again. Happy endings still happen. Why can't Connor see that, especially when it's right in front of his face?"

"I fear it's because he doesn't have a romantic bone in his body," Megan replied sorrowfully. "He's become cynical when it comes to love. Mick and I did that to him, and that job of his—dealing with bitter divorces every single day—has reaffirmed his jaded views."

"Then what makes you think he'll ever come around?" Heather asked.

"Because I *am* a romantic," Megan said, smiling. "I believe in the power of love. And I know how deeply he cares about the people he has let into his heart—his sisters and his brother, his grandmother, even Mick when they're not battling over one thing or another."

"I saw that side of him, too, or thought I did," Heather said softly, though her voice lacked the conviction of Megan's.

"Then don't give up on Connor," Megan advised. "He'll find his way back to you. I believe that, too."

As much as she admired the older woman and respected her opinions, Heather wished she could share Megan's faith where Connor was concerned. So far she hadn't seen even the tiniest chink in his well-established armor. He was dead-set against letting emotion overrule his very stubborn head, at least when it came to her.

Connor stood in the middle of his townhouse in Baltimore and wondered why it no longer felt like home. The furniture he and Heather had chosen was still in place. She'd taken nothing when she left, and yet without her the place felt empty. The kitchen cupboards were filled with dishes, the refrigerator stocked with food, albeit mostly of the frozen variety. In fact, despite her departure several months ago, Heather's touch was everywhere, right down to the framed photos of his son scattered over just about every surface.

Heather's glowing face beamed back at him from many of them, as well. It always made his heart catch when he caught an unexpected glimpse of her. She was the most beautiful woman he'd ever known, inside and out. Most people saw the shining blond hair, hazel eyes and delicate features and focused on those, but he knew she had the most generous heart on earth. She'd put up with him long enough to prove she was a saint.

And then she'd gone. Just like that, on Thanksgiving Day while he'd been out nursing his wounds over a glass of Irish whisky with a couple of buddies, decrying his parents' plan to remarry, Heather had packed up their son and left. To add to his dismay, she'd dropped the baby off on his parents' doorstep, dragging both Mick and Megan into the middle of the drama. Connor wasn't sure he'd ever be able to forgive her for that.

Disgruntled just by the thought of the humiliation he'd felt having to go home to Chesapeake Shores and explain himself to the mother from whom he'd been estranged for years, he poured himself another glass of Irish whisky. He went into his office hoping to push all of his sour thoughts out of his head and get some work done. Before he could cross the room, though, the doorbell rang. He opened it to find his brother Kevin standing there.

"This is an unexpected surprise," Connor said, regarding Kevin warily. His brother wasn't in the habit of dropping in. The last time he had, he'd found a very pregnant Heather on the scene and nearly been struck dumb by the awkward moment. He'd mostly stayed away since.

"You feel like some company?" Kevin inquired, moving aside to reveal two of their oldest friends, Will and Mack, along with Connor's brothers-in-law, Trace Riley and Jake Collins.

Connor scowled, his worst fears confirmed. They were here on some kind of mission. It was anyone's guess who'd put them up to it. His money was on his father.

"And if I don't?" he asked.

"Hey, Baltimore's a big city. I'm sure we can find someplace else to hang out," Jake said. "I'm not wasting this chance for a guys' night. The only reason your sister let me out of our regular date night is because Kevin told her we were coming to see you."

Connor stared at Jake incredulously. "You let Bree tell you what you can and can't do? Come on, man, that's just pitiful." It reaffirmed his low opinion of marriage as well, even if they were talking about his sister.

Jake grinned. "I let her think that's how it works," he corrected. "And, to be perfectly honest, this date night idea of hers has some amazing benefits, or at least it did until she got so pregnant she can barely move. She blames the huge belly, the baby's constant kicking and the swollen ankles all on me. These days I can pretty much forget about sex."

Connor clapped his hands over his ears. "Too much information," he protested. He turned to Trace. "And Abby? Does she have to give you permission to go out with the guys?"

"No way," Trace said forcefully. "However, it helps that she's staying in Baltimore tonight herself because of work, so the subject didn't really come up."

"What did you do with the twins?" Connor asked, referring to Abby's very precocious daughters who were now nine-going-on-nineteen. "They're a little young to be left on their own."

"They're staying with Grandma Megan and Grandpa Mick," Trace said. "The only drawback is that tomorrow I will once again have to explain that ice cream and candy are not the two most important food groups. I'll have to try to convince them of that before Mommy gets home."

"You two do have your trials, don't you?" Connor said to his brothers-in-law with amusement. "You're not exactly walking endorsements for marriage."

Trace and Jake exchanged a worried look that said it all. Obviously at least some part of their mission was to convince him what a mess he was making of things with Heather.

Still, since the men were on his doorstep and he was in desperate need of company, Connor stepped aside to let them enter. "I don't suppose any of you thought to bring food, did you? I have a freezer full of frozen dinners, but that's about it."

"Mack has the closest pizza place on speed dial," Kevin assured him. "His cell phone allows him to find that in any city in the country. He may be lonely, but he'll never starve."

"I'm not all that lonely," Mack retorted.

"Even though he still claims he's not dating your cousin Susie, they seem to spend every spare minute together," Will taunted. "I'm thinking of writing some kind of case study for a psychology journal on the whole phenomenon of delusional nondating."

"Bite me," Mack replied cheerfully, then took out his phone. "Pizza okay for everyone?"

"Works for me," Connor said, then looked pointedly at his unexpected guests. "As long as it doesn't come with a side order of meddling."

"Absolutely not," Kevin said solemnly.

"Agreed," Trace said.

"No meddling with dinner," Will said, then grinned. "We're saving that for dessert."

"How'd things go with Heather today?" Mick asked Megan when they met for dinner at one of the small cafés along Shore Road in the same block as her gallery.

"She's getting settled in," Megan told him. "I think her business is going to be wildly successful. She showed me her apartment upstairs today, too, and it's adorable, just right for her and little Mick."

"I still don't understand why she wouldn't move into the house with us," Mick grumbled. "Little Mick's already comfortable there. We have plenty of room."

"And it would put the two of them right in Connor's face every time he comes home," Megan said. "Is that what you were hoping for?"

"Well, why not?" Mick replied testily. "If those two would spend a little more time together, they could work things out. You know it as well as I do."

"I also know they can't be rushed. Time apart may be the best thing for them right now."

Mick regarded his wife with amusement. "Don't act as if you're not doing your share of manipulating, woman. I know all about the way you put a bug in Kevin's ear to spend some time with Connor tonight. The way I hear it, he, Jake, Trace, Will and Mack have all been dispatched to Connor's place to extol the joys of married life."

Megan regarded him innocently. "Will and Mack aren't married."

"Maybe not, but Will's a shrink, so he has all sorts of insights to offer, I'm sure. As for Mack, he might as well be, for all the time he's spending with Susie these days." He shook his head in bewilderment. "I have no idea why my brother hasn't stepped in and taken control of that situation. It's time for Mack to get off the dime and propose to that girl, or at least admit he's dating her."

"Your brother is not the natural-born meddler that you are," Megan reminded him. "I'm sure Susie and Mack are very grateful for that."

"There you go, sounding all superior again, when I

know for a fact you're every bit the meddler that I am," Mick accused.

Megan laughed. "What can I say? I want all of our children to be as happy and settled as we are."

Mick studied her face, looking for any sign of discontent. After missing too many hints of unhappiness during their first marriage, he was determined to be attuned to every nuance of their relationship this time around.

"You mean that?" he asked directly. "You're happy?"

"Of course I am. I have everything I could possibly want. You and I are back together. I've opened a business I love, and it's gotten off to a solid start. And my relationship with each of our children is getting stronger every day. What could I possibly have to complain about?"

"Maybe the fact that you never did get that honeymoon I promised you," Mick suggested.

Megan shrugged as if having the honeymoon of her dreams was of no consequence, even though they'd only been able to afford a trip to Ocean City for a weekend when they'd first wed all those years ago.

"That's my own fault, not yours," she told him. "Everything started coming together for the gallery right after the first of the year. There was no time to get away."

"And now?" he asked. "You think you could spare a little time for me?"

"The gallery's opened. My assistant's trained. I suppose I could get away," she said thoughtfully, then met his gaze with a sparkle in her eyes. "I'm quite sure that wasn't an idle question, Mick O'Brien. What did you have in mind?"

"A week in Paris," he said at once. He pulled two tickets out of his pocket and set them on the table. "And before you get all worked up over me being presumptuous, note that they don't have a date on them. We can go whenever you say the word."

Megan reached for his hand. "Who could have imagined that you could still learn a thing or two at this late date?"

He laughed at that. "When the motivation's powerful enough, a man can always learn something new. I hope Connor figures that out before it's too late."

Megan's previously lighthearted mood visibly darkened at his words. "Oh, Mick, I hope so, too, but there's only so much you and I can do to make sure that happens. The rest is up to him and Heather."

Mick knew that, but nevertheless it went against the grain to leave something so important to chance.

"You won't object if I do a thing or two to nudge things along, will you?" he asked.

She gave him a stern look. "Nudge all you want, but pay attention to the signs, Mick. When they're all but shouting to back off, do it. I mean that." She grinned at him. "And something tells me this is definitely an ideal time for me to get you out of town before you do something we'll both regret. Make those reservations for Paris. I'll try to keep you preoccupied over there, so Connor and Heather can have a little breathing room back here."

"A sneaky approach," he said approvingly, "but you're forgetting one thing."

"What's that?"

"I'm great at multitasking."

Megan met his gaze, laughter lurking in her eyes. "Is that so?" she inquired softly as she deliberately ran her hand along the inside of his thigh. "Do you really want to bet that I can't make you forget all about Chesapeake Shores, much less meddling?"

Mick swallowed hard. Sadly, she had a point. The good news was that they were going to have one helluva time while she set out to prove it.

2

The combined efforts of the men in his family and his friends convinced Connor to make the drive to Chesapeake Shores on Saturday. He hadn't been home since his parents' wedding on New Year's Eve. Though he'd made his peace with both Mick and even Megan, things seemed to go better between them when he kept his distance. Their capacity for meddling was beyond his for resisting. They'd made their opinions of his relationship with Heather crystal clear.

The drive home had been pleasant for a change. Although the weather was especially mild for late March, it was too early for most of the tourists and weekenders who flocked to the small towns on the Chesapeake Bay later in the season.

Arriving in Chesapeake Shores to discover all the hints that spring was just around the corner, he realized how much he missed being home. This time of year the town green was edged with beds of daffodils, the salty air of the bay beckoned and there was something special about the way the morning sun filtered through a haze and sparkled on the dew that covered the fresh green lawns.

With temperatures hovering close to seventy, he actually had visions of taking his old rowboat out for a lazy day of fishing. Maybe he could even convince Kevin to come along. It had been ages since they'd spent an idle day out on the water together.

Before heading toward home, he made the drive along Main Street, then turned right onto Shore Road. It was practically a ritual to take a tour of the town his father and uncles had built, to see what was happening. There were always one or two changes that caught him by surprise, especially in spring, when most new businesses chose to open in time for the summer tourist season.

He spotted the "Open" flag fluttering outside his mother's new art gallery and resolved to make his duty call there later in the day, since he'd missed the official opening. He was anxious to see if she was as knowledgeable about art as his father and the rest of the family seemed to think she was.

Before he drove on, Connor caught a glimpse of another new store right next door. A beautiful handmade quilt hung in the window, a quilt, he realized with a sense of shock, that looked very familiar because it—or one exactly like it—had once hung on the wall in his townhouse. It was the one thing that had gone missing after Heather's departure.

Slamming on the brakes, he looked around until he spotted a parking place up the street. He swung into it, then tried to still the sudden racing of his heart. He knew that quilt because Heather had made it. He'd watched her in the evenings as she'd stitched every seam, quilted every square, while he'd been studying for his law school classes. He'd been captivated by the contentment on her face as she'd worked quietly, happy just to be in a room with him.

Spotting that quilt in a store window shouldn't throw him like this, he thought as he strode across the street. It shouldn't matter to him that she'd apparently put it up for sale. But it did.

It offended him to think that maybe she was giving it up because she needed cash. How much could a quilt bring in, anyway? He thought he'd been giving her generous support money for their son, enough for both of them really, but maybe it wasn't covering expenses, after all. He knew, though, from their heated exchanges, that she was too proud to take more.

Worse, of course, was the idea that she was selling the quilt because she couldn't bear to look at it anymore, because it reminded her of him. Had she grown to hate him so much? It was true that most of their conversations recently had been brief and edgy, but he'd convinced himself they'd eventually move past the cool civility of late. Maybe that was just another of his many delusions where Heather was concerned, right up there beside the idea that she would change her mind and move back home with him.

He glanced at the sign on the window, which he hadn't noticed earlier: COTTAGE QUILTS. For some reason that struck a distant chord as well. Had Heather ever mentioned opening a shop like this one? Was it one of the dreams she'd had before setting them aside to be with him? He'd known how much she'd hated teaching, but he couldn't recall what she'd hoped to do instead once the baby was a bit older. That just reminded him of how many conversations they'd avoided over their years together. Anything involving the future had presented a minefield.

Just then he saw and heard her, Heather, standing amid a sea of fabric with a customer, talking animatedly about which colors worked well together and which ones clashed. With a sense of shock, he realized that not only was her quilt for sale, but that she was working here. How had that happened? Filled with questions, he stood where he was, just outside the open door, and waited.

When the customer left with a heavy bag filled with fabric, Connor stepped inside. Heather looked up, a smile on her face that faltered at the sight of him.

"Connor," she said, a catch in her voice. "I wasn't expecting to see you here."

"Chesapeake Shores is my home," he reminded her, his own tone testy. "What the devil are you doing here?"

She gestured around her. "What does it look like? I've opened a business."

A thousand questions came to mind, but he blurted only one. "This is yours?"

She nodded, her expression defensive.

"You opened a business here? In my town?" he said incredulously.

She smiled at his reaction. "Actually if the town belongs to any one person, it would be your father, but I'm pretty sure it's open to new residents."

"You didn't think you needed to tell me you'd moved here?"

"I would have as soon as we got settled. Getting this place open has taken a lot of my time."

"Don't tell me you're living with my folks," he said, regarding her with suspicion, already sensing a plot afoot to throw them together. After all, wasn't that exactly what his mother had hinted at her wedding, that she intended to see that he was next to walk down the aisle? And it would definitely explain the unexpected visit by all the men in the family the previous weekend and their push to drag him down here.

"No. Believe me, I know that would have been a bad idea. I have my own apartment upstairs. Your mother and I…"

He frowned at the mention of his mother. "What does my mother have to do with this? Was it her idea?"

"In a way, yes," Heather admitted at once.

"And you went along with it," he said with a dismayed shake of his head. "Haven't I told you she can't be trusted?"

Heather visibly stiffened. "You told me a lot of things, Connor, all probably valid from your perspective, but I prefer to form my own opinions of people. I happen to like your mother, and even you have to admit she's been a godsend in recent months, looking after little Mick."

Connor bristled. "That still doesn't mean you should take her advice. Did she tell you if you settled here, eventually I'd cave in and marry you?"

Heather frowned at him. "Trust me, I know your position on marriage, Connor. You've stated it often enough and in no uncertain terms. It's ingrained in my head."

"Then what are you doing here?" he asked again, genuinely bewildered about why she'd pick this town if not because it was his hometown.

"This decision was all about me and what I want for my future. Your mother saw my quilts and thought I had talent. When I was here for the wedding, she mentioned this space and the apartment upstairs. It seemed ideal for me, especially since it meant our son would get to be around his grandparents, aunts, uncles and cousins. It was a far better option than going back to Ohio to be around my family, as I'm sure you can imagine."

As rational as all that sounded, Connor couldn't get over the fact that she'd kept this from him. "We've seen each other at least a half-dozen times since the wedding when you brought little Mick to spend the day with me, yet you never said a word about any of this. Why not?"

"You've always known exactly how to reach me on my cell phone. You haven't missed a minute with your son. I didn't think you'd be interested in knowing where I'm living," she said with a shrug.

"Of course I'm interested. We're talking about my son!" he said, his voice climbing.

He saw a bit of light die in her eyes at his words and knew he'd said exactly the wrong thing. It was a habit he'd inadvertently gotten into and couldn't seem to break. When he should have been telling Heather he missed her, he couldn't seem to choke out the words. The admission would have revealed a vulnerability he wasn't prepared for her to see.

"Nothing's changed where little Mick's concerned," Heather assured him, her voice tight. "You'll still see him whenever you want to. This might not be as convenient as having us in Baltimore, but we're hardly at the ends of the earth. Besides, other than giving him a chance to get to know his family, this move wasn't about him, either. It was about me, and it's been clear for some time now that I don't matter to you. It was past time for a fresh start. Chesapeake Shores had a lot of advantages that other places wouldn't have had. I'm sure even you can't deny that."

He understood why she thought she didn't matter to him, but it annoyed him just the same. "Don't be ridiculous. I love you. We have a son together. And what kind of fresh start is it, if you're surrounded by *my* family?"

"This is where I need to be right now. Deal with it," she said.

Her tone was surprisingly unyielding. What had happened to the accommodating woman he'd known so well? Before he could ask, she held up her hand to stop him.

"I am not having this discussion here, where a customer could come in at any moment," she said firmly. "Please go, Connor. If you want to spend some time with your son today, he's with your dad. I think Mick planned to take advantage of the weather and take him and his cousins Davy and Henry out on the dock by the house to fish."

Connor wanted to stand here and argue with her, tell her that moving here, getting close to his family was a mistake, but he didn't have the right. His stubborn refusal to take the next step and marry her had cost him the chance to have any say over her decisions beyond those directly related to their son. And how could he possibly argue that a place as serene as Chesapeake Shores with his own family all around was anything other than a perfect place to raise a child? He dropped the argument.

"Will I see you at the house later?" he asked.

"I doubt it. Shanna will bring little Mick home when she picks up Davy and Henry."

"Tomorrow?" he pressed, not sure why he wanted to

know just how deeply she'd insinuated herself into his family's routines. "Will you be at Sunday dinner?"

She held his gaze. "Will it bother you if I am?"

"Of course not," he said, managing to utter the lie despite a boatload of regrets. Seeing her, knowing he'd lost her, was some kind of sweet torture.

"Then we'll see you there. Maybe we'll have a chance to talk about how we're going to make this work." She gave him a hesitant smile. "Connor, I don't want it to be awkward every time we run into each other. I really don't."

He sighed. "Neither do I."

He just wasn't sure it was possible to act as if everything between them had never mattered. Because the truth was, he'd realized months ago that she and his son were the *only* things in his life that did matter. He just didn't see any way to hold on to them without betraying his core belief that most marriages were a sham and led, not to happily-ever-after but to misery.

Back at the house his father had built when he was first developing Chesapeake Shores, Connor paused long enough to throw his bag into his boyhood room, which still had his old sports posters on the walls. In the kitchen he grabbed a handful of Gram's cookies, relieved to find that she hadn't stopped baking, even though everyone, including her, had moved out of the main house, leaving it to his father and mother. Apparently Gram still made sure the cookie jar was stocked for visits by all of her great-grandchildren.

Crossing the wide expanse of lawn toward the bay, he could hear the laughter of children coming from the dock, followed by the low, surprisingly patient voice of his father. Stepping out onto the weathered gray boards, warmed by the midday sun, Connor stood unnoticed as his father baited hooks and helped his three grandsons cast their lines, one arm firmly around little Mick at all times. Only Henry and Davy had any real hope of reeling in a fish, but even from his spot in his grandfather's lap, little Mick dangled his line into the calm waters of the bay, chattering happily to himself in nonsensical words, to which Mick replied as if he could understand him perfectly.

"I wish I had a camera," Connor said quietly, causing Mick to glance up with a broad smile. "I can't recall a time you ever spent the day fishing with me and Kevin."

Mick's smile faded at the barb. "You're probably right. And it was my loss. I thank God every day that I have another chance with these boys."

Up until now Davy and Henry had been totally absorbed with watching the water for some evidence that fish were nearby. When they looked up and spotted Connor, grins broke across their faces. Here was the uncle who was more grown-up playmate than authority figure.

"Uncle Connor, sit with us," Davy pleaded. "You can put the worms on my line."

"Big boys put their own bait on the hooks," Mick told him firmly. "I just showed you how to do it."

Davy wrinkled his nose. "But it's yucky."

Connor grinned. "That it is. Give me a minute with your granddad and little Mick, then I'll come help you."

While listening to the exchange, Mick studied Connor

curiously. "What brings you home? Were we expecting you?"

"Do I need to make a reservation these days?" Connor asked defensively. For a time he'd been banished from his home for trying to interfere in his father's plan to wed his mother again, but he'd thought his exile was in the past. In fact, he'd even moved in for a time when Heather had left his son here for several weeks. He'd commuted to work in Baltimore during that time.

"Of course you don't need a reservation," Mick said impatiently. "You just haven't come back here since the wedding. Or should I say since Heather took your boy to be with her?"

"I was persuaded that I was overdue for a visit," Connor admitted wryly.

Mick chuckled. "Then the mission was a success. You can thank your mother for pulling that together."

Connor frowned. "Mom sent Kevin and the others to Baltimore? I'd figured *you* were behind it."

"Not this time. It was your mother who planted a few seeds here and there," Mick admitted.

"I suppose it was all about getting me down here so I could discover that Heather's living in town with my son."

"Wouldn't surprise me," Mick agreed.

Connor directed a sour look at his father. "It's not going to work, you know."

Mick reached over to put another worm on Davy's hook when he saw the boy struggling with it, then glanced up at Connor. "What's not going to work?"

"Throwing Heather and me together. We're not getting married."

Mick shrugged. "Up to you, though it seems a shame for this boy of yours not to have a full-time daddy in his life." He frowned at Connor. "And before you say a word, I may have been gone too much, but I was a full-time father, and all of you knew it."

Back on the defensive, Connor said, "My son knows I love him."

"How's he supposed to know a thing like that when he never sees you?"

"I see him all the time," Connor said. "Heather brought him for a visit just last week."

"For an hour or two, I'll bet," Mick scoffed. "What kind of parenting is that?"

"He's little more than a year old," Connor protested. "Right now he needs his mother more than he needs me. When he's a little older, he'll spend more time with me."

"And he'll still grow up to complain that he hardly knew his daddy," Mick said, then held up a hand to forestall Connor's retort. "Pot calling the kettle black, I know, but that makes me the voice of experience. Don't let these precious years pass by without being a part of them. Learn from my mistakes."

Connor considered another quick, heated comeback, but instead dropped down onto the dock next to little Mick. "Hey, buddy, catch anything?"

His son gave him a wide grin and happily waved his tiny fishing rod in the air. He crawled off Mick's lap to lean into Connor's side, snuggling close, and reminding Connor in ways that Mick's words never could, of just what his stubbornness was costing him.

* * *

When the quilt shop had emptied of customers around lunchtime, Heather called next door and reached Megan. "Do you have a minute?"

"Jane's about to go pick up a couple of sandwiches, so I can't leave just now. What's going on?"

"Could you just meet me out front? We'll both be able to see if any customers come this way."

"Sure. Do you want Jane to bring back something for you, too?"

Food was the last thing on Heather's mind. All she'd been able to think about for the past hour was Connor's unexpected appearance earlier.

"If she's going to Sally's, have her bring me back a tuna fish sandwich on a croissant," she said eventually. "I'll bring the money outside with me now."

"Will do. See you in a minute," Megan promised.

One of the improvements the town had made along Main Street and Shore Road had been to add benches in front of many of the shops. It allowed weary shoppers to rest for a few minutes, but even more essential, it allowed bored husbands to relax outside, instead of pacing around casting daunting looks that cut short their wives' shopping sprees.

Though the sun was warm, the breeze off the bay was cool. Heather pulled on a sweater, then sat outside to wait for Megan. When Connor's mother joined her, she sighed as she sat down.

"This feels so good," Megan said. "I've been on my feet all morning. I shouldn't complain, because that means business has been good. How about you? Were you busy?"

"Swamped," Heather said. "Mostly lookers, but I did have a couple of nice sales."

Megan regarded her intently. "Then why don't you look happier?"

"Connor's here," she announced, watching Megan closely for a reaction.

"Really? He didn't let any of us know he was coming."

"But you knew he might be coming home, didn't you? You don't sound all that surprised."

Megan shrugged. "I hoped he'd be home soon, of course, but I didn't know his plans."

Heather still didn't believe Megan was as clueless as she was pretending to be. "Why didn't you warn me? He walked in here this morning, spoiling for a fight. I'm not even sure how he knew this shop was mine, since you said you hadn't told him."

"I hadn't said a word," Megan reiterated. "He might have recognized the quilt in the window. Didn't you tell me it used to hang on the wall in your apartment?"

Heather couldn't believe Connor had paid that much attention to the quilt she'd made. When she'd worked on it in the evenings, his head had mostly been buried in law books. He'd barely even commented when she'd hung it in their townhouse.

"I suppose it's possible," she conceded slowly. "Are you sure you didn't let something slip about the shop?"

"I told you I wouldn't," Megan said, clearly not taking offense at the question. "But I did warn you he was bound to find out about it sooner or later. Is he upset?"

Heather nodded. "I'm not entirely sure if it's because it caught him off guard or because I'm here in *his* town."

"Probably a little of both," Megan assessed. "Did you talk?"

"Not really. I didn't want to get into anything here when a customer could walk in at any second. We agreed we'd talk some more when I bring little Mick over for dinner tomorrow."

The look of satisfaction in Megan's eye suggested she'd been hoping for exactly that. Heather studied her suspiciously. "Are you sure you didn't have anything to do with luring him down here this weekend?"

"I can honestly say that I haven't spoken to him in days," Megan said.

"I think there's a loophole in there somewhere, but I swear I can't spot it," Heather said with regret. "I suppose it doesn't really matter what Connor's doing here. Like you said, he was bound to turn up sooner or later. I guess I'd just been hoping for later. I'm not quite ready to go head-to-head with him. I'm still feeling my way with this new life of mine. I might not be strong enough to defend every decision."

"Of course you are," Megan said. "You've started a whole new life for yourself and your son. You can handle anything Connor dishes out. You were strong enough to walk away, after all. That took courage, Heather, especially when your heart wanted you to stay."

"I only did it because I felt I didn't have any other choice. Your son is a very smooth talker. If he puts his mind to it, he can destroy all of my rational reasons for being here and convince me I belong with him."

Megan regarded her curiously. "Are you really worried that he'll talk you into something you don't want to do?" she asked, then added gently, "Or that he won't try at all?"

Heather sat back with a heartfelt sigh. There it was, the undeniable truth. As smart as she knew her decision to move out and leave Connor had been, a part of her still desperately wanted him to fight to get her back. If he didn't, the part of her heart that wasn't already broken would finally shatter.

Connor's plan to take his rowboat out for the afternoon had pretty much gone up in smoke when he'd discovered Heather was now living in town and his son was hanging out with his grandfather.

When little Mick tired of being outside with his cousins, Connor scooped him up and headed for the house. "I'll make some sandwiches, Dad. Will you and the boys be up soon?"

"A half hour," Mick said. "Then we're all going to take naps, right, boys?"

Henry regarded him with a serious look that puckered his brow. "I don't take naps anymore, Grandpa Mick."

"Me, either," Davy chimed in.

"Well, I do," Mick said.

"So does your cousin," Connor told the boys. "If you're not sleepy after lunch, I'll play a game with you, okay?"

"Henry'll beat you," Davy boasted of his older stepbrother. "He's good at games."

Connor laughed. "Then I'll need to be very careful which game I pick to play. I hold the record at some of them."

Mick shook his head. "Are you still that competitive

kid who hated having anyone beat you at anything?" he asked Connor.

"Sure am," Connor replied, giving him a wink. "See you at the house."

An hour later Connor had fed the kids, then sent both his son and Mick off for naps before settling down in the den with Davy and Henry. Despite his protests, Davy fell asleep before he could even get the video system set up. Connor carried him upstairs, returned, then turned to Henry.

"You sure you wouldn't rather rest for a while?" he asked him.

Henry regarded him eagerly. "I'd rather play," he said at once. "Davy's not much competition, and Grandpa Mick and Kevin don't really understand how the game works."

Connor made a big show of sizing him up. "You any good?"

"Really good," Henry said in a rare show of confidence from a boy just starting to find his place in his new family.

"Want to place a little bet on the outcome?" Connor taunted. "You win, I'll take you into town for ice cream. I win, you treat."

"Don't do it," Kevin said, wandering in with a handful of cookies just in time to overhear. "Your uncle Connor cheats."

Connor turned on his brother indignantly. "I most certainly do not. If anyone cheats, it's you, big brother."

"Since when?" Kevin said, snatching up the remote.

Behind them Henry giggled. "You guys are crazy."

Kevin grinned at his stepson. "You are not the first

to notice that, my boy. How about you and me team up against this hotshot? I think we can take him."

Henry nodded eagerly. "Awesome!"

"That doesn't strike me as fair," Connor said, "but bring it on."

An hour later, he'd destroyed the two of them. He regarded Kevin with satisfaction. "Who's crying now? I see a double hot fudge sundae in my future."

"Okay, okay, we bow to your superior expertise," Kevin said, winking at Henry. "Why don't you run upstairs and see if Davy's awake? We should probably get home." He glanced at Connor. "I was supposed to take little Mick back to Heather, but I assume you'd rather do that yourself." He studied him pointedly. "Or am I wrong?"

"I'll take him," Connor said, his voice suddenly tight as he scowled at his brother. "So, you knew when you came to Baltimore the other night that Heather and little Mick were living here in town?"

"Guilty," Kevin said.

"Yet you saw no need to mention it," Connor said accusingly.

"Hey, all of this is between the two of you. The rest of us are innocent bystanders."

"Innocent, my behind," Connor said. "Since when has any O'Brien ever stood on the sidelines when it comes to stuff like this? You're all a bunch of meddlers."

Kevin didn't even attempt to deny it. "You know now—isn't that what counts? Well, that and what you're going to do about it. Any idea about that?"

Connor sighed. "Not a clue."

Kevin's expression brightened. "I have a thought or two."

"Says the man who was not meddling," Connor said. "Forget it, big brother. Keep your ideas to yourself. If I want your opinion, I'll ask for it. You might circulate that message to the rest of the family, as well."

Kevin laughed. "You have to be kidding. You said it yourself, meddling is the family hobby. The only way you're going to deal with Heather in private is if the two of you move cross-country."

Connor thought of the shop Heather had just opened. It was as cozy and welcoming as their home had once been. He doubted she'd be open to abandoning it, and he was in no position to make such a suggestion anyway. What could he offer her except more of the same? Sadly, all of his vows came with conditions, conditions she could no longer accept.

And that meant they were at a stalemate, with no obvious solution in sight.

3

At six o'clock, with the last customer gone, Heather locked the shop's front door and began counting her receipts for the day. Sales had been decent for this early in the season, but things were going to have to get a whole lot better if she was to pay the bills and support herself with this business.

At a tap on the front door, she looked up, expecting to see Shanna with the boys, but it was Connor who stood there, their son in his arms.

"Shanna got held up at the store, so Kevin picked up Davy and Henry. I said I'd bring little Mick to you." He set his son down on the shiny wood floor.

Though he'd started walking weeks ago, when he wanted to move fast, Mick had reverted to crawling. Now he fell to all fours and shot across the room to grab on to her leg.

"Hi, big boy," Heather said, scooping him up, then meeting Connor's gaze. "Thanks. Anything else?"

"I thought maybe we could grab a bite to eat," Connor said, hands shoved into his back pockets. He looked surprisingly vulnerable for a man who could command a courtroom and sway juror opinions.

"Why?" she asked.

"To catch up?"

It was more of a question than an answer, which again showed just how ill-at-ease he was. Heather smiled despite her determination to keep him at arm's length. It would be way too easy to forget all about her resolve and drift back into a relationship with this man, a relationship that would go nowhere, not because they didn't love each other but because he wouldn't allow it. No matter how much it hurt, she had to keep reminding herself that what he was able to give wasn't enough.

"Thanks, but I don't think so," she said softly.

"It's a burger and some fries, not a lifetime commitment," he protested.

"And isn't that exactly the problem?" she replied. "Have dinner with your family, Connor, or a friend. I'll see you tomorrow."

"You and I are friends," he said stubbornly. "I miss my best friend."

"So do I," she admitted, "but things aren't that simple, Connor. Not anymore. What you're offering just isn't enough for me. I owe it to myself and little Mick not to settle for so little."

"Friendships last a whole lot longer than most marriages," he countered, as he had all too often in the past when defending his decision never to wed.

"Probably because friends are more forgiving than spouses," Heather replied, as she had before. "Or because people don't understand that they have to work at marriage. Relationships are never static. They have to evolve over time as the individuals in them change."

Connor frowned. "You still believe in marriage, don't

you? Despite all the evidence you've seen that it never lasts or that people wind up being miserable, you still have this optimistic view that love can conquer everything."

"I do," she said. "I know I grew up with a lousy example in my own life, but that just made me want to try harder to be sure my own marriage is everything it can be. I know I have what it takes to get through the rough patches."

"Then why not look at this as one of those rough patches and work through it?" he asked with apparent frustration.

"Toward what?" she asked reasonably. She waved her hand when he didn't come up with an answer. "Never mind. We've been over all of this before. Why belabor it? I respect your decision, Connor. I just don't agree with it."

"I never lied to you, Heather," Connor said, his voice again filled with frustration. "You knew how I felt almost from the day we met. I didn't change the rules at the last minute."

"I'm not accusing you of that. I just think it's sad that you made such a rule based on what happened with your parents. They've gotten over the past. Why can't you?" She tilted her head and studied him. "You know what I hope? I hope you don't go through your entire life not taking chances, not grabbing on to life. If you keep holding a part of yourself back, never committing to anyone, it would be such a waste."

"You act as if marriage is the only commitment that matters," he said irritably. "It's a piece of paper, Heather. That's all. It's only as strong as two people want it to be."

"Oh, Connor," she said, shaking her head sorrowfully.

She knew he believed that, which was probably the saddest part of all. "We're never going to agree about this. I think you should go. I have things to finish up in here, and then I have to feed little Mick and put him to bed."

For a moment, he looked as if he might prolong the argument, but then he just gave her a curt nod and left.

"Daddy!" little Mick said mournfully, staring after him.

Heather hugged her son just a little bit tighter. "You'll see Daddy again tomorrow, sport. Grandpa Mick and all your uncles will be there, too."

Whether Connor was around or not, at least her son wouldn't be lacking when it came to strong male role models. She just couldn't help wishing that his daddy would be the most important one.

Rather than going home, Connor drove over to The Inn at Eagle Point, hoping to find his sister Jess there. Jess was younger, which meant she still thought he hung the moon, despite all evidence to the contrary.

Better yet, she was single, which meant she had little to say on the subject of his reluctance to wed the mother of his child. All of his other siblings were now so happily wed and starry-eyed, they could no longer seem to grasp his point of view. How they'd accomplished that given the example they'd all grown up with was beyond him.

He found Jess in the inn's cluttered office with a mountain of paperwork spread out on the desk in front of her.

"This is what you do for excitement on a Saturday night?" he taunted, settling down in a chair and propping his feet on the desk.

"It is when it's the end of the month and I haven't touched any of these papers until now," she said. "If Abby catches sight of this mess, I'll never hear the end of it."

"I thought our big sister hired an accountant to take care of the bills," Connor said, referring to Abby's intervention a few years earlier to keep the inn from bankruptcy before it even got its doors open.

"She did, but there are still some things only I can handle," Jess said with a sigh. "It's the most boring part of the job."

"Which is why you neglect it," Connor guessed.

She nodded. "Exactly. At least you're not blaming it on my attention deficit disorder," she said. "Everyone else does. Any time I mess up, it's because of the ADD. I'm tired of people using that as an excuse when I let things slide. Sometimes a screwup is just a screwup."

"Are you referring to a specific mistake or yourself?" Connor asked, his gaze narrowing. "Because nobody calls my sister a screwup."

She grinned. "Thanks, but sometimes that's exactly what I am. I'm sure Abby would be happy to fill you in on all the ways I've messed up. I'll bet she keeps lists."

He hated hearing Jess talk about herself in such disparaging terms. She'd overcome a lot of difficulties to achieve everything she had. "In the end, though, you've made a success of the inn, Jess," he reminded her. "You should be proud. All the rest of us are, Abby included."

"Mostly I am," she admitted, then sighed. "I suppose I'm just having those end-of-the-month blues tonight."

She leaned back and propped her own feet on the desk. "So what brings you to town, especially on a Saturday night? Did you come to see Heather and your son? It's about time, if you don't mind me saying so."

"Honestly, I didn't even know they'd moved here," he admitted. "How awful is that? Heather never said a word."

"She probably thought you wouldn't be interested," Jess said.

"Yeah, that's what she said."

"Are you? Interested, I mean?"

"If it were up to me, she and little Mick would still be living with me in Baltimore," Connor said candidly, then sighed himself. "But I do understand why she bailed. I won't give her the one thing she wants."

"A ring on her finger?" Jess guessed.

"Exactly."

"Is it about a ring or a commitment?"

Connor considered the question. "I'd say the ring. I was committed to her a hundred percent, and she knew it."

"But don't you see, Connor, the ring is proof of that," Jess said, leveling a look at him he hadn't expected. "I get where she's coming from."

Connor frowned. "I thought you'd be on my side."

"Hey, I am always on your side," she told him. "It doesn't mean I can't see another point of view. Plus, I actually get how women think, which is more than you can say or you wouldn't be in this mess."

"Then you think I should marry Heather?" he asked.

"Not if you don't love her," his sister responded at once, then grinned. "But I think you do." She shrugged. "Then again, what do I know about that? My own experience with grand passion is seriously in need of a major overhaul. I haven't stuck with anyone for more than a minute. It's making Dad very nervous. One of these days he's going to take on my love life and try to fix it. If you can keep him distracted from that with your situation for, say, another ten years, I'd appreciate it."

Connor studied her with amusement. "Dad has someone in mind for you?"

"No one specific, but I've seen him looking long and hard at every single man who's ever in the same room with me, weighing what kind of candidate they'd make." She shuddered. "It's embarrassing. I wouldn't put it past him to come up with some kind of dowry to get me down the aisle."

Connor gave her a thoughtful look. "You've got to be worth at least a couple of cows and a herd of sheep, don't you think?"

She scowled at him. "You are not even remotely amusing."

"Look, if you don't want to risk Dad getting involved, then go find the man you want," Connor said. "That'll put a stop to it."

"You say that as if it's as easy as plucking the ripest, sweetest peach from a tree in mid-July. In this town the pickings are pretty slim."

"You run an inn full of tourists," he reminded her.

"Available men do not come to a romantic little seaside inn alone," she replied. "Would you?"

Connor winced. "Now that you mention it, no. Okay, start offering packages for business meetings. The new golf course should be opening soon. I'll bet you could attract a law firm, for instance, to come for a weekend of meetings and golf."

Jess's eyes immediately lit up. "That's a great idea! I could design a special brochure advertising small corporate retreats, then send it to all of the law firms and other corporations in Baltimore and Washington."

She shoved aside papers on her desk, found a notebook and jotted down notes, her brow knit in concentration. Connor might as well have been in Baltimore.

Eventually, his subtle cough caught her attention. She grinned sheepishly.

"Sorry. I got caught up in the idea. You should be proud, since it was yours. And you know I have to write everything down when it's fresh, or it will have flown right out of my head by morning."

"I'd sit right here and brainstorm with you all evening, but to be honest, I'm starved. Can I interest you in dinner?"

Her expression brightened. "Let's go to Brady's for crabcakes. Now that you're a big-time lawyer, you can buy."

"It'll be mobbed on a Saturday night," he protested. "We could just eat here. Word is you have a first-class chef."

"Our kitchen's already closed. We don't stay open this late until the season kicks in. Don't worry about getting into Brady's, though. Dillon lets me sneak in the back way. Oh, he yells at me for doing it, but he hasn't stopped me yet."

"All because you introduced him to his wife," Connor replied. He stood up. "Okay, let's do it. We can sit in the bar and check out the other singles. Maybe one of us will get lucky."

Jess patted his cheek. "You're already luckier than any man has a right to be. You just need to wake up and see it."

Connor groaned. "Are you really going to hop on this bandwagon, too?"

"Of course I am. I like Heather. I love your little boy. And you, big brother, should claim them before some- body else snaps them up." She gave him an impish grin. "Not that I'm meddling, of course."

"Of course," he said wryly.

In the O'Brien family, everyone had an opinion, and not a one of them was shy about expressing it. More's the pity.

Overnight the springlike weather had taken a turn back toward winter. Temperatures dropped, dark clouds rolled in and what started as rain on Sunday morning had turned to sleet by lunchtime. Heather thought about call- ing Megan to cancel, but she knew that not only would she be depriving Connor and their son of time together, but it would look as if she were running scared.

She had little Mick bundled up and was about to head out, when Connor appeared at the door.

"What are you doing here?" she asked, letting him step inside but no farther. It wasn't just that he was soaked from the run from the car to her apartment. She didn't want him in this new sanctuary of hers.

"The roads are getting slick. I didn't want you to drive over to the house. I figured I'd pick you up." He hunkered down in front of little Mick. "Hey, buddy, you ready to go to Grandpa's?"

"Ga'pa," little Mick echoed, nodding eagerly.

Even though Heather hated admitting it, the thought- fulness of the gesture wasn't lost on her. "Thanks, but it's just a couple of miles, Connor. I'm sure it would have been fine. Besides, the car seat's in my car."

"I have one, too," he said, shrugging at her look of

surprise. "I got it awhile back. It just made sense so we wouldn't have to transfer the one from your car to mine if little Mick's with me."

"You're right. It does make sense. Okay, then, we'll ride with you."

Connor frowned at her. "Where's your winter coat? It's turned really cold out there. I wouldn't be surprised if we had snow before tonight."

"This late in March?"

"It can happen," he insisted. "Grab a scarf, too. And some gloves. You never remember your gloves."

Heather hid a smile as she dug in the closet for her warmer coat, scarf and the gloves that had somehow ended up on the floor instead of in her pockets. Connor was right. She rarely wasted time hunting for them. And he was always pestering her about them. It was one of so many little ways he'd tried to take care of her.

If she'd been keeping a ledger, the list of positives in their relationship would have covered pages, but even at that it couldn't make up for the one huge negative—his refusal to consider marriage.

Water under the bridge, she told herself, following him to the car.

"What did you do last night?" she asked as they headed toward his house. "Did you spend time with your mother and father?"

He shook his head. "Jess and I went to Brady's for dinner. It was jammed, so we wound up sitting in the bar."

"Looking for singles?" she asked, knowing that the bar was often packed with the town's available men and women on a weekend night.

Connor shot a hard look in her direction. "Would you care if we were?"

She thought about it. Truthfully, she absolutely hated the idea of Connor being with another woman or even looking at one, but how could she tell him that? She was the one who'd dumped him.

"Hey, you and Jess are young, attractive professionals. You'd both be great catches."

"Do I detect a hint of reservation in there?" he pressed.

She forced herself to meet his gaze. "I don't have a right to criticize anything you choose to do, Connor. We're not together anymore."

"But would it bother you if I started dating someone else right here in Chesapeake Shores?" he persisted.

She frowned at him. "Why are you pushing this? Does your ego need me to admit I'd hate it? Okay, I'd hate it, but we're both going to move on eventually. That's just the way it is."

Now it was his turn to frown. "Are you seeing someone else?"

"Oh, for heaven's sake," she said impatiently. "It's not some sort of contest to see which of us will start dating first, Connor. I've barely had time to take a deep breath, much less think about meeting men. Do you have any idea how much work is involved in starting a business and keeping up with a one-year-old?"

He looked relieved by her response, but his tone was apologetic. "I guess it would be none of my business if you were dating," he conceded, then regarded her miserably. "How did we get here, Heather? From the day we met, I never looked at another woman. You never looked at another man. Those feelings haven't changed, and yet here we are, making small talk and asking about each other's social life as if we're barely casual acquaintances. We're trying to act as if the answers don't matter, when we both know they do."

She heard the sorrow in his voice and found herself reaching over to touch his hand on the steering wheel. "We'll always be more than casual acquaintances, Connor. We share a son, for one thing. But it's going to take time to find our way with this new relationship. Sometimes it's going to be awkward and messy and frustrating, but we have to find a way to make it work. I don't want either of us to end up bitter and unable to be in the same room together."

He sighed. "I don't want that, either."

She forced a smile. "You do know that the two of us turning up together today is going to set tongues wagging with your family, don't you? Are you ready for that?"

"Hey, you're the one living here now. You'll have to deal with the nonstop pressure and meddling more than I will. Are you up to it?"

"I guess I'll have to be." Sobering, she met his gaze. "We made the right decision, Connor."

"You're the one who made the decision," he corrected, his tone suddenly edged with annoyance. "Don't lay this on me. I was happy with the way things were."

"Sure, hiding me and your son from your family was working just fine for you," she retorted sarcastically. "It meant no one except me could tell you what you were doing was wrong. And of course I couldn't say a thing, either, because essentially I made a pact to play by your rules the day I agreed to move in with you."

He frowned at the accusation. "Did I force you to move in?"

"Of course not. You just counted on me loving you so much, I wouldn't be able to turn you down."

"You never once said a word about being unhappy with our situation," he complained. "Not even once."

"And that's all on me," she agreed. "I weighed the options of living with you on your terms or without you, and I chose you. I don't regret that, Connor. I really don't. The years we spent together were amazing."

"What changed?" he asked.

"When little Mick came along, I began to see things differently," she conceded. "I wanted more for all of us."

"You should have told me that," he said.

"Oh, please. Every single time I tried to tell you what I was feeling, you'd get this look on your face as if I were betraying your trust, so I shut up," she said. "And when I saw your attitude toward marriage getting darker and darker every day with every divorce case you handled, I had to accept that you were never going to change. That meant it was up to me to make a choice, and the only one that made sense for me was to move out and move on."

She regarded him with real sorrow. "And just so you know, it wasn't easy, and there are times when I regret it, but I still know in my heart it was the right thing to do."

"Maybe for you," he said grudgingly. "But what about our son? Was it best for him?"

"In the long run, it will be," she insisted. "If you and I cooperate, he'll grow up knowing we both love him."

"The way all of us wound up knowing how Mom felt

about us?" he scoffed. "We grew up thinking she'd abandoned us. Neither she nor Dad tried all that hard to show us otherwise."

"Which is exactly why you and I will do everything we possibly can to make sure little Mick doesn't feel abandoned by anyone," Heather countered. "We have to try, Connor. We're the grown-ups, and we can do this, because we both understand how important it is, right?"

He glanced over at her, then sighed. "Right," he said with obvious reluctance.

He pulled up in front of the house. "I'll let you out here with the baby, then park."

Trying to inject a hint of humor into the suddenly somber mood, she teased, "You just don't want to get caught walking in the door with us. You know I'm right about the hornet's nest that will stir up."

He gave her a rueful smile. "Yeah, that's it."

Again, she placed her hand over his. "We're going to make this work," she reassured him. "I don't know how, but we will, because we have to."

"Sure," he said, though he sounded doubtful.

Heather hesitated, thinking she should say something more, something to put a real smile back on his face, but nothing came to mind. Because the one thing he wanted, for her to cave in and move back to Baltimore on his terms, was the one thing she could never agree to do. At least, not if she were to live with her conscience.

4

Thomas O'Brien wasn't sure what had drawn him home to Chesapeake Shores, especially on such a dreary Sunday morning. Usually he confined his trips to the holidays and the occasional visit to his mother. Now that Nell was in her eighties, he tried to make those visits more frequently, but usually at a time when he wouldn't have to deal with his brother Mick and the rest of the family. He and Mick could pick a fight in ten seconds flat on their best days. On their worst, they barely managed to exchange a civil word. Lately things were better, but he didn't like pressing his luck.

Despite that concern, when he'd awakened this morning in his cramped apartment in Annapolis, Thomas had wanted to go home. Lately, he'd been feeling especially restless. His work with the foundation that studied the bay's environment was frustrating and time-consuming, but his passion for it hadn't waned. Most of the time, it was rewarding enough to keep him going through any rough patches. Usually it even filled the tremendous gaps in his social life since his last divorce.

Recently, though, he couldn't help recognizing that

something was missing from his life. In fact, every time he spent a few hours around Mick, now that Mick and Megan were back together, he could easily pin a label on it. He wanted a family of his own. Hanging around his older brothers—Mick and even Jeff and his family—reminded him of all that he'd missed out on while focusing on work. Both of his marriages had been so brief that he'd never considered children, and he was feeling that lack now more than ever before.

In truth, though he was only in his early fifties, he'd blown both marriages due to his obsession with environmental issues and protecting the bay that he loved. Lately, other than having an occasional drink with a coworker or one of the volunteers working on the foundation's fund-raising efforts, his personal life was deader than the bay's waters had been a few years back. Now the ecosystem was slowly coming back into balance, but his life wasn't.

When he knocked on Mick's door, it was Megan who answered. She beamed at him and immediately dragged him inside.

"Get in here out of that nasty weather," she said at once, her expression welcoming.

"You have room for one more at the table today?" he asked, lifting his sister-in-law off the floor in a bear hug.

"We always have room for you," she assured him. "Why didn't you call and let us know you were coming?" She grinned. "Or do I need to ask? Were you afraid Mick would tell you to stay away?"

Thomas laughed. "He can't scare me away anymore. With our mother and you around, and Kevin working for me, I have allies here."

"You certainly do," Megan said. "Now come in. We're just about to sit down, so your timing's perfect."

"Maybe I'd better find Mick first, so he doesn't keel over in Ma's pot roast at the sight of me." He regarded her hopefully. "That is what we're having, right? I thought I sniffed it in the air when you opened the door."

"It is, indeed. Mick's in the den. Go on in, while I start rounding up everyone else. That can take awhile when the kids are absorbed in one of those video games they seem to love."

Thomas wandered down the hall to his brother's den. He found Mick behind a closed door, puffing on a pipe.

"If Ma catches you in here with that thing, she'll have a fit," he taunted as he walked in. "She only put up with Pop smoking a pipe because she never could deny him anything. He always claimed it reminded him of being back in Ireland."

"It does the same for me. It reminds me of the trips they took us on," Mick said, while regarding him with surprise. "What brings you down here? You usually don't show your face except on holidays."

"Only time I know for a fact I'm welcome," Thomas admitted. "Is it okay? Do you think you and I can be civil today?"

Mick shrugged. "That's always an iffy proposition, but I think we've done a pretty good job of mending fences recently. You were there when I needed you when I was trying to get Megan to marry me again. I won't forget that."

"Of course you haven't forgotten all of my sins from the past, either, have you?" Thomas said, referring to the fact that he'd taken the drastic step of turning Mick in to the authorities when he'd wanted to take some short-cuts in protecting the environment back when all three of them—he, Mick and Jeff—had been developing Chesa-peake Shores.

"You're right. I'm not likely to forget that," Mick said. "But the truth is, now that I've had time to think things through, I admire the way you stood up for what you be-lieved in, even if it was a darned nuisance at the time."

Thomas stared at him incredulously. "You mean that?"

"I do, but I'll call you a liar if you repeat it. The family enjoys thinking we're at odds."

"O'Briens do seem to enjoy their little feuds, don't they?" Thomas agreed. "Have you seen Jeff lately?"

"Here and there around town. We're not sitting around sipping coffee at Sally's, if that's what you're asking. And he does manage our properties in the business district, though most of the time when I have questions about that, I ask his daughter. Susie's a smart girl."

"She is, indeed," Thomas concurred. "Think she'll ever marry that young man who claims he's not dating her?"

"That's a puzzler," Mick said. "I'd have had them in church by now, but Jeff seems to be oblivious to the situ-ation." He gave Thomas a quizzical look. "So, why are you here? You didn't come for a sparring match with me, did you? Was Ma's pot roast the lure?"

"Truth be told, I was lonely," Thomas admitted. "But if you tell anyone *that*, I'll call you the liar."

Mick's expression registered surprise. "I've never heard you say such a thing before. What's going on?"

"I woke up this morning and realized there wasn't

a single person in my life who cared what I was up to today," he admitted with rare candor. "I hope you know how lucky you are."

"Believe me, I know I'm blessed," Mick said, eyeing him worriedly. "What you need is a woman in your life, maybe even kids. You're not too old to have it all, if that's what you want. I thought you were happily married to your work. Your wives certainly thought that, too."

"It's true. There's no question that I sacrificed two good women to spend all my time with it," Thomas lamented. "That doesn't mean I don't miss having a person to confide in, someone to share my bed or a laugh at the end of the day. You must have missed that when Megan was gone."

"No question about it," Mick agreed. "Neither of your ex-wives had remarried last I heard. Give 'em a call."

Thomas shook his head. "It's a rare thing to be able to go back again. You and Megan have pulled it off, and believe me, I envy you for that, but it won't work for me. Those ties are good and broken. My own fault, too."

"Well, surely there are available women in Annapolis who'd jump at the chance to go out with you. You've a successful career. And you have those handsome O'Brien genes, so you're not too hard on the eyes. If you need a little coaching when it comes to charm, I could give you a few tips."

Thomas laughed. "Charm is not my problem. Neither is a lack of abundance of available women."

"Then what's wrong?"

"I just haven't found the right one," he told his brother. "And since she's unlikely to be sitting at your dining room table, we should probably let this drop for now. Ma's pot roast and your family's company will be enough to console me for one more day. Thanks for not tossing me back out your door."

Mick threw an arm around his shoulder as they left the den. "Ma wouldn't allow it," he said. "And if it comes down to it, I wouldn't want to try."

Thomas savored the rare moment of peace between them. Coming here today had been the best decision he'd made in a while, even if it meant going home knowing just how much his own life was lacking.

Somehow Heather had ended up at the dining room table sandwiched between Connor and Mick, who'd ceded his usual spot at the head of the table to his brother Thomas. She cast a desperate look across the table in Shanna's direction, but Kevin's wife only grinned. Next to her, Connor squirmed, which proved he was no more comfortable about the situation than she was.

Mick passed her a plate of home-baked yeast rolls, the kind few people bothered to make anymore.

"Have two," he encouraged her. "You need to put on a couple of pounds. Chasing after that son of yours requires stamina."

"Heather looks just fine, Dad," Connor contradicted. "Leave her alone."

"I'm just saying, she should keep up her strength, especially when she doesn't have a man around to help her out," Mick countered.

"Lots of single women manage careers and kids just fine," Heather said, but neither man paid a bit of attention. They scowled at each other over her head.

"You making ends meet with your shop?" Mick asked.

Heather flushed. "It's doing better each week."

"You need to speak up if you need anything," Mick said. "I'll see that you have it. You're part of this family now, even if your name's not O'Brien. That boy of yours has O'Brien blood."

Connor started to rise out of his chair, but a warning glance from his grandmother had him sitting back down. "Dad," he said tightly, "if Heather and little Mick need anything, I'll take care of it. They're not your concern."

Mick scowled at him. "Family's family," he responded flatly. "No matter how they came to be that way."

Sensing that an explosion was just seconds away, Heather looked from one man to the other. "My son and I are just fine. If we need help from anyone, I know how to ask for it. Now, why don't we enjoy this meal that Nell has made. The pot roast is delicious."

"It is, indeed," Thomas chimed in enthusiastically. "Ma, you still make the best pot roast I've ever tasted."

"And I want you to teach me, Gram," Bree said. "Jake says I'm a disaster in the kitchen."

"You don't have any patience," Nell told her. "And it'll only get worse once you have that baby you're carrying. You won't have two seconds to concentrate on the meal you're preparing."

"Now that's discouraging," Jake said with an exaggerated groan.

Nell gave him a chiding look. "Stop your complaining. That baby is yours, young man. And I'll see to it the two of you don't starve to death, the same way I did around here when Megan had her hands full with all of you."

Bree grinned. "Thanks, Gram."

Abby had listened to the exchange quietly, then turned to her grandmother. "You haven't offered to set foot in my kitchen," she said, feigning a pout. "I'm a working mother, too."

"With a husband who works at home," Gram said. "And a nanny." She wagged a finger at the rest of them. "Don't any of you be getting ideas about this. I'm not providing meals on wheels at this stage of my life. One of these days, I expect somebody to take over these Sunday dinners as well."

Heather laughed at the audible groans from around the table.

"Please don't let it be Mom," Kevin pleaded.

Megan looked up at the comment, chuckling. "Little chance of that, I assure you. Like Bree, I can probably keep us from starving, and maybe not even poison anybody along the way, but it won't be anything like Nell's meals. I vote we nominate and train someone else." She turned her gaze to Kevin. "Didn't you have to prepare meals for a crowd when you were an EMT? There's nothing that says a man can't take over these family meals, right?"

Kevin looked a little pale. "Now, hold on here," he began, but Shanna was already nodding. "He makes a terrific spaghetti and meatballs, and his lasagna's not bad, either."

Mick scowled at his older son. "Where'd you learn to cook, boy? At the Gianellis'? You didn't learn Italian cooking from Ma, I guarantee that."

"Hey, you put me in the kitchen, you eat what I know how to cook," Kevin retorted.

Heather chuckled at the exchange. There was something about this family that never failed to enchant her. Growing up as an only child, she'd envisioned scenes just like this one. And here she was, in the middle of one of them…yet not quite a part of it.

She risked a glance toward Connor and saw that he was studying her, sympathy in his eyes. He knew how much she'd wanted this, understood what moments like this meant to her. And yet he'd still denied her the right to claim this family as her own. Even if they'd stayed together on his terms, she'd have felt like an outsider here, no matter how welcoming everyone tried to be.

Suddenly fighting tears, she pushed back her chair, murmured an excuse, then fled the dining room.

Grabbing her coat from the hall closet, she went outside and ran across the yard, oblivious to the rain. Standing on the edge of the cliff, she studied the pounding whitecaps on the normally placid bay. The tumult matched the feelings roiling inside of her.

"Heather?"

Connor, of course. She turned to find him holding her scarf, her gloves and an umbrella. It was almost enough to put a smile back on her face. Almost, but not quite.

"You should come back inside," he said, a worried frown on his face.

She shook her head. She didn't want to face the curious stares or the unspoken questions about what had upset her. She saw the same puzzlement on Connor's face, even though he should have known exactly what sent her running from the house.

"Want me to drive you home?" he asked. "I can bring the baby back later."

She regarded him gratefully. "Would you mind?"

"If that's what you really want, I'll be happy to take you."

"It's what I want," she said at once.

"Okay, then," he said, though he looked vaguely disappointed.

He led the way to his car, settled her inside, then turned on the heater. It was mostly a wasted effort, since they'd be at her apartment before it warmed up much. They rode in silence for the few minutes it took to reach the alley that ran behind the shops and apartments.

"I'm sorry," he said as she was about to open the door.

She paused and met his gaze. "For?"

He seemed to be struggling to find the words. "I know how badly you wanted to be part of a big family. It must be hard to be there in the middle of mine."

She nodded. "It just makes me think about what could have been, that's all. Don't blame yourself. It's not as if you dangled some promise in front of me and then yanked it away."

He shook his head. "But in a way, that's exactly what I did, and I am sorry. I never meant to hurt you."

Heather sighed. "I know that. Sometimes things just happen. I should go inside, and you need to get back. Please apologize to everyone for me."

"No apology necessary. I'll see you in a couple of hours, okay? I'll wait till after the baby has his nap before I bring him home. That way you'll have time to get some rest, too."

"I'll probably go downstairs," she said. "I need to catch up on some things in the shop."

"You need rest more," he said.

"Looking after me isn't your job any longer," she told him, trying to protect herself from the way his caring made her feel. It might be an illusion, but she felt cherished.

He shrugged. "I can't help it. Old habits are hard to break. I'll bring some leftovers when I come. You barely touched your meal, and you completely missed dessert. Word is it's Gram's apple pie. There's none better. I'll bring you a slice."

She chuckled. "You're no better than your dad, you know. You're trying to fatten me up."

Connor winced at the comparison, then shrugged it off. "I'm bringing the pie, and I'm going to sit right here while you eat every bite. You'll thank me later."

The temptation to slide over and kiss him was suddenly so overwhelming, Heather forced herself to throw open the car door and bolt without responding. Only after she was upstairs in her apartment, with the door safely locked behind her, did she release the breath she'd been holding.

Heaven help her! When an O'Brien turned on the charm and showed his soft, caring side, what mortal woman could possibly resist? And yet somehow, she knew she had to. Her future depended on it.

When Connor had seen Heather standing on the edge of the cliff with rain soaking her, he'd wanted desperately to sweep her into his arms and carry her into the house, into his bed and spend the rest of the afternoon warming her up with his body heat. He'd settled for handing her gloves and scarf to her and holding an umbrella over her head because he'd known she would allow no more. Her wary gaze had been a warning to tread carefully.

Driving away from her apartment just now, knowing she was upset and that he was responsible, had been just as hard.

But neither of those things prepared him for walking back into his house and facing down the judgmental stares of his entire family.

"Where's Heather?" Megan asked, her expression filled with concern.

"I drove her home," he told his mother. "She apologizes for running out. She wasn't feeling well."

"Feeling left out, more than likely," Mick said, showing surprising insight for a man who was usually oblivious to subtleties.

From across the table, Abby scowled at him. "Connor, I just don't understand why you're being so pigheaded. Anyone can see that you love this woman."

"I do," he agreed readily. "It's not enough."

"Well, of course it's not," Mick said with undisguised disgust. "She had your baby. She has a right to expect you to make an honest woman of her. That's what I expect from you, too." He frowned at Connor. "And I don't want to hear any more of this garbage about not believing in marriage."

"Well, I don't," Connor said belligerently, turning to the rest of his family. "No offense intended to those of you who do. You get to live your lives the way you want to. Show me the same courtesy."

"Even if your stance is costing you the woman you claim to love and your son?" Thomas asked mildly. "Everyone here just wants to see you happy. If you can tell us that you are, then God bless."

"Well?" Mick prodded, picking up where Thomas had left off. "Let's hear how happy you are."

Connor remained stubbornly silent. Only the knowledge that bolting from the room would be an act of cowardice kept him in place.

"Enough," his grandmother said. "Connor has to find his own way, the same as the rest of you have. Megan, Jess, why don't you clear the table, and I'll bring out the pie and ice cream."

Relieved to have a reprieve, Connor sighed. Kevin gave him an amused look.

"You don't actually think you're off the hook, do you?" his big brother asked.

"I was hoping," Connor admitted.

"Not likely," Trace told him.

"In fact, something tells me the crowd's just getting warmed up," Jake added.

Sensing unity, Mick gave him a benevolent look. "You won't win this one, Connor. Marry the woman."

"Even if I think marriage inevitably leads to heartache?" he asked. "Even though I see proof of that every single day?" He turned to his uncle. "What about you? Back me up here. You've divorced twice. You know a piece of paper doesn't guarantee anything."

Thomas gave him a pitying look. "Being married was the happiest time of my life. I loved both of my wives. You won't find me arguing against the potential joy of marriage. When it works, it's worth every bit of struggle it takes to get it right."

"And yet, here you are, with *us* on a Sunday afternoon," Connor retorted.

"And I'd give anything to have it otherwise," Thomas said. "I'd go back to either one of my wives, if they'd have me, but sadly I burned those bridges. If the opportunity arises and I find another woman to love, it won't take me but a minute to take that walk down the aisle again."

"Don't say that in front of Gram," Kevin warned. "You know how she feels about divorce because of the church. In her eyes, Dad and Mom were never divorced in the first place, so that wedding they had back on New Year's Eve was nothing but a renewal of vows. She's probably lighting candles right and left for you after two divorces."

Thomas grimaced. "Believe me, I've heard Ma's opinion on the subject more than once. I'm just saying that when it comes to marriage, I'm a believer. People were meant to go through life with a partner at their side who loves them unconditionally."

"Yet another triumph of hope over reality," Connor said cynically.

Again, Thomas's expression was filled with pity. "What do any of us have if we don't have hope?" he asked. "Why, even at the bottom of Pandora's box, there was hope."

Connor glanced around the table, looking for an ally, but everyone there was nodding at Thomas's remark. Abby grinned at him.

"You're outnumbered, little brother. Give in gracefully."

"Never," he said out of habit. Let them all live their lives blinded to the pitfalls of marriage. He wasn't going to fall into that trap. For every happy couple they could point to, even in this room, he could find another five who were miserable. If they spent even a day in his office, listening to one tale of misery and heartbreak after another, they'd be stripped of these rose-colored glasses they were wearing.

"Live in your dream world," he told them, standing up. "I'm going upstairs to check on my son."

"You'll miss Gram's pie," Bree said, looking shocked. "You *never* miss Gram's pie."

"The peace and quiet will be worth the sacrifice," he declared. "Just be sure there's a slice left over for me to take to Heather later."

A grin spread across his sister's face, as she patted her belly. "But I can have yours, right? After all, I'm eating for two."

Despite his sour mood, Connor chuckled. "It's all yours, Bree, as long as Jake thinks he can roll you home after lunch."

"I've got it covered," Jake said, sliding an arm around his wife's shoulders. "That's why I brought along the wheelbarrow."

Bree poked him in the ribs. "You'll pay for that."

Connor regarded them triumphantly. "See what I mean? A couple of ill-considered words here and there, and even the happiest marriage can teeter on the brink."

Bree gazed up at her husband with a totally smitten expression. "I don't think you have to worry about that with us, little brother. We're in this for the duration."

"Amen to that," Jake agreed, kissing her soundly. "The occasional spat or even a poke in the ribs just livens things up."

A grin spread across Bree's face. "We get lively all the time."

"Which is how she ended up pregnant," Jake said.

Connor listened to the exchange, expecting to hear a false note, something to indicate that things weren't as rosy as Bree and Jake would have everyone believe. Apparently they were exactly as they appeared to be, blissfully happy.

And he was happy for them. He really was, even if it put a tiny nick in his rock-solid theory. After all, every rule had its exceptions.

5

After drying off and changing her clothes, Heather went downstairs to the store just as she'd told Connor she'd planned to do. Truthfully, her motivation was less about the work that needed to be done than it was about not being in her apartment when Connor returned with little Mick. Right now that apartment was her haven, someplace with no memories whatsoever of Connor. It was exactly what she needed if she was to have her fresh start.

If Connor visited, even for a few minutes, there was a huge risk that it could change the way she felt about her new home. She'd have to grapple with images of him being there, seated, if only for moments, on her new sofa. His scent might linger in the cushions. It was hard enough to keep him out of her head as it was. That's why she hadn't let him past the threshold when he'd arrived unexpectedly earlier.

Downstairs, she spent an hour on paperwork, opened a box of new fabric and put the bolts on display, then found herself at loose ends. She picked up the quilt she'd promised to make for Megan, another Chesapeake Shores scene, this time of the family's home overlooking the bay. She'd worked on simplifying the design for days, using photos to get not only the images she wanted but the colors that would capture the scene. She'd assembled her fabrics and started the work during lulls in business the day before.

Though she'd made several traditional quilt patterns over the years, she found special satisfaction and creative freedom in doing this kind of folk art quilt. If Megan was right about her talent, these would distinguish her shop from any others in the immediate region.

And if she decided to do custom scenes for her customers, she could probably charge even more for them. Or she could assemble a collection of such quilts and even have a show. She could do it right here, or she could have a more formal showing next door at Megan's increasingly respected art gallery. That could boost prices even higher, she suspected, still a bit stunned by Megan's assessment of her quilts' worth.

Sitting in a rocker she'd placed near the front window for better lighting, she pieced together a section of the O'Brien house with the kind of tiny, neat stitches she'd learned from her mother.

As always, any thought of Bridget Donovan filled her with nostalgia. How had they let things get so far off track? Of course it was because they'd both taken strong positions from which there was no backing down, pretty much the way she and Connor had done.

Ironically, she'd always thought herself capable of reason and compromise. Maybe, though, when something mattered so much, there was no room for compromise.

She wondered how her mother would feel if she knew that Heather had left Connor. Would she rejoice, or would she find it one more thing to criticize? There was no way to know without picking up the phone or going for a visit, and Heather simply wasn't ready to do either. Not yet, anyway. She needed to get her feet back under her, to establish herself in her new life. Then, perhaps, she could withstand one of her mother's pointed interrogations or her father's disappointed looks.

A tap on the front door had her glancing up to spot Connor with their son in his arms. She put aside the quilt and let them in. Connor set little Mick down in his playpen, where he was immediately absorbed with his toys. Connor nodded toward the fabric she'd had in her lap.

"You working on something new?"

"It's for your mother," she said. "She admired another one of my quilts, so I'm doing something similar for her. It's not very far along, though."

Connor walked over and took a closer look, then turned to her with a surprised expression. "It's our house!"

Heather grinned. "Thank goodness you recognized it. You have no idea what a relief that is."

"It's actually amazing. Have you done others like this? I only remember when you worked on the one that's hanging in the window."

"That's a more traditional design," she explained. "It's the kind of quilt you'd find in a beach cottage, I think. At least that's your mother's theory, and I have sold several to the weekenders who have homes here. They love the old-fashioned look and feel of the cottage quilts, and they're perfect for the old iron and brass beds so many people have found in antique shops in the area."

"Did you make them all?" he asked. "When on earth did you find the time?"

She laughed. "Heavens, no. I'm not that fast. I've found several excellent Amish quilt-makers in the area, and I've bought quite a few quilts from them. So far I've resisted buying the machine-made quilts, but I may have to if I can't keep up with demand."

A frown knit his brow. "Can you make enough money selling quilts?"

She shrugged. "I hope so, but I'm also starting classes. Not only do I have several people signed up already, but they'll all need supplies. And I've put out some flyers, so word's getting around that I have fabric available, and a lot of women have been coming in to buy patterns and fabric for their own quilt projects."

He hesitated, then said, "I suppose I have no right to say this, but I'm proud of you, Heather. Clearly you're excited about this and have a vision to make it succeed."

Heather was pleased by his approval. "Keep your fingers crossed that it goes well, or I'll wind up back in a classroom."

She was half-joking, but Connor apparently took her seriously.

"Would that be so awful? The schools around here won't be as tough as the ones in Baltimore," he said. "It would be a whole different experience. Don't you have regrets about wasting your college degree?"

"Not really," she said candidly. "I never felt about teaching the way I do when I walk in here every morning, knowing this business is mine. Connor, I doubt you can imagine what that's like, to discover something you're passionate about and turn it into a career. I never imagined that my love of quilting could be anything more than a hobby, yet here I am."

He frowned. "You don't think I understand that kind of passion? It's exactly how I feel about law."

Heather regarded him with skepticism. "I'm not a hundred percent certain about that."

"Meaning?"

"To be honest, I've always thought you liked law as a way to get even, not as a way to ensure justice."

He looked taken aback by the comment. "You don't think much of me, do you?"

She saw the hurt in his eyes and regretted being so candid. "Oh, Connor, it's not that. I love you. That's why it's so hard to see what you're doing to yourself with the kind of cases you take. I know it sounds dramatic, but I almost feel as if you're selling your soul."

"The cases I take—and win, by the way—will get me a partnership in a very prestigious law firm, which means you and our son will never want for anything," he responded defensively.

"I appreciate that you want to support little Mick, but we could get by on less. I'd rather have you truly happy."

"You could ensure that if you'd just come home," he said, then waved off the remark before she could respond. "Never mind." He regarded her with resignation. "I know that's not happening, not now that you've apparently made a new life for yourself here."

He looked for an instant as if he wanted to say more, maybe even to plead his case once again. Heather waited, wondering if he was about to take a step closer and kiss her the way he might have done a few months ago. His kisses, always intoxicating, always persuasive, never failed to move her.

But the joy and contentment she found in his arms was fleeting. Once her feet touched down on solid ground again, she had to face the same reality. She and Connor were as close as they would ever be. They couldn't grow together as married couples did.

Instead of reaching for her now, though, he backed away. He shoved his hands in his pockets as if he feared making a move that would be rebuffed.

"I suppose I should get on the road," he said. "I have some case files I need to go through tonight."

"More divorces, of course," she said. As soon as the words were out of her mouth, she regretted the bitter, judgmental tone of them.

As she'd expected, his expression immediately turned defensive again. "Of course. That's the kind of law I do."

"And you're very good at it," she admitted. "Your clients are lucky to have you. I just think it's sad to be surrounded by people who are so miserable and embittered."

He held her gaze, tried to make his case. "Heather, don't you get it? People who are going through a tough time emotionally need to have someone in their corner they can count on to protect their interests."

"Of course I get that," she said. "But it's as hard on you as it is on them. Every time you get caught up in their stories, you become more and more disillusioned about marriage."

"Don't be ridiculous," he said impatiently. "I'm the objective outsider, remember?"

She smiled wearily at the characterization. "If only that were true."

"It is true," he insisted.

"No, Connor, you take every case personally and add it to that mental ledger you keep as proof that marriage can't work. Tell me, whose side are you on these days? Always the husband's? Or have you started taking the wives as clients, at least some of the time?"

He seemed thrown by the question. "Most of my clients are men. What's your point?"

"That in every single instance, you're still trying to get payback for what you believe your mother did to your father all those years ago. As I said earlier, you're still that little boy trying to get revenge because his mom walked out on his dad and on him."

"That's absurd!"

She held his gaze. "Is it?"

He was the first to blink. "I'm not having this discussion again," he said finally. "I need to get on the road."

She let the subject drop and nodded. "Drive safely."

At the door, he hesitated again, looking torn, but then he walked out without another word. Heather stared after him and sighed.

Forget their fractured relationship, she thought. How could he not see that as long as he focused his law career on disintegrating marriages, he'd never find the kind of happiness he deserved?

One of little Mick's toys landed at her feet just then. Relieved by the distraction, she laughed as she walked over to his playpen and picked him up.

"Tired of being ignored?" she teased, holding him close.

"Mama," he said, patting her face.

She breathed in the scent of baby shampoo and powder. "No matter how bad things are for your daddy and me," she told her boy, "I have you, and that's the greatest gift anyone could ever have given me. I will always love your daddy because of that."

"Da?" Mick said, looking hopefully toward the door.

"He'll be back soon," she promised. And she had to figure out how she was going to prepare herself for the next encounter, because clearly they weren't getting one bit easier.

Thoroughly disgruntled by the parting conversation he'd had with Heather and by the way his family seemed to have accepted Heather and his son into their lives, Connor returned to Baltimore determined not to give any of them another thought. He had plenty of work to keep him occupied, including a couple of high-profile cases that were going to be very complicated and messy.

In fact, first thing Monday morning he had an appointment with a film director who'd been working on location in Baltimore, had established a residence here and then moved the movie's star in to share the place with him. Naturally the tabloids had gotten wind of it. The director's wife back in Los Angeles had been furious about the publicity, if not about the infidelity, and intended to take him apart in the divorce. Despite the man's egregious behavior, Connor didn't intend to let her get one penny more than she deserved.

To be honest, he'd taken the case more for its publicity value than out of any desire to defend the man's bad behavior. If he could keep Clint Wilder from being taken to the cleaners, it would seal his status as the top divorce attorney in the region. He'd make partner at the law firm by the end of the year for sure.

Even as the thought occurred to him, he remembered Heather's disdain for his motives. Okay, she was right, at least to an extent. But what was wrong with wanting to be successful? Wasn't that what most people wanted, to be the best at whatever career they'd chosen?

Still, on Monday morning as he listened to Wilder's side of the mostly sordid tale, he couldn't help thinking what Heather's reaction would be. She'd be horrified that Connor would take the husband's side over his wife's. Connor had a momentary twinge about it himself, especially as Wilder boasted that it wasn't the first time he'd slept with the leading lady in his films, just the first time his wife had gotten wind of it and been publicly humiliated.

"I don't know what she expected," the director said, sounding genuinely bewildered. "She stays at home with the kids. What am I supposed to do? Look, just offer her the house, support money for the kids and some kind of monthly alimony. Make it all go away."

He handed Connor a piece of paper with some suggested figures. Connor glanced at them and shook his head. Even by his usually conservative standards, these would never fly. Not when this man made millions.

"Look, I'll do what I can, but it may not be so easy to make this go away. You've been married a long time, and this isn't the first time you've strayed. Her lawyer could rip you apart. If she gets a sympathetic judge, you'll wind up paying three or four times this amount."

The director leveled a look at him that probably intimidated every actor on his set. "Don't let that happen," he said quietly. "Understand?"

Connor nodded. All he could do was offer his best

advice. In the end, it was his client's decision. "I'll be back in touch as soon as I've spoken to your wife's lawyer."

"Tell that little weasel I have plenty of dirt of my own I can throw at her," Wilder told him. "If he wants to get tough, I'll be tougher, and I'll walk away with the house and the kids. She'll wind up with nothing. She was barely one step out of the gutter when I met her, and I can see that she winds up back there."

Connor felt his blood turn cold at the man's vicious words. For all of his go-for-the-jugular tactics, he still clung to at least some sense of respect for women. Sadly, though, he had dealt with enough men who thought their own behavior should be exempt from scrutiny to recognize a man willing to play hardball. Usually he liked having the kind of leverage necessary to make the other side squirm. Maybe because of last night's conversation with Heather, today he was the one squirming. The whole thing suddenly seemed so darn sleazy and cruel.

Ironically, it wasn't Heather's face he saw in his head, but Gram's. He heard her reminding him over and over that Megan deserved his respect, even when he was angriest at what she'd done to the family. Gram would be appalled by Clint Wilder, a man willing to publicly sully his wife's reputation out of greed.

In the end, though, Connor knew he would win for the director in court, because that's what he did. But for the first time, at the end of the day, he didn't feel entirely good about it.

When the firm's senior partner, Grayson Hudson, walked into his office and asked about the case later, Connor shrugged. "It'll get a lot of publicity," he said, as if that were all that mattered.

"Just make sure the firm looks good," Grayson told him. "You're very good at what you do, Connor. That's why I used you myself when Cynthia and I split up. But your tendency to go for broke can stir up sympathy for the other side. You make sure that man's wife isn't going to come through this looking like Mother Teresa, you hear?"

Connor thought about Wilder's veiled references to his wife's past. "Doubtful, sir," he said confidently.

"Just do your homework, that's all I'm saying."

"Not to worry. I always do."

After all, Connor reflected, wasn't he the one who was known in his family for having very little faith in the human race? He left next to nothing to chance. Even though he had Clint Wilder's word that his wife had skeletons in her closet, he'd put a private detective to work checking her background within five minutes of the man walking out of his office. He wasn't about to enter a mediation room or a courtroom without knowing everything there was to know about the other side.

Using the dirt, though? That was another matter and one he had no idea how he would handle.

Though he was immersed in work, Connor still wasn't able to keep Heather out of his head. Every time he drew up a line of attack in another case, he heard her voice questioning his tactics and his motives. It was getting annoying.

In fact, just being unable to get her out of his head was annoying. The only way he could think of to change that was to put his social life on a fast track.

For the next couple of weeks, he spent his evenings

hitting every bar in town with various colleagues from his law firm. Though he met plenty of attractive, intelligent professional women, not a one of them held a candle to Heather. Her image haunted him.

He reached for the phone a half-dozen times a day, tempted to call so he could hear the sound of her voice. He even had a built-in excuse, wanting to get updates on their son. It was downright pitiful that he even considered resorting to that.

In the end, he resisted because he knew she'd see through the excuse. Anyone in his family could tell him what was going on with little Mick. It wouldn't take frequent calls to Heather to learn how his son was doing. Besides, she left him regular messages herself. They were too short, too unsatisfactory. What he needed was a real conversation.

His inability to get on with his life clearly meant that he needed to try harder.

The next woman he met, he asked on a date, then spent an evening in one of Baltimore's finest restaurants being bored out of his mind. It seemed all she cared about was whether he'd met any of the stars in Clint Wilder's movie. He repeated the pattern for another couple of weeks, then finally conceded he was wasting his time.

On the Saturday morning of Easter weekend, he got in his car and drove once again to Chesapeake Shores, using the excuse that it had been too long since he'd seen his son. He somehow managed to blame Heather for that, even though several of her messages had included an offer to bring little Mick for a visit.

When he arrived at the house, he found Gram in the kitchen with all of the kids coloring Easter eggs. Though the room was a disaster and Gram looked harried, her eyes were twinkling when she spotted him. She handed off his son, who clung happily to his neck. The boy's smile of delight at Connor's arrival immediately improved his mood.

"Get out of those fancy clothes and come in here to help me," Gram commanded. "If I'm not careful, I'm going to wind up with my hair dyed pink."

"It would be beautiful," Caitlyn told her solemnly.

"We can do mine, too," Carrie said. "But I want blue." She danced around. "Don't you think I'd be beautiful?"

"Gorgeous," Connor agreed, laughing. He felt lighter than he had in days. His twin nieces, with their unexpected observations and uncensored comments, could lift his spirits in a heartbeat. Spending time with them and the rest of the family was exactly what he'd needed.

"I'll be right back," he promised his grandmother.

Taking little Mick with him, he changed into an old T-shirt and a pair of cutoff jeans, then hurried back to the kitchen and settled his son in a high chair.

"How'd you get roped into doing this?" he asked Gram.

"Everyone's working today," she explained. "It's a busy weekend in town, so Shanna, Heather, Bree and your mother are all at their shops. Abby went to help Bree deliver flowers. It seems everybody in the universe is sending an Easter bouquet to someone in Chesapeake Shores this weekend."

"Where's Dad?"

"Mick took one look at the mess in here and mumbled something about checking on one of his Habitat for Humanity sites." She chuckled. "I'll have my revenge, though. Once we're finished, I can walk off and leave this for him to clean up. That's the joy of being able to go back to my own place these days. Now, you help your son. He doesn't quite have the knack for dying eggs, instead of his hands."

"Help me, too, Uncle Connor," Davy pleaded.

Henry, who was still adjusting to this boisterous new family of his, stood back, looking on shyly.

Connor plucked three boiled eggs from a basket on the table. "Come on, guys, let a master show you how it's done. Each of you grab a crayon. We'll draw on a design first, okay?"

The designs weren't much, but it hardly mattered. Connor guided little Mick's tiny fingers as they drew a barely recognizable duck. Davy drew something that looked like Santa, though turned upside down it could have been a bunny. It was impossible to tell and probably risky to ask.

Connor glanced over to check on his other nephew, Kevin's adopted son. Henry printed his name with careful letters, then thoughtfully did two more eggs for Kevin and Shanna. It hurt Connor's heart to see how hard the boy was trying to fit in with his new family. All the caution was his. Kevin and Shanna, who'd been Henry's stepmother in a previous marriage, adored Henry. And Davy was thrilled to have a big brother.

Henry glanced hesitantly at Connor. "Do you think I should do one for my dad, too? I sent him and my grandpa and grandma a card already. Shanna helped me pick it out."

"If you want to make an egg for your dad, we'll find a way to get it to him," Connor promised, trying to imagine how hard it must be to be separated from his biological family because his father's alcoholism and failing liver had made it impossible for Henry to remain with him.

Henry's little face immediately brightened. "Cool!"

In the meantime, Carrie and Caitlyn were drawing elaborate patterns with bright colors, then dipping the eggs into the brightest dyes.

"Ours are best!" Carrie announced, jumping up and down.

"It's not a contest," Gram chided.

"That's right," Connor told her. "The contest comes tomorrow, when we see who can find the most eggs in the yard." He tickled his boastful niece. "And I guarantee you I'll win."

"You're too big to play," Caitlyn said, dodging his attempt to tickle her. "Only kids get to hunt for eggs."

"Hey, I'm a kid," Connor protested.

"Are not," Carrie said, giggling.

"Oh, honey, I'm afraid your uncle Connor is just a big kid," Gram said sorrowfully. "I haven't seen a sign of maturity yet."

"Hey," he protested.

"I doubt you want me to explain all my reasons for feeling that way," Gram said, her gaze steady.

Connor sighed. "No need."

"I didn't think so."

"Maybe I'll get my boy here cleaned up and take him back to his mother," he said.

"That sounds like a fine idea to me," Gram said approvingly. "Be sure she's going to join us for Easter dinner tomorrow after church."

Connor nodded. Somehow the prospect of issuing

that invitation to a simple family gathering and getting the hoped-for "yes" held more allure than all those endless bar crawls and dates he'd been on for the past few weeks.

And spending a carefree afternoon dying Easter eggs with his son, his nieces and his nephews was a thousand times better than dealing with the Clint Wilders of the world. Apparently, despite Heather's oft-stated fears, he hadn't gone so far over to the dark side yet that he couldn't see that.

6

During Connor's absence over the past few weeks, Heather had once again been able to establish a new rhythm for her life and put him out of her mind. Her days were occupied with the store, getting to know her regular customers, even making a few friends among them, and keeping her son out of mischief. Nights were harder, when the darkness settled around her and the brand-new bed she'd purchased felt too big, too empty.

Of course, there were reminders everywhere. For one thing, her son looked exactly like his daddy and his granddaddy, but she'd gotten better and better at keeping the two separate in her head. Little Mick was her life now. Connor was her past. She just needed to keep reminding herself of that. She assured herself she was getting better at it every day.

Unfortunately, though, there was more she couldn't control. Connor's family tended to pop up everywhere she turned. It was both a blessing and a curse.

Still, with every day that passed, she felt herself growing stronger, her initially uncertain resolve deepening into real conviction that she was on the right path with her life. Everything was falling into place just as she'd hoped.

And yet, all it took to change her perspective was one quick, unexpected glimpse of Connor in the doorway of her shop, holding their exhausted son in his arms. Her resolve immediately turned to mush, and her traitorous heart skipped several beats.

Why did the man have to look so darn good, even with his thick hair mussed and his rumpled clothes apparently plucked from the back of his closet, most likely left over from high school? It was one thing for him to turn her head when he was clean-shaven and wearing Armani. It was quite another to have her heart catch when he'd taken zero care with his appearance. It was just one more reminder that it was the man and his charm, not anything else, that had captivated her.

She tried to hide her reaction by turning quickly to one of the students in her newly organized quilting class to answer a question. Bree's sister-in-law, Connie, and Abby's sister-in-law, Laila, had been two of the first to sign up for the class, and Heather sensed they were going to become friends well beyond the fact that they were part of the same huge extended O'Brien family. They'd lingered after class with a barrage of questions.

Connie seemed to sense Heather's sudden distraction, turned and caught sight of Connor in the doorway.

"Well, well, look who's here," she taunted, then started laughing as Connor actually came inside. "Looks as if somebody got more Easter egg dye on himself than on the eggs."

Heather followed the direction of her gaze and noted that Connor's T-shirt did indeed look as if it had been tie-dyed by an amateur…or a pair of tiny hands. There was a streak of bright blue dye on his cheek, too. His hair, normally carefully groomed, stood up in spikes with the occasional wayward curl. Once more she noted that he looked charmingly rumpled and devastatingly sexy.

"Happy Easter, Connor," Laila said, then grinned. "I wish somebody would tuck a man like you in my Easter basket tomorrow morning."

Connie nudged her in the ribs. "Watch it! He's taken." She cast a warning look in Heather's direction.

"Actually, he's not," Heather said mildly, taking her son from his arms.

"Hey, I never said I wanted Connor," Laila protested. "I said I wanted a man *like* him." A grin spread. "But minus the flaws."

Heather noted that Connor's cheeks were flushed, even though he'd obviously known both women for most of his life, was indirectly related to them, and had to be used to their teasing.

"Hey, let's not be passing me around like some old football, ladies," he grumbled. "I have feelings. Let's talk about your love lives for a minute."

"Sadly, I have none," Laila said, then brightened. "Maybe you could bring home a couple of your lawyer friends one of these days. We need some hot new blood in this town, right, Connie?"

"That would definitely work for me," Connie confirmed.

Connor's gaze landed on Heather. "And you?"

"I know your colleagues," she said, holding his gaze. "I'm not interested." She turned to Laila and Connie. "Boring workaholics."

"Ah, been there, done that," Laila said with regret. "Well, I'd better take off. I promised Abby and Trace I'd watch the girls tonight so they can have an evening to themselves."

"And I have to get home before Jenny goes out on her date," Connie said. "Even though her curfew hasn't changed in two years, if I don't repeat it ten times before she leaves the house, she'll claim she didn't remember. Then we get to fight over whether she should be grounded for being late."

"See you next Saturday," Heather called after them, watching ruefully as they left her alone with Connor.

"Watch it with those two," Connor told her, a grin tugging at his lips. "They'll fill your head with all of my youthful misdeeds."

"I pretty much know everything I need to know about you," Heather replied. "I doubt they could say anything to sway me for or against." She studied him curiously. "Did you ever date either one of them?"

His gaze locked with hers. "Would it bother you if I had?" he asked, almost sounding hopeful.

"No, I'm just wondering. They're both beautiful, intelligent women."

"They are," he agreed. "But Connie's a few years older, and by the time I was dating, she was already pretty serious about the man she eventually married."

"They're divorced now," Heather reminded him.

"A single mother with a teenage daughter's not going to be interested in me," he said candidly. "Besides, Jake would beat the living daylights out of me if I led his sister on. Ditto with Trace. He's very protective of Laila. Both of my brothers-in-law know how I feel about marriage.

They'd definitely object to me getting involved with either of their sisters."

"You know what I don't understand," she said, carrying the now-sleeping Mick into the back room and settling him into his portable playpen, "How can you spend time with Jake and Bree, Trace and Abby, Kevin and Shanna and even your parents, and not see how happy they are?"

"I can't deny they appear to be happy now," Connor admitted, surprising her.

"Really?"

Then he had to go and ruin it by adding, "But it won't last. It never does. Besides, appearances can be deceiving. Look at all the years my folks made each other miserable. The world thought they were just fine, and then it all blew up and my mom walked away."

"And yet somehow you thought you and I could go on forever, as long as we didn't legalize it," she said. "Can't you see how absurd that is?"

"Maybe it doesn't make any sense to you, but I can't change how I feel," he said defensively. This time he put a halt to the topic. "Look, Gram wanted me to be sure you're coming for Easter dinner tomorrow. Will you be there?"

Heather thought of how wonderful it felt being part of that big, rambunctious family, especially on holidays, but it was wrong. She wasn't an O'Brien, and keeping up the pretense that she was hurt too much. She'd learned that on Connor's prior visit.

"I think tomorrow little Mick and I will spend Easter on our own," she said.

Connor's gaze narrowed. "Because of me," he guessed.

"Look, please don't stay away and keep little Mick from being there to hunt for eggs with his cousins. If it'll make you more comfortable, I'll go back to Baltimore in the morning. No one was expecting me to be here this weekend, anyway. It won't be a big deal if I take off."

"Absolutely not. This is your family, and you should spend the holiday with them. I'm the one who doesn't belong."

"That's not true," he argued. "You've come to mean a lot to all of them, especially my parents. And our son should be there."

He held her gaze. "Please, Heather. Don't let me chase you away."

She sighed and relented, though not without real regret. Every time she saw him, it was now clear it was going to reopen old wounds. "Okay, we'll come as long as we don't chase you away, either."

Connor regarded her with relief. "Fine. I'll be there, too." He pulled a stool over to the counter, sat down and studied her with an intense expression. "You know what I don't get?"

She regarded him with amusement. "What's that?"

"We were together for years. I thought we knew each other inside out, that we could talk about anything. Now we can barely be in the same room without things turning awkward."

"That's what happens when people break up, Connor. Some manage to reestablish the relationship on new ground. Others don't. Even the ones who pull off becoming friends take some time to do it. Can you imagine some of the couples whose divorces you've handled sitting down for a holiday meal with the whole family?"

"Not a chance," he admitted with a rueful grin. "Right now, for instance, I'm handling the Clint Wilder divorce. I'm not sure *I'd* want to have a meal with him. I can't even imagine how his wife must feel."

Heather regarded him with shock. "You actually recognize that she has a right to be furious about what he did?"

"Well, of course I do."

"And yet from what I read in the paper, you seem to think she's going to get very little in the divorce settlement."

"You're following the tabloids?" he asked, looking startled. "That's not your usual reading material."

She shrugged. "I couldn't miss it when I was standing in line at the checkout counter. A very compromising picture of Wilder and the other woman was splashed all over the front page. I recognized the name and had a feeling you'd be involved since he's been living in Baltimore."

His lips curved into a satisfied smile. "You checked it out because of me?"

"Don't let it go to your head. Of course I was curious." The truth was, a feeling of dread had settled over her when she'd looked for Connor's name in the article. Finding him linked to the messy divorce was one more depressing example of the kind of choices Connor was making in his career, the sort of people by whom he was surrounded.

"And you don't approve?" he said, his tone suddenly flat.

"It's not up to me to approve or disapprove," she said.

"But you do have an opinion, and I'm sure I can guess what it is. You think I'm working for one more sleazy guy who's trying to get out of a marriage without paying for the consequences of his actions."

She saw no reason to deny it. "Aren't you?"

"Heather, you're not my conscience," he retorted.

"Believe me, I know that. Didn't I just say it wasn't up to me to approve or disapprove?"

He sighed. "And yet your opinion still matters to me," he admitted. As if he hated having made the admission, he held up his hands to ward off a response. "I'd better take off now. Gram wants my help tonight. She's cooking a ham down at her cottage and she wants me to carry it up to the house."

Heather considered trying to stop him, trying to make him understand her point of view, but she knew it was pointless. They'd had the same conversation too many times before and it almost always ended the same way... in a bitter standoff. Even when she thought she'd gotten through to him, his choices proved she'd wasted her breath.

"See you tomorrow, then," she said, instead.

As soon as he'd gone, she locked the shop door behind him, then gathered up little Mick and took him upstairs to their apartment to face another lonely evening. It didn't help knowing that it didn't have to be this way. If only she were willing to compromise on what she wanted, she could be with Connor tonight and every night for the foreseeable future.

As tempting as that was, though, she knew it would never be enough without a real commitment for a lifetime. And she simply had to accept that such a commitment was something he was incapable of making.

* * *

An hour later, Heather had fed little Mick and put him down for the night when her phone rang. To her surprise, it was Connie.

"I hope I didn't wake your son," she said. "I was sitting here feeling sorry for myself now that Jenny's out of the house for the evening, and thought you might be feeling a little blue, too. Bumping into Connor all the time can't be easy."

"It's awful," Heather said at once, then sighed. "And wonderful."

"Oh, sweetie—do I remember what that's like!" Connie said sympathetically. "When Jenny's dad and I first split up, it was some kind of torture every time I saw him at the gas station or in the grocery store. It does get better, I promise. Of course, in my case, it helped that he eventually moved to Michigan, where now, if God is truly good, he is freezing his butt off at least ten months of the year and thoroughly miserable."

"Not that you give a hoot," Heather said with a laugh.

"Not even a tiny one," Connie said. "I really called to see if you'd like to grab a pizza or something. I can come over there if you don't want to wake little Mick and bring him out."

"I would love the company," Heather said at once, relieved not to be facing another lonely night. "I'll call and order the pizza."

"Don't bother. I'll pick it up on my way. Do you have sodas or wine, or should I get that, too?"

"I have diet sodas, but no wine."

"That works for me. See you soon."

Heather started straightening up her apartment, only

to have the phone ring again. It turned out to be Bree, Connie's sister-in-law and Connor's sister.

"What are you up to?" Bree asked. "I know Connor's in town, so I thought you might need cheering up."

"I see the family grapevine is alive and well," Heather said wryly. The O'Brien grapevine worked faster than the internet.

"Of course. Truthfully, though, I was looking for something to do. Jake's painting the nursery tonight, and he doesn't want me breathing in the paint fumes. I swear, it's a good thing this baby is due in less than a month, because I'm not sure how much longer I can handle the way he hovers over me."

Heather chuckled. "I think it's sweet. You should have seen your brother when I was pregnant with our baby. Even though he was swamped with work he'd bring home from the office, I'd catch him staring at me as if he was afraid my belly was going to pop open. And the night I actually did go into labor, he was such a wreck I almost had to drive myself to the hospital."

"Oh, just wait till I see him," Bree gloated. "I am so going to hold that over his head. Anyway, if you're not busy, I thought I'd drop by."

"Come on over," Heather said at once. "Connie's picking up pizza. I'm sure there will be enough for one more."

"Have you seen the way I eat these days?" Bree asked. "I'll call her on her cell phone and tell her to pick up two."

"See you soon, then."

When she hung up, Heather couldn't seem to stop the smile that spread across her face. For the first time practically since college, she was making friends. Okay, Bree was Connor's sister, so that was probably a little risky. Connie had O'Brien in-law status through Jake's marriage to Bree. Still, these were women whose company she could enjoy, women who clearly understood the emotional roller coaster she'd been on.

"This is good," she murmured as she put ice into tall glasses and poured their sodas.

And for the first time since moving to Chesapeake Shores, she truly felt as if she were not just launching a business, but settling into a community that would be home.

When Heather answered the first knock on her door, she found not only Bree, but Jake.

"He insisted on walking me up the stairs to be sure I got here okay," Bree explained, exaggerated disgust in her voice but a telltale glint of delight in her eyes.

"Stop complaining, little mama," Jake said. "Until this kid of ours is out here in the world where I can look out for him directly, the two of you are a package deal. Get used to it."

Bree scowled at him. "Does that mean all the attention will shift to the baby as soon as he or she is born? Am I just some sort of incubator to you?"

He fought unsuccessfully to stop a grin. "I thought that's what you wanted, to be free from my hovering. I heard you say that very thing not ten minutes ago."

Heather held up a hand. "Truce, you two. The goal is a happy, healthy baby and a contented mother, am I right?"

"Yes," they agreed at once.

"Ah, unity. It's a blessed thing," Heather said, then nudged Jake toward the door when he showed no inclination to leave. "Your sister and I will take very good care of her for the next couple of hours. Go, paint, have a beer and relax."

Reluctantly, Jake backed away. "You need me, you call, okay?" he said to Bree just as his sister climbed the steps with the two big pizza boxes. He sniffed the air. "Or I could stick around."

Connie stared him down. "Do you really want to tell your friends that you spent Saturday night at a chicks' gabfest? I brought my DVD of *Love Story*. Think about your image, little brother."

He groaned at the mention of the guaranteed tearjerker movie. "I'm out of here." He still couldn't seem to tear himself away. He stepped back inside and kissed Bree. "Call when you're ready to come home."

"I'll drop her off," Connie said.

Jake looked uncertain.

"I promise she'll be in one piece," Connie said impatiently. "Now get out of here, or I will start to tell embarrassing stories about you that even your wife doesn't know!"

That finally got him out of the apartment.

Bree sank onto the sofa. "I do love that man, but I need breathing room."

"Just wait till you need him to help with the middle of the night feedings and the dirty diapers," Connie predicted. "You'll have trouble figuring out where he's hiding."

Heather thought back to the early days at home with little Mick. Connor had handled his share of feedings.

"Actually Connor was amazing about that kind of thing," she said as she bit into the still-steaming pizza. After chewing thoughtfully, she added, "Maybe it helped that he was usually burning the midnight oil going over case files, but I can't tell you how many times I found him half-asleep in a chair with a file in one hand and the baby sleeping on his chest."

"And the diapers?" Bree asked skeptically.

"He changed his share."

Connie regarded her incredulously. "And yet you still left him?" As soon as the words were out of her mouth, she looked chagrined. "Sorry. None of my business."

"It's okay," Heather told her. "Sometimes I wonder if I was out of my mind, too."

"Well, Connor is my brother and I love him to pieces," Bree said as she plucked another slice of pizza from the box, "but I get why you did what you did. Marriage matters. It means something when two people stand in front of a priest or a judge and say, 'I do.'"

"It certainly should," Connie agreed, sipping her soda. "Of course, when I got married, all it meant to my husband was that he was buying into a permanent cooking and cleaning service. Jenny required too much of my time and attention." She shook her head. "He was a selfish pig. How I'd missed that is beyond me."

"As great a believer as I am in love," Bree said, "I think we all delude ourselves sometimes and see what we want to see in a man. Look at the mistake I made with my so-called mentor at the regional theater in Chicago. I convinced myself he was madly in love with me, when he was really in love with the sound of his own voice. I was just his adoring audience." She looked chagrined. "To think I could have lost Jake forever for a man like that."

Heather listened to the two of them and found solace in what they were saying. "So you've both been down some bumpy roads and survived," she commented.

"Better than survived," Bree said. "I've thrived. I'm happier now than I ever imagined being. I love the flower shop, and having my own theater is challenging and amazingly rewarding. I've actually written my first new play in ages and hope to produce it next season."

"And I may not have met an exciting new man in, oh, the past five years or more," Connie added, "but I have a great daughter, a wonderful brother and a really good life. I even enjoy working at the nursery for Jake."

She frowned, set aside the slice of pizza she'd just picked up, then confessed, "I honestly don't know what the dickens I'll do once Jenny leaves for college next fall. I can't imagine rattling around in that house by myself."

"You could sell your place and buy one of those snazzy new townhouses being developed just outside of town," Bree suggested. She eyed the pizza longingly, grimaced as she apparently lost the battle with her willpower and took another slice.

Connie shook her head. "Empty is empty. I'm afraid the empty-nest syndrome is going to hit me harder than most," she said disconsolately.

"You need a hobby," Bree said.

"I've already signed up for quilting classes with Heather," Connie said.

Bree shook her head. "No offense, but that's a hobby for women. You need one that will help you meet men."

Connie regarded her with amusement. "Do you happen to have one of those?"

"You could volunteer at my theater," Bree said at once. "We have lots of things you could do."

"And how many men who aren't married or gay?" Connie inquired reasonably.

Bree winced. "You have a point. Okay, what else are you interested in?"

When Connie remained silent, Heather prodded, "Do you like to read? Shanna has a book club at her store. She mentioned it to me the other day."

"I don't think so. I don't like the pressure of having to read anything on a deadline," Connie said. She glanced at Bree. "I did pick up some of those books on the bay that your uncle Thomas recommended when he did that talk for Shanna. I like the work he's doing."

"Then volunteer," Bree said excitedly. "That's perfect. It's a really great cause. Kevin can fill you in, or you can drop by the house tomorrow. Uncle Thomas will be there for Easter dinner, I'm sure. He never misses a holiday. You can get some ideas directly from him. Bring Jenny along, too."

"You can't just add two people to Easter dinner," Connie protested.

"Of course I can," Bree said. "If there's one thing we O'Briens love, it's a jam-packed holiday table. It diverts Dad's attention from us, so there's less meddling. And Gram thinks having company keeps us all on our best behavior." She shrugged. "I'm not so sure about that, but there's always enough food for an army. Promise me you'll be there. I don't want to think about you and Jenny having lunch all alone, anyway. Heather will be there, too, right?"

Heather nodded. "Do come. It'll be nice to see another friendly face in the crowd. I feel outnumbered by O'Briens."

"Clear it with Megan and Nell and I'm in," Connie said finally. "Now let's pop this movie in. Maybe if we shed enough tears, we'll work off a few of the calories we've just consumed."

"Not much chance of that," Bree said, patting her belly. "If I so much as look at food these days, I gain weight."

"Of course, you did slightly more than look at the pizza," Connie teased. "I'm pretty sure you ate a whole one all by yourself."

"Guilty," Bree said unrepentantly. "Could you not tell my husband that, please? He'll just start obsessing and insist I take some awful walk with him first thing in the morning."

"Your secret's safe with us," Heather promised.

They settled into their seats as she turned on the movie, then passed around a box of tissues. "We know how it ends," she said. "We might as well be prepared."

"What about chocolate?" Bree asked. "Do you have chocolate?"

Heather laughed as she fetched a bag of dark-chocolate candies from a drawer. "Here you go, though how you can eat them after all that pizza is beyond me," she said as Bree took several from the bag.

"There's always room for dessert," Bree said.

In less than two hours, they were all sobbing openly as the movie's closing credits rolled.

"Just what I needed," Connie declared, wiping the tears

from her cheeks. She stood up. "Now I'd better get you home, Bree, or Jake will be over here pounding on the door. And I need to be home to make sure Jenny meets curfew."

Her own cheeks still damp, Heather walked them to the door. "Thank you so much for coming by. This has been fun."

"We'll do it again," Connie promised. "See you tomorrow."

Bree tried to hug her, but her belly got in the way. She shrugged and settled for kissing her cheek. "See you tomorrow."

Heather watched until they'd made their way carefully down the stairs and into Connie's car before closing the door with a smile. She'd been right earlier. Chesapeake Shores was rapidly becoming home.

7

When Connor arrived at Gram's, to his surprise he found Jess and Will there. He bent down and kissed his grandmother, then gave his sister a hug.

"You always did like to sneak a taste of ham the minute it came out of the oven," Connor accused his sister, then turned to Will. "What brings you by?"

"I'm hoping for the second taste," he said. "And rumor had it you'd be stopping by and would be at loose ends. I thought maybe we could all go out for a drink after we take care of whatever chores your grandmother has for us."

"The ham needs to go to the main house," Gram said. "The pies, too. After that, you all are free to get on with your evening."

Will's eyes lit up. "There's pie, too?"

Gram gave him a warning look. "Don't you dare try to sneak a taste of any of them. If you want pie, you'll be at the table tomorrow."

Will grinned, his expression hopeful. "Is that an official invitation?"

"Of course," Gram said. "You should know by now that

you're always welcome. You were underfoot enough as a boy to count as family. Now that your folks have moved to Florida, I imagine holidays are lonely. You just think of our house as yours."

Will kissed her cheek. "Thank you." He turned to Connor. "So, now that I've successfully angled for an invitation to tomorrow's festivities, what about tonight? Are you available?"

"Count me in," Connor said at once. "Jess, how about you?"

She shot a distrustful look in Will's direction. "That depends. Are we going to hang out and have some fun, or are you going to start psychoanalyzing me again?"

Will frowned at the comment. "I do not psychoanalyze you," he retorted indignantly, then amended, "At least not all the time."

"Oh, please, you can't help yourself," Jess retorted. "If I want advice from a shrink, I'll hire one."

Despite the animosity in her tone, Will winked at her. "But I'm the best one around and, lucky for you, I'm free for friends and family."

Connor looked from his sister to Will, then back again, noting Jess's tension and Will's amusement. "Am I missing something here? Why are you two suddenly at each other's throats?"

"Oh, these two have been going at it like this since they were teenagers," Gram said. "One of these days maybe at least one of them will wake up and smell the roses."

Jess whirled on Gram, her expression dismayed. "What are you suggesting? Not that I'm interested in him, I hope, because nothing could be further from the truth."

"Ditto," Will said, though he looked a little less certain.

With sudden insight into the situation, Connor chuckled, then draped an arm around his grandmother's frail shoulders. "I have no idea why I never noticed it before, but you are absolutely right. I'm suddenly feeling a little overheated in here myself. Should we leave them alone to work this out?"

"Don't you dare," Jess snapped. "And if it's hot in here, it's because the stupid oven is on." She threw up her hands. "I am so out of here. You two guys go hang out together. I have no desire to spend my Saturday evening with such a pitiful pair."

Connor winced as she flounced from the kitchen. He heard the screen door at the front of the cottage slap closed behind her. He turned to Will. "Sorry, pal. I had no idea."

"You're imagining things," Will said. "Jess is like a kid sister to me. That's it."

Gram shook her head pityingly. "And you're the one with the fancy Ph.D. In my day men weren't half so dense. They fought for the women they wanted, instead of acting like lovesick fools till it was too late." Her look of disgust took in both Will and Connor. "Take the ham and pies on up to the house. I'm going to bed. I want to get to the early Mass at church in the morning."

When she'd gone, Connor exchanged a look with his friend. Normally he admired his grandmother's insights into people, but it was more difficult to handle when her scathing comments were directed at him. "Are we really the fools she just accused us of being?" he asked Will.

"More than likely," Will confirmed.

"That's what I was afraid of."

Unfortunately the only way to change the path he was on—by ignoring everything he believed in about marriage and simply taking the plunge—was completely unacceptable.

Connor was on his third drink in the bar at Brady's when he turned to Will. "So exactly how long have you had a thing for my sister?"

Will refused to meet his gaze. "I don't."

"Look me in the eye and say that," Connor ordered.

Will sighed deeply and turned, still not quite meeting Connor's eyes. "I do not have a thing for Jess," he said as if he'd repeated it a thousand times for his own benefit.

Connor chuckled. "You need a lot more practice lying to pull that off, my friend. So, have you ever done anything about it? Have you asked her out?"

"Jess has made her opinion of me perfectly clear," Will said. "You heard her tonight. She's terrified I'll put her under some shrink microscope, dissect every word she says and turn her into a case study or something."

"Is that what you want to do?" Connor asked.

"Have you looked at your sister?" Will asked, his tone incredulous. "Is that the first thing that would come to your mind?"

Connor felt it was his brotherly duty to swallow the laugh that was bubbling up. "Hey, that's my sister!" he protested. "Watch it."

Will sighed. "I'm just saying, I do not think of Jess as a case study."

"Then tell her that."

"Don't you think I have?" Will held up a hand.

"Enough. Let's talk about you and Heather. How's that going?"

"It's not," Connor admitted. "And it won't as long as I refuse to cave in and marry her. I just don't see why it's not enough that I love her and want her and our son to live with me. As far as I'm concerned, I've offered her a lifetime commitment."

"And of course she disagrees," Will guessed.

"Of course, though for the life of me I don't get it."

"Maybe because she sees the obvious loophole. You could change your mind tomorrow and kick them right back out."

"I could do the same thing if we were married," Connor argued. "People do it all the time."

"But if they have to untangle all the legal ramifications, sometimes it makes them stop and think twice about it," Will said. "They can't just show the other person to the door."

Connor regarded him with disbelief. "Oh, no? Do you know how many of the people who come to me have really tried to work things out? Maybe ten percent. Most of them bail at the first sign of trouble."

"Come on," Will protested. "That can't be right. They probably don't tell you all the details about what they've tried to do to resolve the issues in their marriage. By the time they see you, they're ready to take that next step."

"I actually ask how long they've felt their marriage was in trouble and what they've done to make things better," Connor said.

"And?"

"For way too many of them, divorce is the first option, not the last."

Will looked troubled by his response. "That's sad."

"I agree," Connor said. "Despite my own beliefs and what everyone in my family thinks about my opinions on the subject, I even encourage clients to seek counseling. After all, I know what it's like to be a child caught up with parents who are divorcing. I don't wish that on anyone. But almost no one takes me up on the idea. They just want the marriage to end. Maybe I should insist, but I don't."

He eyed Will curiously. "What about you, though? Do you do much marriage counseling?"

"Some," Will said. "But often it's only one side who seeks help and the other refuses to participate. When that happens, divorce is pretty much inevitable."

"Well, there you go," Connor said triumphantly. "You see it, too. Marriage is pointless, when it too often will end with heartbreak."

Will shook his head. "Sorry, pal. I just don't see it that way. I think it's the only step to take when two people really love each other."

"It's a ring and a piece of paper," Connor argued.

"They're symbolic of much more," Will insisted. "They represent commitment and security and feelings that are worth nurturing for a lifetime."

"Or until they're not," Connor corrected cynically. He sighed. "This is depressing. Let's talk about something else."

"But this is the conversation that matters," Will said, giving him a penetrating look. "Come on, Connor. You know it is. Your future with Heather and your son is at stake. She's already left you. Unless you meet her halfway, one of these days she'll meet somebody else, and it will be too late for you."

"Meeting her halfway is one thing," Connor said. "She wants me to give in."

"I suppose in this situation, there is no halfway," Will admitted. "But mark my words, stick to your guns and she will move on. Can you live with that?"

Connor didn't want to think about it. "Careful, or I'll refuse to hang out with you, too. Jess isn't the only one who doesn't want to spend an evening being psychoanalyzed."

Will backed off at once. "In the interest of hanging on to that invitation to dinner tomorrow, I won't say another word about love and marriage. How about the Orioles? Think they have a chance this season?"

Connor grinned. "It's early in the season. I'm always optimistic now. I went to Camden Yards for the home opener. The firm has season tickets for box seats. We'll have to get Mack, Kevin, Trace and Jake together one of these days and go to a game."

"Sounds great," Will said. "Do you ever regret not trying for a career in pro baseball? You were good enough."

Connor shook his head. "No I wasn't. I might have pulled off a season or two in the minor leagues, but I couldn't see wasting the time. I decided to get my law degree and start a career that would last a lifetime."

"It's interesting that you chose matrimonial law," Will began, only to have Connor cut him off with a look.

"There you go again, analyzing," Connor said.

"What can I say? It's what I do. Some people actually view it as friendly input, rather than a threat."

Connor scowled at his choice of words. "I do not view your insights as a threat."

"Really? Not even when they challenge your nice, tidy view of your world?"

Connor forced a grin, because any other response would be too telling. "Nope. That's just annoying."

Will shook his head. "Maybe we'd better confine ourselves to checking out the women in here for the rest of the evening."

"Finally a plan I can get behind," Connor said, swiveling his stool around for a better view.

Sadly, though, at this hour on the Saturday night of a holiday weekend, the place was nearly empty. Next to him, Will heaved a sigh, finished his beer and set the bottle on the bar.

"I'm out of here," he said. "Not that your company's not scintillating, but at least if I'm home and asleep, a sexy woman might appear in my dreams."

Connor nodded. "Right behind you."

Besides, the only woman he really wanted to be with was no doubt home in bed. Sadly, though, not *his* home and not *his* bed.

"Do you actually know where you hid all the eggs?" Kevin asked Connor as the family assembled outside for the traditional Easter egg hunt on Sunday morning after church. He looked like a director at a recreation center with his whistle hanging around his neck and his clipboard in hand.

"What does it matter?" Connor replied. "They're plastic. They're not going to stink up the yard the way the real ones did that year you were in charge of hiding them."

"We've all learned a lot since then," Kevin said grimly. "At least some of us have. You, apparently, not so much."

Heather listened to the exchange with amusement. She turned to Bree, who was sitting next to her in an Adirondack chair on the porch. "Have those two always been like this?"

"Worse, actually. Connor is a natural-born competitor. He wants to win at everything. It's probably why he's so good in a courtroom. Losing is never an option. Normally Kevin is quiet and laid-back, but Connor has always been able to get a rise out of him. Most of the time I think he does it deliberately, just to see how long it takes before Kevin loses it."

Now the brothers were standing practically toe-to-toe. Kevin had an exasperated expression on his face. "Plastic's great," he told Connor. "It won't stink, you're right about that. But while most of the eggs have candy inside, which is no big loss, some of them have money."

Connor suddenly looked vaguely uneasy. "You mean like a quarter, right?"

Kevin nodded. "Some of them. And some have dollar bills. Dad even tucked a five-dollar bill into a couple of them. Now maybe losing track of five bucks doesn't mean much to a big-shot attorney, but to these kids it's a big deal." He tapped his clipboard. "That's why I had Dad write down what he put in the eggs, so we could check 'em off at the end of the hunt. There are thirty with candy, twelve with quarters, five with a dollar and four with five dollars. I told him it was a bad idea hiding that much cash, but he insisted."

Connor looked encouraged. "The point is that you'll know if any are missing."

"But not where they are, you moron."

Heather laughed, then tried to cover it when Connor scowled in her direction.

"Okay, okay," Connor said. "If any of the eggs with money don't turn up, I'll replace the cash."

"And give it to whom?" Kevin asked. "Dad? You certainly can't randomly pick a kid and give it to him or her. We'll have a rebellion."

Bree looked over at Heather and rolled her eyes. "Somebody needs to stop those two and tell them to get on with the hunt. The kids are getting restless."

"Don't look at me," Heather said. "They're your brothers. I'm an innocent bystander."

Bree gave Heather a chiding look. "Then I suppose it's up to me," she grumbled. "Haul me out of this chair."

Heather helped her up, then watched as she inserted herself between her brothers. She reached for the whistle hanging around Kevin's neck and blew it.

"The hunt has officially begun," she called out, even as Kevin and Connor regarded her with dismay.

"Hey," Kevin began. "I'm in charge of the Easter egg hunt."

"Then run it," she said.

Of course, the advice was a little late, because whooping kids were running in every direction, snatching up eggs and putting them into their baskets. Little Mick was crawling after them, but had absolutely zero chance of competing.

"Connor!" Heather called and gestured toward their son. "How about some help?"

Spotting the problem, he scooped up his son and took him directly to the flower beds along the path beside the house, where they immediately found several of the brightly colored plastic eggs.

"Hey, no fair," Caitlyn called out indignantly, her hands on her hips. "Uncle Connor knows where all the eggs are."

"Not all of them," Kevin muttered.

Abby came out of the house in time to hear the exchange. "Caitlyn, you just worry about finding your own eggs. We always helped you when you were your cousin's age."

Caitlyn looked momentarily taken aback by the rebuke, then shrugged and ran off, yelling with glee when she found another egg just moments later.

"Do Megan and Nell need any help in the kitchen?" Heather asked Abby.

"Nope. They just kicked me out," Abby said. "Gram has a system. She barely tolerates Mom being underfoot."

"I love your family," Heather said, then immediately regretted it when both Abby and Bree regarded her with sympathy. She held up a hand. "Forget I said that. I'm sure you both know how lucky you are. That's all I meant."

"No, it's not," Abby said, casting a disgusted look toward Connor. "If it weren't so plain to me how much he loves you and the baby, I'd kick his butt for how he's treating you. Even for an O'Brien, he's taking stubbornness to new heights."

"We could gang up on him," Bree suggested.

"Absolutely not," Heather said, horrified by the idea. "I may not agree with Connor's views on marriage, but I can't deny that he believes every word he utters on the subject. It's pointless to try to change his mind. I've certainly given up."

"Well, that's just sad," Abby said.

Connor, carrying an exhausted little Mick, overheard as he joined them on the porch and sat down next to Heather. "What's sad?"

"Never mind," Heather said hastily.

Abby immediately stood up and held out her hand to Bree. "We're needed in the kitchen," she said, despite having told Heather only moments ago that she'd been kicked out.

Connor stared after his sisters in bemusement. "What's up with them? Were they bugging you?"

"Of course not. I like your sisters."

"So do I," he said. "That doesn't mean they can't be exasperating. If they're on your case or making you uncomfortable, I'll put a stop to it."

"Leave it alone," she said tersely.

"But—"

Determined not to go down that road, she glanced pointedly at little Mick who looked to be just seconds from nodding off. "So, how many eggs did you and Daddy find?" she asked.

He grabbed a bright green one and held it up. "Egg," he pronounced happily.

"Does he know there might be candy inside?" she asked Connor.

"No, thank goodness, and the others have been forbidden to eat any now. If these kids get any more wired, we'll never get them settled down for dinner."

"How's the hunt for those big-ticket eggs gone? Are all the dollar and five-dollar bills accounted for?"

Connor grinned mischievously. "Of course."

"What do you mean, 'of course'? Kevin was about to have a fit not a half hour ago." Her eyes widened as understanding dawned. "You said you didn't know where all the eggs were hidden just to tick him off, didn't you? Did you make a map?"

He pulled a detailed sketch from his back pocket. At her shake of her head, he said, "Hey, I had to have some fun, didn't I? They wouldn't let me hunt for eggs this year."

Heather laughed. "You're terrible."

"That seems to be the consensus," he agreed, then held her gaze. "You used to like the bad-boy side of me."

She still did, but she knew that admitting it would be a huge mistake. "No comment," she said, instead.

He grinned. "Sweet pea, don't you know that an evasion is as good as an admission?"

"Don't apply your courtroom logic to me," she retorted.

"That's not courtroom logic," he scoffed. "That's human nature. People who can't bring themselves to utter a real lie, evade." He gave her a thoughtful look. "I could prove it, you know."

"Prove what?"

"That you still like the impetuous bad boy in me."

She frowned at the taunt. "I don't think so," she said, not about to get drawn into whatever scheme he had in mind.

But before she knew what he intended, he was out of his chair and leaning over her. One arm cradled their son, but the other was braced on the arm of her chair. He hesitated just long enough for her pulse to scramble, then sealed his mouth over hers.

Heather willed herself to sit perfectly still, to not respond in any way to the kiss. Connor, though, was cleverly patient. He lingered. He coaxed. Eventually her willpower was no match for his ingenuity or the power his lips had over her. She felt herself responding.

The kiss seemed to go on for an eternity…and not nearly long enough. It reminded her of all there was between them, and all there wasn't.

Eventually, he backed away, his eyes twinkling wickedly. "I rest my case."

When she could catch her breath and keep her voice steady, she said, "You do realize you've just stirred up a hornet's nest, right?"

He regarded her blankly.

She nodded toward their suddenly silent audience— Mick, who'd just stepped outside to call everyone to dinner, Kevin, Trace, Jake and all the kids returning to the porch to count their eggs in hopes of winning the big prize of the day, a gift card for the toy store. They were all standing there staring in openmouthed astonishment.

"Well now," Mick said, beaming. "Nice to see you've come to your senses, son."

Connor frowned at his father. "It was a kiss, Dad. Don't make too much out of it."

"Doesn't matter what I make out of it," Mick said. "It's what Heather believes. What's she to think about a man who makes his intentions quite clear on the one hand, then goes around stealing kisses on the other?"

"Heather knows exactly what's going on," Connor said, though he regarded her uncertainly. "Right?"

Though a part of her ached to believe something had changed, she knew better. "Everything is crystal clear," she said tightly.

Mick regarded her with a look that was entirely too sympathetic. It made her want to cry. To avoid making an idiot of herself, she stood, took her son from Connor and headed inside.

"I need to put him down for his nap," she said, though she doubted anyone entirely bought the excuse, no matter how true it might be. Everyone there knew she was running away from Connor and the feelings that simply wouldn't go away.

8

Megan regarded Nell with concern. Her mother-in-law had been on her feet in the kitchen for hours following the Easter Mass and, though she showed no signs of slowing down, there was an unmistakable hint of exhaustion in her eyes, and her skin was paler than usual. It struck Megan that they all needed to be more considerate of Nell's age, though Nell herself would be appalled by the idea.

"Nell, sit down with me and have a cup of tea," Megan insisted, already heating the water. "I've been on my feet too long, and so have you. We deserve a break before the real madhouse begins. If this family gets much bigger, we'll need to hire a caterer and rent a hall to handle these holiday events."

"Come now. You know I wouldn't have this any other way," Nell said. "And this is no time for a break. We need to get this meal on the table." Despite the protest, she did sink down gratefully onto a chair at the kitchen table. She closed her eyes for a moment, then conceded, "This does feel good."

"And we're not going to feel guilty about this for a single second," Megan told her. "The kids are perfectly happy hunting for the last of the Easter eggs. None of the rest of us are going to starve if you and I relax for a couple of minutes."

Nell accepted the cup of tea Megan had prepared, then sighed. "I hate to admit it," she said eventually, "but you are right about one thing. This may be getting to be too much for me."

The admission itself was less of a surprise than the fact that Nell had made it. Megan had never heard her mother-in-law acknowledge that she was getting older. It also wasn't like Nell not to criticize the shortcut Megan had taken with the tea, using teabags rather than the loose tea Nell preferred. She was clearly not herself, which worried Megan more than ever.

"Well, it'll be a while before we have this kind of family holiday celebration again," Megan told her, choosing her words carefully. "Not that Sunday dinners are any less chaotic. How would you feel about cutting back on those, maybe only having them once a month?"

"Heavens, no!" Nell said at once, looking dismayed. "That's not a tradition I intend to break. I like having everyone around this table. And I think it keeps the younger ones grounded, reminds them that family's important."

"Okay," Megan said, backing off at once. Truthfully, she agreed—she just didn't like seeing Nell looking so worn out. She phrased her next suggestion even more cautiously. "But why don't we put our heads together before the next one and come up with a new approach, something that's less demanding of you?"

Nell looked skeptical. "Such as? Don't tell me you want to split the family up and let everyone do their own thing? Didn't I just say no to that?"

"Actually, I was thinking that we'd host the meals here, as usual. You could prepare one of the family's favorites, like your pot roast or corned beef and cabbage, and then everyone else could bring a dish."

Nell looked horrified. "Pot luck suppers are for church, not family gatherings."

Megan persisted, despite Nell's strenuous objections. "You said yourself not long ago that everyone needs to start learning how to make your specialties. Don't you think this would be the ideal way to teach them? Give each one of the grandchildren a recipe, then spend some time teaching them how to make it. They should be involved in the preparations for these family occasions."

After her initial negativity, Nell looked faintly intrigued. "That would give me a chance to see a bit more of these busy young women," she conceded, her expression thoughtful. "I can't tell you the last time I had a few minutes alone with Abby, now that she's always running off to that office of hers in Baltimore. And Jess may be right up the street, but the inn takes most of her time. As for Bree, she has her theater and her flower shop now and a baby on the way. Her time will soon be at a premium. It would be nice if I could be sure of carving out a bit of alone time with each of them."

"Exactly," Megan said, sensing triumph. "And I'll handle getting the house ready for all the company, since we're agreed I'm hopeless in the kitchen."

"We've agreed to no such thing. You are not hopeless," Nell chided. "In fact, next Sunday I'm going to devote myself to teaching you to make my pot roast. That was always Mick's favorite. Thomas's, too. Jeff, he prefers my roasted chicken with mashed potatoes and gravy. I'll show his wife the secret to getting the gravy just right."

"Then you like the idea of passing on your recipes to the next generation?" Megan asked.

"I do, as long as no one starts thinking I'm getting old and frail and starts treating me as if I'm on my last legs," Nell said with renewed spirit.

Megan grinned at her. "No one would dare. You've plenty of life left in you, Nell. We're all in awe of you."

"Then I suppose I can't let you down," Nell said, standing. "Let's get this food on the table. I think I've worked up an appetite. That's a rarity these days."

Megan noted that her color had returned and her eyes were bright once more. She'd have to remind all the others—very discreetly, of course—that Nell wasn't invincible. They needed to look for subtle ways to take over for her without making her feel for one single second that she was no longer needed. Because the truth was, Nell had always been the glue that held the O'Briens together.

As everyone was coming inside for Easter dinner, Heather sought out Megan.

"I hate to make a big deal out of this, but please do not make me sit beside Connor," she pleaded.

Megan regarded her first with surprise, then understanding. "No problem. You'll sit at the other end of the table by me," she said at once, then added wryly, "That'll guarantee Connor doesn't join you." Megan gestured to a chair between hers and Nell's. "Here you go," she said.

When Connor came inside and spotted Heather at the far end of the table, he frowned, but he made no attempt to join her. He took a seat between his cousin Susie and her brother Matt.

Once grace had been said and the food passed around the table, Megan set down her fork and regarded Heather closely. "Did something happen earlier? Did you and Connor have an argument?"

Heather shook her head.

"Whatever it is, you can talk to me about it," Megan reminded her. "I'm Connor's mother, but I'd like to think that you and I are becoming friends."

"Not here and definitely not now," Heather said, forcing a bright smile. She deliberately turned to Connor's grandmother. "The ham is absolutely delicious," she told her.

Nell patted her hand. "Thank you, my dear. Connor's always loved my baked ham. Would you like me to teach you how to make it?"

Heather knew what she was doing, making an assumption that Heather would someday need to know how to please Connor with his favorite meals, but she couldn't resist nodding. "I'd love it." On the rare occasions when she'd had a chance to be alone with Nell, she'd found her counsel wise and her warm demeanor comforting.

"Then we'll set a date and I'll show you," Nell said, then clasped Heather's hand. "It's all going to work out, you know. My grandson may be foolish, but he has a good heart and it's filled with love for you."

"I know he has a good heart," Heather agreed, ignoring the claim that Connor loved her. "But I'm not sure *he* knows it. I'm convinced he believes he hasn't any heart at all, that no one does."

"Then you'll prove to him how wrong he is, won't you?" Gram said.

Heather was pleased by Nell's faith in her abilities, but she didn't share it. "I've tried."

"Then try harder. That boy the two of you share deserves no less."

"Yes," Heather said softly, stealing a quick glance down the length of the table toward Connor. "Yes, he does."

But it seemed increasingly unlikely that she could find any way at all to ensure that little Mick got the family he should have.

Connor wasn't sure how he choked down his holiday meal. He knew that once again he'd managed to upset Heather, but he wasn't entirely sure whether it was the kiss that had infuriated her, her own reaction to it or the fact that they'd had an audience. He'd just been trying to prove a point, and, in fact, he'd succeeded, but the momentary glow of triumph had faded when he'd walked into the dining room and seen her settling at the table between his mother and grandmother. He recognized a deliberate snub when he saw one.

As soon as the meal ended, there was chaos as some family members left, some retreated outside for a game of tag football and several got started on clean-up duty. Connor assumed Heather was hiding out in the kitchen, but when he checked, he found only his sisters Jess and Abby and his cousin Susie.

"Have you guys seen Heather?" he asked.

"She took little Mick and went home," Abby said, then

gave him an innocent look. "Didn't she tell you she was leaving?"

"No, or I wouldn't be in here asking, would I?" he retorted irritably. "Wasn't she feeling well?"

"I imagine she'd just had enough of your mixed signals, big brother," Jess told him. "I heard about that smoldering kiss you laid on her in front of God and everybody."

"We all did," Abby said. "You embarrassed her."

He sat down at the kitchen table. "I was trying to make a point."

Abby tossed him a dishtowel. "Well, if you're going to hang out in here and expect advice from us, you can at least dry the pots and pans."

"I didn't ask for advice," he grumbled, but he stood up and reached for one of the pans, then gave Abby an appealing look. "Do you have any?"

"There's always the obvious," Susie chimed in. "An engagement ring would be an excellent start." Her expression turned wistful. "I wonder if I'll ever get engaged."

"Of course you will," Abby said, then grinned. "It might happen sooner if you and Mack would stop playing games and just admit you're crazy about each other."

Connor listened to the teasing exchange, then reminded them, "Hey, we were supposed to be talking about me and Heather."

"The same advice applies," Abby said. "Stop playing games and get on with it. Otherwise, I intend to introduce Heather to the first sexy available man I run across."

Connie walked into the kitchen just then. "Did I hear you offering to find sexy available men for people? Put me on the waiting list."

"Me, too," Jess said.

Connor scowled at the whole lot of them, then focused on Abby who, as the oldest, usually did exactly what she said she was going to do. "I do not want to hear about you setting Heather up on any dates," he warned.

Abby gave him another of her innocent looks. "Why not? If you're not interested..."

"I never said I wasn't interested. I love the woman, dammit!"

When applause broke out, he shook his head. "You all are absolutely no help. It's like you belong to some sort of sisterhood."

"Hey, big brother," Jess said, "you wanted advice and you got it. Don't blame the messenger if it's not what you wanted to hear."

Connor saw little point in sticking around for more of the same. The woman he actually needed to be talking to was not in this room.

But, when it came right down to it, he had no idea what to say to her, either.

Thomas could only take so much of the commotion at the house. As much as he loved the frequent Sunday dinners and family holidays, it didn't take long before he found himself gravitating toward the water. Since the tide was high, leaving only a narrow strip of sand along the shore, he settled for walking out onto the dock and sitting on a bench.

On days like today, he regretted not keeping one of the houses Mick had built in Chesapeake Shores for himself. He'd had that option as one of the developers, but he and Mick had been at odds, and he hadn't been able to envision a time when he'd want to be within spitting distance of his impossible older brother. His wife at the time had wanted to be in a bigger city as well, so settling in Annapolis had made more sense. At least he'd remained on the bay, although he now found himself in a tiny condo because most of his income went to support two ex-wives.

At the sound of footsteps on the weathered gray boards, he looked up and saw Jake's sister, Connie, hesitating halfway out onto the dock. He patted the seat next to him.

"You needed to escape, too? Come on. There's room on the bench."

"Are you sure? You looked as if you were lost in thought."

He shrugged. "I suppose I was." Not wanting to admit where his thoughts had truly gone, he improvised. "Whenever I'm around the bay, my mind tends to wander over the list of things I should be doing to ensure it gets healthy again. Since I can't accomplish a one of them today, a distraction would be welcome."

Connie sat down beside him. "It's beautiful out here," she said. "Sometimes I forget how lucky I am to live in such an incredibly lovely place."

"I wish more people appreciated the Chesapeake and would do their part to make sure it stays that way," he said with real regret.

He noticed that the young woman's eyes lit up at his comment.

"Actually, I'd hoped to talk to you about that today," she admitted. "I heard your talk when you and Shanna organized that fundraiser last year. I bought several of the books you recommended, and I'd love to figure out some way I could be involved. I don't know that I have any of the skills you might find helpful, but I'm willing to do whatever you need. Stuff envelopes, make calls, anything like that."

Thomas regarded her with surprise. "You're really interested in volunteering? Am I remembering correctly that you're a single mom and that you work for Jake? Do you have the time?"

"Actually my daughter will be going off to college in the fall, so I'm thinking ahead to what it's going to be like once she's gone. I need to develop some outside interests, and preserving the bay really matters to me."

Thomas never turned down an eager volunteer. The fact that this one was in Chesapeake Shores was even better. He'd been toying with an idea ever since he'd done that talk for Shanna. Perhaps this was the perfect time to implement it.

"How are your organizational skills?" he asked.

Connie laughed, which put a sparkle in her dark brown eyes. "You said it yourself, I'm a single mom with a job. I'm very good at juggling things."

"Get along with Shanna?"

"Sure."

"What would you think about the two of you putting together some more of those events like the one we had here? I'll talk, she'll sell books, and we'll try to raise not only money, but awareness of the cause. I'd like to do maybe a half-dozen of them during the summer in small towns all along the bay."

"It's a fantastic idea!" Connie said at once. "I'd love to work on it. Do you think I could come to the foundation's headquarters sometime so you could bring me up to speed on all the research that's being done? And I'd love to go out on the boat when you're working on one of your studies. I think I'll be more effective if I actually know what I'm talking about."

Thomas was pleased by both her enthusiasm and her businesslike approach. "Just call whenever you have the time and we'll make it happen. You, Shanna and I should get together soon, too, to talk about all this. I've mentioned it to her, but I could see she was a little overwhelmed by the thought of doing this all on her own. And Kevin would kill me if I stole too much of his new wife's attention."

"Shanna and I can handle this, no problem," Connie said eagerly. "And I'll put my daughter to work on it, too, until she leaves for college. It'll be good for her to think about something other than boys this summer."

Thomas laughed. "I doubt you can stop a teenage girl from thinking about boys for even a minute."

Connie sighed. "But I can dream, can't I?"

"Of course you can," he said. "Seems to me that not nearly enough dreaming goes on these days." He gestured around. "After all, it was Mick's dreaming that created this town. Shanna's bookstore is her dream, and that new quilt shop is Heather's. Even Megan has fulfilled a dream with that art gallery of hers." He studied Connie. "Other than trying to keep your daughter out of mischief with boys, what's your dream?"

Her expression sobered, and the light in her eyes died. "I gave up on those kinds of dreams a long time ago," she said quietly.

There was no self-pity in her voice, just a hint of regret that nearly broke his heart.

"One of these days maybe you'll tell me about those long-ago dreams of yours," he said kindly. "You see, the thing about dreams is that it's never really too late to make them come true."

Connie shook her head. "Sometimes it is." She forced a smile and waved off the gloomy moment. "Enough of that. Not only have I had a lovely day with family today, but I have something exciting and worthwhile to look forward to. I'll be in touch with you soon about that visit."

Thomas nodded. "I'll look forward to it."

To his surprise, as she walked away, he realized it was the first time in ages he'd looked forward to something besides work. Of course, a case could be made that this was work, too, but it didn't feel that way. It felt hopeful, as if he'd just met a kindred spirit under very unlikely circumstances.

Heather wasn't entirely surprised when she opened her door and found Connor on her doorstep. She'd been half-expecting his arrival ever since she'd left the O'Briens' Easter celebration.

"I wanted to stop by before I head back to Baltimore to make sure you're okay," he said.

She folded her arms around her middle. "I'm fine."

"Aren't you going to invite me in?"

"No."

Ready to step inside, Connor regarded her with shock as her refusal registered. "Why not? Do you have someone in there you don't want me to meet?"

"Don't be ridiculous."

He frowned. "Well, what am I supposed to think? People don't just turn away friends for no reason."

"Friends don't embarrass friends in front of other people, either."

"So, you are ticked off about the kiss," he concluded. "I figured as much."

"Connor, why would you do such a thing in front of your family?" she asked, thoroughly exasperated with him. "It's hard enough for me without you blurring the lines. I'm doing my best to make sure your son is surrounded by extended family, and you're about to make it impossible for me to spend any time at all with you *or* your family."

"I'm sorry. I didn't think about any of that," he admitted candidly. "I was just trying to prove that your feelings for me haven't changed."

"I never said they had," she said. "I just told you I was no longer going to act on them, that our relationship wasn't healthy the way it was. Kissing me to prove some stupid point is hardly likely to get me to change my mind."

"Again, very sorry," he said contritely. "If you let me in, I'll write it a hundred times on a piece of paper. That's what Mrs. Brinkley made me do when I misbehaved in class."

Heather bit back a smile. "Then I'm surprised you had time to do anything else."

"It was a challenge," he admitted, a grin tugging at the corners of his mouth.

When she didn't budge, he sobered. "Why don't you want me in your apartment?" he asked. "The truth, please."

Heather hesitated, then opted for candor. "It'll make it too hard. This apartment is mine and little Mick's. You've never been here. I don't see you everywhere I look. If I invite you in, all that will change."

Connor immediately looked chagrined. "I should have thought of that. Heaven knows, I see you in every square inch of our townhouse. It drives me crazy sometimes. Everywhere I look there's some picture with a special memory tied to it."

Heather was surprised that he actually got it, even more surprised that he was willing to admit it. When she'd left, he'd feigned indifference. Oh, he'd asked her to stay, argued with her about her reasons for leaving, but in the end he'd shrugged off her actual departure. She wasn't sure what she'd expected, but not that. It felt good to know that her absence wasn't something he'd gotten over easily.

"Thank you for understanding," she said. "This transition is hard enough. Learning to find my way with your family without letting them overpower me is tricky. They're everywhere. I need some space that's just mine."

"A Connor-free zone," he joked, though there was sorrow in his eyes when he said it.

"It won't always be this way," she said. "At least I hope it won't."

"We'll find a way to make sure it isn't," he told her, then framed her face with his hands and kissed her forehead. "I'll be back next weekend, Heather."

Startled, she could only stare before she finally found her voice. "Next weekend? But I thought…"

"What? That you'd be safe here for weeks on end? Sorry, but I've discovered a sudden need to be around family. And as my father has taken to pointing out at every opportunity, I have a son who needs to spend time with his dad."

"You could have little Mick for the whole weekend," she said, unable to keep a desperate note from her voice. "I could send him to Baltimore with Abby on Friday morning."

"His life has been disrupted enough. His home's here now. Since Mom and Dad are heading for Paris this week on that delayed honeymoon of theirs, I'll have the house to myself. Little Mick and I can be bachelors for a couple of days."

He almost looked as if he expected her to argue, but Heather simply nodded. "Fine, but if I hear about you introducing our son to beer, poker and wild women at his age, you'll be in a heap of trouble."

A startled expression passed over Connor's face, but then he laughed. "I think that's one worry you can cross off your list," he assured her. "When we're not fishing or hanging out with the other kids, I have a stack of cases needing my attention. It'll be a very low-key weekend." He held her gaze. "Feel free to stop by at any time, day or night, to check it out."

"Oh, I'm sure I can trust you," she said, resolving not to get within a hundred yards of Connor next weekend, especially in private and after dark, when her willpower tended to be weakest and his charm most devastating.

He regarded her innocently. "You don't think I'd try to seduce you, do you?"

"I *know* you'd try," she said tartly. "The bigger question is what I'd do about it."

"Now you're just taunting me," he joked.

"Sadly, I'm not." She knew the admission had been a

mistake, when she spotted the immediate glint in his eyes. Stepping back inside her apartment, she said, "Goodbye, Connor," then closed the door very firmly behind her.

It was several minutes before she heard his footsteps going down the stairs. Something told her he'd been debating knocking on her door once more and trying to press the advantage she'd foolishly given him by admitting the power he still had over her.

The more important question, though, was how she was going to manage to avoid him next weekend. Or, worse, whether she even wanted to.

9

Megan had clothes strewn all over the bed as she tried to decide what to take with her to Paris. Mick sat in a chair, observing the scene with the kind of masculine amusement that could set a woman's teeth on edge.

"Don't you dare laugh at me," she muttered. "I can still decide to stay right here. The truth is, I think this is a bad time for us to be going away, even though the thought of Paris in April is just about the most romantic thing I can think of."

"You don't want to go because of Connor and Heather," Mick guessed at once, proving that he was more attuned to the family nuances than she'd given him credit for being.

"Mick, I just don't like the way things stand between those two," she said, sitting down on the side of the bed clutching an armload of lingerie. "At this rate, I'm very much afraid they'll never find common ground."

"Since you're the one who's always telling me not to meddle, I'll turn the tables and tell you the same thing. Connor will do whatever he wants to do. We can't influence him. We should both know that by now."

"It's just so sad, and I feel as if it's all our fault for setting the example that made him so cynical."

"We may have laid the groundwork, but it's his job that's sealed the deal," Mick complained. "I wish he'd come back here and set up a law practice. For one thing, it would put him and Heather in close proximity. With the strong bond they already have over their son, I think that's all it would take to get them back together."

"What kind of law could Connor practice in Chesapeake Shores? Real estate closings and wills? Defending people ticketed for traffic violations?" Megan scoffed.

"It would be an improvement over what he's doing now," Mick insisted.

"I don't disagree, but you know our son, Mick. He'd be bored to tears in a few weeks."

"Not if he's back with his family," Mick said.

Megan regarded him incredulously. "Surely you know better than that. You had your very large family right here, and that wasn't enough to keep you from chasing from one end of the country to the other on development jobs. You needed the challenge those jobs provided. Connor's the same. He needs to have a demanding, fulfilling career."

"My work was entirely different," Mick claimed. "That's just the nature of the kind of architecture and urban design I did. I had to go where the work was."

Megan backed down. "Fair enough. Let's not have that discussion again at this late date. I'm just saying that Connor's a lot like you. He needs a challenge. As much as I'd love to have him living here, I don't know if he'd find that kind of challenge practicing law in Chesapeake Shores."

But Mick already had his teeth into the idea. "I'm

pretty sure old man Porter's going to retire one of these days. The town will be without an attorney. Oh, there are others in nearby towns, of course, but people like trusting their business to someone they know. Seems like the perfect opportunity for a young man just starting out."

"Do you really believe that Connor will trade the partnership he's worked so hard for in a prestigious Baltimore law firm for a private practice in Chesapeake Shores? He's ambitious, Mick."

"Only one way to find out," Mick said, not backing down.

Megan frowned at him. "Don't you dare go to Joshua Porter and try to manipulate him into offering some deal to Connor."

"Of course not," Mick said indignantly. "Porter and I are barely on speaking terms, anyway." He winked at her. "I'll send Ma. He's handled her legal affairs for years."

"Please don't drag Nell into this," she pleaded.

"I won't 'drag' her into anything. I'll plant the idea. She'll do what she wants to do." He gave her a knowing look. "You should understand all about that kind of thing. You planted the notions that had Kevin and the others luring Connor down here to discover Heather was living in Chesapeake Shores, did you not? You're not above a little meddling, Megan O'Brien, so don't pretend you are."

"Guilty," she admitted. "I just worry that one of these days it will all blow up in our faces."

"Then it's a good thing we'll be out of town," he said, grinning. "Now, why don't you forget all that packing that seems to have you completely befuddled and come over here?"

She saw the glint in his eyes and immediately felt her blood stir. Someone, though, had to be practical. "But we're leaving tomorrow," she protested.

"And whatever there's no time to pack, we can buy in Paris. We'll find you a whole new wardrobe from the skin out," he said, reaching for her and pulling her into his lap. "Then, again, we could spend the whole vacation naked. It is, after all, our honeymoon."

She settled against his chest. "If you think I'm going to miss one single second of Paris by staying shut up in a hotel room, you're crazy as a loon, Mick O'Brien."

He laughed. "If that's the case, all the more reason to start the honeymoon now."

She smiled at his eagerness. "You have a point."

When Mick kissed her, she forgot all about Connor, packing and even Paris. And that was probably exactly what he'd intended.

The mediation with Clint and Barbara Wilder was not going according to plan. Armed with reports from his private investigation that showed Mrs. Wilder had, in fact, come from a troubled past, Connor had pressed her attorney for a meeting and a quick, amicable settlement. The director's wife had flown in from Los Angeles on the red-eye and arrived in his office looking exhausted.

A petite wisp of a woman with eyes too big for her small face, Barbara Wilder looked fragile and younger than her years. That weariness and impression of fragility vanished in a heartbeat, though, when Clint walked into the conference room. She stood up straighter and stared him down, fiery sparks of anger in her eyes. Her attorney gently touched her arm and she sat back down.

"Babs," Wilder said coolly. "You look beat."

"How gallant of you to mention it," she retorted. "You beckoned. I came. Let's get this over with."

For one brief instant, Connor thought he saw an unsettled expression in his client's eyes, as if he'd never expected his wife to have any fight left. Before Wilder could respond and start an argument, Connor stepped in.

"I believe all of us want to wrap this up as fairly as possible," he began.

"Maybe you do," Barbara Wilder snapped. "I doubt Clint does—not if that offer he put on the table is any indication."

"It's a generous offer," Connor insisted.

She whirled on him. "In what universe? We have documents showing the millions of dollars in assets he's hidden away. Has he mentioned those to you? Did he admit to you the long list of affairs he's had during our marriage?"

Clint sat back, listening, his expression smug. When she'd wound down, he turned to Connor. "I assume you can counter that."

"I can," Connor confirmed. "But I'd rather this not get ugly." He took a longer look into Barbara Wilder's eyes and saw not avarice, but sorrow, not revenge, but fear. Out of the blue, for the first time since he'd been handling divorces, he saw the other side more clearly, in human, rather than monetary terms.

When she met his gaze, there were tears in her eyes. "Obviously you have the pictures," she said. "I was sixteen years old and living on the streets when I resorted to letting myself be photographed in the nude. At the time, I thought it was better than the alternative."

Connor winced at her matter-of-fact recitation. "The alternative?"

"Prostitution. Pictures of myself were one thing, but I don't think I could have sold my body to one man after another the way so many young girls in my position wound up doing. I was a naive kid from Wisconsin. You've heard this story before, I'm sure. I came out to Los Angeles with such high hopes. I didn't know that it would be impossible to get an audition with no agent and no experience. Everyone back home said I was beautiful, that I ought to be in the movies. I'd gotten the lead in my school plays practically since first grade. When things got bad at home, I ran toward a dream. It turned out to be a nightmare."

She regarded Connor with defiance. "I'm not proud of those pictures, but I'm not ashamed, either. I did what was necessary to survive."

That, of course, was the part Connor couldn't have known. Once again, he had to face the human side of a very real tragedy. Sympathy wasn't in his client's best interests, but he could practically hear Heather yelling in his ear that he had to take this woman's story into account, not use it against her.

Mrs. Wilder gave him a plaintive look. "I hate what I did. I certainly don't want it to go public so that my kids will find out about it." She turned to her husband. "But if that's the way it has to be for me to get what's fair, then you go for it, Clint. I'm not the one who'll come out of this looking sleazy—it'll be you. See how many of your leading ladies will crawl into your bed once they've seen how you treated the mother of your children."

Connor drew in a deep breath. "She's right," he told his client.

"I don't give a damn," Clint exploded.

"You have two children," Connor reminded him. "*They* will care if their father drags their mother through the mud just to save a few bucks he can well afford."

Barbara Wilder regarded Connor with surprise, while his client stared at him with barely banked fury. They all waited.

"Okay, fine," Clint said, shoving back his chair. "Double it, but that's my final offer." He stormed from the room.

Barbara Wilder stared after him.

Her attorney stood up and shook Connor's hand. "You did the right thing. Thank you."

"Yes, thank you," Mrs. Wilder said softly, tears in her eyes. "The saddest part of this is that even now, after everything he's done, I'd still rather have him than all the money in the world."

"You're better off without him," Connor told her candidly.

She gave him a rueful smile. "You're not the first to tell me that. I suppose one of these days, I'll believe it."

After everyone had gone, Connor walked back into his office and sat down. He found himself wanting to pick up the phone and call Heather, to tell her about what had happened here today, the epiphany he'd had. Okay, maybe *epiphany* was too strong a word for what had happened. He'd simply opened his eyes and seen two sides to a very sad story. He couldn't help wondering if that was an entirely good thing. It might make him more human, but it could make him a less effective attorney, at least when it came to divorce law.

He supposed the old saying was true—time would tell.

* * *

As Friday drew closer, Heather became more and more anxious. Though she was pretty sure she could avoid most contact with Connor, they were bound to be thrown together more than she'd prefer. She had a hunch he'd see to it.

When Bree popped in on her way to her theater company rehearsal, she regarded Heather with curiosity. "Why are you so jumpy? Is it because Connor's coming down tomorrow for the weekend?"

"I just didn't expect him to start spending so much time here," Heather admitted, unable to keep a plaintive note out of her voice. "He hardly ever came to Chesapeake Shores before."

"Because you and his son weren't here," Bree said. "You're the big draw."

"It's little Mick who's the draw," she contradicted, though she knew otherwise, too. She just didn't want to acknowledge the truth—it was too disconcerting. "I don't know why Connor wouldn't let me send little Mick up to Baltimore tomorrow with Abby."

Bree gave her a disbelieving look. "Really? You have no idea why he preferred coming here to that option? Do you really need me to spell it out for you?"

"Okay, maybe it is about me," she conceded reluctantly, "but why now? And to what end? Nothing's changed. I still want a future. Connor doesn't."

"Oh, Connor wants a future with you," Bree said. "He just wants it the easy way."

She pulled out a chair at the table where Heather gave her quilting lessons and lowered herself slowly into it.

"Let me give you a little insight into my brother," Bree said. "Things have always been easy for him. He cruised through school without having to study too hard. He was a star ballplayer without much effort. He even managed to get himself noticed by a big law firm without much of a struggle. He wins some huge percentage of his cases in court."

"I think he's worked harder for all that than you're giving him credit for," Heather said. "I was there when he was studying until all hours in law school. I saw the time he put in to win those cases in court."

"My point is that he doesn't have a lot of experience at losing or having to fight for things. The minute he realized he wouldn't go straight into the majors playing baseball, he walked away. He takes high-profile, tough cases, but only if he's convinced he can win. You've been a surprise to him, Heather. He actually lost something that mattered. At first, I suspect he was flat-out stunned. Now that he's getting his feet back under him, he's decided that losing is not an option."

"It's a fight he can't win," Heather told her determinedly. "Not without compromise."

"He'll figure that out," Bree assured her. "Eventually. Until then, you might as well accept that he's going to be in your face. If you can't deal with that, you'll need to be somewhere farther away than Chesapeake Shores."

Heather sighed. She knew Bree was right. She'd just have to toughen up and not let Connor's presence get to her. Because losing the future she truly wanted for herself—Connor and her son—was simply not an option. Neither was running away.

* * *

All day Friday, Heather jumped every time the door of her shop opened; but by closing time there was still no sign of Connor. Nor had he called.

Fortunately, little Mick was too young to really grasp that Daddy was supposed to be coming to pick him up, but she could envision a time in the future when Connor would be setting their son up for disappointment with this kind of behavior.

Annoyed, at least in part because she'd gotten herself all wound up over nothing, she decided to take her son to Sally's for dinner. He could smash an entire plate of French fries if he wanted to, and she could have the burger she'd been craving all day. She figured they deserved to splurge by eating out.

A half-hour later, their food was barely on the table when little Mick began excitedly waving a French fry in the air and shouting, "Da!"

Heather looked up and saw Connor emerging from his car in front of the restaurant. He waved at his son, as if meeting them here had been the plan all along.

Inside, he nudged Heather until she moved over to make room for him.

"You're late," she announced testily.

He gave her an innocent look. "Am I? I don't recall mentioning when I'd be here."

She opened her mouth to argue, then realized he was right. "Okay, whatever."

He grinned at her. "Careful, Heather, or I'll start to wonder if you missed me."

"Not likely. I just didn't want your son to be disappointed."

He didn't look as if he bought the explanation. In fact, he merely grinned impudently. "Maybe this was just my sneaky way of getting to have a meal with the two of you."

She frowned at the suggestion. "You couldn't possibly have known I'd bring Mick here for dinner."

"I found you, didn't I? That indicates a certain understanding of your behavior patterns."

"My behavior patterns?" she repeated indignantly. "What does that mean?"

"When you're upset, you always crave hamburgers. I'm late. You're upset. *Voilà,* here you are at Sally's."

She scowled at his observation. "Do you have any idea how incredibly annoying you are?"

"You've mentioned it a time or two," he said readily, beckoning to Sally and indicating he'd have a burger and fries as well. "I'd like a chocolate milk shake, too."

Heather's gaze narrowed. "You don't like chocolate milk shakes."

"No, but you do. I'm being thoughtful, since I know you'll never order one for yourself."

"Once again, annoying," she declared, though she was touched by the apparent effort he was making.

"I don't even get one brownie point?" he asked, his gaze on her, even as he moved his son's French fries from reach. Too many were being scattered onto the floor. Connor had always been a stickler for not letting little Mick throw his food around. Once the fries were out of reach, Connor handed him one, then gave Heather a beseeching look. "Come on, one point's not a big deal. Give me something to work with here."

"Maybe one point," she conceded, then regarded him

warily. "Connor, you can get a thousand and one points and it still won't be enough."

He shrugged off her warning. "We'll see."

Sally dropped off his meal. When she was gone, he took a bite of his burger, then met Heather's gaze. "How was your week?"

"Fine. Yours?"

"Interesting." He met her gaze. "Do you really want to hear about it?"

She hesitated. "The Wilder case, right? You had your mediation session?"

He nodded.

"I'm not sure I want to know anything about that."

He grinned. "It'll save you picking up the tabloids this week."

"As if," she muttered. "Okay, tell me what happened."

Connor never revealed the details of his cases, and he didn't this time, either. Instead, he told her about how he'd felt during the proceedings. Her surprise mounted as she listened.

"You're serious?" she asked when he'd finished. "You went to bat for his wife?"

"Very carefully," he said. "After all, he was my client. I just tried to make him think about his children and pointed out that he needed to be reasonable for their sakes."

"And he didn't slug you? The world didn't come crashing down on your heads?"

Connor laughed. "No. In fact, other than Wilder slamming a couple of doors on his way out, it went pretty smoothly."

"And therein lies a lesson," she told him. "I am so proud of you."

"I almost called you," he admitted. "It went down the way it did because of you. I kept thinking about how you'd feel if you knew all the facts that I knew."

She was more pleased than he could possibly imagine. "You tapped into your compassion, Connor. Isn't that really the best kind of justice?"

He didn't immediately respond, which suggested he wasn't quite ready to go that far, but that was okay. If this case had taught him there were two sides to every story, perhaps he'd be looking for one with his next case. After all, what was the old saying—every journey begins with a single step? Connor had just taken his first step.

Connor took hope from the fact that his impromptu meal with Heather had gone well. He'd actually done exactly as he'd told her, calculated his arrival to make sure they'd meet on neutral turf. There'd been a small risk, he supposed, that she wouldn't behave true to form, but Heather had always been a creature of habit. It was another of the things he loved about her. He usually knew exactly what to expect, which was just one reason why her taking off on him had shaken him so badly. He hadn't anticipated it.

"Feel like a walk?" he asked when they'd finished eating.

She studied him as if seeking an ulterior motive. "You should probably take Mick home and get him into bed."

"He'll fall asleep while we're walking. Remember how we'd take him out and walk around the block when he wouldn't stop crying? It always worked like a charm."

Heather finally nodded with undisguised reluctance. "Okay, just a short walk. I'm beat."

At the end of the block, they crossed Shore Road, then took the sidewalk that ran along the bay. It was balmy for late April, and the pleasant night had drawn a crowd of people for an evening stroll. Connor recognized several locals, even though he'd been mostly away for years now. Surprisingly, Heather seemed to know as many people as he did, possibly more. She greeted many of them by name.

"You astonish me," he said. "You've only been here a few months and you already know half the people in town."

"It comes from having a store. You know how curious everyone in this town is when a new business opens. They all stop by to check it out, even if the thought of owning or making a quilt never crossed their minds. Add in my connection to the O'Briens and they can't seem to stay away. I'm sure they're all dying to ask questions about the two of us, but most have been too polite to do it."

"Most?" he said. "Have some been hassling you?"

"Not really. Some people just can't seem to censor their words."

"How've you handled that?"

"With the truth—that you and I have a son together. There's no point in denying that."

"People aren't judging you, are they?" He was prepared to leap to her defense, if need be.

"No, everyone's been wonderful, Connor. Really."

He studied her intently. "Then you're happy with your decision to move here?"

She turned to him, her eyes shining. "I really am,

Connor. I already feel so at home here, and your family has been remarkable, your mom especially."

"I'm glad," he said.

Her gaze narrowed. "That didn't sound particularly convincing. Did you want me to be unhappy?"

"Of course not. I guess on some level I was hoping that if this didn't work out, you'd consider coming back to Baltimore."

"To what?" she asked pointedly.

"Our life," he said, unable to keep an impatient note out of his voice. "The terrific, perfect life we had not so very long ago."

"It was terrific," she admitted, "but hardly perfect, Connor. At least not from my point of view."

"And living here, away from your son's father, being completely on your own, scrimping to make ends meet, that's better?" he asked incredulously.

"Yes," she said flatly.

"I see."

She regarded him with a penetrating look. "Do you really? Do you actually get that relying on myself is better than relying on someone who could bail the first time things get tough?"

"Have I ever once bailed on you when things got rocky?" he demanded, offended that she would think he might.

"No, but—"

He cut her off. "'No' is answer enough. I think my actions speak for themselves, Heather. I've proved my commitment to you time and again. A piece of paper wouldn't make that bond one bit stronger or guarantee

I'd behave differently at some crisis that may or may not come along in the future."

Her expression turned resigned. "Here we go. It's the same old song and dance, Connor. You have your point of view, I have mine. We're never going to agree, and we need to stop trying. It just ends in frustration for both of us."

"Not a chance," he said flatly. "We have a son. I love you. I'll never stop trying."

"But don't you see? You'll be wasting your breath. It's time to move on." She reached up and touched his cheek, her eyes brimming with tears. "I'm going home, Connor. You need to do the same."

Before he could react, she cut across the street and disappeared into the alley behind the stores. He could have taken little Mick and followed, but to what end? She wasn't going to change her mind just because he wanted her to. Pressure wouldn't help. Sadly, he realized, neither would time. Which left him at a complete loss. Capitulation seemed to be the only option, and for him, it remained unacceptable.

10

On Saturday morning, Heather looked up at the sound of the shop's bell and was surprised to see Abby.

"What brings you by?" she asked. "I didn't think you had two spare minutes in your life these days, much less enough time to take up quilting."

Abby shuddered at the suggestion. "Believe me, I don't. Besides, I'm hopeless when it comes to any kind of handiwork. Gram tried to teach me to embroider a sampler when I was around seven. Not only did I bleed all over it, but almost every stitch turned out to be some kind of big, ugly knot. There was an equally disastrous attempt at crocheting. After that, she gave up. She had slightly better lucky with Bree, but Jess couldn't sit still long enough. We were mostly huge disappointments to her."

Heather laughed. "Then I go back to my original question. Since you're not here for quilting class, which starts in a half hour, why are you here?"

"Just touching base," Abby said, though her guilty expression suggested otherwise. "How are you?"

"Fine."

"Connor has little Mick this weekend, right?"

"He's in town, yes."

"Does that mean you're free this evening?"

Heather stilled. "Abby, what's this really about? If you're trying to set me up to spend time with Connor, the answer is no."

"Not Connor," Abby admitted, then smiled brightly. "Actually, one of my colleagues from Baltimore is in town for the weekend. I thought you might like to join us for dinner."

If she'd suggested they spend an evening bungee jumping, Heather wouldn't have been more shocked. "You're trying to set me up on a blind date?"

"Sure," Abby said as if the idea of her setting up the mother of her brother's child on a date weren't totally ludicrous. "Glenn's terrific. I think you'd like him."

"Not that I don't appreciate the thought," Heather responded carefully, "but what do you think Connor would say about this? Do you really want to get caught up in our drama?"

"I already ran the idea past him," Abby said blithely, though she didn't quite meet Heather's gaze when she said it.

Heather couldn't imagine how that conversation must have gone. "And?"

Abby hesitated, then grinned. "He hated it, which is why I think you have to say yes. It will drive him nuts."

"So you're sacrificing a colleague to make your brother jealous?" Heather asked. "Who does that?"

"Someone who cares about the two of you," Abby said without so much as a hint of remorse. "Somebody has to kick this thing between you into gear."

"And what about Glenn? Is he just collateral damage?"

"Oh, Glenn has an on-again, off-again girlfriend," she said airily. "I think that's insane, too, for the record, but the important thing is he knows this is all for show. He's happy to help out."

Heather shook her head. "This is a very complicated and dangerous game you're playing, Abby. I don't want any part of it. If nothing else, Connor and I have always been honest with one another. I don't want to change that now."

Abby looked disappointed. "Not even to drive my brother crazy? Focus on the goal, Heather."

"Any means to an end? No thank you. You O'Briens really do play hardball, don't you? I knew Connor did, but I hadn't realized it was a family trait. I find that a little scary."

"But we're a great family," Abby said, her tone cajoling. "You know you want to be a part of it. You *deserve* to be a part of it. Your son is an O'Brien, after all."

"Not this way," Heather insisted. "I'll take my chances on Connor coming to his senses eventually. I'm fully prepared to move on if he doesn't." Brave words, but she wanted them to be true.

Abby sighed. "I hope you're not counting on that, because if there's one thing aside from playing hardball that O'Briens are known for, it's our stubbornness."

"Yeah, I've noticed," Heather replied just as people began showing up for her beginners' quilting class.

Abby paused to hug Connie and Laila, then turned back to Heather. "The offer's on the table if you change your mind. Dinner's at seven."

"I won't change my mind," Heather assured her. "And for your sake, I won't mention this conversation to your brother."

Abby merely chuckled. "Connor and I have been at odds since he found out I could hit a baseball farther than he could. One more argument won't destroy us. In fact, I kind of like the idea of him finding out I made good on my threat."

Heather merely stared at her. "So, when you said you'd run the idea past him, that's what you meant, that you'd threatened to fix me up? You deliberately tried to shake him up?"

"That's exactly what she did," Connie confirmed. "I was there. The look on Connor's face was priceless." She faced Abby. "I have to admit I didn't really expect you to go through with it, though."

"Somebody had to do something," Abby said again. "I've been very aboveboard about my intentions. Fair warnings and all that."

Connie chuckled. "By O'Brien standards, maybe. By most people's, you're being sneaky and underhanded." She eyed Heather curiously. "Did you say yes?"

"Of course not," Heather said indignantly.

"More's the pity," Abby said, then sighed. "Oh, well, this is just going to take a little longer than I'd hoped. Have fun quilting, ladies."

She breezed out the door the same way she'd breezed in. Heather stared after her.

"What did she mean, it might take longer than she'd planned?" Heather asked warily, looking from Laila to Connie and back again. "What might take longer?"

"Getting you and Connor together, of course," Laila said, grinning. "Abby has a bit of a determined streak, in case you haven't noticed. It took her, what, fifteen years or more, but she got Mick and Megan back together. Her track record for persistence is solid."

"Sweet heaven," Heather muttered. "Do I need to warn Connor?"

"Trust me, he knows," Connie said. "When Megan left, it was Abby as much as Nell who held that family together. Not only is she strong, she's fiercely protective. Right now, you and her baby brother seem to be her pet project."

Heather whirled on Laila. "You need to go over to their house right this minute and tell your brother to do something to distract his wife."

"Such as?" Laila asked, clearly amused by Heather's panic.

"Tell him they need to make a baby," Heather said, seizing on the first thing that came to mind. "I don't care. Just keep her occupied."

"While I think Trace would get behind that idea," Laila said, "I'm not sure even he can save you and Connor now that Abby's on a mission."

"I agree," Connie said, grinning. "You're doomed, sweetie. You might as well hang on and enjoy the ride."

Laila's grin was even broader. "In fact, you might want to buy some Dramamine if you're inclined toward motion sickness."

Even though little Mick had cooperated by going down for his morning nap right on time, Connor couldn't seem to get any work done. He had problems concentrating. He kept thinking about how his evening with Heather had gone so far off course, just when he thought they'd been making progress.

He was sitting on the porch with a stack of case files,

the baby monitor beside him, when Trace came up the steps from the beach and crossed the lawn.

"You busy?" his brother-in-law asked as he sat down.

"I should be, but I'm not. What are you up to?"

Trace glanced around as if he feared spies might be hiding in the bushes. "I came to warn you that Abby's up to something."

Connor's gaze narrowed. "Such as?"

"She brought some guy from her office home for the weekend."

"That's a little in-your-face, even for Abby," Connor commented. "Have you punched the guy out yet?"

Trace chuckled. "I don't think he's here to get me all riled up and jealous."

Understanding immediately dawned. "My sister is actually making good on her threat to fix Heather up with someone else," Connor concluded.

"That would be my guess," Trace said. "Just so you know, I told her days ago that it was a bad idea. Obviously she didn't listen. You know how your sister is once she gets an idea in her head. She can plot and scheme with the best of the family."

Connor wasn't sure he wanted to know the answer to the most obvious question, but he asked it anyway. "Did Heather take the bait?"

"Abby's over at her shop now." He met Connor's gaze. "You ever known your sister not to get what she wants?"

"Well, what the devil am I supposed to do about it if Heather wants to go out with some slick stockbroker?" Connor asked in exasperation. "I can't very well order her not to, can I?"

"Not under current circumstances," Trace agreed. "Quite a quandary for you, isn't it?"

"Instead of gloating, you could at least pretend to be on my side," Connor grumbled.

"I am, which is why I'm here warning you about what's going on. Beyond that, what can I tell you? I have to live with my wife." He stood up. "See you, pal. Good luck."

Connor stewed about Trace's news for an hour. The second he heard his son stirring, he ran upstairs, changed him and loaded him into the car.

"You and I have to go save Mommy from the evil big sister," he muttered as he drove into town.

Hopefully it wasn't too late.

"Gee, what a surprise!" Laila said mockingly when the bell rang over the door at Cottage Quilts just as the quilting class was wrapping up. "Here's Connor."

Heather's head snapped up. Indeed, there he was. There was no sign of their son.

"Where's little Mick?" she asked, deciding to focus on first things first, especially the least controversial things.

"I left him with Bree for five minutes so you and I could talk."

Before Heather could respond, Connie said, "Judging from the sour expression on his face, he must have heard about Abby's big plans."

"You two are not helping," Connor said. "Isn't class over with? Go home. I didn't ditch my son so I could contend with two opinionated observers."

"He seems a little agitated," Laila commented, not even trying to control her smirk.

"He probably rushed right over to protect his turf," Connie added knowingly.

Though the two of them seemed to be having a very good time at Connor's expense, Heather decided it was time to call a halt. "Stop tormenting him, you two."

"Connor can defend himself," Laila said. "We're just trying to be supportive of you."

Heather laughed. "No, you are deliberately taunting him."

"Hello!" Connor muttered irritably. "I'm still here, though I'm beginning to wonder why."

"Would you like me to guide you through the reasons?" Connie asked. "You want to know if Heather accepted a blind date with Abby's friend."

He scowled at her, then turned to Heather. "Actually, yes, I would like an answer to that."

"No," Heather said.

"No what? No, you're not going to answer me, or no, you didn't accept the date?"

"I told Abby I wasn't interested," Heather said, "though it really wouldn't be any of your business if I had said yes."

He frowned. "You don't see anything wrong with accepting a blind date set up by my sister?"

"Philosophically, no."

"Then why didn't you say yes?"

"Because Abby obviously has an agenda. It's going to put the two of you at odds. I saw no point in encouraging that. She's your sister."

"Something she's apparently forgotten," he grumbled.

"She thinks she's helping," Laila said.

"I don't need her help," Connor said.

Connie and Laila exchanged a meaningful look laced with amusement.

Hoping to put an end to the entire discussion, Heather turned to Connor. "Did you stop by for something specific or are they right? Are you here just to protect your turf, which, frankly, isn't yours to protect?"

"I thought maybe you'd like to have dinner at the house with me and little Mick," he said, turning his back on Laila and Connie, who hadn't budged.

"No, thanks," she said.

"But—"

"Not a good idea, Connor."

He looked thoroughly thrown by her flat refusal. "Okay, then," he said, backing toward the door. "We'll see you tomorrow. I'll bring little Mick back around four before I drive back to Baltimore."

She nodded. "That would be great."

On his way out the door, he paused to scowl at Laila and Connie. "You were a big help. Thanks," he said sarcastically.

"Not in your booster club at the moment," Laila told him.

"I'll keep that in mind," he said.

After he'd gone, Laila and Connie turned to Heather. "Maybe you should have gone to dinner with him," Connie suggested. "He is trying."

"Trying to do what?" Heather asked. "Connor and I were great at dating. We were good living together. But sadly, there is no evidence to suggest we'll ever get to the next level. If he's trying at all, it's to get back what he lost, not to move forward."

"But he is a good guy, and he obviously loves you,"

Connie said. "Do you know how many of us would kill to find that?"

"And you'd be content even if the relationship was heading nowhere?" Heather asked skeptically.

"Of course not," Laila said, frowning at Connie, then assuring Heather, "You're right to want it all. We all do."

"I'd just settle for a date on a Saturday night," Connie said wistfully. "It has been way too long."

"But you still wouldn't settle for a man who couldn't commit," Laila told her. "You know you wouldn't."

Eventually Connie nodded. "You're right. Stick to your guns, Heather, even if it means drinks with Laila and me is the only excitement in your life on a Saturday night."

"Great idea," Laila said at once, seizing on the innocent comment. "How about it, Heather? We know you're free. Let's go to Brady's for a couple of hours tonight and have some fun."

Heather hesitated, then thought of how long it had been since she'd gone out with friends for a drink. "Count me in."

"Seven o'clock?" Connie suggested.

"Perfect," Heather said. "I'll meet you there."

As she agreed, she knew that she'd made the right choice. Being with Connor might have been more exciting. Meeting Abby's friend Glenn might have stirred up some interesting complications. But going out with Laila and Connie would be totally uncomplicated fun, something she'd had far too little of in recent months.

In a serious funk over being turned down by Heather, Connor scrapped the idea of cooking hamburgers on the grill in favor of grabbing a crabcake dinner at Brady's. He called his sister—the one who *hadn't* betrayed him—to see if she could join him.

"Just us?" Jess asked carefully.

"And little Mick," he said, puzzled by the question until it dawned on him she was referring to Will. "Are you still avoiding Will?"

"I'm not avoiding him. I'd just prefer to spend time with people who don't try to pick me apart and examine all my flaws."

Connor chuckled.

"It's not funny," she said indignantly.

"It is, because never once in all the years that Will has been hanging around the house have I ever heard him say a negative word about you."

Jess was silent for a moment. "Really? Are you sure?"

"Of course I'm sure."

"He was probably just scared you or Kevin would beat him up," she suggested.

"I don't think so, sis. He likes you."

"Then why does he always pick on me when we're together?"

"Are you sure that's what he's doing? You can be a little sensitive when it comes to certain topics, like your ADD. You get all prickly even when someone makes an offhand comment that isn't meant to offend you."

Jess sighed. "You're right about that. Oh, well, never mind. It doesn't matter if Will's not joining us, anyway. What time do you want me to meet you?"

"Seven okay? I don't want to keep little Mick out too late. He starts getting cranky, and Dillon will kill me if my kid starts wailing in his restaurant."

"We'll just get Kate to protect us," Jess said blithely, referring to Dillon's wife. "Hand the baby off to her. Her biological clock is ticking, so she's into babies these days. Dillon's a little freaked by it."

"He's probably more freaked by the thought of what a pregnancy would do to his efficiently run restaurant," Connor said. "As temperamental as Dillon can be in the kitchen, Kate's the one who smoothes everyone's ruffled feathers and keeps the customers happy."

"You are so right about that," Jess said with a chuckle. "See you at seven." She hesitated, then asked, "By the way, was I your second choice for tonight?"

"What do you mean?"

"Why aren't you with Heather?"

"Not an option," he said tersely.

Jess gasped. "Don't tell me she accepted Abby's invitation to have dinner with that guy!"

Connor wasn't all that surprised that Jess knew about the plot. "No, she turned her down," he said. "But she turned me down, too."

"Sorry, big brother."

"I don't know why I was surprised," he admitted. "It's not as if she hasn't made herself perfectly clear. I keep thinking she'll change her mind, but so far she's sticking to her guns."

"Gee, a stubborn woman!" Jess said, feigning astonishment. "Who'd have thought a mule-headed O'Brien could be taken in by one of those?"

"Well, apparently I was," Connor grumbled. "She's caught me completely off guard."

Jess laughed. "Good for her."

"We'll discuss your lack of family loyalty when I see you," he told her, then hung up.

Oddly enough, though the evening wasn't turning out exactly the way he'd planned, he was still surprisingly content with the prospect of spending it with his sister and his son in a restaurant as good as any of the seafood places in Baltimore. In fact, a relaxing Saturday night in Chesapeake Shores, where he didn't have to be alert to his public image everywhere he went, especially after the Wilder case, held a certain appeal. He wasn't quite sure he could handle a steady diet of peace and tranquility, but for now it suited him.

As always on Saturday night, as the summer season approached Brady's was packed. Heather inched her way past the line of people waiting for tables and slipped into the bar. She found that Connie and Laila had already claimed a booth in a corner.

"This place is a madhouse," Heather said. "It's good to see they're doing well despite the economy."

"Dillon's managed to keep his prices reasonable," Laila said. "He said he'd rather have a packed restaurant than increase his profit margin on every meal. So far, it's working for him. Locals know he has the best food around, and he's not trying to gouge them."

Connie and Laila exchanged a conspiratorial look. It was Connie who spoke.

"Did you happen to catch a glimpse of who else is here tonight?" she asked Heather, leaning across the table and lowering her voice.

"In the restaurant? I couldn't see past the hostess station."

"No, in here," Laila said. "The booth just across from us."

Heather turned and spotted Connor, Jess and little Mick. "Oh dear," she murmured.

"It's not as if they caught you out on a date," Laila said, even though Connor was scowling as if he had. "Just because you turned down his invitation doesn't mean you had to sit home all alone tonight. Just tell him we'd made these plans earlier, if he asks."

"Not that I owe him an explanation," Heather said. "But it's awkward. Have they been here long?"

Connie shook her head. "They came in when we did. I thought about asking them to join us, but that needs to be your call. We got a big booth, just in case."

Heather debated with herself, then looked at Laila and Connie. "It would be the civilized thing to do, wouldn't it? I mean, it's not as if I hate Connor's guts or anything, and that is my son over there."

Laila's lips quirked. "Feeling territorial all of a sudden?"

"Only about my child," Heather said.

"Well, for what it's worth, I say invite them over," Connie said. "Why create some issue over it? We're all here. We're all more or less family. There's no need to stir up some feud like the one between Mick and his brothers that lasts forever."

"I agree," Laila said, then studied Heather. "Unless you'll be uncomfortable."

Heather sighed. "I'm a big girl. I can handle it. I'll go invite them myself."

She crossed the restaurant and focused her attention on Jess. "You look great," she said. "How's business at the inn?"

"Hopping since the season's starting," Jess said, though there was amusement in her eyes over the small talk and over Heather deliberately ignoring Connor.

Finally Heather forced herself to look at him. "We were wondering if you all would like to join us. There's room at our booth and, as packed as this place is, I'm sure they'd appreciate it if they could free up a table."

He regarded her with surprise. "You sure?"

"Of course."

He glanced at Jess, who was openly smiling now. "Is it okay with you?"

"As if I'd dare to say no," she murmured, already picking up her purse and drink and heading across the room.

Heather plucked little Mick from the high chair, and Connor followed with the chair. When they settled into the booth, she found herself squeezed between Jess and Connor. She frowned at Laila, who'd slipped in next to Connie in order to accomplish that. Laila merely gave her an innocent look and lifted her beer in the air in a silent toast.

"To happy families," she said, drawing a scowl from Heather and a sharp look from Connor.

Beside Heather, Jess chuckled, then enthusiastically tapped glasses with the traitor across the table.

Heather sighed. If dinner at Abby's with a strange man would have been awkward, this promised to top it.

11

Though Connor had been pleased by Saturday night's turn of events, he regretted that he'd been with Heather by happenstance rather than her choice. He supposed he should be grateful that she hadn't chosen to ignore his presence or bolted from the restaurant when she'd first seen him there with Jess. Still, he was vaguely disgruntled when he stopped to drop off little Mick on Sunday and all too ready to pick a fight.

As soon as his son was happily settled in his playpen, he turned to Heather. "Why didn't you just tell me you were going out with Laila and Connie yesterday when I asked you to come to dinner?"

"Because we hadn't made our plans at that point," she said with exaggerated patience. "Don't you see, Connor? It doesn't matter whether I have other plans. I can't accept dates with you. I don't want to lead you to believe that we're going to get back together."

He shook his head in disbelief. "This isn't some misguided attempt to protect me, Heather. You're scared if we spend time together, you'll cave in."

She actually smiled at that. "No question about it,"

she said readily. "Right now, though, my willpower and convictions are strong. That doesn't mean I want to put myself into temptation's path."

"Me being temptation?" he said, oddly pleased by that. It was pitiful that he was grateful for even such a tiny bone being tossed his way.

"Yes, Connor, you being temptation."

"Good to know. I'll have to figure out how to capitalize on that."

"Maybe you should spend more time trying to figure out why you're really so determined not to do the one thing that might really get me back," she suggested.

"Reevaluating my views on marriage," he said.

"Of course." She gave him a wide-eyed look meant to indicate, he supposed, that she'd just been struck by something. "What about counseling? Let an objective outsider work through your issues with you. I'd suggest Will, since you're already comfortable with him, but that might not be the best thing. He might let you off the hook too easily."

He regarded her with annoyance. "I'm not the one with a cockeyed view of the world. Evidence backs me up. You're the one wearing rose-colored glasses."

"I'm hardly the Lone Ranger when it comes to believing in love," she said. "Thousands of people take that leap into marriage every single day."

"And get divorced a year later," he retorted. "Lucky for me."

She simply stared at him, clearly not amused. "Do you hear yourself?" she asked in dismay. "Is it any wonder I don't want to be with someone who's that negative and cynical? How do you stand yourself? In fact, how do you stand living in a world that's so dark and gloomy? I suppose I can't drag you out of all that dreariness, but I surely don't want to live there with you. And I will not have my son raised with those beliefs."

Connor felt as if a cold fist were squeezing the life out of him. "You're not about to ask for sole custody of little Mick, are you?"

"Of course not. I figure I can counteract whatever message he hears from you."

"But that's it for you and me?" he pressed. "You've fallen out of love with me because I don't share your idyllic view of love and marriage?"

"Sadly, no," she said quietly. "I will love you forever. You have so many wonderful qualities that I admire. You're a great father. You're funny and smart. You're thoughtful and considerate."

He made another attempt at humor. "Then I'm astonished you haven't snapped me up."

"Oh, Connor, how can I? I can't accept a relationship that's less than everything it could be. I don't want that for myself. I don't want it for little Mick. And, believe it or not, I don't want it for you, either." She pulled her gaze away. "You should probably leave now."

Connor started to argue, but in the end, what was left to say? That he thought what they had was worth fighting for? It was. That he loved her? He did. She knew all of that.

And it still wasn't enough.

Thomas had a pounding headache, the same one he usually got when he went over research that showed pollution levels in the Chesapeake Bay weren't improving as quickly as they should be. The problem, he believed, didn't lie with lax laws. It was with erratic enforcement by all of the states with tributaries that fed into the bay.

He'd pushed aside the report and was about to ring for Kevin to join him to hammer out a new battle plan, when someone tapped on his office door and stepped inside.

"Connie!" he said, his mood brightening at the unexpected sight of her, the way it did when the sun unexpectedly peeked out from behind a cloud an a dreary gray day. "Was I expecting you today?"

She laughed. "Now that's a question I can't answer, can I? I did speak to your receptionist a few days ago, and she put me on your calendar."

He winced. "I suppose I should pay more attention to that, but distraction's a bad habit of mine."

"Is this a good time?" she asked.

"If you'll go with me for a cup of coffee and some conversation, it's an excellent time," he said. He gestured to the research papers on his desk. "I've just spent the morning trying to absorb more depressing news."

"Would you share it with me?" she asked eagerly.

He regarded her with amazement. "You actually want to read a bunch of statistics and dire predictions?"

"The whole point of me coming up here is to get up to speed on the latest research," she said. "It seems as if my timing is perfect."

Thrilled by the idea of a captive audience, Thomas grabbed the papers, then showed her out of his office. They walked to a small waterfront café mostly frequented by those who worked along the nearby Severn River. It didn't have much atmosphere, but the tables were clean and the coffee was strong and plentiful.

"I am so excited about this," Connie said, sitting across from him. "I spoke to Shanna yesterday, and she's ecstatic that we're going to be doing these speaking events. She and I even roughed out a timetable for you. We weren't sure how many you wanted to schedule, so we just listed all the bay-front towns that might be receptive to such an event. We can schedule as many or as few as you'd like."

Thomas chuckled at her enthusiasm. "I knew I'd chosen the right people to do this. You'll have me working every Friday night and Saturday if I'm not careful."

"The way I hear it, you work all the time, anyway," she said, then blushed. "That's the family view, anyway."

"It is, indeed," he said, not denying it.

"Is that what happened to your marriages?" she asked, then clapped a hand over her mouth. "Sorry. I have a habit of talking before my brain engages. It's just that I know you've been married twice, so I wondered if being a workaholic contributed in some way…" Her voice trailed off as she flushed with embarrassment.

Thomas couldn't seem to tear his gaze away from the sudden pink in her cheeks. When was the last time he'd met someone who spoke with such an intriguing blend of candor and naiveté?

"I'm actually surprised the family grapevine didn't supply that bit of information as well," he said with humor. "It's true. My wives tired of me being married to my work. It was worse, as you might imagine, when I was actually working on the Chesapeake Shores development with Mick and trying to fight for the bay's preservation at the same time. If my wife saw me one night out of seven, it was a bonus," he admitted ruefully. "It took her a year to tire of it."

"That seems awfully quick to bail on a marriage," Connie said.

"Not when the handwriting's already on the wall," he said.

"And wife number two?"

"Oh, she came in with her eyes wide open, claimed to love the fact that I was so passionate about my work. It turned out that gave her plenty of time for a few little dalliances on the side. We agreed to end it after nine months. I'll never know if she might have been faithful if I'd been around more. I like to think so."

"Then I suppose you're as jaded when it comes to marriage as Connor?" she said, looking saddened by the idea.

"No, indeed. I'm an optimist. Or is it called crazy when a person keeps doing the same thing and expecting a different outcome?"

"I'd call it hopeful," she said. "Why do you suppose Connor can't see that?"

"Because he's not ready to admit he's been wrong," Thomas said. "O'Briens hate acknowledging their weaknesses. He'll come around and marry Heather, if that's what's worrying you."

"It just seems such a shame that he's throwing away this incredible chance at happiness," Connie said, then held up her hand. "I didn't come up here to discuss all these personal O'Brien family dynamics. Tell me what that impressive pile of papers says."

Thomas nodded. "I'll try to give you the short version,

but my enthusiasm is likely to get the better of me. When you've heard enough, just say the word."

She leaned closer, as if trying to read the papers upside down. "Not going to happen." She squinted. "What does this say? Something about the oyster population?"

Thomas nodded, then turned the pages so she could see them more clearly. There was nothing he liked more than an eager student, especially one as lovely as this one was.

When the thought struck him, it gave him momentary pause. Connie Collins had to be young enough, what, to be his daughter? No, of course not. She had a daughter of her own about to go off to college, which meant she had to be forty or close to it. And he wasn't that far on the other side of fifty.

Still, she was of the generation of his nieces and nephews. Thinking about her as anything other than a volunteer would be insane. Despite that reminder, when he looked into her bright, curious eyes, they inevitably brought on a smile. And maybe a little bump in a heart rate that had been slow and steady for way too long.

On a Friday morning two weeks after Connor's visit, Heather was surprised when Megan walked into the shop wearing what had to be an outfit she'd picked up in Paris. She looked more stylish than ever with her frosted blond hair and trim figure.

Heather came out from behind the counter to hug her. "Welcome home! I didn't think you were due back here till next week."

"We weren't," she said, her expression chagrined.

Heather frowned. "The honeymoon didn't go well?"

"Oh, the honeymoon was fantastic, thank you very much," Megan said with a laugh. "The French food was amazing, the wine was superb, the scenery spectacular and the art amazing. Mick was on his very best behavior and at his most charming."

"If it was all so wonderful, then I'm a little bit surprised you didn't buy a place and stay there," Heather teased.

"The truth? I missed my family," Megan said. "I've just gotten them back, and being away right now, especially with everything that's going on, was killing me. Mick, too, though he wouldn't admit it. He made a big show of sacrificing the last few days of our trip to cater to my whim to be back here in the thick of things."

"We would all have been right here with nothing changed if you'd waited to come back," Heather told her.

"Maybe that's what worried me most," Megan admitted. "Some things need to change."

"If you're referring to Connor and me, forget it," Heather said. "I will not discuss that with you."

Megan's face fell. "What's happened now?"

"Absolutely nothing, really. He's in his dark world and determined to stay there. I refuse to join him. Why keep fighting it? Now, let's move on. Tell me everything about Paris. I've always wanted to go there."

"Then you can join us tomorrow night to look at the hundreds of pictures Mick took. Or you can say no, and I'll bring the pictures in here when you won't have to listen to his travelogue."

"Oh, no. I want the full commentary," Heather said. "What time?"

Megan hesitated. "Connor said he couldn't make it till six or so. Is seven okay?"

Heather's enthusiasm died at the unexpected mention of Connor. "Maybe I will look at the pictures here, after all."

Megan didn't even attempt to hide her disappointment. "Sweetie, you can't avoid him forever."

"It's hardly forever. He was here less than two weeks ago."

Megan looked surprised. "While we were gone? That's great."

"Not really." She touched Megan's hand. "It's okay. I don't mind waiting to see the pictures. Then you'll have another chance to talk about the trip. I don't want to spoil the evening."

"You could hardly do that," Megan said. "I swear that son of mine needs to have his head examined."

Heather laughed. "Don't mention that to him. I suggested the same thing, and he didn't take it well."

Megan stared at her. "Seriously? You told him to see a shrink?"

"I thought maybe somebody objective could help him sort through his issues," Heather responded with a shrug. "Suffice it to say, he didn't like the idea."

"No, I imagine he didn't," Megan said. "You see, years ago I had the bright idea that perhaps the children should all go to counseling to deal with the divorce. Mick ranted and raved that I was the crazy one and that *his* children didn't need a psychologist to tell them anything. It was quite a tirade. I'm quite sure the kids all overheard this because Abby mentioned it to me years later. Connor might have gotten the idea from his father that seeing a shrink is a weakness. You'd think he'd have outgrown that view, especially with Will as a friend, but sometimes the wrong lessons stick."

Heather shook her head. "Which is all the more reason why he needs to see one."

Megan smiled. "You could have a point, at that. Perhaps I will push the idea myself, after all. He's always annoyed with me, so what do I have to lose?"

Impulsively, Heather hugged Megan. "I am so glad you're home."

"Me, too, sweetheart. Me, too."

Connor thrived on work, and in his drive to make partner, he'd been taking on more and more cases. Lately, when he didn't want to think about Heather and the mess that was their relationship, work had been his solace, a crammed calendar a boon.

Today, though, for some reason he was barely able to contain himself as yet another client outlined his wife's flaws and his own justifications for wanting out of the marriage. That's what they were, too—self-righteous justifications for breaking their wedding vows. It was the first time Connor had looked at them that way, which meant Heather was in his head again.

He looked at the man seated opposite him, the CEO of a local company who'd found excuse after excuse for the affairs he'd been having. Now that his wife had filed for divorce and was seeking a huge settlement, he wanted to blame all of his bad choices on her.

Normally Connor would have focused solely on the man's complaints about his wife, but as with Clint Wilder, all of a sudden he wondered about her side of the story.

Had anything she'd done—or not done—really justified the man cheating on her repeatedly?

"So, you can get me out of this without me losing everything, right?" Paul Lacey asked. "Everyone says you're the best at making sure we guys don't get taken for a ride by our ex-wives."

"How many kids do you have?"

"Three."

"How old?"

"Six, ten and twelve," he said.

"Spend much time with them?"

The man squirmed a bit. "As much as I can, given the kind of schedule I have to keep at work."

"What are you thinking about custody?"

Lacey looked surprisingly thrown by the question. "Visitation, I guess," he said, sounding disinterested.

Connor was taken aback. "Not even joint custody?"

"Like I said, I don't have a lot of spare time," Lacey replied defensively.

Right then, Connor decided he didn't like his client. What kind of father could be so dismissive about being part of his children's lives? No matter what happened between him and Heather, he would always want to play a huge role in little Mick's life. So far they'd been able to work out a fair schedule, so he hadn't seen a need to legalize his rights, but if it came to that, he'd insist on joint custody.

"Okay, here's how I see it, Paul," he began. "You're going to abdicate the major responsibility for raising your children to your wife. She's going to ask for a substantial amount in child support, and the court will approve it. Given the facts of the situation, which you've admitted to me and of which she's apparently well aware, she's likely to get more alimony than you want to pay. Before this goes any further, why don't you take a step back, go home and try to work things out? It's the only way you're going to come out of this a winner."

It was the first time in his career that Connor had made such a recommendation wholeheartedly. In the past, he'd made the suggestion, then quickly dropped it when his client demurred. Usually he was all too eager to rush into court or mediation and fight for his client's financial rights.

Paul Lacey looked thrown by his advice. "I came here so you could represent me in my divorce and you're advocating that we reconcile? What kind of lawyer are you?"

"An honest one. I can take your case and promise to do my best, but you're going to come out a loser if what matters to you is preserving your bank account. If you ever cared about your wife and family, maybe you should take another stab at remembering why. That's all I'm saying. If things don't work out, divorce will still be an option."

Even as the words came out of his mouth, Connor was surprised by them. What? Was he channeling Heather all of a sudden? It was disconcerting, to say the least.

Lacey stood up. "I'll think about it. If I call you on Monday and tell you to proceed, you'll handle it, right?"

"Sure," Connor said, though without much enthu-siasm.

As soon as Paul Lacey had left, Connor grabbed his briefcase full of case files and headed for the door.

"Marjorie, I'm done for the weekend. If you need me, call my cell."

"But you have a four o'clock appointment," she protested. "And I thought you'd scheduled several meetings for tomorrow, too. What should I do about those?"

"Call and reschedule. I need to get down to Chesapeake Shores." He should have canceled the appointments the minute his mother had called about the honeymoon travelogue she had on tap for tomorrow night, but at the time he hadn't been overjoyed by the prospect of an evening of cheesy family photos.

Worry immediately creased Marjorie's brow at his response. "A family emergency?"

"In a way, but nothing for you to worry about."

He just wanted to see Heather and his son. After a couple of weeks of dealing with nonstop ugliness, he needed to be reminded that innocence still existed. Seeing little Mick would accomplish that.

As for seeing Heather, despite how he fought her, even he was starting to appreciate the way she clung to all that was good and hopeful in the world. After the past couple of weeks, he needed that balance even more than he'd realized. And maybe he needed some time to think about why that was.

Heather had finally allowed herself to be persuaded to join the family for dinner. She pulled into the winding driveway at the house just behind Connor. He came over to help her with little Mick.

"Just getting here?" she asked.

"Actually, I came down last night," he said as he tickled his son and set off delighted giggles.

She regarded him with surprise. "I thought you were jammed up at work."

"I was, but I had Marjorie reschedule a few things. I needed to get down here for some peace and quiet and a fix of my guy here."

"Really? That's new."

"Never let it be said I can't learn an occasional new trick." He met her gaze. "I'm glad you're here. Mom said she was inviting you, but I wasn't sure you'd say yes."

"Your mom was so excited about the trip, how could I say no?"

"And you knew I'd be here?" he asked.

She smiled. "Yes, Connor. I knew."

"And you came anyway," he said with exaggerated shock.

"I weighed the wisdom of staying away against the delight of hearing absolutely everything about Paris. Paris won."

"I just hope they leave out the details about the honeymoon itself," Connor said with an exaggerated shudder.

She laughed. "I don't imagine they'd want to share those, so I think your delicate ears are safe." She studied his face, then sobered. "What's going on, Connor? Have you had a bad day at the office?"

"One too many cheating husbands who expect me to save their hides, if you must know."

She actually stopped in her tracks. "Did you just sound as disillusioned by your clients as I think you did?"

He shrugged. "Probably. I'm sure it's just two weeks of back-to-back consultations with new clients, who mostly have the same old story." He held her gaze. "And maybe one more thing."

"What's that?"

"You whispering in my ear that they're whiny jerks," he admitted.

"I have never once called your clients whiny jerks," she protested, though she couldn't help smiling. "Even if that is what some of them are."

"All of them," he conceded with shocking candor. He looked at her with bemusement. "Why couldn't I see that before?"

"Because you thought you were put into the legal world to defend the rights of all men who'd been mistreated by conniving women. You saw them through the prism of your own experience or, to be more precise, your dad's."

"Maybe," he said, which amounted to a huge concession coming from him. "All I know is that for two weeks now, I've sat there listening and taking notes, all the while wondering why any woman would want to stay married to these men." He met her gaze. "I think you've ruined my career."

"Not that I necessarily think that would be a bad thing," she said at once, "but I doubt it's true. There are plenty of men who deserve to have someone like you fighting for them in court. Maybe you just need to be more discriminating about the cases you take."

"I'm trying to make partner. The heavier my caseload, the better my chances."

She halted him by putting a hand on his arm. "Is it worth it?" she asked. "I know making partner is like the Holy Grail or something, but what if you lose your soul in the process?"

Now Connor laughed. "Despite your low opinion of what I do, I'm not selling my soul to the devil."

"If you say so," she said, not entirely convinced.

"Seriously, Heather, I'll be fine. I just had a rough couple of weeks. Seeing you and little Mick is just what I needed. You'll ground me again."

She wanted to believe she provided some kind of balance to his life, but she was one person, little Mick only a baby. They couldn't be responsible for saving him from the gloomy aspects of the kind of law he'd chosen to practice. Only he could do that.

But from what she'd heard him say tonight, perhaps he was actually starting to do that.

12

After rushing to get to Chesapeake Shores on Friday, Connor had deliberately made himself wait until Saturday evening to see Heather. He'd needed the time to think. Discovering that he was suddenly disenchanted with some aspects of his career had come as a shock to him. He suspected it would pass once he'd had a weekend filled with watching his parents make fools of themselves under the guise of having fallen in love all over again.

To his surprise, though, they actually seemed to be genuinely happy. He couldn't deny the glow on his mother's face or the light in his father's eyes every time he caught a glimpse of Megan. And their teasing banter as they showed the stacks of photos they'd taken in Paris, tripping over each other's words as they shared their honeymoon memories, was a revelation to him. He couldn't recall a single time from his childhood when there had been so much rapport between his parents or so much laughter in their house.

There had to have been, of course. People didn't stay married for nearly twenty years before divorcing without at least *some* joy to keep them hanging in for so long.

Had Connor been too young when there'd been laughter, instead of tension, or had he blocked it out in his zeal to blame his mother for tearing the family apart?

He'd certainly managed to turn a blind eye to every single good time he and his mother had spent together. He grudgingly admitted that her recent gentle nudging had stirred a few of those happier memories. He'd have to ask Abby or Kevin, who were older, about the laughter one of these days. Of course, to ask would be to risk having the rest of his bitter memories of the past shattered.

As he sat off to one side, in place for the honeymoon reminiscing but not quite part of it, Carrie came over and snuggled up beside him.

"Hey, short stuff, what's up with you?" he asked, studying his niece's pensive expression.

"Caitlyn and me have been thinking," she told him solemnly.

It was practically a given that those two thought in unison, Connor thought, restraining a smile. "Is that so? About what?"

"We really, really liked being in Mommy's wedding to Trace. And we liked wearing the pretty red velvet dresses for Grandma Megan's wedding to Grandpa Mick."

"And you looked beautiful," he assured her, having no idea where she was heading with this. But all women, even at nine, loved being told they were pretty. Of that he was sure.

She beamed at him. "You thought so?"

"Of course."

She gave him a wistful look. "We'd like to do it again," she said.

Connor was lost. "What? Wear pretty dresses? I'm sure

you have a whole closet full of dresses that you can wear anytime. I know how much your mom and your grandmother like taking you shopping. And if you want to go someplace where you can dress up, maybe your mom will bring you and your sister up to Baltimore, and I'll take you out someplace fancy for lunch. Or we can go to one of the hotels for afternoon tea. You can pretend you're princesses."

She shook her head fiercely. "No, silly. We don't want to wear just *any* dresses. We like the kind for weddings." She gave him a sly look. "Lunch would be good, too, or even tea, but weddings are the best."

He stared at her blankly. "Why tell me?"

"Because we heard Mommy talking, and she says you and Heather should get married. So we think when you do, we ought to be in the wedding." She regarded him hopefully. "What do you think? Will you ask Heather if it's okay?"

"I think your mommy talks too much," he said, scowling at his big sister across the room. Abby managed to pull off a totally innocent expression, as if she weren't perfectly aware that Carrie had just put him on the hot seat.

Caitlyn suddenly appeared and snuggled close on his other side. She regarded her sister eagerly. "Did he say yes?"

"No," Carrie said sorrowfully. "Not yet, anyway."

Caitlyn stared up at him. "How come? We did a good job in Grandma Megan's wedding to Grandpa Mick. Everybody said so."

"You did a fabulous job," he agreed. "But I'm not planning to get married."

Both girls blinked at him, their expressions shocked. "Not ever?"

"Not ever," he confirmed.

"But you and Heather have a baby," Carrie said, puzzlement written all over her face. "Aren't you supposed to be married to have a baby?"

"That's certainly the way it should be," Abby said, joining them. "Right, brother dear?" The look in her eyes dared him to say otherwise to her impressionable nine-year-old girls.

Connor was so far out of his depths he wanted to bolt, but how could he with his nieces staring at him with such earnest expressions?

"Your mother is absolutely right that people should wait until they're married to have children," he said eventually, then regarded Abby with a touch of defiance, "or at least until they're old enough to understand the responsibilities that come with being parents."

"But you have a baby and you're not married, so isn't the baby illegal?" Caitlyn asked worriedly. "That's what someone at school said."

"It was that dumb Tommy Winston," Carrie added. "He called Jimmy Laughlin illegal, 'cause he doesn't have a dad. You don't want Mick to be illegal, do you?"

"Not illegal, illegitimate," Abby corrected, her gaze commanding Connor to talk his way out of this.

Connor drew in a deep breath. "What's important is that your cousin has a mommy and a daddy who both love him more than anything in the whole wide world," he told them, hoping that would put an end to it. He should have known better. These were the girls who'd asked *why* so incessantly it had nearly driven everyone in the family berserk.

"But if you don't live together and be a family, how's he supposed to know that?" Again it was Caitlyn, the little worrier, who asked.

"You don't live with your dad, but you know he loves you, right?" Connor explained.

"I guess," she said after several seconds of thoughtful deliberation.

Connor scrambled to reassure her. "And you know that all of us, your aunts and uncles and your grandparents, we love you, but we don't live in the same house with you."

Carrie's expression brightened. "That's true."

"Well, that's the way it is for little Mick. He lives with his mom, but I see him as much as I can so he'll know how much I love him, too. And he has all of you in his life, so he'll always be surrounded by lots of love."

"Will he get more presents?" Carrie asked. "Me and Caitlyn get lots and lots of presents because we have a dad and Trace, too."

Connor hid a smile. "Sometimes it works that way."

Apparently satisfied at last, they stood up. "I want ice cream," Carrie announced.

"Me, too," Caitlyn said, right on her heels as they raced toward the kitchen.

Connor glared at his big sister. "Thanks. I know you put them up to that."

"Actually, I didn't. They caught wedding fever all on their own and figured out you and Heather were their best bet."

"But you knew we weren't," he charged.

Abby shrugged. "Not necessarily. Things change. You could come to your senses any minute now."

"Bite me," he said cheerfully, then sobered. "By the way, I hope you're not planning another blind date for Heather. She's not interested."

Abby merely smiled. "Like I said, things change."

His heart thudded dully at the glint in her eyes. "What does that mean?"

"It means that life isn't static, little brother. Heather might have said no last time, but who knows what tomorrow might bring?"

"Abigail, do not start messing in my life!"

She grinned. "I wouldn't dream of it. Heather, however, as you very well know, is her own person."

Before he could decide whether throttling a meddling big sister would be considered assault, she sashayed off. Not five minutes later, when he saw her huddled with Heather, his temper stirred, but he managed to bite his tongue. Seething, he left the house before he could do or say anything that would be way too revealing about the state of mind he was in where the mother of his child was concerned.

Heather knew exactly what Abby was up to. She'd seen Connor's sister obviously taunting him, then making a beeline straight across the room in Heather's own direction. She had no idea what the two O'Brien siblings had been discussing, but it had sent Connor storming from the house. Now Abby was trying to persuade Heather she needed to go after him.

"Why?" she asked, studying Abby with blatant skepticism. "Are you meddling again?"

"Who me?" Abby asked, all innocence. "I'm just worried about my brother. Something's on his mind this weekend."

"He had a tough couple of weeks at work," Heather said.

Abby seemed to take great comfort in her response. "Then he's talked to you about it?" she said eagerly. "That's progress."

"He mentioned a few things," Heather admitted, immediately realizing her mistake. "I'd hardly call that progress."

"Of course it is," Abby said. "It just proves when the chips are down, you're the first person he thinks of. You've been with him all through law school and the bar exam. You know how difficult it is. He came to you because he knows you'll understand."

"What's your point?"

"That everyone needs a special someone who really gets what they're going through. It's good that Connor has you."

"He doesn't have me, Abby," she said patiently. "Not anymore."

"You wouldn't be there for him if he was going through a crisis?" Abby asked, feigning shock. She shook her head then. "I don't believe that. Whatever else has happened, I know how deeply you care about him."

"Connor's not going through a crisis," Heather said, though she did wonder a bit about that. He'd certainly seemed shaken by some of the things he'd discovered recently. "He's just seeing a few things from a different perspective."

"A better perspective?"

"Possibly."

"Then maybe you should stick around and encourage that," Abby said. "That's all I'm saying. Forget whatever's going on between the two of you for a minute. Don't we all want him to take another look at this depressing career track he's on? It's practically our duty to do anything we can to encourage that."

"Your brother is actually on a very successful career track," Heather corrected.

"In the wrong kind of law," Abby insisted. "And for all the wrong reasons. I know you don't disagree with that."

"No, I don't," Heather admitted reluctantly. As much as she liked Abby, she was uncomfortable with this sudden feeling that Abby saw them as coconspirators.

"Then go out there and talk some sense into him," Abby told her. "However his second thoughts started, press the advantage."

Heather smiled. "Don't you think if I'd been able to get through to Connor, it would have happened a long time ago? When it comes to his job, Connor pretty much tunes me out."

Of course, earlier he'd actually said he'd been hearing her voice in his head. Maybe now *was* the time to press the advantage, as Abby had just said. Before Abby could summon more arguments, Heather caved in.

"I'll go and talk to him," she said. At least she wouldn't have to listen to any more of Abby's less-than-subtle attempts at persuasion.

Abby beamed. "Good for you! We're all counting on you."

Heather frowned at her. "Don't. I'm not doing this for

you or your family. It's only because I care as much about Connor as you do."

"Whatever," Abby said blithely. "At least you'll be talking. That's what counts."

Heather sighed. Perhaps in the world of a sneaky O'Brien it really was all that mattered.

Heather found Connor sitting at the top of the steps leading down to the beach. High tide had waves lapping all the way up to the bottom step, completely obliterating the narrow strip of sand beyond. She dropped down beside him.

"Who's Abby fixed you up with now?" he asked without looking at her.

"I beg your pardon?"

"That's what she's up to, you know. She's determined to set you up with some rich investment guy just to make me crazy." He scowled at her. "It's not going to work."

Heather smiled. "And yet here you are, sitting out here all alone with a nasty attitude."

"My attitude's just fine."

She swallowed a laugh. "Yes, I can see that."

He faced her then. "Why are you out here? Did you come to gloat about the hot new man in your life?"

She did laugh then. "No, actually I'm here because your sister seemed to think you had a lot on your mind. I was persuaded, however, to think it had something to do with second thoughts about your career."

His mouth gaped. "That's how she got you out here?"

"Pretty much. Since it fit with the conversation you and I had earlier, I thought I'd check it out."

"Then there's no man?"

"Not at the moment."

His gaze immediately narrowed. "You're leaving the door open?"

"It seems wise," she said, her tone casual. "And your career? Are you thinking of abandoning it?"

"I'm a bit disillusioned, not crazy."

"Which means your sister is up to another of her manipulative tricks," Heather concluded.

"I swear I'll never trust another word out of that woman's mouth," Connor declared with feeling. "You probably shouldn't, either. She stirred the twins up about being in our wedding. Did you know that?"

Heather chuckled, knowing how Carrie and Caitlyn could get carried away when they wanted something. "How'd you handle that?"

"With the truth. I said we weren't getting married, which led to a whole discussion about having babies without the sanctity of marriage." He shuddered. "It was not the happiest few minutes of my life."

"I can imagine."

He turned and studied her face. "I know I'm making light of this, but do you hear much about the fact that we have a baby and aren't married?"

"Nothing I haven't been able to handle. It helps that your whole family is so openly supportive. I doubt anyone in town would dare to say much behind my back, much less to my face."

"I'm sorry if anyone's ever made you uncomfortable. It's not fair."

She shrugged. "I knew when I moved here that there could be questions. It's actually been better than I expected. I hear a whole lot more from my mother."

Connor grimaced. "I can imagine. Have you spoken to her recently?"

"Why? So I can hear another lecture? I'm not interested. She's made her opinion plain."

A guilt-stricken expression crossed his face. "Heather, you have to know that I never meant for things to turn out like this. I thought we'd be together forever, and eventually that would be enough to silence all these people who think marriage is the only way to be happy."

"Hey, we both made our choices, Connor. And little Mick is a blessing. I won't let anyone, especially not my own mother, say otherwise."

"Of course he is," he said just as vehemently. "Still, I can't help being sorry that there's a rift between you and your mother, and it's my fault."

"It's not all your fault. I knew what I was getting into practically from our very first date. By the time we moved in together, I'd accepted the way things were. It would be totally wrong for me to cry foul now. If anyone changed the rules, it was me."

A breeze stirred off the water and blew a strand of hair into her face. Connor reached over and tucked it behind her ear, his knuckles grazing her cheek. Even such an innocent touch sent heat and need spiraling through her. She told herself she should get up and go back inside, but when he met her gaze, she couldn't even make herself look away, much less move.

"God, I miss you," he said quietly.

Tears stung her eyes. "I miss you, too."

He skimmed a finger across the dampness on her cheeks. "Why do you have to be so beautiful?"

She smiled at that. "Just to torment you, I guess."

He leaned closer then. Her breath caught in her throat as she waited for him to kiss her, but at the last second he pulled back.

"Sorry," he said, his voice gruff. "I'm not playing fair, am I?"

Sadly, right at that moment, she didn't want him to play fair. She wanted his mouth on hers, his arms around her. She wanted to feel the strength that had always made her feel so safe.

"No," she conceded, her voice shaky. Had she admitted to the need, she would have gotten what she wanted, a kiss that stirred memories…and heartache.

Instead, she forced a smile, rose to her feet and walked back to the house, settling for the heartache alone.

Connor stayed by the bay a while longer before finally going back up to the house. When he got there, Heather had already left with their son.

"Little Mick had a bit of a fever," his mother told him. "Heather thought she ought to get him home and into bed."

Connor regarded her with alarm. "He's sick?"

Megan put a reassuring hand on his arm. "Kids spike fevers all the time, Connor. I'm sure it's a routine childhood illness. If it turns out to be more, Heather will call."

"I'm not waiting around for that," he said. "Tell Jess I had to leave. She and I were going out for a drink at Brady's after things wound up here. She needs to go without me. Will's meeting us there."

His mother's eyes lit up. "Really? Is there something going on between those two?"

"Not if Jess has her way," Connor admitted.

"But Will's crazy about her, isn't he?" she pressed.

He nodded. "Seems that way to me. I'm trying to remain neutral."

Megan's expression turned thoughtful. "If what you say is true and I tell Jess you're not going, she won't go, either."

Connor hadn't considered that. "You're right. I should probably call Will and cancel."

"No," his mother said hurriedly. "I'll tell Jess you're running by Heather's and will meet her at Brady's." She looked especially pleased with her solution.

Connor laughed. "Nice to know the meddling gene hasn't missed anyone in this family."

"Certainly not me," Megan said. "I just try to be a bit more subtle than some other people we could both name."

"Be careful with Jess, Mom. She's more vulnerable than she pretends."

"I know that," she said quietly, then touched his cheek. "Thank you for looking out for her." She studied his face for a moment. "Who, I wonder, looks out for you?"

Connor chafed at the idea he needed looking after. "My life's under control. I don't need looking after."

She shook her head, a sad expression on her face. "If only that were true. Run along and check on your son. Call me if you need me."

Connor left the house with the oddest feeling that he'd just had a totally honest conversation with his mother for one of the few times in recent memory. He not only appreciated her genuine concern for Jess, but he actually felt better knowing she would come running if his son was truly ill.

When he reached Heather's apartment moments later, the upstairs lights were on. He parked in the alley behind the shops and took the steps two at a time. He would have banged on the door, but then worried that little Mick might be sleeping. He tapped gently, then tried the knob. It opened at once, which was an issue for another discussion. Tonight he needed to focus on his son.

Heather was halfway to the door when he stepped inside. She studied him with surprise.

"What are you doing here?" she asked suspiciously.

"Mom said little Mick had a fever."

She seemed to relax at his response. "She shouldn't have worried you. It's nothing," she said. "His temperature is already back to normal and he's sound asleep."

He stood where he was, suddenly uncomfortable. "Oh." He was all too aware that he'd invaded her space, space she'd been trying to preserve as a sanctuary, free from any memories of him. "I should go, then."

As if she'd guessed what he was thinking, she managed a half smile. "It's okay. You're here now. Would you like something to drink? I'm afraid I don't have any beer or wine, just sodas."

He searched her face. "You don't mind?"

"Well, you've crossed the threshold and the world hasn't come to an end, so I suppose it's okay."

He thought of the kiss they'd almost shared earlier. Being here, alone with Heather, even with little Mick in the next room, might be tempting fate.

"It's probably not a good idea for me to hang around," he said eventually. "I wanted to do a lot more earlier than just kiss you. If I stay here now, who knows what I might do?"

She looked into his eyes. "God help me, but I kind of like the idea that I can still make you lose control."

His gaze narrowed. "What are you saying, Heather?"

"Only that I'm willing to take the risk of letting you stay," she said hurriedly. "Not that I'm encouraging you to try something."

He smiled at the breathless note in her voice. "So it's okay with you if we hang out for a while and torture each other with thoughts of all the things we're *not* going to do?"

She nodded. "Shall I pour you a soda?"

He met the challenge in her gaze. "Sure. Why not? A little seductive torture is probably good for the soul."

"I'm almost certain it builds character," she agreed with a grin as she flipped open the tab on a soda and poured it over ice, then handed him the glass.

"You do realize there's not enough ice in that pitiful little fridge of yours to cool the thoughts going through my mind right now, don't you?"

She gave him a purely feminine, wicked smile. "I'm actually counting on it," she admitted. "What does that say about me?"

"That you're a tease," he said, amused despite the agony he was bound to be suffering if they kept up this game. "How did I not know that about you?"

"Because in the past you always got what you wanted in the end," she said. "Then it's not teasing."

"But not tonight?" he concluded.

"Not tonight," she confirmed.

"Then I'll make do with the company," he said,

choosing a chair that put him halfway across the room from the sofa where she'd chosen to sit.

Distance might keep him from acting on the temptation she represented, but, he discovered, it didn't do one blasted thing to cool him down.

13

"Wasn't that Connor's car I saw parked in the alley late last night?" Laila asked when she stopped by Heather's on Sunday morning.

"He came over to check on little Mick," Heather said, turning pink with embarrassment even though he'd had a legitimate excuse for being there. It wasn't as if there'd been some secret rendezvous. Still, she felt compelled to add, "Megan told him Mick had a fever."

"And that required him to stick around half the night?" Laila inquired, her expression bland. "I had no idea he was such a devoted father."

"Well, of course he is," Heather said defensively. "He adores that boy."

"Just not enough to marry his mother," Laila commented, then added with a shake of her head, "The man's an idiot."

"Hey, don't say stuff like that about Connor," Heather protested. "I knew the score from the beginning. I just hoped for a different outcome."

Laila shook her head. "I've known him longer. I say he's an idiot. You're not at fault for wanting what any woman would want, a husband and family, especially when the family part has already happened. I can't believe he's behaving so irresponsibly and selfishly."

"He supports his son, so he's hardly being irresponsible. He'd support me, too, but I've refused to take anything more than child support from him. Keep in mind he wanted us to stay with him. I chose to leave."

Laila rolled her eyes. "Sure. Having you stick around with no commitment would have worked out nicely for him, wouldn't it? He'd have had it all his way. What would you have had?"

Heather found herself in the awkward position of feeling she needed to defend the very behavior that had sent her fleeing. Since she couldn't do that, she retorted, "Is that why you came by, Laila? To call Connor names? If it is, you can leave."

Laila immediately held up both hands. "Sorry," she said. "If you've accepted the situation, far be it for me to criticize. Actually, I came by to invite you over to Abby and Trace's today. They're having a barbecue on the beach. Everyone agreed Gram needed a break from dealing with Sunday dinner this week."

Heather shook her head at the invitation. "I think I've had about as much of the O'Briens this weekend as I can handle. Besides, I have a ton of paperwork to deal with in the store."

"Then why don't I take little Mick along?" Laila offered. "He'll be able to spend a couple of hours with his dad before Connor goes back to Baltimore this afternoon."

"Given your earlier comments, I'm surprised you're willing to entrust my son to Connor," Heather said.

Laila grinned. "Just my way of making sure Connor gives you a break. I'll get a great deal of pleasure out of it if little Mick throws a tantrum or two and runs him ragged."

"As long as your motives are pure," Heather said wryly.

Still, no matter how it came about, the thought of having even a couple of hours entirely to herself was like a gift from heaven. Forget the paperwork. She could spend that amount of time soaking in a bubble bath until every bubble popped and she shriveled up like a prune. When was the last time she'd allowed herself time to indulge in some pampering? She couldn't remember.

"Pure enough," Laila assured her. "I'd love to take him. And it'll do Connor good to wonder why you've stayed away, especially if anything interesting went on here last night." She gave Heather a sly look. "Did it?"

"Laila Riley!"

Her friend chuckled. "Just checking. I thought you might slip up and reveal something spicy."

"There's nothing spicy to reveal," Heather insisted. Unless, she amended silently, the sparks continuously flying between herself and Connor counted for something. Of course, sparks had never been the issue with Connor. It was turning them into an eternal flame that was the problem.

"Oh, well," Laila said, clearly disappointed. She walked over to the playpen. "Want to go to the beach with me, big guy?"

Mick's eyes lit up at the mention of his favorite place. "Beach," he repeated excitedly.

"Your daddy will be there, too," Laila said.

"Da," he echoed, holding up his arms.

Laila scooped him up, nuzzling his neck as she did so. "There is nothing like the way babies smell," she said, a telltale hitch in her voice.

"So when are you going to settle down and have some of your own?" Heather asked.

Laila laughed, but the sound seemed forced. "Who knows? It's certainly not in the cards at the moment. I haven't met anyone interesting in months. It's almost enough to make me regret breaking up with my last boyfriend." She sighed. "But even when I'm at my lowest, I know I would have eventually died of boredom if we'd stayed together. Settling's never the answer."

"The right person could be just around the corner," Heather consoled her.

"In Chesapeake Shores?" Laila scoffed. "We don't have that many corners."

"Seems to me that Abby, Bree and Shanna would probably disagree," Heather said.

"No doubt," Laila said. "What time should I have my little buddy here back home?" She grinned. "Or should I encourage Connor to drop him off?"

"You take him, you bring him home," Heather said. "Sort of like a date."

Laila nodded. "I'll do my best, but if I know anything at all about Connor, he's the one you'll be seeing a couple of hours from now."

Heather knew her friend was right, which meant she needed to use the next couple of hours wisely. Even though seducing Connor was out of the question, it didn't mean she wouldn't like to torment him a bit more by looking her sexiest before he left town again.

* * *

Connor stood on the staircase outside of Heather's door, his son sound asleep in his arms, and waited for Heather to answer. When she did, he nearly swallowed his tongue.

Her hair was tousled, the way it usually was after sex. Her cheeks glowed the same way, too. Her lips even looked plumped up, as if she'd been soundly kissed recently. And she was wearing next to nothing—a silky robe he'd never seen her wear before. It barely came to midthigh, and she wore not one single thing underneath, unless his eyes were deceiving him.

"What the hell have you been doing?" he demanded, wondering if she had some man hidden away in the bedroom. "You shouldn't come to the door looking like that."

"Like what?" she asked, her expression innocent.

"As if you've spent the afternoon making love," he said irritably. "That's how. Should I take our son around to Sally's until you can get yourself dressed and get rid of whoever's in there with you?"

To his shock, she laughed.

"I am not amused," he informed her.

"Perhaps not, but you obviously have a very vivid imagination," she said, holding the door open wider. "Take a look. No men here."

"Then why do you look like that? Did you see me coming and shoo whoever it was out the door?"

She gave him a bland look. "Why are you so worked up over this, Connor? You and I are over. What I do doesn't concern you."

"Of course it concerns me," he snapped, his voice rising.

"Why?"

"Because I still love you, dammit!"

"Nice to hear," she said, as if he'd merely complimented her lipstick. "But actions speak louder than words. I know you understand that because you use it in court all the time. It's part of your standard strategy for putting the women on the stand in their place."

Connor frowned at her. "What's gotten into you today? We had a perfectly civil conversation last night. In fact, I thought we were getting along better than we had in a while."

"I thought so, too," she admitted. "And then you came over here just now, making assumptions and hurling accusations at me about my behavior."

He drew in a deep breath. Apologizing didn't come easily to him, though lately it seemed he'd done more than his share of it. "Sorry. I overreacted. I just saw you and went a little crazy." He wasn't a hundred percent sure, but he thought he detected a glint of satisfaction in her eyes. "That's exactly what you wanted, isn't it?" he asked suspiciously.

She held her fingers a scant inch apart. "Maybe just a little," she admitted.

"We have to stop this game we're playing," he said eventually. "One of these days one of us will do or say something and ruin what little we have left between us."

"What's that?" she asked.

"Our friendship and respect." He met her gaze. "I don't want that, Heather. We have to think of little Mick."

Her expression sobered then, too. "I agree. I'm sorry. It won't happen again. Next time you're in town, I'll be on my friendliest behavior."

"Why doesn't that entirely reassure me?"

"I don't know," she said. "I meant it to. When will you be back? It may take me awhile to adopt more appropriate behavior."

Connor thought about it. Though he wanted to see his son—wanted to see Heather, as well, to be honest about it—something told him that the distance he'd sought last night wasn't nearly far enough. He needed to keep miles between them for the time being.

"I'll let you know," he said eventually. Weeks might not do it. Months might be smarter.

She reached out and took little Mick from his arms, then met his gaze. "Don't make it too long, okay? He'll miss you."

He sighed heavily. "That works both ways. Maybe Abby can bring him up to Baltimore and drop him off for a weekend."

There was a flicker of disappointment in her eyes, but she nodded. "Just say the word and I'll make it happen," she promised agreeably.

Though there were a lot of words on the tip of his tongue, things he wanted to say but knew he shouldn't, Connor turned and walked away. Unlike so many times when they'd parted, for some reason this time felt a whole lot more like goodbye.

"What is wrong with that son of ours?" Mick grumbled when Megan told him that once again Connor wasn't

coming home for the weekend. He'd been avoiding Chesapeake Shores for the past month.

"He's stubborn, that's what's wrong," Megan said.
"He's too proud to admit that he misses Heather and that
he's made a dreadful mistake."

"How the devil are we going to fix this?" Mick
asked.

"I don't know that you can," his mother said as she
sipped a cup of tea while the three of them sat at the
kitchen table on a Friday morning. "Connor's a grown
man and a father. It's time he figures things out for
himself."

"At this rate, his son will be a grown man himself
before Connor comes to his senses," Mick retorted.

"Nell's right," Megan said. "Our meddling will only
make things worse. Let's just concentrate on supporting
Heather and our grandson in whatever ways we can."

Mick shook his head. "That's not good enough. We
discussed a strategy a while back. I say it's time to implement it."

Megan frowned. "Are you talking about trying to lure
Connor into moving back to town? I'm still not so sure
about that, Mick. I'm afraid he'd be miserable practicing
law here."

To Mick's surprise, his mother looked intrigued by the
idea. "Joshua Porter's bound to retire one of these days,"
Nell said, immediately putting two and two together.
"He's been making noises about it for years. Maybe I
could give him a little push, suggest that the timing is
right and the perfect person to bring into his practice is
available."

Mick cast a triumphant look toward Megan. "Exactly

what I was thinking. Connor could step right in and take over for Joshua. Whether my son knows it or not, this town is in his blood, just the way it's in mine and the rest of the family's. He could make a good life for himself here."

Megan looked resigned. "If you two want to plot, go right ahead. Set things in motion. In the end, though, this has to be Connor's decision. No pressure from either one of you. Is that understood?"

Nell scowled at her. "When have you ever known me to pressure anyone in this family? I'll put a bug in Joshua's ear. What happens after that is up to the two of them."

Megan turned to Mick. "And you?"

"I'll stay out of it," Mick promised. "Trust me, Connor's going to see the advantages of this all on his own."

Megan gave a nod of satisfaction, obviously pleased by his response. To his shock, though, tears welled in her eyes. "I do hope you're right about this, Mick. There's nothing I'd like more than to have Connor home again. I feel as if all the unfinished business between us will never be settled until we spend more time together. Even though things have been better lately, with Connor living in Baltimore he can still avoid me whenever he wants to."

"It'll happen," Mick said confidently. He'd see to it. Not only was his wife's peace of mind at stake, so was Connor's future.

In mid-June Connor had an unexpected call from Joshua Porter, who'd established his law practice in Chesapeake Shores the year the town was founded.

"Next time you're in town, I'd like to meet with you," the attorney said. "I have a proposition for you."

"What kind of proposition?" Connor asked skeptically. Porter was older than his father, and they'd never exactly traveled in the same circles. In fact, Connor seemed to recall some animosity between Porter and Mick when Porter had helped Uncle Thomas with a legal action that had backed Mick into a corner during the development of the town. Mick had never forgiven either of them for that.

"I'm thinking of retiring, and I'm looking for someone to take over my practice," Porter said. "You're the first person I thought of."

"I don't do estate law, property law or traffic cases," Connor said, knowing that was the backbone of a small-town practice. "And I live in Baltimore."

"Your roots are here," Porter reminded him. "And the way I hear it, you have a boy here who could use more of your attention."

Connor sighed. "You've been talking to my father."

The older man gave a dry chuckle. "To your grandmother, actually. She seems to think you might be ready for a change. Is she right? Can we meet or not?"

Connor hesitated. The idea of moving back to Chesapeake Shores had never occurred to him, not when he was on a trajectory to make partner at the firm in Baltimore within the next year or so. Then again, Heather and his son were there, and if nothing else, the past few months had taught him that being separated from them wasn't going to get easier. Add in that he'd had another week of dealing with the likes of Paul Lacey and his on-again, off-again decision to divorce his wife, and Connor was more open to Porter's suggestion than he otherwise might have been.

"I'll drive down tomorrow afternoon," he said eventually.

After the troubling thoughts he'd been having lately, maybe the fates were conspiring to show him the path his life could take. More likely, though, it was just Gram taking matters into her own hands and showing her unique intuition about what he needed even before he'd recognized it himself.

Connor had hoped to slip in and out of town without anyone in the family being the wiser. He didn't want to stir up false hopes. Nor did he want the pressure of all the O'Briens chiming in with their two cents about the decision he might be facing. Until he actually met with Porter, he had no idea if moving back to Chesapeake Shores was a realistic option or not.

Connor had thought the location of Porter's office, which was attached to his home on a side street a few blocks from Main, would work to his advantage. He'd even scheduled the appointment for late in the day. What he hadn't counted on was the attorney's lack of discretion or the town's grapevine, one of which had to be responsible for the sight of a very familiar classic Mustang convertible sitting in Porter's driveway—which meant Mick was inside. Connor heaved a sigh and almost drove right on by, but cowardice wasn't in his nature.

He parked on the street, then walked past the weathered shingle hanging on a post in the yard and into the office, where he was greeted by Chelsea Martin, who'd been a cheerleader back when Connor was playing ball. She beamed at him.

"When I saw your name on today's schedule, I couldn't believe my eyes, Connor," she said, bubbling with enthusiasm. "How long has it been?"

"I'm guessing high school graduation," he said.

"You've forgotten the bonfire on the beach a few days after that?" she teased. "I do believe we made out that night. I thought for sure you'd call."

Connor winced. "What can I say? I was a cad back then."

"Word around town is that you still are," she said cheerfully. "Everyone just loves Heather and that adorable son of yours."

"So do I," he muttered, wondering if Chelsea was likely to be part of the package he'd be inheriting if he came back to town. Her clear-eyed view of him and his transgressions might be awkward.

"By the way, your father and grandmother are in with Mr. Porter now. I'll let them know you're here. They should be wrapping things up soon."

Okay, so maybe Mick's presence wasn't part of some conspiracy, he concluded. Perhaps he'd just driven Gram over for an appointment. Then again, the timing was suspect.

As soon as Chelsea buzzed her boss, the door to the office opened and Joshua Porter waved him in. He looked to be at least eighty, with stooped shoulders, thick glasses and thinning hair. But behind the horn-rimmed glasses his eyes were bright, and he studied Connor shrewdly.

"You don't look old enough to be out of law school to

me," Porter said. "Then again, everyone's looking like a kid to me these days."

"I assure you I have the degree and the experience with a major law firm that Gram probably told you about," Connor said.

"Oh, she's been singing your praises for the past hour," Porter said. "Of course, it made me wonder why she was in here seeing *me,* if you're so darn good."

"Because I prefer to keep my business private from family," Nell said. "Even an old woman should have a few secrets that no one will learn about till she's gone."

Connor laughed and leaned down to kiss her cheek. "What kind of secrets have you been hiding from us, Gram? And why would you let Dad, of all people, in on them?"

She waved off the question. "Oh, we just let Mick through the door a minute ago. He wasn't in here while Joshua and I were going over my affairs."

Mick scowled at her. "Hey, I can keep a secret, Ma. You have no idea of all the things people have entrusted to me over the years."

"Name one," she said, then laughed at her own taunt.

Mick laughed, too. "You'll not catch me that way." He turned to Connor. "What brings you down here?"

Connor shook his head. "You actually managed to ask that with a straight face, Dad. Maybe you should ask Bree about joining her theater company."

"Connor and I have some business to discuss," Porter said. "And since it's late in the day, we should get to it." He took Nell's hand in his. "That is, if our business is concluded."

"You've done everything I requested, as always," Nell told him. "Come along, Mick. Maybe we can go for a drive with the top down. It's been a while since I've been out in that fancy old convertible of yours."

"Absolutely," Mick said eagerly, always happy to show off his classic car, though he was fiercely protective when it came to letting anyone in the family drive it.

Suddenly Connor recalled his mother sneaking the convertible out of the garage on occasion, almost always when Mick had done something to displease her. He regarded his father innocently, then addressed his grandmother. "Gram, I'll bet Mom would take you for a ride in it anytime you'd like."

His father scowled at him. "Don't try to stir up trouble, young man. I know all about your mother taking this car joyriding on the sly."

"And yet you remarried her anyway," Connor teased.

Mick scowled. "Don't think that same forgiveness extends to you. You're just lucky you never put a scratch on it."

Connor had only *borrowed* the car once. His mother had covered for him, or at least until this very moment, he'd thought she had. Apparently those two had no secrets, after all. He decided that shutting up would be wise. Mick seemed amused by his decision.

"Will we be seeing you at the house later?" Mick asked.

"I thought I'd stay for the weekend, if that's okay," Connor told him, changing his mind about hightailing it straight back to Baltimore. His presence was bound to be noted, anyway, thanks to this chance encounter with

Gram and his father. And it had been several weeks since he'd spent any real time with his son.

"Of course it's okay. I'll let your mother know. We'll hold dinner till you get there." Mick gave him a sly look. "Unless you have plans with Heather."

"No plans," Connor said, holding his gaze with a touch of defiance.

Mick muttered something under his breath that Connor couldn't quite decipher, though he was pretty sure his father might have just called him an idiot. Mick left before Connor could confront him on it.

As Porter walked out with Mick and Connor's grandmother, Connor looked around the office. The oversize leather furniture looked comfortable, if worn. The law books lining the wall behind the desk appeared well-used. Light flooded the room from a large bay window. He hadn't noticed a room for a second office, which made Connor wonder if Porter intended him to work here or to set up a practice elsewhere, then funnel clients to Connor slowly as he phased out his own practice.

A moment later, Porter returned and closed the door. "So, let's get acquainted. Why don't you tell me about what you've been doing in Baltimore?"

Connor described the practice and his client list.

"Sounds depressing, if you ask me," the old man said.

"Lately, I've been thinking the same thing," Connor admitted, much to his own surprise. "But I'm not sure estate law and real estate transactions will be any better."

"Want to know how I see it?" Porter asked.

Connor nodded.

"You practice law in a big city like Baltimore,

especially when most of your cases are divorces or custody battles, you see people at their worst. You get to
know them just long enough to navigate them through a
rough patch in their lives. That's the last you see of most
of them, am I right?"

"Pretty much."

"Here, you're going to be dealing with people you
know. If you're the kind of man I'm sure your grandmother tried to raise, you'll care about what's happening
in their lives. It won't be a bunch of filings and motions
for you. And when all's said and done, you'll see your
clients again tomorrow, in church or on the street or
at Sally's. You'll know how things are going for them.
They'll invite you over for a drink in their new house that
you helped them get. You may be around when they've
had a run of bad luck, but you'll also be around for the
happiest moments of their lives." He met Connor's gaze.
"You see what I'm trying to tell you?"

"I think so," Connor said.

"Are you a part of the community like that in Baltimore?"

"No, sir."

"You like it that way?"

Connor thought about the life he had, especially now
that Heather and little Mick were gone. He was making
good money. He had a great career. What he didn't have
was a life, not the kind that Joshua Porter was describing. Suddenly he knew what he had to do. Still, he was
cautious.

"If I say yes, how will this work?" he asked the older
man.

Porter outlined the ideas he had about a partnership.

"There's another office in the back here. That'd be yours. Chelsea can probably handle working for both of us, but if that doesn't pan out, we can always bring in someone else. I'll start scaling back. I can't say how much or how fast. Some of my clients may not want to change, and I'm not sure I'm ready to call it a day entirely, either."

"Are you sure there's enough work for two of us?" Connor asked.

"I know there's more than I can handle," the attorney said. "I say yes to everybody who walks through that door because right now I'm not willing to send them out of town to some stranger. There are plenty of other good lawyers in the area, but most folks like dealing with someone they know."

What he was describing was a much slower pace than Connor was used to, but maybe having time for other priorities would be a good thing. Taking the job would mean a cut in pay, too, but the cost of living here would be much less. There were a lot of things he needed to weigh and consider.

"Let me think about this over the weekend," Connor suggested. "Can we talk again on Monday morning before I go back to Baltimore?"

"Works for me," Porter said, then bellowed in a surprisingly strong voice, "Chelsea, come in here!"

She popped her head in the door. "Yes?"

"Put Connor on my calendar for Monday morning." He glanced at Connor. "Eight o'clock good for you?"

"I'll be here," Connor said.

"You have any questions over the weekend, give me a call. Otherwise, I'll see you Monday morning first thing."

Connor took another look around the office, then met Joshua Porter's gaze. He thought of all the mentors he'd had in Baltimore. The men might be more polished and a whole lot wealthier, but few of them had told it like it was the way this man had. Connor instinctively liked and trusted Porter, and he liked even more the picture Porter had painted of practicing law in Chesapeake Shores.

He already knew what he was going to do, but he also knew he needed the weekend to let the idea percolate. It was a huge decision with lots of ramifications, including the fact that Heather and his son would be in his life on a daily basis.

That could be sweet torment or, if he let it, the best thing that had ever happened to him.

14

Heather was in the middle of teaching her quilting class on Saturday morning when Megan dropped into the shop, her eyes alight with excitement.

"Do you have a minute?" she asked Heather, after greeting Laila, Connie and the other women in the class.

"We'll be wrapping up in another hour," Heather said. "Could it wait?"

"Go ahead, Heather," Laila said. "We're all ripping out stitches, anyway. It'll just make you insane to watch us."

Heather chuckled. "Who knew I'd wind up with a beginners class filled with perfectionists? Okay, I'll be back in a minute."

She joined Megan on the sidewalk outside the store. It was one of those rare spectacular days in June when the air was soft and springlike, rather than oppressive. It felt good to be outside, even for a few minutes. Heather studied Megan, who was barely managing to contain some kind of big news. "Okay, what's up?"

"Have you spoken to Connor lately?"

Heather shook her head. "It's been a couple of weeks. In fact, I was about to call and bug him because he hasn't seen his son."

"Not to worry. I imagine you'll be seeing him before the weekend's over."

Heather regarded her with surprise. "He's in town?"

"Came down yesterday. And do you want to know why?"

"To see little Mick, I imagine."

"That, too, of course, but he was here to meet with Joshua Porter," Megan announced, clearly brimming over with delight.

Heather shrugged, not getting what the fuss was about. "Who's that?"

Megan looked disappointed by her reaction. "Oh, wait, I forgot that you weren't actually here when all that paperwork for the shop and apartment was being signed. Porter's an attorney, the only one we've had in town for years and years."

"Why was Connor meeting with him? Does he need an attorney?" Unexpected panic suddenly tore through her. "He's not going after full custody of our son, is he?"

"Heavens, no," Megan said, looking horrified. "Connor would never do such a thing. He knows you're a wonderful mother."

Heather's pulse slowed at Megan's reassurance. "Then what's this all about?"

"Well, Connor hasn't said a word to me, but I do know that Porter was going to ask him to join his practice," Megan told her. "They met yesterday afternoon to discuss it."

Heather's eyes widened, and her heartbeat accelerated

all over again. "Here? Connor might practice law in Chesapeake Shores? I don't believe it! For as long as I've known him, all he's talked about was making partner in a big-time law practice."

"Well, apparently he's reconsidered. At least he seems to be taking Joshua's offer seriously," Megan told her, then studied her worriedly. "You'd be okay with that, right? I mean, you do think it would be for the best if he moved back here."

Heather didn't know what she thought. It would be great for little Mick to have his dad close by, but for her? It would mean facing, every single day, the fact that she and Connor weren't going to have the life she'd once dreamed of. And it would be happening before she really had her feet solidly under her and had established a new and totally fulfilling life of her own.

"It's not a done deal?" she asked eventually, hating that her reservations had put a damper on Megan's excitement.

"No, I don't think so," Megan said, frowning. "Oh, Heather, will it be too hard for you? We, none of us, thought of that."

Heather stared at her. There was something in Megan's voice that suggested she'd had something to do with this unexpected turn of events. "You're behind this?"

"In a way," Megan admitted. "Not me so much as Mick and Nell. Mick had the idea and Nell went to Porter."

"Does Connor know that?"

She nodded. "Apparently, it didn't take him but a split second to figure it out."

"Then I'm surprised he didn't run the other way," Heather said.

"Frankly, so am I, but he hasn't. I find that encouraging. Not only would this be a fresh start for Connor—perhaps change the way he looks at the world—but I believe it could finally turn things around for the two of you."

Fighting off a quick burst of hope, Heather shook her head. "Connor's core values aren't going to change, no matter where he's living, Megan."

Megan sighed. "I hope you're wrong about that."

"I wish I were," Heather said. "But I don't think I am."

And that meant if Connor made this move, she was going to be right back where she started, in the middle of a life that would never be everything she'd once hoped for.

Connor had found an old T-shirt and a pair of khaki shorts in his closet to wear on Saturday morning. He planned to call Heather and make arrangements to pick up Mick for the weekend, then spend the day with his son fishing on the dock or hanging out at the house. The less he saw of Heather while he was pondering this move back home, the better. He didn't want her presence to influence his decision one way or the other. The move had to be right for him. It would require some serious adjustments of his career ambitions that he wasn't entirely sure he was prepared to make.

He'd just fixed himself a bowl of cereal and poured a cup of coffee when the kitchen door opened and Kevin came in, looking harried.

"Boy, was I glad to hear you're in town," his brother said. "I have a crisis."

Connor regarded him with concern. Kevin was a former EMT and had been a medic in Iraq. He was usually unflappable. "What kind of crisis?"

"Have you heard about these speaking engagements Uncle Thomas has lined up all over the region?"

Connor shook his head. "But I assume he's doing talks about preserving the bay."

"Exactly. He did one for Shanna here last year, and it went so well, he enlisted her and Connie to put together a whole string of them. There's one this afternoon over in Easton."

"I'm still not hearing anything about a crisis."

"They sell books at these events and sign people up for memberships in the foundation. There needs to be a couple of people to handle that. I'd told Shanna I'd stay here and run the store, but now Henry's sick with some kind of stomach virus and this morning Davy threw up, too. I can't watch them and the store, so she's staying home with the boys, I'm taking over at the store and you're going to pitch in by helping Connie at the event."

"But I'd planned on spending the day with little Mick," Connor protested.

"Take him along. He'll have a great time. It's outdoors and somebody's bound to be selling hot dogs and stuff." Kevin gave him an imploring look. "Please, bro. You've got to help me out. Otherwise we have to close the store and I have to watch the boys so Shanna can go. I do not do well with sick kids."

"You're a former EMT, for heaven's sake," Connor said.

"Not the same when it's your kid throwing up and looking miserable," Kevin told him. "You'll see when you start spending more time with your son." He grinned. "I hear it won't be long before that happens."

Connor frowned. "I see the O'Brien grapevine is working at warp speed these days. I haven't said yes to Porter's offer yet. I might not."

"Of course you will," Kevin predicted with confidence. "So, can I count on you today, bro? It's about time you pitched in with a few family obligations."

Connor gave him a mock scowl. "Watch it, or you could provide me with a reason to stay right where I am in Baltimore."

Kevin shook his head, his expression serious. "You're smarter than that. Not that you've shown much evidence of it recently, but we're all betting on that changing."

"Yeah, that's what I'm afraid of." Connor sighed. "Okay, count me in. Tell me where I need to go and when I need to be there."

"Connie has the information. You can ride over with her. The books are already packed in the trunk of her car." Kevin hesitated, then said, "There's one more thing."

"Uh-oh," Connor replied, regarding him warily. "What's that?"

"Keep an eye on her and Uncle Thomas," Kevin requested.

Connor stared at his brother in shock. "Connie and Uncle Thomas? You have to be kidding me!"

Kevin shrugged. "It's not like there's anything official going on. It's just a vibe I got when I saw them together recently in Annapolis. But I'm a guy. What do I know?"

"I'd like to point out that I'm a guy, too. I may not be any better than you at assessing the situation."

"You're a lawyer. It's part of your job to read people.

And nobody knows these two particular people better than you do."

"Jake knows his sister. What's his take?" Connor tried to imagine what Jake's reaction would be. Given the age difference between Connie and Thomas, it probably wouldn't be good. "He might have quite a lot to say about this."

"I'm not sure there's anything for Jake to have a take on," Kevin warned, "so don't go spreading tales. I just want to hear your assessment after you've spent some time with them. I'll let Connie know to pick you up—be ready to go in a half hour. I think that's when that quilting class over at Heather's store wraps up."

"Tell Connie I'll meet her there. I have to grab little Mick anyway, if Heather agrees."

"Perfect," Kevin said. "Thanks for doing this, bro."

"Not a problem," Connor told him. In fact, he was just discovering that Chesapeake Shores might have more fascinating things going on than he'd ever envisioned.

Thomas finished his speech, then took time to talk to anyone who lingered afterward with questions. He couldn't seem to stop himself from glancing across the green to where Connie was doing a brisk business selling books about the Chesapeake Bay. While watching the piles of books dwindle was satisfying, he realized he was more interested in the woman selling them. She had a smile for everyone, and her laughter rang out whenever his nephew made some comment to her.

Thomas had been surprised when he'd seen Connor and his boy arriving with Connie. In fact, he'd even had a momentary pang at the thought that even though Connor was a bit younger than Connie, the two of them made much more suitable companions than he ever would with a woman her age. Of course, Connor's heart belonged with the mother of his child, whether he wanted to admit it or not. Still, Connie no doubt had opportunities to meet many men closer to her own age than he was.

When the last of the stragglers had wandered off, Thomas crossed the green. Connie looked up from her sale and smiled at him, then went back to writing the receipt. He glanced toward Connor and saw that his nephew was watching him intently.

"How'd we do with donations and memberships today?" Thomas asked, forcing his attention away from Connie.

"I don't have anything to compare it to, but it seemed okay to me," Connor said. "About forty people signed up for the foundation, and donations topped a thousand dollars. I think there are additional pledges on some of the membership applications, too."

"Fantastic!" Thomas said enthusiastically. "I knew this was going to work after the event Shanna held last summer. Can't imagine why none of us ever thought of it before."

"Connie seems very excited about being a part of it," Connor said, glancing her way.

"She's been a godsend," Thomas said, then added quickly, "As has Shanna."

Connor smirked. "Of course."

Thomas heard the suggestive note in Connor's voice, latched on to his nephew's arm and dragged him away from the table where Connie was still making book sales.

"Is there something on your mind?" he demanded irritably. "If there is, out with it."

"Not a thing," Connor swore, but there was still a glint of amusement in his eyes. "Anything you want to tell me?"

Thomas studied him with a narrowed gaze, wondering just what Connor was not saying. He certainly wasn't going to be the one to bring Connie's name into the conversation.

"Nothing," he said stiffly. Although he was surprisingly disappointed not to have the opportunity to share so much as a cup of coffee with Connie, he could see that today wasn't the day. "I need to be getting back to Annapolis."

"Since you're this close to Chesapeake Shores, why not come on over for the rest of the weekend?" Connor suggested. "There's plenty of room at the house. I don't think Dad would throw you out. Or perhaps there's someplace else in town you could stay," he added suggestively.

"You know, if you were my son, I'd have plenty to say about all these looks and innuendoes of yours," Thomas told him.

Connor actually had the audacity to laugh. "But then Dad doesn't know what's going on, does he? I'm sure if he did, he'd have a few things to say to you himself."

"There is nothing going on," Thomas said in a fierce undertone, glancing over to make sure that Connie couldn't overhear. "And if you suggest otherwise, I'll call you a liar. Don't be stirring up trouble, young man."

Connor's expression sobered. "Hey, I'm just giving you a rough time. If you've got a thing for Connie and she's reciprocating, I think it's great."

There it was, spelled out in plain English, Thomas thought with a sigh. "She's a lovely woman," he conceded cautiously. "I've noticed that. It's gone no further. I doubt it will."

"Why not?"

"Because I'm not about to make a fool of myself at this stage of my life," Thomas said. "Now, can we let this go before she wonders what the two of us are whispering about?"

"I think it would be a crying shame for you not to at least spend a little time getting to know each other," Connor argued. "Why don't we all go for something to drink? Little Mick could use a snack before we head back anyway."

It was an invitation Thomas couldn't bring himself to turn down. "A half hour, just so we can tally the results of the day," he said finally.

Connor grinned. "Whatever you need to tell yourself."

Sadly, right at this moment, that excuse was the only thing that kept Thomas from feeling like an old fool.

Connie was quiet as she and Connor drove back to Chesapeake Shores. Little Mick had fallen asleep in his car seat the minute they'd hit the road. Connie had agreed to let Connor drive. She'd spent most of the ride staring out the window, her expression pensive.

"Something on your mind?" Connor asked eventually.

"No, just a little tired," she said. "It was an exhausting day."

"But an incredibly productive one," Connor observed.

"At least that's what Uncle Thomas said. He's very grateful for everything you and Shanna are doing."

Her expression brightened. "Working with him…" She actually blushed, then amended, "I mean for the cause, well it's incredibly rewarding. For the first time in ages, I feel as if I'm doing something that really matters. I wish my daughter would help out. I tried to get Jenny to come today, but she'd rather work more hours at Bree's flower shop than volunteer for anything."

"She's saving for college, right?" Connor said. "That's a responsible thing to do as well."

"I suppose."

"Did you want her to get to know my uncle better?" he asked, staring straight ahead at the road when he said it.

Connie seemed to choke. "Excuse me?"

He glanced over at her. "I was just wondering if you thought maybe he'd be a good influence on her."

"Well, of course he would be, but that's not why," she said hurriedly. "It's about making her think about something besides clothes and boys."

"Sure."

"Connor, is there something on your mind?"

"Not a thing," he swore. "It's just that I think Uncle Thomas is great, and of course Kevin thinks the world of him. We'd all like to see him happy."

Her gaze narrowed. "You don't think he's happy now?"

"Generally speaking, yes, but unlike me, he's one of those men who actually is happiest when he's married. He just hasn't had much luck staying married, because he cares too much about his work."

"I don't understand how any woman couldn't appreciate the passion he has for such a wonderful cause," Connie said, jumping to Thomas's defense in a way that Connor found telling. "What he does is admirable."

"I didn't know his first wife very well," Connor admitted. "I was just a kid when they got married and divorced. The second one had some issues of her own that made them a very bad match."

She nodded. "He mentioned something about that," she told him.

"Really? Then you've talked about personal issues?"

She peered at him with undisguised amusement. "Yes, Connor," she said with exaggerated patience. "We've talked about more than bacteria in the water."

"Good to know," he said.

"Connor, you're not going to make too much of this, are you?" she pleaded, a frantic note in her voice. "Not that there's anything to say, of course, but I wouldn't want anyone in your family—or mine—to get the wrong idea. Or Thomas, either, for that matter."

"And what would be the wrong idea?"

"That there's anything ..." She blushed furiously. "You know, anything *personal* going on between your uncle and me. We've spent very little time together, and the focus has been almost exclusively on this project."

"Too bad," he said, then glanced over and held her gaze for just an instant. "If you ask me, there should be something personal going on. You're both great people."

And that was the last thing he would say on the subject. Anything else was up to the two of them.

With her son spending the weekend with Connor, Heather was at loose ends Saturday night and all day

Sunday. She found she wasn't very good at it. By Sunday evening, she was going a little stir-crazy. She decided to have dinner at Sally's just to get out of her small apartment. She considered calling Laila or Connie for company, but instead opted for walking around to the café on her own. It was ironic in a way how few times in her life she'd actually eaten alone in public. She probably ought to get used to it.

She took a book along to read while she ate, but once seated at a table she couldn't seem to focus on it. She kept staring out the window, watching the people walking by. It seemed they were almost all in pairs. She sighed as she acknowledged that was the way she'd always imagined her life, as part of a couple.

She'd been seated for fifteen minutes or less and had just started on her hamburger when Connor walked in with little Mick.

"Mama!" little Mick called out, then released his father's hand and toddled unsteadily straight toward her.

Heather stared at him with a mix of wonder and tears. "You're walking," she whispered, then gathered him close. "Good for you, my big boy!"

She turned to Connor. "When?" she asked, unable to stop the jealousy that streaked through her as she acknowledged that she'd missed this big milestone. Oh, little Mick had come close before, but mostly he'd clung to surfaces as he teetered around their apartment. These had been real steps, taken all on his own.

"This morning," Connor said, clearly reading the disappointment in her expression. "I'm sorry you missed it. He spotted something he wanted across the kitchen and just went after it."

"I wish I'd been there," she admitted.

"You've been there for all of his other firsts," Connor reminded her. "I've missed more than my share."

"I know. It's silly of me, but this was such a big one."

"It could have happened with a babysitter or Mom and Dad instead of either one of us," he consoled her, then reached in his pocket and pulled out his cell phone. "I took pictures, though."

She scanned through the pictures, smiling at the one in which little Mick seemed to realize he was standing on his own in the middle of the room and, in the next, plunked down on the floor, the toy he'd gone after clutched in his hand.

"I'll have prints made for you," Connor promised. "Do you mind if we join you?"

It was a moot point, since Mick had already scrambled into the booth beside her. "Of course not."

Connor slid in opposite her, then fell silent.

Eventually, when she couldn't bear the quiet for another second, she met his gaze and asked the question that had been troubling her all weekend. "Is it true what I heard? Are you seriously thinking of moving back here?"

He nodded. "How would you feel about that?"

"I'm not entirely sure," she said candidly. "I think it would be wonderful for you to have a fresh start practicing a different kind of law, and it would be fantastic for little Mick."

"But not so much for you," he guessed, showing surprising perceptiveness.

"I just don't know how I feel about it," she admitted. "I'm barely getting used to being on my own. In fact, right before you got here, I was thinking about how few times I've ever eaten alone in public. It felt a little awkward when I first sat down, but then I realized no one was paying a bit of attention to me. Do you know, until now I've never lived independently? I went from home to my college dorm to your apartment."

"How do you like it?" he asked.

"I'm not really sure. It's lonely sometimes, and overwhelming, but I am discovering things about myself. I'm stronger than I ever thought I was." She said it with pride.

"You've always been stronger than you realized," Connor said. "And you'd still be on your own, if that's the way you want it. I'd just be close by if you need something."

"I think I'd feel odd about going on a date knowing I might bump into you," she blurted before she could stop herself. "I mean, in Baltimore, I suppose it could have happened, but the odds would have been against it. Around here, it's almost a certainty."

Connor frowned. "Have you started dating then? Last time I was here, you acted as if that was the last thing on your mind."

"It is. I'm just saying it could happen down the road and I'd feel weird about it."

The waitress came over with a booster seat for little Mick, then took his order and Connor's, giving Heather time to summon her composure. When the teenager had left, Heather said, "Look, how I feel—or might feel at some point in the future—really isn't the issue. You need to do what's right for you."

He studied her face. "I hope you mean that, because I

think this is the right thing. The idea's been growing on me all weekend—I can see the real advantages of practicing law here. I'm planning to tell Joshua Porter yes when I see him in the morning."

Heather swallowed hard against the tide of hope and dread that warred inside her. "Then you have decided," she said flatly.

"Unless you tell me right now, straight out, that you don't want me around, yes."

She tried desperately to form the words that would keep him away, but the part of her that longed for him to be involved in some small way in her life again—hers and their son's—couldn't do it.

Somehow she'd just have to find a way to cope, and to lock away the old dream that still had absolutely no chance of coming true.

15

Connor's decision to leave the Baltimore law firm shocked the partners. It was gratifying to have them try to persuade him to stay.

"You'll be a junior partner here by the end of the year," Grayson reminded him. "How can going into practice for yourself in a town the size of Chesapeake Shores come close to matching that, either in income or prestige? You're an ambitious young man, Connor. We've all seen that. It's one of your most admirable traits. Leave now and you won't have an opportunity like this again. You'll have thrown away the past few years of hard work."

Connor didn't see how all the experience he'd gained working for a major law firm could ever be considered a waste.

"This is what I have to do," he said. "I want to be near my son. He's my priority."

"And Heather?" the older man asked perceptively. "You've been restless ever since she left. We've all noticed that. I've never understood why you won't just give her what she wants. Marry her. I'm sure she'd be willing to move back to Baltimore if you do. She's a lovely young woman. She'd be a tremendous asset to an up-and-coming young attorney. There's no limit to what you could accomplish here with a woman like that by your side."

Connor shook his head, not just at the suggestion of marriage but at the idea that Heather would be some kind of trophy wife. The idea was laughable.

"She'd never agree," he said flatly. "She has her own dreams, and she's achieving them in Chesapeake Shores." He couldn't say he entirely understood it, but it was evident that the quilt shop had fulfilled her in ways that teaching never had.

"Of course she would. She's very bright. I'm sure she understands what's at stake here. Talk it over with her. I'm sure she'll want you to be successful."

Connor chuckled. "Heather doesn't care whether I'm successful or not, and she'd see right through it if I had some sudden change of heart about getting married. She knows how I feel about marriage. I can't deny that I love her. But if I won't get married for love, then I certainly won't do it as some sort of career move. I'd like to think I still have some integrity left."

"Then if you're not chasing after her, what is this really about?" Grayson asked, obviously bewildered and not considering a toddler son motive enough for making such a drastic change.

"It's about getting my priorities in order. It's about being closer to my family." He gave his boss a rueful look. "And it's about me being sick to death of listening to men trying to excuse the crummy way they treat their wives. I want to practice a different kind of law." He would have described Joshua Porter's vision, but he doubted Grayson would understand. To a man totally focused on the accumulation of billable hours and the right kind of publicity, it would be sentimental hogwash.

"That would be a crying shame," Grayson said. "You've made a name for yourself handling high-profile divorces. What about your current caseload? What are you going to tell the men who are counting on you to extricate them from their marriages and get them the best possible settlements?"

"We have other attorneys who can take over. Or I can simply stop taking on new cases and refer any inquiries to someone else. I'll finish up with the clients I already have, however long that takes. It's up to you how you want to handle that. I haven't set a specific timetable for leaving, but I won't abandon anyone unless that's your preference."

Grayson shook his head. "I'll have to think about that. These men sought you out. They may not be comfortable with another attorney taking over in the middle of things. On the other hand, when they learn what you're planning, they could lose faith in your judgment."

"Like I said, it's up to you, or we could meet with each client and handle them on a case-by-case basis once we determine what they want," Connor said, trying to be reasonable. Although he was anxious to get started on this new venture, he didn't want to leave bad blood behind. If things in Chesapeake Shores didn't work out as he'd envisioned, he could someday be back in Baltimore looking for work.

"I'll talk this over with the other partners and get back to you," Grayson said. "They're not going to be one bit happy about this, Connor. We've all invested a lot of time and energy in bringing you along with the firm. You've been our rising star."

"And I appreciate that," Connor told him. "I really do."

Of course, what *they* appreciated was that from the beginning he'd been not only ambitious, but aggressive in building his caseload. They might have mentored him in many ways, but he'd brought that trait into the firm with him. While some of his colleagues might genuinely miss him, most would miss the income he'd generated. He had no illusions about that.

Less than an hour later, Grayson was back in his office. "If you refuse to reconsider, we're agreed that it's best for this to be a clean break. Mitch Douglas and Frank Helms will take over your caseload effective immediately. Their secretaries will notify the clients of the changes. You can transfer the files to them by the end of the day."

Connor knew he shouldn't be shocked, but he was. "You want me gone today?"

Grayson's expression was cold and unyielding. Connor had seen him look the same way when going for a witness's jugular in court.

"We think it's best not to drag these things out," Grayson said. "I'm sure you understand."

Gone was any pretense of affection or even graciousness. It was clearly all business. Connor's decision was viewed as a betrayal, and the partners were quickly cutting their losses. He was almost relieved by that. It told him a lot about the attorneys with whom he'd worked the past few years.

"Oh, believe me, I do understand," Connor said just as coldly.

Something told him that not only had he made the right decision, he'd made it in the nick of time—before he turned into the kind of money-driven, unfeeling men he'd once admired.

Megan looked up from her book in surprise when she heard a car pull to a stop in front of the house. She was even more surprised when she saw Connor emerge. She'd taken a rare day off and had planned to spend it enjoying the quiet outside doing next to nothing. Her life had been an endless whirlwind since she'd moved back to Chesapeake Shores, remarried Mick and opened the gallery. Today, with Mick out at one of the Habitat for Humanity sites he oversaw, she'd envisioned an afternoon with no interruptions, least of all from her son.

"What brings you here in the middle of the week?" she inquired as he crossed the lawn. "Not that I'm not delighted to see you. I'm just surprised."

"You can't be too surprised," he said, settling into a rocking chair beside hers. "The entire town seems to be in on the secret that I'm moving home."

"Today?" she asked, stunned.

"No time like the present," he said wryly. "That seemed to be the general consensus yesterday around my law firm, anyway."

She regarded him with shock. "They kicked you out?"

He smiled at that. "Since I'd just quit, I don't think you could say that, but they were surprisingly eager to have me gone."

"Well, that hardly seems fair after all the hard work

you'd done for them," she said indignantly. "What kind of people are they?"

"Greedy and self-protective," he assessed. "I think they were afraid I'd sneak off with all my clients if they gave me a chance to speak to any of them."

"That's absurd. You're an honorable man."

He laughed. "Thanks for the vote of confidence. The truth is, I felt an amazing sense of freedom when I walked out the door for the last time yesterday. I figured I might as well load up my car with a few things this morning and head on down here." He turned to her. "Will you and Dad mind if I stay at the house for a while?"

"Of course not," she said, her expression brightening. "I'd love it."

"And Dad?"

"Your father always loves having any of you underfoot. He likes to have someone other than me he can boss around."

Connor regarded her with surprise. "Dad bosses you around?"

She laughed. "He tries. Occasionally I even let him think he's getting away with it."

Connor fell silent. "Can I ask you something?" he said after a while.

"Of course."

"How do you all do it?"

She regarded him with puzzlement. "Do what?"

"Make a marriage work, especially after letting it fall apart the first time."

Megan sighed. "Oh, Connor, there's not a magic formula. I think your father and I both learned a lot from the mistakes we made during all those years we were married. I learned that I need to speak up if I want some-thing. For way too long I expected your father to know I was unhappy without telling him what needed to change. Men aren't mind readers. None of us are, for that matter. He needed to see that his compulsive drive to support his family, combined with a healthy level of ambition, was costing him too much time away from the very family he cared about. We needed to figure out the kind of balance and compromise that makes a marriage work."

She met his gaze. "And just so you know, every couple is different. The need for compromise, however, is universal."

"But you really believe it's going to work this time?" he asked, a surprisingly wistful note in his voice.

"Not without hard work, but yes, I think it will work this time. We never stopped loving each other, you know. We just lost sight of that because of all the other things going on. I felt abandoned and overwhelmed. Instead of explaining that, though, I let the frustration build until the only thing left seemed to be divorce. I see now that it was a drastic and very foolish attempt to get your father's attention, but once I set off down that path, it was too late to turn back."

Connor stared at her with shock. "You didn't really want the divorce?"

"Not if I'm being totally honest," she said. "In the end, I think it worked out for the best, but it came at a huge cost. I lost all of my children because of it. I'm still trying to win you all back. I thank God every day that I'm get-ting a second chance."

She studied him for several minutes. "You seem especially introspective today. Is it because of the job or does it have something to do with your feelings for Heather?"

"It's Heather, actually."

Megan was surprised. She hadn't expected him to admit it.

"I love her," he said quietly.

"I know that."

He gave her an imploring look. "Then tell me why I can't give her the one thing she wants?"

"Because you're not ready," she said candidly, regretting that he was struggling so hard to deal with so many contradictory feelings. She patted his hand. "But you will be. Moving home was the first step. I predict you and Heather will find your way back to each other, and when you do, it will be right for both of you."

"You believe that even though we've done exactly what you said you and Dad did, taking stances from which it's all but impossible to retreat?"

"But we did retreat," she reminded him, then smiled. "Eventually."

"Were you always such an optimist?" he inquired, sounding amused.

She took his question seriously. "Not always. I gave up on your father, didn't I?" She shrugged. "These days— yes, I believe in happy endings. Now go on inside and get settled. I'll fix your favorite dinner for tonight. Why don't you invite Heather and your son to join us? We can celebrate the start of a whole new chapter in your life."

He gave her a curious look. "What's my favorite meal?"

"Spaghetti and meatballs," she said at once, then grinned. "You didn't think I knew that, did you?"

"Not really," he admitted.

"You'd be surprised by how much I remember about each one of you, Connor. Maybe one of these days, you'll learn to trust that I never stopped caring about you."

"Maybe I will," he said. Then, looking vaguely uncomfortable at the rare moment of intimacy between them, he bounded off the porch and went to his car to unload his things.

Megan watched for a moment, then sighed. One step at a time, she reminded herself. And having Connor back here, under the same roof, was going to give her the time she desperately needed to make things right with her younger son.

Heather was startled to see Connor walking into the shop in midafternoon on a Tuesday. "This is a surprise," she told him.

"You sound just like Mom. I am obviously way too predictable."

"As a matter of fact, you are," she said. "What's going on?"

"Long story short, the firm wasn't happy about my decision to leave, so they suggested I take off now, rather than after the two weeks or longer I was willing to give them to wrap up my cases."

"Jerks," she said succinctly. "I always told you Grayson wasn't half the man you thought he was."

"I get why they did it," he admitted. "And it's probably for the best. I can get started down here that much sooner. Joshua Porter was thrilled when I stopped by there to fill him in on my way over here. He'd have me start tomorrow morning, if I agreed to it."

"Will you?"

"I think I'll use the rest of this week to haul my stuff down to the house and get the townhouse on the market, then start next Monday."

"Makes sense. Did you want to take little Mick back to the house with you tonight?"

He shoved his hands in his pockets, looking surprisingly uncomfortable. "Actually, I came to invite you both over for dinner. Mom's making spaghetti and meatballs."

Heather's eyes widened. "Your favorite. I'll bet hers is a whole lot better than mine ever was."

He laughed. "Not touching that one," he said. "So, will you come? I think she wants it to be a quiet celebration. Just us, not the whole family."

Heather hesitated, but in the end she couldn't resist. "Sure, why not? What time?"

"Early, because of little Mick. How about six-thirty? You close here at six, right?"

"That'll work. Shall I bring anything?"

"Just your protective armor," he said wryly. "I'm sure Dad will be at his matchmaking best."

"I can handle your father," she said bravely. Connor was the one to whom she had no immunity.

He laughed. "That's what you think. He's been subtle up to now. With me moving back here, I'm anticipating a full-court press."

She studied him with a narrowed gaze. "Are you trying to warn me away?"

"No, indeed. Just alerting you to the danger. Don't count on Mom protecting you, either. She's almost as bad as he is."

"Your mother and I have an understanding," she said confidently.

Connor laughed. "Don't count on it. She's been lulling you into a false sense of complacency. I'm just discovering that she's almost as much of a master manipulator as Dad is."

"Then I suppose we're in for an interesting test of wills," Heather said. Oddly enough, she realized she was looking forward to it.

And *that* was probably a huge mistake.

Connor had been wrong about it being a quiet evening. When he got back to the house, Gram was in the kitchen with his mother, his nieces were in the den with his dad, and everyone else started turning up one or two at a time until the place was chaotic. Though he was momentarily thrown, he realized this was one of the benefits of moving back home. He'd missed these impromptu gatherings, and now they'd be a regular part of his life again. Before, he'd been the visiting brother or uncle. Now he was in the thick of things again.

"What time will Heather be here?" his mother asked.

"Six-thirty," Connor told her, only to have Trace give him an amused look.

"Not wasting any time, are you?"

"Meaning?"

"Just that things should always start the way you intend them to continue. Draw Heather into the fold from the get-go."

"Inviting her was Mom's idea," Connor told his brother-in-law.

Trace merely laughed. "It might have been her idea,

but you obviously made no attempt to talk her out of it. In fact, you're the one who issued the actual invitation, am I right?"

"Yes," Connor said, then scowled. "What's your point?"

"Everyone in this family seems to see the handwriting on the wall except you," Trace explained patiently. "Have you even admitted that you're making this move because you can't live without her?"

"I'm making this move because I want a different kind of lifestyle," Connor insisted. "I want to live in a small, friendly community again. I want to be around my family, though right at this moment, I have to wonder why."

Trace laughed, then glanced toward the door as Heather walked in with little Mick. Connor followed the direction of his gaze and couldn't seem to tear his own gaze away. Just a glimpse of her was enough to take his breath away. Apparently she caught him staring, because the smile on her face died.

"I rest my case," Trace said, nudging him in the ribs to get his attention. "You're a goner, man. Admit it and get on with your life."

"I've never denied being crazy about her," Connor said defensively as he watched her mingling with his family. And then she moved on to somewhere beyond his view.

Trace rolled his eyes. "Marriage is just a piece of paper, right? How many times have we all heard you say that? If it's so damned insignificant, then why are you fighting so hard to avoid signing it? That piece of paper is your ticket to happiness."

Connor wished he could believe that was all it was. Too often, though, it was a surefire path to misery. Passion turned to hatred. Children suffered. And nothing any of these happily-ever-after relatives of his said was going to convince him otherwise.

Trace gave him a knowing look, as if he could read his mind. "Unless you think Abby and I, Jake and Bree and your folks are all doomed," he said slyly.

Connor didn't deny it.

"Well, your sisters and your parents might take exception to that," Trace told him. "Hell, I take exception to it. Abby and I have our moments, but most of the time we are blissfully happy. If I could get her to slow down long enough to add to our family, I think our lives would be close to perfect."

"Look, you know I wish you all nothing but the best," Connor told him. "I hope your marriages last forever. I just think the odds are against it."

"So it's better not even to try?" Trace asked.

"That's the way I see it," Connor insisted, though he couldn't deny a moment of envy when Abby came over and wrapped her arms around her husband's waist and gave him a smoldering kiss. Across the room, Jake was bending over Bree, checking on the two-week-old baby girl in her arms, his expression filled with awe, especially since they'd been half convinced they were having a son. Connor recalled feeling exactly like that when he and Heather had brought their son home from the hospital. Her pregnancy with little Mick had happened by accident. Knowing there'd never be another one filled him with unspeakable sorrow.

"I need some air," he said suddenly to no one in particular, then walked outside.

To his dismay, he found Heather on the porch. In his

current mood, it was more temptation than he could resist.

Before he could think about what he was doing or why, he tucked a finger under her chin and kissed her, just a quick graze of his lips across hers. She blinked at him in confusion.

"What was that about?" she asked, a hitch in her voice.

"I'm not entirely sure," he admitted.

"Then maybe you shouldn't do it again," she said, rubbing at her lips as if to wipe away the feel of his mouth on hers.

"Probably not," he agreed, then met her gaze. It was doubtless a bad idea to admit right now that he was lying. Wise or not, there were going to be more kisses if he had his way. And one of these days very soon, he was going to have to figure out just where he intended them to lead.

Having Connor back in town was not going to be easy, Heather concluded a few weeks after the welcome-home dinner that had turned into a major celebration. Oh, the dinner itself had been fine, no more uncomfortable than all the other O'Brien family occasions to which she'd been invited. It was the kiss that had left her shaken and confused.

She hadn't wanted to feel the surge of hope that welled up inside because she knew better than anyone that a mere kiss meant nothing. As for the move, it might not be anything more than just that, a relocation to Connor's hometown. Not an hour went by that she didn't dissect the meaning of it all or stare dreamily out the window thinking about the feel of his lips on hers. She was clearly out of her mind. Nothing had really changed.

Still, in the three weeks he'd been back, Connor had been finding more and more excuses to spend time with her and little Mick. There'd even been another stolen kiss or two, not the kind that had once taken her breath away, but the kind that stirred her senses and filled her with longing just the same. Her protests had been ignored, most likely because they hadn't been very convincing. She had no idea what any of it meant.

As a result, though, she'd been more distracted than usual. Laila and Connie had called her on it more than once. It was a good thing she had only to walk downstairs to get to work, because heaven knew where she'd wind up if she had to drive.

Today, though, with the quilt shop closed for the day, she had to head over to one of the big box discount stores to pick up everything from detergent and junior baby food to diapers and toilet paper. She'd left little Mick next door at the gallery with Megan and promised to be back in a couple of hours.

She'd chosen a lousy day to make the trip. It had been pouring rain most of the morning, which made visibility on the winding road even worse than usual. She was tense behind the wheel, clutching it tightly as she watched for oncoming headlights. She wasn't sure she'd ever get used to driving on these narrow, two-lane country roads. Give her a traffic jam on the interstate any day.

Worse, there was a car behind her. Though for once the driver didn't seem to be impatient about her cautious pace, she kept glancing in her rearview mirror as well as ahead, which just added to the tension.

Then, not even five miles out of town, she rounded a curve in the road to see another car coming straight at her in the wrong lane. Intuitively, she swerved to avoid a collision, but on the narrow road there was no place to go. Her tires skidded on the gravel shoulder, then lost traction as the car veered wildly off the road.

Everything seemed to move in slow-motion after that. Though she jammed on the brakes, the car kept moving, skidding across the soaked ground directly toward the trees that lined the roadway.

Panicked, she knew a crash was inevitable. Her last thoughts were of her son and Connor. A prayer that she'd see them again.

She barely heard the sickening crunch of metal as she crashed into a tree, then careened into a second one. The airbag deployed with astonishing force.

The pain was nearly blinding. Her head. Her leg. Her chest. She hurt everywhere.

And then, blissfully, nothing.

16

It was midweek of his third week back in Chesapeake Shores and Connor was arranging law books in his new office, when Mick walked in. Connor studied his father with concern. Not only had he apparently gone out in the pouring rain without an umbrella, but Mick's expression was more somber than Connor had ever seen it except during those awful days when his mother had first left home. He stopped what he was doing and crossed the room.

"Dad, what's wrong? You shouldn't be walking around in weather like this. You're soaking wet."

"Don't worry about me. I'm fine, but I think you need to sit down," Mick said, though he was the one who looked as if he might pass out.

Connor's entire body seemed to go numb at the dire expression on his father's face and the gloomy tone of his voice. "What's happened? Is it little Mick?"

Mick shook his head and put a hand on Connor's shoulder, as if to brace him for what was to come. "It's Heather, son. There's been an accident."

Connor's knees buckled as he tried to make sense of

what his father was telling him. It was eleven o'clock in the morning. She should be at work. What kind of accident could she have in a quilt shop, for heaven's sake? "I don't understand. Did she fall off a ladder or something like that?"

"She was in her car, Connor. She skidded off the road and hit a tree. The roads are slick today because of the rain, but I don't know if that had anything to do with it or not. Kevin didn't mention that."

"Kevin? What does he have to do with this?"

"I'll explain in the car," Mick said. "We need to go."

Connor tried to sort through what his father was telling him, but the words just didn't make any sense. Individually he recognized them, of course, but he couldn't seem to grasp the implication. His father regarded him with sympathy.

"Are you okay?" he asked as Connor suddenly sank onto the closest chair. "Want me to get you some water? Or maybe Joshua has something stronger in his office. I'm sorry to come in here and just blurt this out, but we need to get on the road."

Connor shook his head to clear it. "I don't need anything. I'm fine," he insisted. "Is she…?" He couldn't make himself complete the question. He settled for asking, "Where is she?"

"She's at the hospital now, but we need to get there fast. Trace is waiting outside to drive us. Your mother and sisters will meet us there. Gram's going to look after little Mick."

The rallying of the troops scared Connor as much as anything. Tears welled up in his eyes. "She's going to be okay, right? They said she'll be okay? Come on, Dad, don't sugarcoat this. I need to know what to expect."

"Let's just go," Mick said, urging him toward the door. "I'll tell you everything I know on the way to the hospital."

Outside, Trace was waiting for them, the motor running. He gave Connor a quick sympathetic glance, then focused on driving. Connor felt as if he were going to crawl right out of his skin unless he got answers fast.

"Dad, talk to me. What the hell happened?"

"Kevin happened to be on his way to work. He was on the road right behind her. He said some driver coming from the other direction on the two-lane road swerved into their lane. It was right out at that curve by Miller's Creek. I've been complaining for years about it being a blind spot, but the state's done nothing about it. Heather apparently didn't see the car till the last second. She tried to avoid a collision, skidded off the road and hit a couple of trees."

"Oh my God," Connor whispered, envisioning it all. How could this be happening, especially now, when they had a real chance to work things out? "Did Kevin say…?" He swallowed hard. "Did he say if she's going to be okay? Come on, Dad. He knows this kind of stuff. He must have said something."

Mick avoided the question. "Just concentrate on the fact that your brother was right there on the scene. She had a trained EMT with her starting treatment even before the ambulance arrived. You know your brother, Connor. He has years of experience with trauma injuries. There's no question, he did everything he could."

All Connor heard was what his father hadn't said. The

evasion hung in the air until he couldn't stand it another second. "Dammit, Dad, is she going to live or not?"

Mick shook his head, his expression helpless. "I don't know, son. I just don't know."

And with those words, Connor knew that his life could very well be changing forever. "Please give me another chance," he prayed silently. "Please, God. I'll do it her way this time. I'll get down on my knees, propose, the whole nine yards. Just let her be okay."

He remembered how Kevin had barely gone through the motions of living when Georgia, Davy's mom, had died in Iraq. He doubted he'd be any better at being a single dad than his brother had been during that terrible time.

"My son needs his mother," he whispered.

"I know, Connor," his father said, giving his hand a squeeze. "The whole family's praying that he'll have her for years to come. That you both will."

But even with Mick's reassurance and as he himself prayed, Connor wondered if after all the church services he'd missed, the mistakes he'd made, God would even hear him.

At the hospital, they found Kevin and the rest of the family in the emergency waiting room. Connor went straight to his brother. Thanks to his EMT experience and his tour of duty in Iraq, Kevin, as Mick had said, knew trauma injuries as well as any doctor around. Moreover, he'd be brutally honest about what lay ahead.

Connor stood in front of him and held his gaze. "How bad is it, Kev?"

Kevin returned his gaze unblinkingly. "Bad," he said quietly.

Connor tried to hold back a gasp of dismay, but a sob seemed to be wrenched from somewhere deep inside him. Kevin nudged him into a chair, then hunkered down in front of him.

"Tell me," Connor pleaded.

"She has a pretty severe head injury, more than likely a grade three concussion since she was unconscious. Maybe worse," he told Connor, his tone straightforward. "I was focused on trying to get the bleeding to stop, but she probably has a couple of cracked ribs from the airbag, and it looked as if her right leg got jammed under the dashboard. I'm pretty sure there were breaks in her tibia and fibula, just below her knee. I didn't try to move her. I didn't want to make anything worse. There's no way I could tell about internal injuries. Her pulse..." He shook his head. "It wasn't good, Connor, but the EMTs took her vitals and said she was hanging in there during the ride over here."

"Was she conscious?"

"In and out for a couple of minutes, then unconscious."

Connor nodded. "What's happening now?"

"The trauma docs are assessing her, probably taking a CT scan or an MRI of her head. I imagine she'll be in surgery before long, once they can prioritize which injuries they need to focus on first and determine if any of her internal organs were injured."

Connor stood up. "I need to see her. Where is she?" He spotted the double doors to the treatment area and headed in that direction. Kevin stepped in front of him.

"Don't," his brother commanded. "You'll only be in the way back there."

Connor just walked right past him. "There are things I have to say, things she needs to hear in case..." He couldn't bring himself to complete the thought.

Before he could push his way through the doors, Megan appeared at his side. "Connor, sweetheart, listen to your brother. There will be plenty of time for you to say all the things you want to say," she assured him. "Let the doctors do their job. Right now, saving Heather's life is the only thing that matters."

Mick joined them. "Why don't you and I go for a walk?" he suggested, putting his arm around Connor's shoulders.

"I'm not leaving here," Connor said, regarding all of them with defiance. "Not until we have answers, not until I've seen Heather for myself."

"I'm not suggesting we go far, just get some air," Mick coaxed. "You need to hold it together for Heather and for your son. We could be here a while. Someone will come for us if anything changes, right, Kevin?"

"Absolutely," Kevin said. "I'll get you myself."

Connor didn't want to leave, but sitting around in this cold room filled with plastic chairs and frantic people would only increase his anxiety.

"Okay, okay, I'll go," he murmured and followed his father into the courtyard outside. He paced for a few minutes, but the frustration of not having any real information finally got to him.

"Dammit, I need answers," he said.

"And you'll have them," Mick promised. He settled onto a concrete bench, then patted the spot beside him.

"Come on and sit here beside me." When Connor had complied, Mick met his gaze. "Did you know what a difficult time your mother had the night you were born?"

Connor blinked at the information. "What are you talking about? I never heard anything about that."

"You were a breech birth, and it wasn't going well. I was in the delivery room, freaking out, and then they made me leave. I thought I was going to go out of my mind waiting for information. Your uncles sat out here with me, trying to convince me that everything was going to be fine, but that was just a bunch of words. After all, what did they know? Thomas had never fathered a child, and Jeff only had Susie back then. I swear that kid popped out like she was in a hurry. Not a bit of trouble. Susie's birth was just as easy as Abby's, Kevin's and Bree's. I should have known that night what a handful you were going to be."

Connor felt the faint curve of a smile on his lips. "Susie hasn't changed much. She's still in a hurry, and she's never caused anyone even a moment's grief." His smile widened. "Except maybe Mack."

"Yeah, those two are quite a pair, aren't they?" Mick said. "What's with spending every spare second together and still swearing they're not dating?"

"They're both delusional, that's all," Connor said.

Mick shook his head. "Crazy, if you ask me. Anyway, my point is that waiting around when someone you love is injured or ill may be one of the toughest things you'll ever have to do, but you get through it, son, because you have to. People are counting on you to be strong. Heather needs that. So does your son."

"I know," Connor said, dragging his hand through his

hair. "I'm just no damn good at waiting. I need to be doing something."

"Then how about this," Mick suggested quietly. "You need to think about calling Heather's family. They'd want to be here." Before Connor could tell him to forget it, Mick held up his hand. "Look, I know there have been some differences there, but we're talking about her mother and father. They have to know what's happened. It's only right."

"Heather wouldn't want them running over here acting all concerned after the way they've rejected her and our son," Connor protested. "And frankly, they'll be none too pleased to hear the sound of my voice."

"Doesn't matter," Mick insisted. "At times like this, families put differences aside. Whatever they decide, you need to do the right thing and at least give them the option of being here for their daughter. I can have Ma or Megan call them, if you don't want to. Just give me a phone number."

Connor thought about what his father was saying and deep down, he knew the call had to be made. He also knew he had to be the one to make it.

"I'll do it," he said eventually.

"You have their number?" Mick asked.

Connor nodded. "It's in my cell phone. You go on back with the others. I'll call and be there in a minute. If you find out anything, if the doctor turns up, come and get me."

"Or I can wait with you," Mick offered.

"No, I swear I'll make the call. You don't have to stand over me the way you did when I slugged Timmy Frost and you made me call to apologize and stood right there until I did it."

Mick smiled. "Don't think I didn't figure out that you were holding down the disconnect button the whole time," he said.

Drawn out of his despair by the memory, Connor laughed. "You knew?"

"Of course. I'd have done the same thing. Why do you think I drove you over to Timmy's house right afterward and made sure you actually spoke to him face-to-face?"

"I thought that was just part of my punishment," Connor admitted. "It was humiliating."

"You learned your lesson, though, didn't you?" He squeezed Connor's shoulder. "Now make that call. I'll be inside."

Connor paced around the small courtyard, ignoring the patients and family members sitting on the benches on the pleasant morning. He dreaded making this call, not just because of the news he had to impart, but because he feared Bridget and Charles Donovan wouldn't react as loving parents, but as the two judgmental people who'd hurt Heather so deeply.

Finally, knowing he couldn't put it off any longer, he placed the call. The phone rang several times before Bridget Donovan picked up.

"Mrs. Donovan, this is Connor O'Brien," he said, then heard her gasp of dismay. "Please don't hang up. There's something you need to know. It's about Heather."

"What about her?" she asked, the question tentative. "We haven't spoken in months."

"I know that, but it doesn't really matter right now.

She's been in an accident. She's in the hospital over here in Maryland. I'm still waiting for word on how serious her injuries are, but it's not good. I just thought you and Mr. Donovan should know." He hesitated, then added, "If you want to fly over, I can make the arrangements and have someone pick you up at the airport."

"She won't want us there," she said, sounding sad.

"Right now, all that matters is that she be surrounded by everyone who loves her," Connor said. "Please, come. I know you'll regret it if you don't."

"It's…it's that serious?" she asked in a choked whisper.

"It is," he said. "Please, come."

"We'll drive," she said decisively. "In the end, that will be faster than trying to arrange for a flight. I doubt I could get Charles on a plane, anyway, not even for this. Tell me where you are."

Connor filled her in. "Do you have a cell phone?" he asked.

"Yes," she said and gave him the number.

"I'll call you the minute I know anything more," he promised. "And you take down my number in case you have any questions or need directions or anything."

"We'll be there by tonight. Shouldn't take more than eight hours or so to get there." She hesitated, then added, "Thank you for calling, Connor. I'm sure it wasn't easy after the way we've treated you both."

"That's not important now," Connor said.

"Can you tell me something before I let you go? Were you in the car with her?" she asked.

"No, she was alone. She was on her way to do some shopping, according to my mother."

"Then—" she began, hesitated and then asked "—the baby? He wasn't with her?"

"No, she'd left him with my mother."

"Thank God for that," she murmured.

"Hurry, Mrs. Donovan."

"We will, and don't you worry. Heather's strong. She'll bounce back from this. Just you wait and see. We'll see you soon."

Connor disconnected the call, relieved to know that the Donovans would be here in a few hours. Mick had been right. This was no time to let ridiculous squabbles, which seemed insignificant in light of the situation, keep them away from their daughter.

Bridget Donovan was a large, raw-boned woman who arrived alone, looking as if she were one step away from falling apart. Connor reluctantly crossed the waiting room to greet her.

"Where's Mr. Donovan?" he asked, steering her toward one of the hard plastic chairs.

"He refused to come," she said tightly. "Stubborn old coot. How is she? How's Heather?"

"She's in surgery," he said. "But the doctors are cautiously optimistic. She had a serious concussion, and there's some swelling of her brain, but they're going to relieve the pressure. They think she'll regain consciousness after that."

Mrs. Donovan sketched the sign of the cross over her chest. "She hasn't been awake in all this time?"

Connor shook his head, trying to hide his own panic over the same information.

"Anything more?" she asked.

"They didn't find any internal injuries, just a couple of cracked ribs, but there are two serious breaks in her right leg, so they're going to put a metal rod in the worst one. She'll be in a cast for a couple of months, they said."

Mrs. Donovan paled at his words. "Oh, my poor child," she whispered.

Connor regarded his mother with relief when she joined them, sitting down next to Mrs. Donovan and introducing herself.

"You must be exhausted," Megan said. "Why don't I take you down to the coffee shop and we can have some soup? Someone will come to get us if there's any news. I think we have a long night ahead of us."

Mrs. Donovan looked too dazed to refuse. As Connor mouthed, "Thank you," Megan led her out of the waiting room.

"At least she didn't shoot you on sight," Kevin said, sitting down next to him. "I was expecting fireworks."

"Oh, there will be plenty of time for that," Connor said, being realistic. "I think she's in a state of shock right now, just like I am." He met his brother's gaze. "Kevin, tell me the truth. Do people recover from injuries like this? I'm talking about the head injury."

"All the time," Kevin assured him. "She's lucky it wasn't anything more than a severe concussion. She'll probably have a few headaches, but since there wasn't any hemorrhaging, her symptoms should be minimal and short-lived."

"Then there's not going to be any...you know?"

"Brain damage?" Kevin said, voicing the words Connor hadn't been able to bring himself to say. "She should be fine, Connor. Of course, there's no way to know if there will be any long-term effects until Heather's awake and can be fully tested, but there's every reason to be optimistic."

"Then the odds are in her favor?" he persisted.

"If I were a betting man, I'd take them," Kevin told him. "Come on, bro, keep the faith. Heather's going to be back to her feisty old self in no time. You'll be longing for the days when she wasn't in your face."

Connor managed a half smile. "I look forward to that."

"Then focus on it," Kevin said.

It was another three hours, nearly midnight, when the surgeon came in and told them that Heather was in recovery and that he was satisfied that things had gone exceptionally well in the operating room.

"It'll be awhile before she comes around, even under the best conditions," he told them. "Go home and get some sleep. This is just the beginning of what could be a long recovery. The ribs will heal on their own, but that right leg of hers is going to take awhile to mend." He looked to Connor. "Any questions?"

"Can I stay here with her tonight?" Connor asked.

"You'd be better off at home in your own bed," the doctor said, then apparently noted the stubborn set of Connor's jaw. "Then again, it'll be good for her to have a familiar face close by if she wakes before morning."

"Thank you." He glanced at Mrs. Donovan. "Do you want to stay, too?"

Megan immediately interceded. "Bridget, I think after driving all that way alone and the stress it's put you under, you should come back to the house with Mick and me and get a good night's sleep."

Though she seemed reluctant to agree, eventually Mrs. Donovan nodded. "I'd be grateful, if you have the room."

"Of course we do," Megan said at once. "Now, let's get out of here. Nell told me she'd made a big pot of her potato soup. I think that's just the thing after the day we've had."

Before she left, Megan crossed the room to Connor and gave him a fierce hug. "If Heather wakes up tonight, you tell her we all love her and are praying for her. Be sure she knows her mother came."

Connor nodded. "I'll tell her. Thanks, Mom." He let his gaze rest on each member of his family. "I don't know what I'd have done today without all of you here."

"This is where we belonged," Mick said. "We stick together in a crisis. That's understood."

"I can stay here with you tonight," Kevin offered.

"No, if the doctor's right about her not waking up till morning, I'll probably just wind up dozing beside Heather's bed," Connor said. "Go home to your family and count your lucky stars they're all safe and sound."

"Amen to that," Abby said, giving him a hug. "Love you, little brother."

When the waiting room had cleared of O'Briens, the doctor regarded Connor with a commiserating expression. "It must be a little overwhelming to have a family like that."

"Sometimes," Connor agreed. "But on days like today, it's a blessing."

Heather felt as if she'd tumbled into a huge vat of cotton and couldn't fight her way out. She tried to open her eyes, but it seemed to require more effort than she possessed. Her body, at least the parts that didn't hurt, seemed weighted down, probably under all that cotton.

"Come on, sweetheart, open those beautiful eyes of yours."

She heard the voice as if from a great distance. Connor, of course. She felt her lips curve into a smile, knowing he was close. Or had she dreamed him?

"Heather!" This time he sounded more impatient.

"What?" she mumbled, her voice as hoarse as a frog's.

She heard a sound and realized he was laughing. "Not funny," she muttered.

"No, it's not funny," he agreed. "It's the most wonderful sound I've heard in the past forty-eight hours."

She tried to make sense of what he was saying. Why had it been two days since he'd heard her speak? Where was she? She tried to struggle into a sitting position, but pain shot through her and she fell back.

She felt Connor's soothing hand on her shoulder.

"Settle down," he said. "You're probably feeling a little foggy about now."

"Too much cotton," she said, trying to shake her head to clear it, but that hurt, too.

"Cotton?" he asked.

"Can't you feel it? It's all over."

"There's no cotton, sweetheart. There are a lot of bandages. You're in the hospital, and they're taking very good care of you. You're going to be fine."

Hospital? "Why?"

"You don't remember the accident?"

She started to shake her head but immediately real-

ized that was a very bad idea when pain shot through it.
"Accident?"

"I'll tell you all about it later," he promised. "Right
now, I need to let the doctor know you're awake."

"Don't go," she pleaded. She didn't want to be left in
this strange place all alone.

"I won't be long. Two minutes at the most." She felt
his lips on her brow, just a whisper of feeling, and then he
was gone. She wanted to stay awake until he came back,
but the pull toward sleep was too strong.

When she woke again, she managed to blink her eyes
open, then regretted it. It was like walking into sunlight
after days of darkness. Everything was too bright.

"Connor?"

"Right here," he said, clasping her hand in his. "How's
the cotton?"

"Not so bad now," she said. "How long was I out this
time?"

"Just a couple of hours. It's Saturday afternoon."

"Saturday? I don't remember anything after..." She
tried to think back. "Tuesday, maybe. Is that when I had
the accident?"

"No, it was Wednesday morning. Mom said you were
going shopping."

She tried to dredge up the memory of any part of that
morning, but it was all a blank. "What's wrong with me?"
she asked the blurry image that she knew to be Connor.
"You're all fuzzy."

"You had a serious concussion, but the doctors dealt
with that. You may have blurry vision from time to time
because of that. You have two cracked ribs and your right
leg's a bit of a mess. It probably feels heavy right now

because you have a cast from the ankle up to your hip to stabilize the bones you broke."

As if to prove him wrong, she tried to move her leg, but it was weighted down. She reached down with her fingers and felt the plaster cast.

"I broke it?"

"Did quite a number on it, as a matter of fact. Apparently it got jammed up under the dashboard somehow and snapped your shinbone and the fibula. Your knee was pretty badly bruised, but they didn't spot any breaks or cracks in the kneecap. They're going to want you up and moving around on crutches soon. Normally they'd push for that sooner, but they've been cautious because of the head injury."

She blinked hard, and her vision cleared a little. She tried to read Connor's expression, but he was keeping it perfectly neutral.

"What aren't you telling me?" she demanded.

"I've told you everything," he insisted.

"No other injuries?" she pressed. "I'm not going to discover tomorrow that there's some major body part I'm missing?"

He smiled at that. "No, I can assure you that all your parts are still there. You have plenty of cuts and bruises as souvenirs, but that's it."

"Then what are you hiding? I know it's something big, because you've got that look on your face."

"What look?"

"The one that you've always had right before you tell me something you know I'm not going to want to hear."

"Oh, *that* look," he said, smiling.

"You're stalling, Connor. Just spill it, whatever it is."

"Okay, here it is," he said. "Your mother's here. She's been staying at the house. I called to let her know you're awake, so she'll probably be back here any minute."

Heather couldn't quite grasp the news. "My mother is here? In Chesapeake Shores?"

Connor nodded.

"Was I dying? Is that how you got her here?"

"You were hurt. That's what got her here. She didn't even hesitate."

"Well, send her home," Heather said heatedly. "If she couldn't be there for me when little Mick was born, then who needs her now?"

No sooner had the words left her mouth than she heard a gasp of dismay and saw her mother in the doorway to the hospital room, her skin pale. Obviously she'd returned at exactly the wrong moment.

Even with her compromised vision, Heather could tell that not only had her mother heard, but that the harsh words had hurt her. "I'm sorry" was on the tip of her tongue, but she couldn't bring herself to utter it. If anyone was owed an apology here, it was her, for months of being treated like she'd shamed her family.

Connor looked from Heather to her mother, then back again. "You two should talk," he said quietly. "I'll give you some time."

"No," Heather protested, grabbing his hand.

He gently extricated his hand, then said meaningfully, "Yes. It's time, Heather. She's right here. You need to have a conversation face-to-face." He turned to her mother. "A brief one, though. Don't upset her."

To Heather's surprise, as Connor left, her mother marched right into the room. She pulled the chair Connor had been sitting in a little closer to the bed, then sat down, gripping her purse tightly in her lap.

"He's right," she told Heather eventually. "We need to mend fences."

Heather sighed. "I doubt that's possible."

"Well, we have to try," her mother said stubbornly. "You're my only child. I want you in my life." She swallowed hard, as tears tracked down her cheeks. "And my grandson…" Her voice trailed off. When she spoke again, she was smiling. "Oh, my, Heather! He's such a wonderful boy. I was a fool to shut him out, to shut you out. This accident, it was a wake-up call. Suddenly I understand that we never know what lies ahead."

"You're the one who cut me out of your life," Heather reminded her, then asked, "Where's Dad?"

"Back home working," her mother admitted, looking chagrined.

"So it wasn't much of a wake-up call for him, was it?" Heather asked wearily, then closed her eyes. "I can't talk about this now."

"Then I'll just sit here while you rest," Bridget said determinedly. "I'm not leaving this room, and I'm certainly not leaving town until I have my daughter back."

Heather noted the unyielding glint in her mother's eyes and recognized it all too well. She'd still be here come Christmas, if that was what it took. Which meant that sooner or later, Heather was going to have to deal with her.

Closing her eyes again and turning away, she opted for later.

17

Connor found his mother in the waiting room, where she'd been stationed every day since the accident. She'd paid an occasional visit to Heather, but mostly she seemed to be here for him, and for the past couple of days for Bridget Donovan.

"Mom, aren't you sick of hanging around this place?" Connor asked, unwilling to admit how relieved he'd been to know she was nearby. "It's depressing."

She smiled at the comment, then glanced around the room, which was long overdue for a paint job and new furniture. "I can't argue with you, if you're referring to the decor. In fact, I've already spoken to your father about having one of his crews come in here and paint the place. Then your grandmother, sisters and I will find some new furnishings. I have a couple of paintings at the gallery that will brighten things up as well."

He stared at her. "Why?"

"Because it needs it, and we have the means to do it," she said simply. "We're all very grateful to everyone here for what they did to save Heather. This is our way of showing it."

"I'm amazed," he said.

She smiled at that. "You shouldn't be. You have a nice family."

He frowned at her. "I know that," he grumbled. "After a couple of days around Mrs. Donovan, I'm more thankful for you all than ever."

His mother's expression sobered. "She's doing the best she can, Connor. This situation—you, Heather and little Mick—it's not what she expected for her only child. We've talked a lot, and I think I have some idea of where she's coming from."

"Would you have ostracized Abby, Bree or Jess if they'd told you they were pregnant and weren't getting married?" he asked, curious about her reaction.

"Absolutely not," she said at once. "I don't care what flaws any of you might have. My job is to advise you if you want to hear it, listen when you need to talk, but most of all to love you, no matter what. Still, I can understand a mother wanting the best for her daughter."

"So can I," he conceded. "It's the my-way-or-the-highway approach that I don't get."

"Because, despite your sometimes low opinion of the upbringing I gave you, you were taught to be more tolerant of other's choices."

"I'm not sure Dad shares your approach," he said. "He hardly ever shuts up about the mistakes he thinks any of us are making."

"But in the end, you all know his love is unconditional," Megan stressed, then studied him closely. "You do know that, don't you? Mick learned that from Nell. She grew up with strong beliefs and did her best to teach them to her sons and to all of you, but right or wrong, you're her family, and she'll go to bat for any one of you against any outsider who dares to criticize you."

"Maybe she's the one whose attitude will rub off on Mrs. Donovan. I'm sure they share the same Catholic values," Connor said wistfully. "And as unhappy as she might be with me, Gram's never made me feel that she was one step from disowning me."

"I think maybe we need to view this accident as a blessing in disguise," Megan suggested. "It's brought Bridget here. I think she'll see how much you and Heather love each other and your son, even if your relationship isn't traditional. Give her that chance, Connor. Make it a point to spend a little time with her, so she can see for herself what a fine young man you are."

Connor squirmed. "About that," he began. "The traditional thing."

His mother tilted her head, clearly puzzled. "What?"

"All of this has made me do some serious thinking," he began, then stopped. If he said the words aloud, his mother could try to hold him to them. What if he then panicked and changed his mind?

She continued to regard him with curiosity. Then, it seemed, a lightbulb went off in her head. "Connor O'Brien, are you saying what I think you're saying?" she asked excitedly. "Are you going to ask Heather to marry you?"

So much for hedging his bets, he thought. "I think so," he admitted.

Her expression fell at his response. "Your enthusiasm is less than overwhelming."

"Look, you know how I feel, but I realized the other day when I could have lost Heather that I didn't want to go through the rest of my life without her. If we don't get married, eventually she's going to marry someone else and I'll lose her. I'll lose both her and little Mick."

"First of all, you will never lose your son," Megan said. "And not wanting to see Heather happy with another man is not a reason to marry her yourself. That's just selfish. Here's the question that counts—do you love her?"

"Of course," he said without hesitation. "I thought that was a given. Everyone's thrown it in my face often enough."

His mother smiled slightly. "Good to know you were listening. My point is that you have to want marriage and all that it entails, not just because Heather insists on it or might move on without it, but because you really want it, too. Do you?"

He held back a sigh. "It's not that simple."

She gave him a sympathetic look. "It should be. Look, I've promised myself that I won't give you unsolicited advice, but I have to say this. Don't ask Heather to marry you unless you're a hundred percent committed to everything that implies. Marriage requires hard work and a willing heart."

Connor knew it was probably good advice; he just didn't think he could take it. He'd made a promise to God in the car on the way to the hospital. Heather was alive, and he intended to keep his word. He might not believe in marriage, but he believed in Heather and their love. Somehow, he'd make it work.

Heather had to admit her mother was persistent. Bridget was at the hospital almost as often and for just as long as Connor, though amazingly the two of them mostly managed to avoid each other. That was getting on Heather's nerves almost as much as the realization that her recovery was going to be slow and tedious.

Worse than all that, though, she missed little Mick. She knew he was in good hands, staying at the house with his grandparents and great-grandmother looking after him, and with Connor there for at least some part of every day. At first they wouldn't allow the boy in ICU. Then Heather had feared that seeing her laid up in bed with bruises from head to toe would scare him. Now, though, she thought she might go crazy if she didn't get at least a brief glimpse of her sweet boy.

She was lying there thinking about him and trying to ignore her mother, when the door opened and Connor peeked in. "Up for some company?" he asked, then opened the door wider to reveal little Mick holding his hand.

"Mama!" little Mick shouted with glee, and toddled across the room. The bed was too high for him to scramble up, but Connor scooped him up and set him gently down beside her.

Her eyes blurred by tears, she met Connor's gaze. "How did you know this was exactly what I needed?"

"Lucky guess," he said. "Besides, he was very anxious to see his mom. He's been asking for you every minute he's awake. It was starting to break my heart."

"It's true," her mother said, regarding Connor with an approving glance. "He surely has missed his mommy."

Sitting quietly beside her, little Mick turned sad. He reached over and touched his finger very gently to a cut on her cheek. "Boo-boo hurt?" he asked worriedly.

"A little bit," she said, then grinned. "How about you kiss it and make it better?"

"'Kay," he said, moving closer and pressing a kiss to the cut. "More boo-boos," he noted. "Kiss, too?"

Heather laughed. "That might take all day," she said, tickling him until he giggled. "I am so glad you came to see me," she told him. "You're the best medicine ever, but I think you should go home. From in here it looks like such a beautiful day outside. I imagine Grandpa Mick would take you fishing this afternoon if you asked him to."

"G'pa," he said, nodding enthusiastically.

Connor chuckled. "Okay, then. Let's go find Grandpa Mick." He leaned down and kissed her cheek, then winked. "Just making you better."

"Thanks," she said, then stared after them as they left.

"That child adores you," her mother said, moving back to the chair beside the bed. "So does his father. I've seen it in his eyes whenever he's here. And the way he talks about you… Oh, my, it's evident how scared he was when he thought he might lose you. He was wearing his heart on his sleeve. Why the two of you can't work things out is beyond me."

"Not discussing this with you, Mom. I've told you how things are for Connor and me. It's not going to change."

Bridget gave her a sharp look. "Are you so sure about that? I've never seen anyone crazier about a woman. He barely slept a wink when you first came to the hospital, and he's still here every spare minute he has. He's even put his new job on hold. That tells me quite a lot about

Connor's devotion to you. Frankly, it's been a revelation to me."

That last was news to Heather. She'd have to tell Connor it was time for him to go to work. She didn't want to stand in the way of this new career of his. Though she was grateful for his visits, she no longer needed him hovering over her or even running interference between her and her mother.

"I'm of a mind to sit him down and have a serious talk with him," her mother said. "It's time he faced up to his responsibilities and did the right thing by you and that boy! I doubt it would take more than a gentle push to move him in that direction."

"Mom!" Heather protested. "Not a word to Connor. Is that clear? We're both adults and perfectly capable of deciding what's right for us."

"I see no evidence of that," Bridget persisted.

"You'll just have to trust me. Stay out of it, Mom. I mean it."

Her mother looked put out by the order, but she nodded eventually. "Okay, fine. Whatever you want. I'll keep my opinions and observations to myself."

"I'd appreciate it," Heather told her.

She didn't want to hear her mother's speculations about Connor's feelings, either, because stirring up old hopes accomplished nothing. She'd accepted reality a long time ago, and nothing had changed.

Unfortunately, accepting reality and figuring out how to live with it, especially with Connor being so attentive lately, were two different things.

* * *

Connor was walking down the hallway on his way to Heather's room when he ran into the social worker.

"Mr. O'Brien, do you have a minute?" Jill Swanson called out to him.

He paused and waited for her to catch up. "What's up?"

"Ms. Donovan's going to be released in another day or two, but we need to make sure she can manage when she gets home. I understand she lives with her son in a second-floor apartment." She met his gaze. "That's just not going to work under the circumstances. She can't possibly cope with either the stairs or a very active toddler."

Connor had anticipated something like this. He'd already decided that Heather would either come home with him where there would be plenty of people around to help, or he would move into her apartment. Unless, of course, Bridget Donovan intended to hang around until Heather was fully recovered. Given the increasingly irritated calls she was getting from her husband back in Ohio, he doubted that was likely.

"I have a couple of alternative options, but I need to run them past Heather," he told the social worker. "I assure you, though, when the time comes, Heather will have all the help she needs."

"You'll need to fill me in on the plan once the two of you have discussed it," the woman insisted. "Otherwise, I won't be able to agree to her release."

"Not a problem," he assured her. At least not if Heather was being reasonable. Since he knew how badly she wanted to get out of this place, he suspected that for once she'd be more agreeable than usual.

* * *

After talking to Jill Swanson, Connor made a U-turn and left the hospital. He drove straight to a jewelry store, picked out a diamond ring, stopped by his sister's shop for a lavish bouquet of bright pink and white peonies, then returned to the hospital. By the time he got back, Heather was napping. Her mother had gone back to the house with Megan for lunch.

Connor sat beside the bed and tried to work out what he was going to say. Proposing was obviously new to him. Did the words matter? Or was it just the intent? For a man who wrote effective opening statements and closing arguments for courtrooms, he was surprisingly inept at putting his feelings into words. Somehow the stakes were way too high.

As he silently rehearsed various options, he glanced over at the bed and saw Heather staring at him, obviously amused.

"Do you have some kind of big court case tomorrow?" she asked.

"No. Why?"

"Because the only time I've seen you muttering so intensely under your breath was when you were trying to get a closing argument down pat."

He met her gaze. "In a way, this is the same thing," he admitted.

"Oh?"

"A closing argument sums up your case. It tells the court what you want them to take away from all the evidence."

"I know that," she said.

"Well, what I have to say to you is a lot like that. I need

to present all my evidence, sum it up and then pray you reach the right conclusion."

She regarded him with a perplexed expression. "You're not making a lot of sense." She glanced past him and spotted the vase filled with peonies. "Where did those come from? They look beautiful and smell fabulous."

"They're part of my evidence," he told her. "I want you to know how much I care about you. I know you love peonies."

She gave him an oddly quizzical look. "Connor, I've never doubted your love. You don't need to bring me flowers to prove anything. The fact that you've been here for hours every day tells me all I need to know."

"Well, here's the thing," he began earnestly. "This accident, it changed something for me. That day, when my dad came to tell me what happened, that you were in the hospital, I can't even begin to tell you how terrified I was. There were a few minutes there when I couldn't even catch my breath, I was so scared. The drive over here was excruciating, with me not knowing what to expect when I got here. For all I knew you could have…" He shook off the words. "Never mind."

The mere idea that she could have been dead was too awful to mention. The point was that she was here, alive and on her way to a full recovery, and he would spend every day for the rest of his life being grateful for that.

She reached for his hand. "Connor, it's okay. I'm right here. The crisis is past. And I've been meaning to talk to you about that. It's time for you to start working for Joshua Porter. I'm sure he must be anxious to have you take on some of his cases."

"Work's not the issue," he said impatiently. "I'm trying to say something important here."

"What's more important than getting off on the right foot with this new job?" she asked.

"You, dammit! You're more important. I'm trying to tell you that the day of the accident I realized just how much I love you. I don't want to lose you, Heather." He reached into his pocket and pulled out the small jewelry box with the ring in it and held it out. She stared at it, shock written all over her face.

"What is that?"

He knew she was neither blind nor stupid. She knew what it was. She'd just never expected to see such a thing in his hand. Maybe the element of surprise would be a good thing.

"Marry me, Heather," he said quietly. "I want to spend the rest of my life with you and our son, taking care of you, making sure you're happy."

She didn't look half as bowled over by the proposal as he'd anticipated. In fact, she looked more confused than anything. Maybe even a little sad, though he had no idea why getting what she'd always wanted would sadden her.

"And you?" she asked. "Will getting married make you happy? Have you changed that much in a week?"

"I'm asking, aren't I?" he said, unable to control his impatience.

"And I love you for asking, but no," she said, her voice filled with so much tenderness that it made him want to scream.

"But I made a promise," he said before he could stop himself.

"A promise?" she asked blankly. "To whom?"

"To God. I told Him if you pulled through, I'd marry you just the way you wanted."

He knew, even as the words crossed his lips, that he'd gotten it all wrong. Telling her he'd made a bargain with God was absolutely the worst thing he could have admitted. It was too late, though, to scramble for another explanation. Nor could he take back the words. At this point, he couldn't even rephrase the proposal and make it more romantic, more believable.

He stared into Heather's eyes, saw the pain there, and knew he'd blown his chance. He might have others—in fact, he would see to it that he had as many as necessary—but this one had slipped away. He was probably lucky she was confined to bed, or she might very well have dumped those beautiful peonies over his head.

"I don't get it," he said, unable to stop himself even though he knew he was only making things worse. "I thought this was what you wanted."

"Not like this," she said softly, then rolled over and turned her back on him, but not before he'd seen the tears that filled her eyes.

Heather should have known that turning down Connor's proposal wouldn't be the end of it. Apparently working up the courage to say the words once had emboldened him. For the past two days he'd been asking just about every time he walked into the room and they were left alone. She finally lost patience.

"Connor O'Brien, I will not marry you just because you had some epiphany on the way to the hospital," she declared, scowling at him. "How many times do I have to tell you that? You're being very sweet, but the answer is still no!"

All of the pretty words he'd been spouting should have been gratifying, but his proposals were getting on her nerves. *Everything* was getting on her nerves. She wanted to go home.

The only way that was going to happen, though, was if someone was there to look after her. Her cracked ribs were going to take time to heal, as was her broken leg. Right now the whole process looked daunting.

The entire O'Brien family had volunteered to help out, but it was Connor's offer that she found most troubling. It came with totally unexpected strings, and it seemed he wasn't above using her release as a means to get what he wanted.

"You want to leave here, don't you?" he asked yet again, a coaxing note in his voice. "You can do it with full-time help. That's what the social worker has said. I can provide that, but only if you'll agree to marry me."

"That's blackmail," she accused, stunned that he could be so sneaky. How dare he make a mockery of the one thing he knew she wanted above all else—the two of them together forever?

"No, it's giving you everything you claimed to want," he countered. "You get to go home and you get me in the bargain. Forever this time, with a marriage license to prove it."

"Why do I feel as if I'm on *Let's Make a Deal?*" she asked, thoroughly disgruntled, even though, as he said, he was offering everything she'd wanted. "A proposal's supposed to be romantic. This one sounds an awful lot like bartering for a few sheep and a couple of cows."

"Hey, that worked in a lot of cultures for a very long time."

She frowned at the flip comment. "Connor, I can't marry you just so I'll have a caregiver for a few months. What happens once I'm well?"

"We'll have the life we deserve," he said as if it were as simple as that.

She shook her head. "No, you'll start having regrets."

"No, I won't," he insisted. "Why are you fighting me so hard on this? You said you loved me."

"I do," she confirmed. "That's beside the point."

"Hardly. And I love you." He held her gaze. "I really don't see the problem."

"Love was never enough for you before," she reminded him. "You've always assumed it would vanish in a puff of smoke by the time the ink dried on the marriage license."

"I've given the matter more thought," he claimed.

She rolled her eyes. If she'd been even a tiny bit stronger and the least bit mobile, she would have crawled out of bed to shake him. "Connor, stop with this nonsense," she nearly shouted instead. "You still don't believe in marriage. That's why this whole idea is crazy."

He reached for her hand. His grasp warmed her, even if the situation sent a chill right through her.

"Look at me," he commanded. She met his gaze, and he continued, "When I thought I was going to lose you, I nearly went out of my mind. It made me realize that I don't want to live another minute without you. Whatever time we have together on this earth, I want to spend it with you and our son. I want to have more kids with you. I could be content to do that without a wedding license, but you can't, so I'm going to focus on how important you are to me and take that walk down the aisle because it matters to you."

Heather wanted so badly to take what he was offering and let it be enough, but how could she? She'd always feel as if she had somehow trapped him into doing something that went against his deepest convictions. She'd always know he'd gone into the marriage under duress.

"No," she whispered, barely able to utter the word. "It won't work that way, Connor. It can't."

He looked thoroughly shaken by her latest refusal, as if she'd finally pushed him too far. He'd put aside his own beliefs and laid himself on the line, and now she'd rejected him.

But what else could she have done? she wondered. She knew him better than he knew himself. If he made this crazy sacrifice and they married now, he'd be miserable.

He stood up, his spine rigid. He started for the door, then stopped and looked back.

"Because I've always been honest with you and told you how I feel, you're going to hold it against me forever, aren't you?" he said, his voice empty of emotion. "I see now that I'll never be able to persuade you that I've changed, that I'm really ready to commit to you for the long haul."

"Maybe not," she admitted, though saying it nearly broke her heart.

And watching him walk out of her hospital room, his shoulders hunched, an air of defeat about him, finished the job.

18

Connor walked blindly out of the hospital, trying to grapple with the fact that Heather had been so adamant in her refusal of his proposal. He thought he'd offered everything she'd ever claimed to want, and it wasn't enough. What was he supposed to do now? Accept that their relationship was well and truly over? He didn't think he could do that, and yet he was out of ideas.

He was walking so fast, he didn't even notice Bridget Donovan approaching.

"Connor!" she said urgently, grabbing his arm just as he was about to step off the curb and into the path of an oncoming car in the hospital parking lot. Her brow creased with worry. "What's going on? You look upset. Is Heather worse?"

He regarded her blankly for a minute, then shook his head. "No. No, she's fine. Stubborn as a mule, in fact."

Bridget actually smiled at that. "Ah, then she's definitely feeling better. What did she say to get under your skin?"

Connor thought about ignoring the question, but perhaps Bridget was exactly the ally he needed. "Could we talk a minute?" he asked.

"Of course."

"Would you like to go inside for a cup of coffee or tea?"

"I'd prefer to sit right out here in the garden in the sunshine, if you don't mind. It's such a peaceful setting."

They found a bench just past the rosebushes and sat down. She studied him curiously. "What's on your mind?"

"You and I got off on the wrong foot," he admitted. "I know the relationship that Heather and I had was a disappointment to you."

"It was," she agreed candidly. "But I've seen a different side of things since I've been here. I've seen just how deep the love between the two of you runs, to say nothing of how devoted you are to your son. I want my daughter to be happy, Connor, and you seem able to accomplish that. It might not be the way I'd have chosen, but I don't think it's up to me to judge."

He gave her a wry look. "Can I assume that my mother and Nell have given you a less than subtle push toward that conclusion?"

She laughed. "Oh, they've sung your praises, no question about that, but it's what I've seen for myself that's done the trick."

"Then perhaps, if the opportunity arises, you could put in a good word for me with Heather," he requested.

She seemed startled by the request. "Why on earth would you need me to do that?"

"I've been proposing for a few days now, and she's turned me down flat each and every time," he admitted in a chagrined tone.

Shock spread across her face. "But why?"

"She seems to think my epiphany is unbelievable or

that it's come too late. I'm not really sure of her logic. I just know she's pretty adamant."

"Well, that's just crazy!" Bridget declared.

Connor smiled. "I was hoping you'd think so. Then you'll put in a good word for me?"

"I'm not sure having me on your side will be much help, but I'll do what I can," she promised. "For whatever it's worth, I do think the two of you belong together. And a word of advice. Give her a bit of time to adjust to this new outlook of yours. It's quite a turnaround, and the girl has already had her share of whiplash lately."

Impulsively, Connor hugged her. "Thank you for the assistance and for the insight."

She patted his cheek. "Let me go in there and see what mood I find her in. No time like the present to start on this mission you've given me."

Connor watched her head into the hospital, her stride purposeful. To his astonishment, he realized that Bridget Donovan wasn't even half the ogre he'd been making her out to be. As his mother had told him, Bridget was just a mother who cared desperately about her daughter's happiness.

After Connor's departure, Heather thought for a long time about what had happened, about how defeated he'd looked when he left. The image was burned in her mind. She couldn't prevent her tears from spilling over, though she certainly tried. Crying seemed like such a waste of energy, but the tears had been bottled up for too long. She cried as she hadn't in all the months since she'd walked away from their home in Baltimore and their life together.

Once started, she couldn't seem to stop, not even when

her mother walked into the room, took one look at her face and gathered her close. If anything, the rare display of unquestioning, unconditional sympathy made her cry harder.

After a while, she wasn't even sure why she was crying—over a lost opportunity, the end of a dream, her mother's unexpected comfort or a mix of everything.

"This is about Connor, I imagine," her mother said eventually. "I saw him leaving here as I was on my way in, and he didn't look a bit happier than you do. He told me his side of things. What's yours?"

Heather stared at her in shock. "He told you that he'd asked me to marry him?" she asked, tears still streaming down her cheeks.

"He did."

Heather tried to make sense of that, but she couldn't. "Did he also tell you it wasn't the first time?"

Her mother nodded, still stroking her hair as she had when Heather had come to her with some childhood hurt.

"I think it will be the last time," Heather told her with a sad sniff.

"And you're unhappy about that?" Bridget said.

Heather nodded. "I'm absolutely certain it would be a huge mistake for us to marry now," Heather said with a touch of her old spirit. "He doesn't really want to get married."

"But he asked. Isn't that cause to celebrate?"

Heather shook her head. "You're not hearing me. I turned him down—not just today but every time he's asked since the accident."

"But why would you do that?" Bridget asked, clearly mystified. "I know you love him."

"He didn't ask because he wants to be married," Heather said. "He asked because he made some deal with God."

To her shock, her mother smiled. "Did he now? To save your life, I imagine."

Heather nodded. "That's what he said."

"Then he's an honorable man, wanting to live up to his end of the bargain."

"Of course he's an honorable man," Heather said impatiently. "There was never any doubt about that."

"From where I sat, there was," her mother said wryly.

Heather scowled at her. "This is so not the time for another lecture on your low opinion of Connor."

Again, her mother's lips curved into a smile. "I might have been wrong about him. Wouldn't you enjoy rubbing that in my face from now till Kingdom come?"

"You're not taking this seriously," Heather accused. "He's furious because I turned him down, and now I can't even go home, because there's no way I can manage on my own. I'll be locked away in this hospital forever."

Her mother actually laughed at that. "You always did have a flair for drama," she teased. "If you want to go back to your apartment, I'll come with you. I can stay on for a while longer."

"I thought Dad was insisting you come back home," Heather said, though she took heart from the unexpected offer. She wanted so badly to be out of this place and back to normal, or at least what passed for normal these days without Connor living under the same roof.

Her mother waved off the concern. "Your father can

manage on his own for a while longer," she declared, an oddly guilty expression on her face. "The truth is, I haven't felt such a sense of freedom in years. Who knows? Maybe I'll settle in Chesapeake Shores, too. It seems like a nice town."

"Without Dad?" Heather asked, unable to hide her shock.

Her mother merely shrugged. "You never know. Maybe it's time to shake things up."

Heather brushed at the last of her tears as if to clear her vision, then stared at her mother. "Are you serious?"

Bridget hesitated, then admitted, "I might be. But I do know I intend to stay right here until you're back on your feet and are able to manage on your own again."

Though she was still reeling from her mother's unexpected offer and the hint that she might make a permanent move, Heather seized on the prospect of an obvious solution to another of her problems. After all, she'd learned quilting from her mother. "Would you be willing to teach the quilting class at the shop for me, just for a few weeks?"

Her mother's eyes immediately lit up. "I'd love it," she said enthusiastically. "Megan took me by to see the shop and showed me some of the quilts you've made. You haven't forgotten any of the lessons I taught you. In fact, your stitches are better than mine and you're more creative than I ever dreamed of being. You're willing to break the rules for your own designs. I never dared."

"But without the basics I learned from you, I never would have risked trying my own designs," Heather told her. "I'm so grateful to you for sharing your talent with me. And I would love it if you'd work with my class.

They're all really nice people. I think you'd enjoy them. Some are around my age, but there are a couple of older women, too."

"I'll be happy to do it, but I think you could teach it yourself, at least in another week or two," Bridget said. "We could find a way to get you down the stairs."

"Oh, I plan to be there," Heather said. "But I wouldn't mind a few of your lessons myself. It'll be like a refresher course for me."

"Then that's settled," Bridget said, looking pleased. "Now let's talk about this latest proposal of Connor's."

"No," Heather said, her good mood vanishing.

"Later, then," her mother said a little too agreeably.

Something told Heather she was just going to lie in wait until Heather was at her most vulnerable before taking Connor's side again. Who would have thought Bridget Donovan and Connor would ever take the same stance? It was one of the more ironic turn of events since the accident. And Heather had a feeling they both still had plenty to say.

Connor couldn't bring himself to go anywhere near the hospital. In fact, even after he discovered a few days later that Heather had been released and had moved back into her apartment with her mother there to look after her and little Mick, he stayed away. So far he'd managed to cajole other people into picking up his son and bringing him over for his visits with his dad.

Though his caseload was already picking up with the kind of legal matters he wouldn't have bothered with in Baltimore, there was still not enough work to distract Connor from the lousy mood he was in. He expected someone in the family to call him on it, but he hadn't expected it to be go-with-the-flow Jess.

He was sitting in the kitchen at the house just after dawn, staring into his cup of coffee, when his younger sister walked in, scowled at him, poured herself some coffee, then sat across from him. It was obvious to someone who knew her well that she had something on her mind. Connor braced himself.

"This has to stop," she said. "You have the whole family tiptoeing around you, terrified they're going to say the wrong thing about Heather."

"Since when has anybody in this family avoided any topic that suited them?" he asked, considering Jess's comment a gross exaggeration. "Everyone in this family is always in trouble with one person or another for being too outspoken."

"Come on, Connor. You snapped at Gram!" she said indignantly. "What has she ever done to deserve that?"

Connor flushed, recalling the incident with immediate shame. "I never meant to," he said. "She made a comment about Heather and little Mick. I took it the wrong way and told her it was none of her business what Heather and I did or didn't do. I apologized almost as soon as the words came out of my mouth. Gram understood."

"Well, of course she did," Jess responded with exasperation. "That's what Gram does, no matter how badly we behave, but, Connor, you have to see how wrong that was."

"I do. It won't happen again."

"It will unless you fix things with Heather. If I loved somebody as much as you obviously love her, and he loved me back, you can bet I wouldn't be dillydallying

around and letting him get away just because I had my
doubts about whether I had what it takes to make a marriage last."

Connor regarded her with surprise. "It's not about me
doubting myself," he insisted. "If I committed to getting
married, I'd make it work."

"Then why don't you?"

"I gather the grapevine hasn't reported that I asked
Heather to marry me," he replied. "Several times, in
fact."

Jess blinked. "Seriously?"

"Yep."

"Well, hallelujah! Why doesn't anyone know about
this? And why are you walking around in a funk?"

"Because she turned me down flat each and every
time."

Now it was his sister's turn to look stunned. "You're
kidding me. Why? Did she say?"

"She didn't believe I'd really done a one-eighty on the
whole marriage thing." He gave her a wry look. "It probably didn't help that I admitted I'd made a pact with God
when I was scared she was going to die."

Jess stared at him. "You told her that?"

He nodded.

She punched him in the arm. "You're an idiot."

"That seems to be the consensus."

"How are you going to fix it?"

"I'm not," he said. "No matter what I say now, she
won't believe it."

"Then stop talking and show her you're ready to be
the kind of husband she's always dreamed about. Actions

speak louder than words. At least that's what a shrink we both know is always telling me."

Connor grinned for the first time since the uncomfortable conversation had started. "How is Will these days?"

"Annoying," Jess said at once. "Irritating. Impossible. Underfoot too darn much, thanks to you."

"If the guy doesn't get to you, why do you waste so much energy making sure you're never alone with him? Seems to me that's a dead giveaway that you have a thing for him."

"Don't be ridiculous!" she said with a dismissive wave of her hand. "Besides, I didn't come over here to talk about Will."

"No, you came as the family's duly designated representative to make sure I straighten things out with Heather. You can report back that it's not going to happen. Not this time. If anything, things between us are worse than ever."

"Because you're too stubborn to swallow your pride and grovel."

"Ask your friend Will what kind of prayer a relationship that requires groveling will have."

She gave him an irrepressible grin. "The way I hear it, most of them do, especially when the man keeps doing really dumb stuff."

"Asking Heather to marry me was dumb?"

"Of course not," she said at once. "But taking no for an answer certainly was. After the way you held out on her for years, I don't blame her for one minute for turning the tables on you."

"I don't think it was about revenge," he said.

"No, Heather's too sweet to want revenge. She just doesn't believe in this sudden change of heart. Not many women would."

Connor sighed. Even though he didn't like what Jess was telling him, he realized there was a kernel of truth in it.

"Actions, huh?"

She nodded.

"Such as?"

"Did you ever really court her?"

"You mean flowers and candy, that kind of thing?" he asked.

"For starters."

"Never. Who had money for stuff like that back in college?" His expression brightened. "I did take her a huge bouquet of peonies from Bree's shop the other day. She'd always talked about how much she liked peonies." He hesitated. "Or was it pansies? Maybe that was the problem. I took the wrong flowers and she concluded I hadn't been paying attention."

Jess merely shook her head. "Sadly, most women learn by the time they're in their teens that men never hear a word we say unless we toss in things like football and baseball scores to get their attention."

"Now who's being downright cynical?" he said.

"Please," she retorted. "We both know Mom left Dad because he never paid a bit of attention to what she said or what she needed."

"Actually, she told me she'd never communicated to him what she really wanted," Connor said. "You can't blame Dad for not getting a message she never delivered."

"Here we go again, with you taking Dad's side over

hers," Jess said. "None of that's the point. I'm telling you that you need to prove to Heather that you know her better than anyone on earth. Anticipate her needs for a change."

"Look, I get what you're saying, but I am clueless about how to do that," he admitted.

Jess rolled her eyes. "Okay, if you were laid up in bed or at least stuck in the house, what would you want more than anything? Think back to when you had that really awful sprained ankle and had to stay off your feet for what felt like an eternity. Remember?"

"It was midway through football season my senior year," he recalled. "That may have been the most frustrating week of my entire high school sports career."

"Exactly," Jess said, obviously pleased with herself for stirring his memory. "Now, what did you want the most?"

He thought about it for a minute before the answer dawned on him. "To get out."

His sister beamed at him. "See, big brother, you're not so clueless, after all. Pack a picnic lunch. In fact, I'll have that done for you at the inn. Then you can go by, pick up Heather and take her to the beach for the afternoon. Let Bridget deal with little Mick. Make the afternoon all about Heather." Her gaze held his. "And whatever you do, do not bring up marriage or your hurt feelings or this deal you made with God."

"Got it," he said. "Anything else?"

Jess's expression turned dreamy. "Just treat her as if she's the most special person in your life."

Connor figured that wouldn't be that difficult, because she was. Always had been.

Jess stood, then leaned down and kissed him on the cheek. "Don't mess this up," she warned.

"Aye-aye, boss."

"Mock me all you want, but I'm your secret weapon."

"How so?"

"I'm female. I know how I'd want a man to court me. I'll coach you through this, one date at a time."

Connor thought she was overly optimistic, but what did he have to lose? If Jess's methods got him and Heather talking again, it would be a start, a step in the right direction. Worst-case scenario, if these tactics didn't work for him, he could pass all the tips along to Will, and maybe his equally clueless friend could finally break the stalemate he seemed to be having with Jess herself.

Heather had thought that being home would cure her gloomy mood, but the truth was that her apartment suddenly seemed too small with her mother living there, too. Heather had made one futile attempt to go downstairs to her shop, but had had to give it up. Standing on crutches at the top of the steps had been too daunting. As unsteady as she was with that ungainly cast, she'd feared tumbling straight to the bottom. She'd vowed to try to work up the nerve another time.

She'd had plenty of company the past few days, but even that had grown tiresome. Truthfully, she thought, there was probably nothing that would improve her mood, not even winning the lottery or being miraculously cured overnight. The problem wasn't really being incapacitated, it was knowing that things were actually over with Connor. His silence since her release from the hospital spoke volumes. And, if she hadn't gotten the message from that, there was the fact that every other O'Brien except Connor had been by to pick up little Mick.

Only now could she admit that even after leaving Connor, she'd harbored a hope that they'd find their way back to each other. Ironically, he'd finally offered her everything she'd always wanted, but only because he was paying back a debt he felt he owed to God. That was no better way to start a marriage than if one person was dragged to the altar unwillingly.

She'd been in such a foul mood just thinking about their last encounter that her mother had actually taken little Mick downstairs to the store with her.

"If you want to sit up here and stew, that's fine," Bridget had said. "Just don't let your little boy see you acting this way. You don't want to change the way he feels about his daddy. Kids pick up on moods, you know."

"You mean the way I always sensed the tension between you and Dad," Heather had retorted.

Her mother had looked taken aback by that. Without saying a word, she'd gathered up Mick, his toys and his snacks and walked out of the apartment.

When someone tapped on the door, then opened it without waiting for a response, Heather scowled as she looked toward the intruder. Then her heart rate bumped up as she realized it was Connor. Then her scowl only deepened.

"Did you hear me invite you in?" she asked, not even trying to hide her irritation.

Connor smiled, clearly undeterred. "No, but then I didn't want to take a chance that you wouldn't. Your mother gave me her key."

"Since when are you and my mother in cahoots?"

"I'm guessing it's since you apparently got on her last nerve this morning. What's going on over here?"

"See how cheerful you'd be if you were confined to this place day after day," she retorted.

He made an unsuccessful attempt to fight a smile. "Gee, and you've been home for what? Three days?"

"Four," she snapped.

He laughed at that. "Sorry. My mistake. It does seem, though, that I've come by just in time to save you from this self-imposed confinement. Who'd have thought that a few measly little stairs would be too daunting for you to tackle?"

"It's not the stairs," she retorted. "At least not entirely. It's the stairs combined with the way I feel on these crutches and with this stupid cast, which must weigh a thousand pounds."

"It doesn't," he assured her. "How are you going to get used to it if you don't practice?"

"I did practice before I left the hospital, but that was on flat surfaces. Those stairs out there look like a death trap to me."

"So, like I said, I'm just in time."

"In time for what?" she asked suspiciously.

"To rescue you."

For some reason the response made her see red. "You did not just say that," she said. "Since when have I ever needed to be rescued?"

"By your own calculations, since four days ago," he taunted.

She was about to snap out a particularly nasty expletive or two, but he waved a finger at her. "Remember, you have a son. You don't want to get in the habit of saying bad words in front of him. Otherwise, we'll spend all our time trying to explain why our kid has a potty mouth."

Even though she was beyond annoyed, even though she wanted desperately to stay mad at him, Heather couldn't help chuckling. "You have a point. He's just starting to mimic everything I say."

"Well, there you go." He met her gaze. "So, how about it? Care to go out with me?"

She thought of declining just on principle, but what would that accomplish? Her already sour mood would only get worse if she rejected her one chance to break out of here. If she didn't accept now, it could prove to be a very long six to eight weeks until the stupid cast was removed.

"Where?" she asked warily. "And more importantly, why?"

"For a ride and then to the beach. The humidity's low, there's a wonderful breeze. It's a perfect day for a picnic. As for why, it's because I thought it might cheer you up to have a change of scenery."

"Who's been complaining about my mood?"

He grinned. "No one had to. I know you. You've never been good at being idle. Me, I would have thought this would be the perfect time for you to create one of those amazing quilts you make, but I remember how your mind works. It's a little twisted."

She scowled at him. "Did you just insult me?"

"Nope, just telling the truth. Instead of seizing this as an opportunity, you can't get past the fact that you're feeling as though you're trapped in this apartment. Am I right?"

"Okay, yes, but you were never one bit better at forced relaxation than I am."

"True, but we're not talking about me. Now, about the beach—yes or no?"

Closing her eyes, she could practically see the waves on the bay, smell the salt air, feel the breeze against her cheeks. It sounded heavenly. Then she sighed.

"I can't."

"Why not? Do you have other plans?"

"Of course not." She gestured toward the door. "In case you haven't noticed, there are steps. Haven't you been listening? I can't manage them," she admitted with frustration.

"Which is why I will carry you in my big, strong arms," he said. "Try not to wiggle and get me too excited."

Again, a laugh erupted before she could contain it. "As if." She looked into his eyes. "Why are you doing this?"

"Because someone very wise asked me what I thought you'd want more than anything about now. I realized you were probably going a little stir-crazy."

"More than a little," she said.

"Then you'll come with me?"

She weighed the danger—letting herself be drawn right back into Connor's world—against her desire for a change of scenery. The danger didn't seem that extreme by comparison with her total boredom.

"Let's go," she said, and struggled to her feet, determined to maintain at least a shred of independence. She made it across the room on her crutches, and Connor let her do it. Only when they'd stepped onto the landing outside did he scoop her up as if she were weightless and carry her down the stairs.

Snuggled against his chest, she allowed herself to bury her head against his shoulder for just an instant so she could breathe in the wonderfully masculine scent of him, a blending of soap and a faint hint of familiar aftershave. Buried deep in her closet, she still had one of his shirts, stolen when she'd left him, that smelled exactly like this. In moments of weakness, she dragged it out and slept with it. It had given her comfort on some of her darkest nights since the separation.

When they reached his car, she caught him grinning. "What?" she demanded.

"You were sniffing me."

"I most certainly was not," she said indignantly and felt her cheeks flush with embarrassment.

"You always did like that aftershave. You said it reminded you of margaritas, which for some reason I could never figure out."

"The limes," she said without thinking, then winced at the revealing statement.

He gave her a smug look. "You know, it was a funny thing. When you left, my favorite green flannel shirt disappeared."

She refused to meet his gaze. "Really? What do you think happened to it?"

He shrugged. "I can't say for sure, but I seem to recall coming home late from the office a couple of times and finding you all curled up in bed in that shirt. You said it smelled like me."

"I'd forgotten that," she claimed.

"I'm sure," he said wryly, settling her carefully into the

passenger seat of the car, which he'd thoughtfully moved back so her casted leg could extend straight out.

"Why are you making such a big deal about a stupid old shirt?"

He leveled a look into her eyes and made sure she was looking back before responding. "It's not about the shirt, and you know it."

She managed a defiant tone. "Then what is it about, Connor?"

"You miss me."

She swallowed hard and prayed that neither her voice nor the color in her cheeks would give her away. "Do not."

"You're lying through your teeth, sweetheart, but it's okay. I've missed you, too. Now let's just go to the beach and enjoy the day."

"If you're going to be making arrogant claims all afternoon, I'm not sure how much enjoyment we'll have."

"Oh, come on," he teased. "There's nothing you love more than bringing me back down to size. I'm doing you a favor by saying stuff like this. It gets you all riled up. I doubt you've felt this alive in ages."

Sadly, it was true, but not even the threat of torture would have made her admit it. "This is a bad idea," she muttered, even as she settled back into the seat, ready to see what the afternoon would bring. Sometimes going with a bad idea was the only way to live.

19

Rather than going to the main beach in the center of town, Connor opted for a more secluded stretch of sand just outside of the Chesapeake Shores city limits. Here the homes were smaller and, in many ways, less pretentious than those in Chesapeake Shores. Many had been around for years, owned by families and passed from generation to generation. In some cases the paint had been neglected and the porches were weathered, but despite that, there was an undeniable, old-fashioned charm about them.

He'd always liked it out here, especially during the week, because the beach was deserted then. He could recall coming here to get some privacy with his latest girlfriend when he was a teenager.

"Why haven't I been here before?" Heather asked, glancing around curiously as they drove along a beach-front lined with weeping willows.

"There's not too much out this way, just these scattered houses on some prime real estate. At one point when he was developing Chesapeake Shores, Dad wanted to buy up the land and incorporate it into the town, but the owners united and held out. Drove him crazy, but personally I'm glad they did."

Heather regarded him with surprise. "Why? You almost sound nostalgic."

"I suppose I am. I like the fact that the houses along here are pretty much the way they were fifty, even seventy-five years ago," Connor said. "Same families, too, at least for the most part. You almost never see a For Sale sign along here."

"Really?" Heather said, then peered through the windshield. "Connor, wait! There's a For Sale sign. It's just up there at the bend in the road. Let's go look."

Admittedly intrigued himself, he drove a few hundred feet, then pulled to the side of the road and turned off the engine. His enthusiasm died as he got a closer look.

"It's not much," he said, disappointed to see how badly the house had been neglected.

"It's charming," Heather contradicted, her eyes alight. "Look at the yard. It's filled with lilac bushes."

"All overgrown," Connor noted. "And I doubt the house has been painted in years. It's probably riddled with termites."

Heather gave him an exasperated look. "Aren't you cheery?" Her expression brightened. "Look, it's called Driftwood Cottage. How perfect!"

Connor finally spotted the sign dangling crookedly from a single nail above the door. "Looks more like it's been cast adrift to me."

"Now you're just being mean," she chastised. "I wish we could see inside. Do you suppose anyone's home?"

"Not if they value their lives," Connor muttered, not sure why he found the place so depressing. Heather was right. It did have the charm he'd been talking about only moments ago, even if it required some serious attention.

"Help me get out of here," Heather said, ignoring his comment. "Let's go knock on the door."

He actually studied her face then, surprised to find that her expression was more animated than he'd seen it in ages. "You're serious about this?"

She nodded. "I can't explain it. I know it's a bit of a mess, but I love it."

"How can you?" he asked, bewildered. "You have a lovely, modern apartment right above your store. I thought you liked it there."

"I do."

"Then why would you be even remotely interested in this?"

She shrugged. "I don't know. I just feel as if it's calling out to me." Her expression turned dreamy. "I'll bet there's always been a family staying here in the summertime. Look at that old porch swing. Can't you just imagine kids in that, or teenagers courting on a summer night?"

"Heather, it's one thing to rescue some mangy little kitten off the street." Something she'd done too often for his comfort, he recalled. At least she'd been persuaded to find homes for them rather than insisting on keeping each one. Using the same firm voice that he'd used when it came to the cats, he added, "It's another thing entirely to try to save a wreck of a house. Making this house livable would cost a fortune. Ask my dad."

She gave him a defiant look. "That's just what I'll do," she said. "I bet it has great bones. Now, are you going to help me get a closer look, or do I have to struggle over there on my own?"

Connor shook his head, but he dutifully climbed out of the car and went around to the passenger side. After all, today was supposed to be all about making Heather happy, and, for reasons beyond him, this house seemed to make her very happy. In fact, she was already trying to stand up and steady herself on her crutches.

"Will you just hold on a minute," he grumbled. "If you're not careful, you'll wind up with your other leg broken."

He walked with her across the street, but halted at the bottom step leading to the porch. "That wood is rotted right on through," he declared. "You're not going up there."

"Then you go. See if anyone's home."

"You expect me to risk my neck…" Her imploring look silenced him. Choosing his steps cautiously, he went up and knocked on the door. "No one's here," he said eventually.

"Let's walk around back. Maybe we can see in the windows."

"Mind if I borrow one of your crutches to beat a path through the jungle?" he inquired, not entirely in jest. The yard was a tangled mess of weeds. If this had been inside the town limits of Chesapeake Shores, the owner would have been put on notice to clean it up immediately.

Amazingly, though, as they slowly circled the house, he began to see why Heather was intrigued. Driftwood Cottage was bigger than it had appeared from the street. Under the out-of-control weeds, the backyard was huge, perfect for children and fenced to keep them from wandering across the road to the beach. Though the windows were grimy, there was a large sunroom across the back.

"Oh, my," Heather murmured when she saw it. "Connor, isn't it wonderful?"

"It has potential," he grudgingly admitted.

Back in the car, she dug in her purse and wrote down the Realtor's name and number. "Do you have your cell phone with you?" she asked. "I forgot mine."

"You want to call now?"

She nodded at once. "Please."

Connor gave in and made the call. Fortunately from his perspective, he got voice mail. Maybe Heather would come to her senses once she'd had a little time to think this through. She couldn't possibly afford a potential money pit like this.

But he could. The thought came to him out of the blue, like a bolt of lightning when the skies were still clear. What was it Jess had told him—to go for broke to prove to Heather that he was listening to her? This ruin of a house certainly had the potential to break a man's bank account, but even he could see it also had the potential to show Heather that he was in this relationship for the long haul.

He left a message for the Realtor, including his own number, rather than Heather's.

When he'd disconnected the call, she was scowling at him. "You should have left my number," she said. "You'll just tell the woman you made a mistake or something."

He frowned at the accusation. "Have a little faith in me. It doesn't really matter which one of us she calls. I know the right questions to ask, and I'll pass the information on to you."

She continued to look annoyingly skeptical, but she let it drop.

"Can we have that picnic now?" he asked. "I remember a perfect spot just up the road."

Heather nodded, but cast one last look of longing over her shoulder as they drove on. Even when they were finally settled on the beach in the chairs Connor had thought to bring along, to sit atop a blanket to avoid getting sand in Heather's cast, she couldn't seem to stop talking about the house. She had a million ideas about what she could do with it if it were hers. By the time they'd finished dessert, Connor could envision it all, from the white paint and bright red shutters on the exterior to the sun flooding into the rooms onto highly polished hardwood floors.

Most of all, what he could see with heart-clutching clarity, was the three of them living there. And no matter what reservations he might have about the soundness of Driftwood Cottage, he knew he had to make that happen.

"There hasn't been a house for sale along that road for ten years or more," Mick said when Connor described it later that evening. "Are you talking about the old Hawkins place?"

"I guess," Connor said.

"Looks like a stiff breeze would blow it down," Mick assessed. "Agatha Hawkins died two or three months ago. She was in her nineties. With her health declining and no family around to help, she hadn't done a thing to keep it up."

"I didn't see any other place in bad shape along there,

so that's definitely the one. If I get in touch with the Realtor, can you go with me tomorrow to take a look at it?"

"Of course, but if you want a house, why not buy one right here in town? They're newer and I can vouch for the quality of the construction."

"Dad, believe me, I know your houses are in better shape, but Heather likes that one," Connor finally admitted. "Has her heart set on it, in fact."

Mick studied him with a narrowed gaze. "So which one of you is considering buying it?"

"I am," Connor said. He hesitated for a minute, then added with a touch of defiance, "For us."

Mick let out a yelp, then shouted for Megan. She came rushing into the living room, looking alarmed. "What on earth is going on in here?"

"Connor's finally seen the light! He's buying a house for him and Heather," Mick announced as if he personally had made it happen.

His mother's eyes lit up. "You are? Oh, Connor, it's wonderful that you two are finally getting married. I'm so happy for you! I'll call Bridget first thing tomorrow and see what I can do to help with the wedding."

Connor closed his eyes against the powerful tide of parental enthusiasm. "Slow down," he warned them, hating to put a damper on their excitement. "I never said anything about marriage."

Both Mick and Megan regarded him with confusion.

"Then what the devil are you talking about?" Mick demanded, looking as if Connor had pulled some sort of bait-and-switch con on him. "Living together didn't work out so well before. What makes you think Heather will agree to that again?"

"She won't," Connor conceded.

"But you're not getting married?" Megan said, clearly bewildered.

"Not yet." He finally sighed. "I'm hoping the house will get her to take my proposal seriously."

"Now I really am confused," Mick said. "You proposed?"

"And she said no?" Megan looked shocked.

"Pretty much," Connor told them. He didn't think his pride could take explaining yet again that she'd turned him down more than once.

His parents exchanged a look. "Buying a house worked for Trace," Mick commented, his expression thoughtful. "It got Abby's attention. No reason to think it won't work in this situation."

"It is a dramatic gesture," Megan added approvingly. "Women love things like that." Then her brow creased with worry. "Are you sure Heather likes this house? I've driven by there. It just strikes me as sad."

"I actually think that's part of its appeal," Connor said. "Against all odds, she's crazy about it. I'm the one who's skeptical. That's why I want Dad to check it out, see if it's worth renovating."

Megan smiled. "If Heather has her heart set on this house, for whatever reason, she's not going to be persuaded by logic if it turns out to be a construction nightmare. You do know that, don't you?"

Connor sighed. "Yes. I just need to know how expensive this nightmare is going to be."

Heather couldn't seem to stop thinking about Driftwood Cottage. She had no idea how she could afford to buy a house, even if she sold her tiny apartment. It wasn't so much the timing. These units in the heart of town were always in demand, and summer, when tourists flooded the community, was the perfect time to sell. The problem was the likely income from the sale compared to what it would take to buy beachfront property, even outside of the town limits. Still, she couldn't seem to keep herself from daydreaming about that house.

Two days later, when she hadn't heard from either Connor or the Realtor, she dug the slip of paper out of her purse and called the Realtor herself. This time Willow Smith answered right away.

"I'm calling about a house on Beach Drive," Heather told her. "I couldn't spot a number, but it's called Drift-wood Cottage. Could you tell me what the asking price is?"

"Oh, I'm so sorry," Willow exclaimed. "I just got a contract on that house yesterday."

Heather's spirits fell. She'd been so certain the house was meant to be hers. "Oh, no, I loved that house."

"To be honest, you can do much, much better," the Realtor assured her. "I have several other properties that might suit you if you're looking for something on the water."

Heather sighed. "No. I had my heart set on that one."

"I suppose I could take your name in case the contract falls through," the Realtor offered, "but I wouldn't hold out much hope. The buyer's background is solid. He's not going to have a bit of trouble getting financing. Of course, you never know. Sometimes people get buyer's remorse. That could happen, especially once they start assessing the cost of doing renovations or a tear-down."

"They might tear it down?" Heather asked, horrified.

"That's certainly what I would do," Willow said. "But I don't know what the buyer has in mind."

"Well, please take my name and number anyway," Heather said, though she knew she was clinging to a false sense of hope. It was obviously too late. The house had slipped right through her fingers. Unreasonably, she blamed Connor for that. He'd jinxed it all with his doubts. If only she'd made that call herself much sooner, instead of leaving it to him.

She was staring despondently at the phone when someone knocked on the door, then opened it with a key. Connor again, she knew. His timing couldn't have been worse. She frowned at him.

"What are you doing here?"

"I came to see if you were in a cheery mood today," he said, grinning at her. "Guess not."

"Go to—"

He cut her off with a chiding look, then asked, "What's wrong?"

"Somebody bought my house," she told him.

"Really?" he asked.

Something in his tone caught her attention. "Do you know anything about that? You'd already talked to the Realtor, hadn't you? That's why you came by, to let me down gently."

He shook his head. "Not exactly."

"Oh? Were you planning to gloat?"

"No." He tossed something at her, which she snatched instinctively from the air.

"What's this?" she asked, clasping what appeared to be a rusty piece of metal.

"The key to your dream house," he told her.

She stared at him incredulously. "It was you? *You* bought my house?"

"I did."

"But why? You hated it. Did you just do it to torment me?"

He seemed startled by the accusation. "Of course not. Why would I want to torment you? You wanted the house. I bought the house for us, for our future."

"But there is no us," she said, unable to stop the sense of betrayal that washed over her. "That means you bought it for you. How could you, Connor?"

He held up a hand. "Hold it a second. You fell in love with that house. Heaven knows why, but you did. I bought it. My dad's going to renovate it to your specifications. I'm not seeing the problem here. I thought you'd be happy."

"Happy to have you living in the house I wanted?" she asked incredulously. "Why would that make me happy?"

Connor shook his head. "Okay, I think we need to back up the train a minute. I thought I explained this. I bought the house for us," he explained patiently. "You, me and little Mick, in case I wasn't clear enough."

"I'm not going to move in with you again just because you bought a house," she said with exasperation.

Suddenly he laughed.

"Now you're laughing at me? Just go away. I don't want to see you right now."

"Not going anywhere," he said, pulling a chair over beside the sofa and sitting down. "I guess I forgot to mention that the house is my wedding present to you. You know, for when you decide to marry me."

Heather tried not to let the suddenly rapid beating of her heart influence her reason. "But we're not getting married," she reminded him.

"Maybe not right away," he said agreeably. "But we will."

"I told you—"

"You've told me a lot of things and, believe me, I've heard every one of them. I'm just choosing not to accept that particular statement. I get why you said no. Who could blame you? I've been a pigheaded idiot for way too long now, but I have seen the light. I want what you want."

She studied him with a narrowed gaze. He seemed sincere. And he had bought her the house she wanted. "What exactly is it that you think I want?" she asked cautiously, wanting more than anything for him to pass the test.

"Happily-ever-after," he said at once. "A family, a house and a husband who loves you to distraction."

"And you think you can give me that?"

"I know I can," he said with total confidence.

"But you don't believe in happily-ever-after," she reminded him.

He hesitated, and that was all it took to ruin everything. That one shining moment of hope dimmed. She regarded him sadly.

"It's okay, Connor. I know you want to want that, but it's just not who you are. I've accepted that. You can stop trying so hard."

To her surprise, his gaze never wavered. "Not a chance, sweetheart. I'll never stop trying to prove that I'm ready for this." He gave her a chagrined look. "It's going to be a little hard to top buying a house for you, but I'll come up with something to convince you."

Heather regarded him with surprise. This was a Connor she'd never seen before. His words were familiar, but there was a glint of determination in his voice, an air of confidence about him that was new. And for the very first time, she wondered if maybe things were different, after all.

Though he'd worked very hard to present a determined attitude in the face of Heather's skepticism, Connor was thrown by the fact that she was still resisting his proposal. He joined Will at Brady's, in need of some masculine company. Men made sense. In his recent experience, women did not.

"So, I go against every instinct I possess to buy that godforsaken house for her to prove just how committed I am to our future, and what does Heather do? She says no. Even worse, she's mad at me for buying *her* house."

Will laughed. "Buying the house was Jess's idea, wasn't it?"

Connor stared at him. "In a way, yes. How'd you know?"

"Your sister is a big fan of the grand gesture. She was very impressed when Trace bought that house for Abby to prove he was ready to settle down."

"Come to think of it, Abby wasn't much happier about that than Heather is about what I did. Maybe I need to stop listening to Jess. She doesn't seem to have her finger on the female pulse, after all."

Will chuckled. "Oh, Abby liked the house well enough."

"Then why did it take so long for Trace to actually get her down the aisle?" Connor asked, thinking back to how rattled Trace had been by Abby's refusal to set a wedding date, even after they'd been living together for ages. He met Will's gaze. "Do you know?"

"Actually, Kevin is the one who nailed it," Will admitted. "He figured out that Abby kept waiting for Trace to morph into some kind of control freak the way her first husband did after they were married. She was sure he'd suddenly start demanding that she quit work, live full-time in Chesapeake Shores and so on. Once Kevin called her on that and told her that Trace was nothing like Wes Winters, she decided it was okay to follow her heart."

"I see," Connor said, considering the information. "Do you suppose something like that's going on with Heather?"

Will looked puzzled. "I'm not following. Heather's never been married before. Her one big relationship has been with you."

"And we both know that I insisted for a very long time that I would never get married. She obviously doesn't think I've changed, even though the words coming out of my mouth say I have." He paused, then added, "Or she doesn't want to believe me."

Will nodded. "Okay, I'm with you so far. What are you thinking?"

Connor wasn't sure he could put his suspicions into words that would make any sense, but if anyone could grasp what he was getting at, it would be Will. He not only had the training, but he had excellent insight into human nature.

"Okay," Connor began slowly, trying to pull together

his thoughts. "Heather's parents have had a rocky marriage. From what I gather, there was always a lot of tension in the house. Heather prides herself on having risen above that. She insists she still believes in love despite all evidence to the contrary in her own home."

Will nodded. "I get that. Keep going."

"But what if that's just a line she's sold herself?" Connor asked, warming to his theory. "What if down deep she's as scared as I am that marriage doesn't stand a chance? She can hardly admit that to me, of all people, not after she's taken such a strong position on the subject."

"Makes sense," Will agreed.

"Wouldn't that mean she has to come up with a thousand and one excuses to keep turning me down, trying to lay the blame right back at my feet?"

"So essentially you're saying that now that she has the real option of getting married to you, she's the one who's gotten cold feet?" Will said slowly, his expression thoughtful. "You know, it could be. She might not even be aware that the tension in her parents' marriage has influenced her so deeply."

Connor's momentary sense of triumph at having unraveled an emotional mystery was short-lived. "So how am I supposed to fix that? I've always been the doubter. I'm new to being the one who thinks marriage is the answer."

Will gave him an amused look. "If I tell you that, I'll have to charge you for a session," he taunted.

"Bite me. Don't start holding out on me now. I'm about to buy a house for my family. I don't want to wait around till we're in our seventies to work things out and move into it."

"You might have to wait a while," Will told him realistically. "Not until you're in your seventies, of course, but it could take time for you to prove to Heather that your sudden turn-about is real and for her to recognize that it's her subconscious that's now holding her back."

Connor frowned. "Isn't there a way to speed up the process? Lately I've been thinking about a fall wedding."

"Then you might have to call her on it," Will said. "Lay out your suspicions. Turn the tables on her. See how she reacts to this theory of yours."

"You really think she'll admit it?" he asked doubtfully. Heather was as stubborn as any O'Brien.

"No," Will said cheerfully. "But once the idea's out there, she'll have to at least consider it."

Connor tried to envision the conversation. He couldn't see any scenario under which it would turn out in his favor. And yet, what choice did he have, unless he wanted to remain in limbo?

"Maybe you could drop by, have a chat with her?" he suggested in desperation.

"I don't do sneak-attack sessions," Will said. "If she wants to come to see me, I'm happy to work through this with her. I'm just not sure I'd want to be in your shoes if you suggest it."

"Believe me, I get that. I didn't take it too well when she told me I ought to see someone to deal with my issues."

"I think on behalf of my profession, I'm insulted," Will said.

"You shouldn't be. Why would I go hire a stranger, when you're my friend?" He slapped Will on the back. "And a darn good one at that!"

"Then you can pay for our drinks," Will said cheerfully. "The check's not as much as I usually charge, so consider yourself as having received the friends-and-family discount."

"Gladly," Connor told him. "But I will remember this moment when you come to me looking for a shoulder to cry on about my sister."

"I don't need anyone's shoulder to cry on about Jess," Will claimed, though his expression turned despondent. "That ship sailed a long time ago."

"Really?" Connor said innocently. "I was pretty sure it was still at the dock. Maybe you need to check."

Will shook his head. "I've already surpassed my threshold for pain in that department. I've moved on."

Connor was about to argue, but then he saw the genuine hurt in Will's eyes. That alone was enough to silence him. He'd always thought of Will as a roll-with-the-punches kind of guy. That Jess had truly hurt him was a little shocking.

After watching everyone in his family do their share of meddling, Connor had vowed never to do the same, but these circumstances were different. It was Will and Jess, for heaven's sake, one of his best friends and his baby sister.

One of these days, when he thought the timing was right, he was going to have a whole lot to say to his sister about being blind to one of the best men he'd ever known.

20

They'd had their morning coffee together and Megan was about to head to work, when Mick decided to join her. He had some things in town that needed doing, and he saw no reason to put them off.

"Mind if I tag along?" he asked, following along as Megan headed for her car.

She stopped and stared. "You want to go to the gallery with me? Since when?"

"To be honest, I was thinking I might drop in next door," he admitted.

Megan's expression immediately turned to dismay. "Mick, you're not going over to Heather's to interfere, are you? Connor will have a fit if you do."

He gave her a defiant look. "Well, somebody has to get those two to work out their differences. This has dragged on long enough. I want a wedding. I want more grand-babies before I'm too old to play with them."

"We have Carrie and Caitlyn, Kevin's two boys and now Bree and Jake's little girl," Megan reminded him. "And, of course, there's your namesake. Let's not forget that little Mick's a part of our lives, mostly because we haven't chased Heather off by pressuring her."

"I'm not going to pressure her," Mick insisted indignantly. "I'm just going to check out the lay of the land, so to speak. Besides, I have the perfect excuse. Connor wants me to renovate that house for her. I need to get her ideas down on paper, don't I?"

"An interesting approach," she conceded. "But the last I heard, Heather was still furious that Connor bought the house she wanted for herself. You may be rubbing salt in a very fresh wound."

"Or giving her some much-needed perspective," Mick countered, convinced that he was doing what needed to be done. His wife might have very fine instincts about people, but she had more patience than he did. "Heather probably just needs someone older and wiser to help her see that Connor was only thinking of her."

"If I were Heather, I'd probably think he was trying to blackmail her into marrying him, just the way he did when he told her he'd get her out of the hospital if she agreed to marry him."

For an instant, Mick was shocked. "He did that?"

"According to Bridget, he did. Oh, he didn't mean it to come out that way, but Heather's obviously touchy about this sudden attitude shift of his. She doesn't trust it."

"Maybe I can make her see that it's real," Mick said optimistically.

Megan didn't look entirely convinced, but she waited until he'd settled in the passenger seat before starting the engine and heading for town. If she'd been truly annoyed, she'd have had time to drive off without him. He took heart from the fact that she hadn't.

After she'd pulled into a parking spot behind the gallery, Mick said, "I think I'll walk around to Sally's and pick up a couple of croissants and some coffee."

His wife regarded him with amusement. "Are you thinking that if you come bearing baked goods, Heather won't toss you back onto the street?"

"It can't hurt," he admitted. Despite his earlier display of confidence, he wasn't all that sure of his welcome. Megan was the one who'd established a real rapport with Heather. Perhaps she was the one who ought to be interceding. He gave her a hopeful look. "Maybe you should come along with me. The two of you seemed to bond after she left little Mick with us."

Megan backed up a step. "Don't involve me in your scheming. I need to keep those lines of communication open. Right now I may be one of the few people in our family Heather trusts."

Mick shrugged. "Suit yourself. Can I bring you anything from Sally's?"

"I'll take a coffee, but you can skip the croissant. I feel as if I've been eating nonstop with Nell fixing all these family meals every couple of days."

Mick nodded. He strolled down the block and around the corner, stopping to greet and chat with a half-dozen friends on the way. It was after eleven by the time he actually made his way back to Heather's, so he stopped and picked up sandwiches at Panini Bistro while he was at it. He might as well arrive well-fortified with bribes.

He dropped Megan's coffee off at the gallery, managed to avoid another of her lectures, then climbed the stairs to Heather's apartment. When he knocked on the door, he heard her shout for him to come in. When he entered, though, she looked startled.

"Oh, I thought you were Connie. She called a short while ago to say she was going to stop by and bring lunch."

"I may not be Connie, but I did bring food," Mick told her. "You have your choice of a ham-and-cheese panini or a chocolate croissant. Or both, for that matter."

Her eyes brightened. "It sounds wonderful, Mick, but I probably shouldn't, since Connie's going to all that trouble to bring something over."

"Then save this for dinner," Mick said easily. He put his offerings in the kitchen, then took a seat across from her. He surveyed her frankly, relieved to see some color—other than black and blue—back in her cheeks. "You look a whole lot better than you did a couple of weeks ago," he told her. "How are you feeling?"

"Physically, not bad, but I'm sick to death of being stuck in here. The only time I've gotten out was when Connor took me." She narrowed her gaze. "I imagine you know about that."

Mick saw no point in denying it. "In fact, it's one of the reasons I came by," he admitted. "I thought we could talk about the changes you'd like to see made at the house."

Her jaw set stubbornly. "It's not my house. Your son bought it. He can do what he wants with it."

Mick held back a grin. "Connor seems to think he bought it for you."

She gave him an exasperated look. "Only because he gets these crazy, impulsive ideas in his head and then expects everyone to go along with them."

"I can see how that would be frustrating," Mick conceded. He'd been accused of the same flaw often enough—justifiably, if he was being honest about it. "But tell me this, do you love that house as much as he thinks you do?"

The wistful expression on her face would have given her away, even if she hadn't nodded.

"Do you love Connor?"

"Not the point," she said, her voice suddenly tight.

Mick grinned. "I'll take that as a yes. So, here's how I see it. You can refuse to give me any input and the house will get renovated the way Connor or I decide it should be done, or you can participate in the process and get your dream house."

"And then watch Connor move into it," she said, sounding resigned.

"Hey, this is my vision, and that's not what I see," he contradicted. "I figure the two of you will eventually work out your differences and you'll be living there together. That's just a matter of time and some careful negotiations over the terms. Personally, my vote's for marriage, but I'm not interfering."

The comment drew a disbelieving chuckle.

Mick continued. "So, as I see it, the only question open for debate is what the house will look like when that happens."

She looked startled for an instant by his assessment, then laughed. "I see now where Connor got his arrogance."

"It's an O'Brien gene, no question about it," Mick said unapologetically. "So, Heather, what's it going to be? You going to let my son decide how that house gets fixed up, or are you going to put your stamp on it?"

She hesitated for so long, he thought maybe he'd overplayed his hand, but then she reached for a folder on the coffee table. Its proximity suggested she'd been through it recently.

"I do have a few ideas," she admitted.

Mick chuckled. "I thought you might."

She held the fat folder tightly before handing it over.

"I've been stuffing pictures into this folder for years now. I dragged them out after I saw Driftwood Cottage. I've already weeded out the ones I don't think will work, but I'm sure I have more ideas than you'll ever need."

"Never hurts to look at everything," Mick said. "Then we can talk it through and revise it to fit the structure we have to work with."

"What's my budget?" she asked, suddenly sounding eager. Her eyes were alight with excitement as well.

"You let Connor worry about that. You just tell me what you want, and he and I will figure out how to make it happen."

She regarded him with amazement. "Are you like my fairy godfather?" she asked.

Mick nearly choked on a sip of coffee. "Those should probably be fighting words, but I think I get your meaning. No, I'm just a man who wants to see three people I love happy. Getting to be a part of that is an old man's privilege."

And it was going to happen. Even the expression on her face when she'd been complaining about Connor buying her house showed how badly she wanted it to be *theirs*, instead. He was more sure than ever that Heather and his son were destined to be together, if only they'd get out of their own way and let it happen.

Connor winced when he saw the rough sketches his father had made of the renovations for Driftwood Cottage. "How much is that going to set me back?"

"You have a trust fund," Mick reminded him. "You're the only one in the family who hasn't tapped into it. And

I can't think of a better use for that money I set aside for you."

"And Heather actually went along with it when you told her what you were up to?"

"I have a whole folder filled with her ideas. It seems she's been tearing pictures out of magazines for years now. It's my job to blend them into a cohesive whole." He met Connor's gaze. "You know the funny thing? That rickety old house looks a whole lot like what she'd been dreaming about all this time. I think it was fate that took the two of you along that road the other day."

Connor wasn't sure how much fate had to do with it. Jess was the one who'd put the notion of a day at the beach into his head. And she'd probably known exactly where he'd go. He wondered if she'd also known about that house being for sale. He'd have to ask her about that one of these days. Her sneakiness quotient was a match for anyone else's in the family.

"Do you really think you can turn that old place into something livable?" he asked his father.

"Against a lot of odds, I built a town, didn't I? One little house renovation isn't going to defeat me." He gave Connor a sly look. "Just so you know, I'm taking Heather along with me tomorrow around ten o'clock, so we can nail down a few of her ideas. I doubt she'd object if you happened to show up."

Connor shook his head. "That wasn't even subtle, Dad. You must be losing your touch."

"No. Just tired of wasting time. I'm thinking the direct approach is called for. You going to be there or not?"

"Since you're spending my money, I'll be there," Connor assured him.

And he wouldn't mind the chance to spend a little time with Heather so he could float some of his theories about her sudden reluctance to marry him. It might be good to do that with his dad around to referee in case she took exception to his attempt to psychoanalyze her. She might thoroughly enjoy dissecting his psyche, but he had a hunch she wasn't going to be quite so receptive to having the tables turned.

The July day dawned with temperatures already near eighty and the humidity levels just as high. Only a faint breeze stirring through the trees kept it from being unbearably oppressive. And yet, Heather thought, as she sat in the shade in a chair Mick had thoughtfully brought along, it was pleasant enough. She could already imagine sitting out here with a book on a summer afternoon. In fact, it would be lovely to have a screened-in gazebo right in this spot, with a view of the water and protection against the mosquitoes.

She'd just swatted viciously at another one when Connor drove up. He frowned as he crossed the yard. "What was Dad thinking, letting you sit out here to get eaten alive by the bugs?" he grumbled.

"He was thinking it would be cooler than inside the house, to say nothing of safer," she replied. "He doesn't seem to have any more faith in the flooring than you did when we first saw this place."

Connor shook his head. "You should have stayed in his truck with the air-conditioning running."

"That from a man who preaches about going green," she responded. "I'm fine. Stop fussing over me."

He sighed. "I'm always going to fuss over you. You

should hear the way Dad goes on about Mom all the time. I think it comes with the territory."

"What territory is that?" she asked, studying him curiously.

"Loving someone." Before she could challenge that, he added, "You fuss over little Mick, don't you? It's the same thing."

"He's a child, Connor. I'm not."

He shook his head. "Then you don't mind the bugs? Fine with me. I was going to at least offer you the can of spray I keep in the car, but if you're not interested…"

Heather wanted to remain stubbornly silent, but the landing of another mosquito on her arm and one on her leg forced her to reconsider. "I'll take the spray," she said grudgingly.

"Now you're being sensible," he praised, trotting off to his car and returning with the bottle of insect repellant. "Let me." He squirted the stuff over every inch of bared skin, then gave a nod of satisfaction. "Now, tell me what you and Dad have decided."

"Nothing yet. The last time I saw him, he was holding the pictures I'd shown him and walking around muttering to himself."

Connor laughed. "The creative genius at work. The good news is I guarantee he'll come back here with rough sketches that will blow your mind. He showed me a few preliminary drawings last night, so I'm sure he's in there right now refining those. For all of the issues I've had with my father over the years, I can't deny he's one of the best architects around."

Heather lifted her gaze and dared to meet his eyes. "Connor, I don't want to take advantage of you. Your dad insisted that I make suggestions about what I want, but this really is your house. It feels wrong for me to have any say at all."

"We both know I have no sense of design or color," Connor reminded her. "Remember when you said you wanted little Mick's room to be yellow and I came home with paint that looked like the mustard that goes on hot dogs at the ball park?"

Heather smiled at the memory. "That should have been a warning," she agreed. "And yet I still sent you out to get the green paint for the living room. If we'd used what you brought back, it would have been like living inside a Christmas tree."

He shrugged. "Well, who knew there were so many shades of green? You said something about sage. I figured herbs are all bright green. What do I know?"

"So you got a couple of things wrong. The point is that this house should be a reflection of what you want."

He held her gaze. "I want what you want. What's it going to take to convince you of that?"

"Spending thousands of dollars according to my preferences is helping," she told him, only partially in jest. "But, Connor, you do know we're not going to be living here together, right?"

He remained stubbornly silent, so she continued, "Now that you're back in Chesapeake Shores for good, it makes sense that you'd want a home of your own, but you shouldn't fix this house up with the idea that I'll love it so much, I'll move in. That would be crazy, for both of us."

Rather than taking offense as she'd feared he might,

he dropped down to the ground beside her, then looked up. "Tell me something."

She regarded him with suspicion. "What?"

"How's it been having your mother here?"

Heather was completely thrown by the change of topic. "It's been good. I'd missed her. Why do you ask?"

"How long is she planning to stay?"

"I'm not really sure," she said. "She's not bad-mouthing you every second of the day and night, if that's worrying you."

"Never crossed my mind," he claimed. "What about your dad? He still hasn't been over here to visit, has he?"

"No." She gave him a puzzled look. "Connor, where are you going with this? Why the sudden interest in my family?"

He met her gaze. "Honestly? I'm wondering if maybe that situation isn't coloring the way you're looking at the possibility of a real future with me."

"How?" she asked incredulously. "One thing has nothing to do with the other."

"Are you so sure about that?" he asked. "You've always said that you believed in love and in marriage, despite the tension you lived with growing up. And yet, despite that tension, your parents did stay together. Now I have the feeling that your mother might be ready to make an official break from your father. She certainly doesn't seem anxious to get back to Ohio."

Heather immediately shook her head in denial. "She's only here because I need her."

"And that's it? She's said nothing about staying on?"

Heather thought about her mother's quick, off-the-cuff

comment a few weeks ago that she liked Chesapeake Shores and might want to stay on indefinitely. Heather hadn't put much credence in it at the time, but her mother was showing no signs of leaving.

She studied Connor with a narrowed gaze. "Do you know something that I don't? I didn't think the two of you had been having talks behind my back."

"We haven't been," he said. Then amended, "Well, just once, but her marriage wasn't a topic of discussion, I can guarantee you that. I'm just making an observation."

"And there's a point to this observation beyond the fact that you're speculating that my parents might be breaking up their marriage?" she inquired testily.

Connor looked a little uneasy. She could almost see him wrestling with the decision of whether to keep pursuing this. She wanted him to see it through, so she waited impatiently for him to get to the point. She had a hunch she wasn't going to like it when he did.

"It just occurred to me that if your mom is suddenly thinking about divorcing your dad, it might have thrown you, even though you've obviously seen something like this coming for years."

Heather thought about all the times she'd overheard her parents arguing deep into the night. When her friends' parents had divorced, she'd always been relieved that it wasn't hers, but she'd waited with a sense of dread nonetheless for that day to come. And even though it had made no sense to remain married and miserable, she'd been glad that they had. Somehow that had gotten all twisted up with her conviction that marriage was meant to be forever. Though her mother might have stayed married because of deeply held religious beliefs, Heather had never been that rigid. She didn't approve of divorce as a quick way out, but she understood that sometimes it was the only solution to a truly terrible situation. What if her parents had reached that point?

Even though she found Connor's comments to be unsettling, she couldn't ignore what he was suggesting. "You think a divorce is inevitable after all these years," she said flatly.

"You know them better than I do," he said, clearly not willing to commit to such a drastic prediction. "I just wonder if you're not shaken up by that possibility. It must call into question a lot of your beliefs."

"*If* my parents were divorcing—and I don't know that they are—sure, it would rattle me," she admitted. "What's your point?"

"That maybe that's why you're so determined not to believe that I've changed," he said, holding her gaze as if trying to gauge her reaction.

"Are you crazy?" she said at once. "Is your ego so huge that you can only imagine me refusing your proposal by laying it on the shaky status of my parents' marriage?"

Connor didn't back down. "The idea's not that crazy," he insisted. "I discussed it with Will and…"

Her temper flared. "You and Will talked about my parents? Their marriage is none of his business. It's none of yours, either, for that matter."

"It is if it's the thing that's keeping you from marrying me. As for Will, he's a really good shrink. I value his opinion."

"Then get him to psychoanalyze you and leave me and my family out of it," she said. "You're the one with issues about marriage. I think that's been pretty well-documented. And nobody turns off beliefs that deep on a dime."

He stared at her indignantly. "And you think that's what I did—turned on a dime?"

"Didn't you?" she challenged. "I had an accident and suddenly you woke up to the joys of marriage? I didn't buy it when you told me at the hospital, and I still don't."

"It wouldn't be the first time a crisis made someone reevaluate his life," Connor said defensively. "It happens all the time."

"Not to you," she countered. "Your beliefs haven't changed in years. You're surrounded by people who are happily married, and even after your own parents reconciled, you still held out. Then, in a flash, it all changed? No way!"

"If you can't buy that I've changed, how do you explain what's happened with you?" he asked reasonably. "Ever since we met, you've been a huge proponent of marital bliss. Then I propose, and suddenly you're not interested."

"Because I don't believe it's what you really want!" she practically shouted at him, her patience at an end.

Connor threw up his hands in exasperation and walked away. She stared after him, stunned to find that tears were rolling down her cheeks. She had no idea why, other than the fact that the man infuriated her, but that was nothing to cry about.

"Heather, are you okay?"

She looked up into Mick's worried gaze. "I will be," she said, brushing impatiently at the tears.

"Where's Connor? I thought I heard his voice out here."

"Oh, he's off somewhere making up excuses for why I won't marry him. He can't seem to believe I turned him down because I know it's not what he wants."

Mick gave her a sympathetic look. "Are you sure that's what you're doing, letting him off the hook?"

"Of course. He just had an attack of conscience or something after my accident."

"I don't think so," Mick said. "Connor's timing might be lousy, but he loves you. There's not a doubt in my mind about it. Don't throw that away."

"I'm not throwing it away," she said softly, then wondered if that wasn't exactly what she had done. She'd thrown Connor's words and his proposal right back in his face. More than once now. Why?

Could he possibly be right that seeing how her mother was literally blossoming away from her dad had shaken her values, made her question everything she'd believed about marriage and the possibility of happily ever after? Had seeing Bridget slowly reach out for her own fresh start reminded Heather of all the reasons she'd had when she first left Connor?

No, she thought fiercely, that couldn't be right. She'd left Connor not because she'd craved independence, not because she didn't love him and want a future with him, but because he wasn't offering one. Now he was, and she'd said no. Maybe she did need to see a shrink, after all.

Or maybe it was time she went back to listening to her heart.

21

Heather couldn't seem to shake Connor's theory about why she was holding back on marriage now that he was ready for it. Did it have anything at all to do with whatever was going on between her mother and father? And what was going on?

Certainly Bridget seemed to be in no big hurry to get back to Ohio. She was going to church on Sundays with Nell and had even joined her women's group at the church on a couple of occasions. Last week, she'd played bingo there one evening, as well. And she seemed to be thoroughly enjoying working at Cottage Quilts and teaching classes. It appeared she truly was settling into Chesapeake Shores.

Feeling oddly disgruntled, Heather watched her mother's efficient movements as she prepared dinner for the three of them. She was making spaghetti. It was one of little Mick's favorites—and also his dad's. Bridget didn't even seem to mind the mess he was bound to make. In fact, she had incredible patience with her grandson, who could test even Heather's nerves from time to time.

Heather maneuvered herself to her feet and used her

crutches to cross the room. She settled on a stool at the kitchen counter. "Mom, can I ask you something?"

Bridget looked up from the sauce she was stirring. "Of course."

"What's going on with you and Dad?"

Her mother's expression froze. "I don't know what you mean."

"Of course you do," Heather said impatiently. "You must. You've been here for several weeks now. He hasn't come to visit. He hardly calls anymore. At least, not when I'm around. Is this some kind of separation?"

To her horror, a tear leaked from her mother's eye and trickled down her cheek. "Mom?" she whispered, shaken by the sight of her mother crying. "I'm so sorry. I shouldn't have asked. I didn't mean to upset you."

"No, it's okay," her mother insisted. "You should know what's going on. The truth is, your father and I separated months ago."

Heather regarded her with shock. "Months ago? And you never said a word to me? Why?"

"You had a lot going on in your own life." Bridget sighed. "The truth is we should have done it years ago, but we thought staying married was for the best."

"Because of me," Heather guessed.

"You, and because I wasn't raised to accept divorce as an option. When I spoke those vows in church, they meant something to me. With divorce off the table, it didn't seem to make sense to disrupt everyone's lives with a separation."

"And now?"

"I just don't know," Bridget said wearily. "I still believe divorce goes against God's will, but it seems wrong for two people to remain tied together forever when they're both so unhappy. It's not that I expect to meet someone new at my age, but just separating indefinitely the way it's been these past few months would be like living the rest of my life in limbo. I honestly don't know what my next step should be. Being here, not having to face that decision right away, has been a relief."

"I wish you'd talked to me about this sooner," Heather told her. "Not that I have any answers for you, but at least I could have listened."

"I didn't want to burden you. I was still struggling to accept that you and Connor had a child together and had no intention of getting married. Because of the way I raised you, I knew you had to have conflicting feelings about that. I thought my problems might just add to your confusion."

Heather wasn't ready to admit that perhaps they had. Instead, she asked, "Mom, do you believe marriages ever work?"

Bridget looked startled by the question. "Well, of course, I do. There's evidence all around of that."

"But there's just as much that proves they don't," Heather reminded her. "Look at the divorce statistics. Look at your own situation, for heaven's sake."

"Too many people run at the first sign of trouble," Bridget declared with feeling. "I'm not saying marriage isn't hard. It is. It requires determination and compromise and enough love to weather the storms. But even with all of that, sometimes people just have to admit they've made a mistake. That's the way it is for your father and me. We were a mismatch from the beginning. I'm a homebody. I like my routines. He's a spur-of-the-moment kind of guy who'd rather hang with his buddies in a bar than sit at home with me. I thought when you came along, he'd change, but that only made things worse."

She gave Heather an apologetic look. "Not your fault, of course. He had no idea what to do with a baby, and I started to resent him not being around to help. I could go on and on. We tried, though. I even got him into counseling for a couple of sessions, but the truth was, he didn't want to change. I just had to accept that."

Heather regarded her mother with sympathy. "I'm so sorry."

"Don't be." She turned the heat under the sauce to low and sat down next to Heather. "I'm painting a picture of all the things that went wrong, but there were some good times. Quite a lot of them, if I'm being honest."

Her expression turned nostalgic. "Nobody could make me laugh like your father could. And there was many a night in the early days when I'd go with him to the Irish pub down the block just to hear him sing. The man has a voice like an angel. I think that's why I fell in love with him."

Heather tried to recall a single time she'd heard her father sing, but none came to mind. "He never sang at home, not even in the shower," she said. "I would have heard him."

"He did in the early years," Bridget told her. "And he sang you to sleep more than once when you were a baby and I couldn't get you to stop crying."

"I wish I could remember that," Heather said wistfully. What she remembered most was a handsome man who seldom smiled and had little to say. Though he rarely yelled and had never lifted a hand to her, she'd always had the sense she needed to tiptoe around him, taking care not to anger him. There were none of the warm, loving memories all of the O'Briens seemed to have of Mick. It was as if her father had been there, but hadn't been involved in her life, almost a stranger on the fringes of it. And yet she had adored him, had longed for his approval just as most young girls did with their fathers.

"Do you want to stay in Chesapeake Shores?" Heather asked tentatively. "You could go on working with me at the quilt shop. It won't pay much, but if you stay here with me, your living expenses will be modest."

Her mother looked touched by the offer. "Sweetheart, thank you for that. I have to admit, the thought has crossed my mind more than once since I've been here, but I just don't know."

"Is that because you don't want to stay?" Heather asked. "Or because you don't think you should?"

"Mostly the latter," her mother said candidly, "though not for the reason you're probably thinking. It's not that I think leaving your father permanently is wrong. I just wonder if I won't be in the way here. I don't want to be the reason you and Connor don't work things out."

"What's happening between Connor and me has nothing to do with you," Heather protested. "We agreed long ago not to get married."

"But things have changed," her mother protested. "That was Connor's decision back then, not yours. Now, it seems he's changed his mind. What I don't understand is your reluctance to accept his proposal."

Heather sighed. "That does seem to be the question of the day," she said. "I'm not sure I have an answer to it."

Her mother patted her hand. "Then you need to spend

some time thinking about it because if I've figured out one thing about that young man of yours, it's that he's not patient."

"Well, I've waited this long for him to come to his senses, now he can wait for me to catch up with him," Heather said with a touch of defiance.

Bridget's gaze narrowed. "So, this is payback?"

Heather was stunned by the observation. "Of course not," she said at once.

But was it? Or was Connor right that the turmoil in her mother's life, which she now understood more clearly, had shaken her faith in marriage? She simply didn't know.

But her mother was right about one thing. She needed to figure it out, and she needed to do it quickly before she lost everything she'd ever wanted.

On Saturday, a few minutes after the quilting class had ended downstairs, Connie burst into Heather's apartment.

"You need to come with me," she declared urgently, pacing from one end of the small space to the other, clearly agitated. "Right now."

Heather gestured toward her propped-up leg. "Hello! Not very mobile here."

"I'll get you down the stairs and into my car if I have to carry you myself," Connie said.

Heather could see that her friend was thoroughly flustered. What she didn't understand was why. "How about you sit down, take a deep breath and tell me what on earth has you in such a state?"

Connie kept right on pacing. "There's no time. I have to

get to one of those events for Thomas's foundation—you know, the ones that Shanna and I have organized."

"Okay," Heather said slowly. "And you want me to come along?"

"You *have* to come along," Connie corrected.

"Why? Do you need extra help? Did Shanna bail on you?"

"Shanna bailed, but that's not the problem."

"Sweetie, you're going to have to spell this out for me, because I'm a little lost here. You know I'm willing to do whatever I can to help, but I need to have some clue about what that is."

Connie stopped, sucked in a deep breath and blurted, "I think I'm falling for Uncle Thomas. I mean Thomas. He's not my uncle, is he? That would be bad. But it's pretty bad anyway because he's my brother's uncle-in-law, and he's older than me." She sighed and finally sank into a chair. "Am I insane or what?"

Even though she knew it was precisely the wrong thing to do, Heather chuckled. She tried to hide it, but the scowl on Connie's face told her she'd been unsuccessful.

"I'm so sorry," she apologized. "You're obviously upset, and all I can think is how fantastic this is."

"It is not fantastic," Connie retorted. "Were you not listening to me? This practically shouts disaster."

"How does he feel about you?" Heather asked.

Connie looked bewildered by the very logical question. "I have no idea. I guess he likes me well enough, but that's the thing. He's smart enough to know this is crazy. Even if there was some kind of attraction, he'd never do anything about it. I mean we're practically family, for heaven's sake. Just think of the furor."

"You are *not* family," Heather said firmly. "Let's get that out of the way once and for all. And you're both consenting adults. I'm not saying it might not get complicated—we're talking O'Briens. Everything about them is complicated."

"That's what I'm saying," Connie said. "I need you with me today. I need you to keep me from doing something I'll regret."

Heather bit back a smile. "Such as? Have you ever thrown yourself into a man's arms out of the blue? Impulsively kissed one senseless?"

Connie looked appalled by both suggestions. "Of course not."

"Then I think you're going to be just fine. You're overthinking this. This project the two of you are working on is the best scenario possible under the circumstances. You'll be thrown together innocently for a good cause, and you'll have time to really get to know each other. If there's something between you, it will develop naturally and when the time is right."

"I suppose," Connie said, then asked plaintively, "Are you sure you can't come with me?"

"Oh, I'm coming," Heather said, struggling to her feet. "Do you think for one second I'm going to miss a firsthand glimpse of what's going on between you two?"

Connie's gaze narrowed. "You're enjoying this, aren't you?"

"It definitely beats sitting around trying to figure out how things got so mixed up between Connor and me," Heather said, heading for the landing. "Grab my purse. I think if I'm really careful and you go down ahead of me, I can make it down these steps without breaking my neck. I've been envisioning the way I need to do it for days now. You've just provided the motivation I needed to try it."

Connie took her place in front of Heather and helped her take each step at an excruciatingly slow pace. Only when they'd reached the bottom and Heather had managed to get into the passenger seat of her car did Connie turn to her with a beaming smile. "I suppose I should tell you that Connor's filling in for Shanna today."

Heather stared at her. "You sneak! Was the whole Thomas thing some kind of subterfuge to get me to go with you?"

"Oh, no. That's real enough. I just figured if I was going to let you watch me squirm, you should know that I'm going to keep my eyes on the two of you as well. I'm today's designated meddler."

Heather wasn't sure whether to take her seriously or not. "Are you telling me the family has drawn straws to see who's going to mess with my head or Connor's on any given day?"

"The arrangement's not quite that formal," Connie admitted. "But we've all taken an interest in the situation. You may as well get used to it. Even if we weren't talking you and an O'Brien, we're talking Chesapeake Shores. It's a town that likes its happy endings."

"Oh, sweet heaven!" Heather murmured. She and Connor were doomed.

Connor had now filled in at a couple of these events to save the bay, and he'd discovered he enjoyed them. He was getting to spend some time in communities around the region, helping a worthy cause, and little Mick loved running around outside and eating hot dogs or whatever else was being served.

Connor's understanding and admiration for the work his uncle and Kevin were doing had deepened as well. He was even thinking of offering to do the group's legal work pro bono as his own contribution to the cause.

Today he'd driven down ahead of Connie and set up the tables for selling books and foundation memberships. He'd toted all the boxes of books over as well. Now he and little Mick were walking around to visit the handful of vendors who'd used the occasion to set up their own booths selling locally grown produce, crafts and even baked goods.

"Cookies, Da!" his son announced excitedly, spotting a tray of big chocolate chip cookies. "Please?"

"After lunch," Connor said firmly.

His son's expression turned mutinous. "Now!"

The woman sitting in the booth gave him a sympathetic look. "At that age, later is not a concept they're fond of. If it helps, you should know that these always sell out early. Maybe if you bought one now and gave him just a bite, it wouldn't spoil his lunch."

"That would certainly be better than sticking to my guns and then coming back to find they're all gone," Connor agreed. He paid the woman, broke off a small piece of the cookie for Mick, then put the rest in a bag. "Thanks."

"I saw you setting up over there. You're with Mr. O'Brien, aren't you?"

"Actually, I'm his nephew, Connor O'Brien."

"Nice to meet you, Connor. I'm Maggie Carter. Please tell your uncle for me that I think the work he's doing is wonderful. I've been a member of the foundation since it was started. I'm sure he'll attract a lot of new members today. I'll certainly send everyone who stops by here over your way."

"Thank you," Connor said. "I'll be sure to tell him that. I know he'll appreciate the support."

Little Mick looked up at him. "More cookie?" he asked hopefully.

"Not yet," Connor told him, then smiled at the woman. "I'd better get him a hot dog. Stop by the booth later and meet my uncle, if you have the time."

"I certainly will."

Connor took little Mick's hand and had started toward the hot dog vendor, when his son broke free with an excited shout.

"Mama!" he said, toddling off toward the foundation's booth.

Startled, Connor stared after him. Sure enough, Heather was hobbling unsteadily across the uneven ground, Connie's hand tucked under her elbow. Connor scooped Mick into his arms and raced toward them, hoping to avert disaster. He thrust Mick into Connie's arms, then put an arm securely around Heather's waist.

"Are you deliberately trying to break your neck?" he asked, trying to fight down the fear he'd felt when he'd seen her awkward progress. The ground simply wasn't made for crutches. "There are all sorts of holes and dips on this green. You could have fallen."

Her gaze clashed with his. "But I didn't, did I? I was very careful."

"Still, it was an accident waiting to happen. What are you doing here, anyway?"

Connie whirled around, a look of alarm on her face that made no sense to him. "I just wanted some company," she blurted. "And Heather felt like getting out."

He got the distinct impression there was a lot more to it, but he let it pass. "Well, I've got everything set up," he assured Connie. "I didn't put the books on display. I thought you'd want to do that, but the boxes are all there. I was just going to buy a hot dog for little Mick. Are you two hungry?"

"Not me," Connie said, looking calmer now. "I'll wait till later."

He turned to Heather. "How about you? You look a little pale."

"I'm fine. I would like some water, though."

Connor nodded, then turned to his son. "Hey, kiddo, you want to come with me?"

Mick shook his head. "Stay with Mama."

"You sure you can manage him?" he asked Heather. She nodded. "We'll be fine."

He handed her the bag.

She gave him a questioning look. "What's this?"

"A bribe," he said, then mouthed c-o-o-k-i-e.

"Ah, I see. Then I *know* we'll be fine."

"The rule is after lunch," he warned.

"That's your rule. Moms make rules of their own."

Connor shook his head. "Sure, undercut my paltry attempt at discipline."

She merely laughed.

When Connor returned, his son was settled in Heather's lap as she read him one of the children's books about sea life that Connie had included in the selection available for today's attendees. He'd discovered that Thomas believed it was sometimes the most basic ecological awareness of kids that actually caught the parents' attention.

As the story ended, he caught sight of his uncle striding across the green. In his khakis and a blue polo shirt and with the tan of a man who worked on the water, he looked younger than his years. Connor noticed that several women turned to watch his progress, but it was the look on Connie's face that really caught his eye. She was clearly smitten. He glanced toward Heather and saw a smile form on her lips. So, she'd seen it, too. He could hardly wait to compare notes with her.

Thomas beamed when he saw them, though his gaze seemed immediately drawn to Connie. "I see you've brought a crowd of helpers with you today." He patted Connor on the back and leaned down to kiss Heather's cheek and ruffle Mick's hair. "How's the healing process going, Heather?"

"Very slowly," she said with obvious frustration. "Though the doctor says I'm right on schedule."

"Has Connor told you how impossible he was when he broke his arm playing baseball in college?"

Heather rolled her eyes. "Believe me, I know. I was there."

Thomas looked startled for an instant, then shook his head. "Of course you were. I keep forgetting what a long way back the two of you go. Well, I hope he's treating you well."

Heather squirmed slightly. "Sure," she murmured.

"I'd be doing a lot more for her, if she'd let me," Connor said pointedly. "She's stubbornly independent."

Thomas laughed. "Well now, you'd know all about that, wouldn't you?" He glanced out over the crowd gathered on the green, his expression pleased. "I should get up there and do my thing." His gaze fell on Connie. "Have I thanked you again for organizing these events? You and Shanna are amazing."

Connie blushed. "I'm glad to help."

When Thomas trotted off to begin his speech, her gaze followed him. Connor saw Heather take note of that and smile once again.

So, he thought, it was official. There was something developing between his uncle and Connie, just as he'd suspected earlier in the summer. He wondered how long it would take one of them to act on it, or if they'd go on pretending it didn't exist.

In the meantime, though, he was grateful for the opportunity they'd presented to him. Under the guise of promoting the budding romance, he'd have the perfect excuse to get Heather to himself later this afternoon.

Heather had been fully aware of the secretive glances being exchanged by Connie and Thomas when he'd first arrived for the event. They were acting like a couple of bashful teenagers, which she found utterly charming. She was pretty sure Connor had noticed as well.

When Connie took a quick bathroom break, she glanced over at Connor. "You saw it, too, didn't you?"

"What?"

"The way those two were looking at each other— Thomas and Connie?"

He grinned. "Oh, yeah. Even Kevin thinks there's something going on, and both of them have admitted to me how they feel. I'm just not sure they're willing to admit it to each other." His gaze narrowed. "Is that why you're here? Did Connie drag you down here to assess the situation?"

Heather nodded. "Something like that. She claimed she wanted me here to keep her from doing something crazy, but I really think she wanted me to observe Thomas's behavior around her and see if she was nuts for thinking there was some kind of attraction going on."

"And?"

"Oh, yeah," she said fervently. "The man definitely has the hots for her."

"And vice versa," Connor said. "So, here's what I'm proposing. When this thing ends, let's encourage the two of them to stick around and grab lunch or something. Then you and I can bail, and you can ride home with little Mick and me."

"Count me in," she said at once, proving that she was more concerned with her friend's happiness than steering clear of him. In fact, she grinned at him. "Nice to see you have the O'Brien matchmaking gene, despite your oft-stated claim that you despise all that well-meaning interference."

"It's my uncle and Connie. It's a worthy cause," he said.

She gave him a sly look. "You do know that Connie had another motive in having me tag along today, don't you?"

"Me?" he guessed at once.

"Of course, and we've just agreed to play very nicely into her hands."

He laughed. "Does that bother you?"

She met his gaze, then sighed. "Not half as much as it probably should."

22

It was nearly two o'clock by the time they'd packed up after Thomas's speech. Connor turned to Heather.

"You ready?"

"Sure," she said at once, then told Connie. "I'm going to ride back to Chesapeake Shores with Connor and little Mick. You don't mind, do you?"

Connie looked immediately flustered by the news, so Connor stepped in. "Uncle Thomas, I know Connie never had lunch. Why don't the two of you grab a bite? It's the least you can do to pay her back for all the hours she's put in to help you out."

"He doesn't have to take me to lunch," Connie protested, her embarrassment evident in the blush that tinged her cheeks.

"But I'd enjoy it," Thomas said, though he avoided her gaze and cast a suspicious look toward his nephew.

Connor barely resisted the desire to say, "I thought you might."

Though she still looked flustered, Connie accepted the invitation. "I am starving," she admitted. "It's been a busy day, and I skipped breakfast, too."

"Then you definitely have to eat," Thomas said. He turned to Connor and Heather. "Thanks for the help today. I'll catch up with you later." The glint in his eye suggested that when he did, Connor was in for a stern talking-to.

Connor stood next to Heather and watched them go. "Worked like a charm, if I do say so myself," he said with satisfaction.

Heather didn't seem quite as impressed with the success of their plot. "It's lunch, Connor. Given how cautious those two are, it could take months before either of them admits to their feelings, much less acts on them."

He turned his gaze on her. "What about you? Are you ready to admit your feelings?"

She frowned at the question. "I've never denied my feelings."

Connor grinned. "Then how about acting on them?" he inquired hopefully.

Rather than responding, Heather glanced pointedly at little Mick. Though he looked to be asleep on a chair, there was no telling when he might awaken and overhear.

"Later," Connor said, acknowledging her concern.

Once they were in his car heading home, he glanced her way. "How about stopping for a late lunch of our own? There's a great place on the water in the next town."

"But I'm all hot and sweaty," she protested.

"It has an outdoor deck. Most people come straight off their boats. It's not fancy. And the crabcakes are excellent. Don't tell Dillon Brady I said so, but I think they're even better than his."

She nodded, though with obvious reluctance. "Okay, then."

Connor wondered when he'd become so easily satisfied

by such small victories. Still, he couldn't deny being pleased that they'd have another hour or two together. He kept hoping they could recapture their once easygoing relationship, the days when they talked for hours about everything going on in their lives.

Now he felt awkward half the time, as if he hardly knew her, much less had shared a home and a child with her. But he was sure if they got back on their old footing, it would only be a matter of time before she'd accept that his proposal was sincere.

At the bayside restaurant, he carried his still-sleeping son onto the deck and settled him in his lap. Mick stirred slightly, then woke. Seeing all the food around them, his eyes widened. "Fries," he pleaded.

"Just like me," Connor said with a laugh. "He's going to grow up to be a fast-food junkie."

"Not on my watch," Heather retorted.

"Who are you kidding?" Connor teased. "You're as addicted to fries as I am."

She laughed. "Okay, maybe just a little. But all the rest of it, no way."

When they'd placed their order, she sat back and looked around at the lively crowd, the serene tree-shaded setting, the boats lined up along the dock, and smiled. "This is nice. Thanks for suggesting it."

"I thought you'd like it. They sometimes have great music on Saturday night. We'll have to come." He kept his tone casual.

Though she looked vaguely disconcerted, she nodded. "Sure. One of these days."

He caught her gaze and held it. "Heather, do we need to start from scratch? Would that make a difference?"

"What do you mean?"

"Go on dates?"

She smiled at the suggestion. "I think we're a long way past the dating stage," she said, glancing toward little Mick.

Connor wasn't going to be put off so easily. "But maybe if we went back, started again from where I am now, you'd be able to accept that I really do want to marry you."

"Do you think my memory is that faulty?" she asked. "Am I supposed to forget how vehemently you've opposed marriage since the day we met?"

Connor regarded her with frustration. "Why can't you see that I've changed? You wear rose-colored glasses when it comes to the whole world, but you're still viewing me through that same old dark lens."

"No, I'm viewing you realistically," she argued. "Nobody changes a core belief overnight, Connor. Core beliefs run too deep. They go into the very soul of who you are."

"And that's that? There's no way to move forward?" he asked, exasperated by her refusal to give an inch. "I've quit my job handling divorces. I've moved down here to be closer to you and our son. I've bought the house you love for the three of us. What else is it going to take?"

Again, probably because she had no rational answer, she looked to their son. "This is not the time to discuss this," she said quietly.

"Will there be a time?"

He could read the sorrow in her eyes, see the confusion as she shrugged.

"I don't know, Connor. I just don't know."

What Connor couldn't figure out was how on earth he was supposed to fight for their future when she didn't seem to want to try.

After their awkward conversation on Saturday, Connor had never felt so defeated in his entire life. He'd seen the future he wanted, reached out to claim it despite all of his long-held misgivings about marriage, and lost yet again. When he wasn't drifting in a sea of despair, he had to curse the bitter irony. Maybe he should give up and accept Heather's decision, but when he floated that thought past his father, Mick was appalled.

"She said no a couple of times, after all the times you said no to her, and you're walking away?" his father asked, regarding him with disgust. "What kind of O'Brien takes no for an answer when it's something that matters?"

"I'm pretty sure she thinks it's like one of those jailhouse conversions, convenient under the circumstances."

"Is it?" Mick asked. "Did you only ask her to marry you because of the accident?"

"In a way, yes, because that's when I realized I didn't want to lose her forever," he said honestly. "In that moment, I couldn't envision my life without her. Once I saw that, it was like the knowledge had been there all along, buried under all that baggage from the past."

"Then keep telling her that until she believes you."

"I don't think she'll ever buy it," Connor told him. "It's ironic really. I did too good a job of selling her on the fact that I don't believe in marriage."

"If you sold her on that, then you can sell her on this," Mick insisted. "It might take a little longer than you'd like and it might require a little creativity, but I've seen you in action in a courtroom. You can win over anyone once you set your mind to it."

Connor still wasn't convinced. "I appreciate the vote of confidence, Dad, but I just don't know. Maybe I have to accept that it could be too late." Despite the words, though, admitting defeat grated.

"It's only too late if you let it be," Mick said impatiently. "Now stop sitting around here feeling sorry for yourself and go after the woman you love." His expression brightened. "I could kick you out of here, if that would help. You could tell her you need a place to stay."

Connor laughed, in spite of his sour mood. "Jess owns an inn. I'm pretty sure Heather would suggest I go there if I'm suddenly homeless."

"Well, I'll speak to your mother. I'm sure between the two of us, we'll be able to come up with a plan."

"Thanks for the thought, but I think I'd better handle this on my own. Sometimes the meddling O'Briens can be a bit much."

"As long as you do," Mick said direly. "Losing that woman and your son is not an option."

Yeah, no matter what he'd claimed just now, Connor had pretty much figured out that much. Obviously what he really needed was a new strategy…and not one invented by his parents.

Heather had an appointment with her orthopedic surgeon, and then, if all went well and her cast was finally removed—or at least cut down to her knee—a physical therapy session to start reconditioning her injured leg. Megan had offered to take her, so she was surprised to find Connor at her door.

"Your chauffeur awaits," he said cheerfully. "Mom's tied up."

She regarded him doubtfully. "Is that so? And you just happened to have the afternoon free?"

"Quite a lucky break, wasn't it?"

"Sure, lucky."

Accepting that spending the afternoon with Connor was inevitable, she allowed him to help her down the steps. It was still an awkward process, despite her improved agility with crutches. Once in the car, though, she fell silent.

Her mood deteriorated rapidly at the doctor's office. She'd been counting on the doctor removing her cast, so when he told her, in an abundance of caution, that he wanted it to remain for another two weeks, she left the appointment bitterly disappointed.

"I had to cancel the therapy session," she told Connor as they drove away. "You can just take me home."

"Not so fast," he protested. "You obviously need cheering up. How about a hot-fudge sundae?"

"It's going to take more than a hot-fudge sundae to cheer me up, but thanks for trying."

"Oh, the sundae's just for starters. I have more in mind," he said at once.

He stopped in front of the ice cream parlor, brought two large sundaes back to the car, then drove along the beachfront to Driftwood Cottage. "I thought you'd like to see how much progress Dad's made," he said as he parked across the street.

Heather turned to look. The exterior already looked exactly as she'd envisioned it, with bright white siding, red shutters and a sturdy new porch with a white railing and Victorian-style trim. Rockers and Adirondack chairs were already in place, as was an old-fashioned, elaborately trimmed screen door, just as beach cottages had probably had years ago.

Connor met her gaze. "Want to have your ice cream over there?"

Tears in her eyes, she immediately nodded. "Oh, Connor, it's perfect, exactly the way I imagined it would be. Can't you just see it with big pots of red geraniums out there?"

"Dad's definitely got the knack for capturing dreams and turning them into reality," he said, plucking her easily out of the car, prepared to carry her across the street. When she opened her mouth to protest, he commanded, "Don't argue. The ice cream will melt if I wait for you to make your way over there on your crutches."

"Good point," she said, smiling as he strode across the two-lane road, opened the gate and settled her into a comfortable rocker with her leg propped up on another chair.

He was back in seconds with their sundaes.

Heather dug into the rapidly melting ice cream, but she was far more captivated by the view from the porch. The bay sparkled in the late afternoon sunlight filtering through the weeping willows along the bank. She spotted a waterman checking the last of his crab pots on his way back into port.

"This is heaven," she said with a sigh. "Connor, you're going to love it here. So is little Mick when he's with you."

He opened his mouth, but she held up a hand. "Don't argue. Not just now. I really want to enjoy this moment.

It's so peaceful and calm. I love the hustle and bustle of being right downtown over the store, but this is just amazing."

"You wouldn't have thought that a couple of hours ago when Dad's crew was at work. This was a beehive of activity. He's anxious to get it finished."

"How's the inside coming?"

"The floors are solid again, and the new drywall is mostly up." He met her gaze. "You want to take a look? It's still pretty rough, but you'll get the idea of what's happening."

"I'd love to see," she said eagerly. "I'll have to take my time, though."

"Forget trying to maneuver around on your crutches," he said. "There are too many obstacles. Dad would have a fit if I let you try to walk around in there, especially without a hardhat. I'll carry you."

"Come on, Connor. There's no need for that."

"It's my way or no way," he said, his jaw set stubbornly.

Since she could see the sense of doing it his way, she agreed, even though being held close to his chest reminded her all too clearly of desires she thought she'd put behind her.

He carried her from room to room, pausing to set her on a chair in the kitchen so she could look around to her heart's content. "It's going to be fabulous, isn't it?" she asked, delighted to see her dream becoming reality. "With all these windows, there will be so much light. I can already see the breakfast nook right over there and the sink with the view of the backyard."

For all of her happiness over seeing how well Mick

had translated her random ideas into a real home, she couldn't help being saddened by the realization that she would never live here.

"Upstairs?" Connor asked, studying her closely.

She imagined seeing the master bedroom that should have been theirs and shook her head. "Not today. I should probably get home."

He looked vaguely disappointed, but nodded at once. "Sure. Whatever you want."

She lifted her gaze to his. "Thanks for bringing me, though. Tell Mick I think it's going to be amazing."

"He'll be pleased you're happy," Connor said.

Heather bit back a sigh. Happy was a far cry from what she was feeling right at this moment. It was just a house, after all. What mattered was that she was alive after a terrible accident, that she had her son and had reconnected with her mother. She had her whole future ahead of her. There would be another house, maybe even another man, though the one she truly wanted was right in front of her.

Her gaze was drawn to Connor, who was looking at her with so much love written all over his face. She could have him, could have it all, but still she held back.

And the worst of it was, even she didn't understand why.

It was the end of the day and Heather had spent the entire afternoon downstairs in the store. She hadn't been able to do much, but it had felt good to see people for a change. It had also been a revelation to see how good her mother was at interacting with the customers. She was a natural-born saleswoman, especially when it came to fabrics and quilt patterns.

"We had a good day today," Bridget announced as she closed out the register.

"I could tell," Heather said. "You're very good at making a sale. Several of those women walked out of here with a whole lot more than they'd intended to buy."

"And they'll be back for lessons," her mother said. "I signed them up for the next session."

"That's fantastic."

"I thought perhaps I could work with an advanced class and you could work with the beginners," her mother suggested tentatively. "Or vice versa. What do you think?"

Heather smiled. "Does that mean you're staying?"

Her mother nodded. "If you're sure it won't be an imposition."

"Absolutely not," Heather said. "You've certainly fit in here. You've been a huge help. And I'd love the company."

"Well, you'll have to forgo my company tonight. Nell and I are going to bingo. In fact, I'm already running late. We're meeting at Sally's first, so I'd better scoot."

Heather regarded her with alarm. "What about little Mick? I can't get him upstairs on my own."

"Oh, don't worry about that," Bridget said blithely. "Connor will be along any second." The door opened and she brightened. "There he is now. Right on time. Enjoy your evening, you two."

Heather stared after her with a frown.

"Don't blame her for conspiring behind your back," Connor said, guessing at the cause of her irritation. "Gram told me about bingo, then suggested I take you and little Mick out for dinner. Seemed like a great idea to me."

"Yet you didn't think to consult me," she said irritably, though she had to admit she was surprisingly happy to see him. These impromptu visits might be disconcerting, but a part of her clearly looked forward to them. She'd missed talking to Connor at the end of the day, missed sharing a life with him. Seeing him now was a teasing reminder of what they'd had and of what they could have again if only she could believe he truly wanted it.

Connor gave her a solicitous look. "Would you rather stay in? We could order pizza."

"Am I to assume that having dinner with you is the price I'll have to pay in order to get back upstairs?"

He grinned. "Pretty much."

"Then let's go out. I'm tired of eating in so much, even though Mom's cooking is a whole lot better than my own." She met his gaze. "She's staying on, by the way."

"I thought she might be. How do you feel about that?"

"I'm sad about what's happened with her and my dad, though not surprised. Still, it'll be good having her here, I think, especially for little Mick."

"And for your relationship with her," Connor guessed. "You seem to have mended fences."

"It's true, we have. We understand each other much better now." She gave him a wry look. "And she no longer hates your guts for leading me astray, so that's a bonus."

"One for which I'm eternally grateful, that's for sure," Connor responded.

Since Connor was making no move to leave and kept

glancing toward the door, Heather finally called him on it. "Are we going to dinner or not?"

"We are, but my mom is supposed to get little Mick and take him over to the house for dinner with her and Dad."

"Another of those decisions to which I wasn't privy?" she muttered testily.

"It's hard to have a romantic dinner with a toddler present," he said.

Heather studied him with a narrowed gaze. "You didn't say anything about a romantic dinner."

"Didn't I?" he asked innocently. "My mistake. We're going to Brady's. There'll be candlelight, wine, the whole nine yards."

"Why?"

"Because you deserve it," he said simply, looking relieved when Megan finally walked in. "Mom, great! Mick's all ready. Since he'll probably be asleep by the time we've finished dinner, he can just stay over, right? He has extra clothes in my room."

"No problem," Megan said.

Heather looked from one conspiring O'Brien to the other. "Hold on. There is no reason he can't come home and sleep in his own bed."

Connor's gaze caught hers and held. "There might be."

A tingle of anticipation shot down her spine at the less than subtle innuendo in his voice, but she couldn't allow him to run roughshod over her. "There won't be," she retorted stubbornly.

He smiled. "We'll play it by ear," he told his mother. "I'll give you a call."

Megan laughed. "Whatever works. I'll wait to hear from you. Now have a wonderful evening, you two, and don't worry about a thing. Mick bought a new toy of some kind today, so I imagine that will keep both of them occupied. I swear, I think the reason he wants all these grandkids is so he can play with all the toys."

Little Mick overheard the mention of his grandfather and ran to Megan. "G'pa Mick?"

Megan scooped him up. "Yes, he's waiting for us, sweet pea. Let's go see him."

Connor turned to Heather. "What about you? Are you ready to go?"

She thought for an instant about saying no, about insisting that he help her back upstairs, then asking him to leave, but temptation won. Romantic dinners had been few and far between in their past. Early on, there hadn't been the money for them, and later there hadn't been the time.

She lifted her gaze to Connor's and smiled. "I'm ready," she said. At least for dinner.

As for what he was so clearly planning afterward, she'd been ready for that since the day they'd met, which was how they'd wound up with little Mick in the first place. No matter how hard she'd fought to put the attraction behind her, it obviously hadn't worked.

Connor wasn't foolish enough to think that a candlelit dinner and some wine would turn the tide for his relationship with Heather, but he was hoping it would shake up the status quo. What he hadn't counted on was running into his sister Jess and Will the minute they walked in the door at Brady's. Jess's eyes lit up.

"You're on a date?" she asked.

"Not really," Heather said a little too quickly. "Why don't you join us?"

Will cast a look toward Connor, seeking a reaction. Connor sighed and shrugged. "Sure, why not?" he said with resignation. Maybe a buffer was exactly what they needed. It might keep the evening from getting more intense than Heather was ready to handle. She certainly seemed to feel the need for someone to intercede, or she wouldn't have uttered the impulsive invitation.

"Will, I think maybe we're intruding," Jess said, holding him back. "We'll all have dinner another time."

"No, really," Heather said, an unmistakable note of desperation in her voice. "It'll be fun."

Jess continued to look uncertain. "If you're sure…"

"We're sure," Connor told her.

Over crab dip and wine, Heather visibly relaxed, and Connor recognized that he'd made the right decision. She was a lot more comfortable having the other couple around. Jess, bless her, told way too many tales about his misadventures as a boy, with Will chiming in to add more. Heather laughed more than she had in a long while.

By the time they left Brady's, her cheeks were flushed and her eyes sparkling.

"That was fun," she declared when they were driving back to her place. "I'm so glad they joined us. They make a cute couple."

"Don't say that to Jess," he warned. "She claims Will drives her crazy."

"But he obviously adores her," Heather said.

Connor shrugged. "That seems to be plain to everyone except my sister."

She hesitated, met his gaze, then looked away. "Thank you for not making too much out of my insistence that they have dinner with us."

"Why did you?"

"To be honest, I think I was nervous," she admitted.

"With me?"

She nodded. "Crazy, isn't it? We know each other so well. We even have a son together, but it almost felt like a first date."

Connor smiled. "That's exactly how I wanted it to feel. It was that fresh start I mentioned to you the other day."

She gave him a skeptical look. "But you didn't have first-date plans for afterward, did you?"

He chuckled. "How'd you guess?"

"Getting rid of little Mick for the night was a pretty big clue. You forgot about my mom, though. Bingo's probably over by now."

Connor pulled into a parking place in the alley behind her apartment, then turned and met her gaze, his expression suddenly sober. "Which is why she's spending the night at Gram's."

Heather swallowed hard. "She is? She actually agreed to that?"

"It was her idea, as a matter of fact. I get the feeling she's pretty confident that she's about to get her wish for the two of us, and she wants to do whatever she can to assure it happens."

He saw the mix of emotions in Heather's eyes. Desire and yearning were there, but fear and confusion were, too.

"I don't have to stay tonight," he said softly, holding her gaze. "But I want to."

She hesitated, then whispered, "I want you to, but, Connor, it doesn't—"

He cut her off. "It doesn't have to be a guarantee of anything. I just need to show you how very much I love you."

He waited for what felt like an eternity before she nodded. "Let's go home."

They hadn't counted on just how awkward it would be to make love with a cast on Heather's leg from thigh to ankle. Though she'd gotten used to the cumbersome weight of it, the once-familiar moves and dexterity they were both used to was next to impossible. At one point, she came close to knocking Connor out when she made a sudden move with her leg. Not that any of her moves could be all that sudden, she concluded, unable to control her laughter.

Next to her, Connor fell back, his chest heaving. Though she wanted to believe he was breathless with desire, she knew he, too, was trying to stifle his own laughter.

"What was I thinking?" he murmured, pulling her next to him and holding her close.

"You? I'm the one who's been living with this cast for more than a month now. You'd think I'd have seen what a ridiculous idea this was. I'm sure we could find a way to get where we both want to go, but I have to admit I'm content just to be right here in your arms again."

"Me, too," he said. "Not that I'm not incredibly frustrated right at this moment."

"Tell me about it," she said ruefully.

He looked into her eyes, his gaze searching and hopeful. "Can I get a rain check?"

"You mean for when it's less likely I'll clobber you with my cast?"

"That would be good."

Heather sobered and looked into his eyes. "Connor, I don't know. What if we start over and it gets complicated and doesn't go anywhere? We have little Mick to think about now. I don't want him to be confused."

"We'll be careful about what we say and do around him," Connor promised her. "We'll make sure he doesn't think anything's changed unless it really has."

"What about me? I'm already confused," she admitted. She gestured at the two of them, half dressed and tangled together. "We were always good together. That was never the issue."

"I think that's the point, though," Connor said, his brow knit thoughtfully. "We always got the sex right. And we've never denied loving each other. Shouldn't those be two of the things that matter the most? We've let all the other stuff get in the way."

"All the other stuff—like you not believing in marriage?" she said wryly. "That's huge, not some petty little difference of opinion over broccoli."

"We've both always loved broccoli," he reminded her.

She gave him a chiding look. "You know what I meant."

"Of course I do. Look, the one thing I know with absolute certainty, the one thing that has never changed, is that I want to spend the rest of my life with you. That was true when we were living together. It was true after the accident, and it's true tonight. The commitment has been real practically from the day we met. With the ring and the piece of paper or without them, that will never change." He looked directly into her eyes. "You are the love of my life, Heather Donovan. I've never doubted that. Not once."

Heather heard something in his voice then that reassured her as nothing else ever had. He had the same passion, the same conviction, he had when he argued a case before a judge. And she knew better than most that he couldn't fake that kind of sincerity. If he said it, he meant it.

And, in the end, wasn't that what marriage was all about—taking a leap of faith that two people could fight for and hold on to the feelings they had in their hearts when they got engaged, on their wedding day and for all the years to come?

"Yes," she said softly, knowing in her heart that it was time to take that leap with Connor. If he, with all of his misgivings, all of his personal history, could do it, then so could she. If he could do it, lying here in her bed without the pleasure and passion of making love to cloud his judgment, then she had to believe in the two of them at least as deeply as he did.

He blinked and stared. For a moment, he looked as if he didn't dare to believe he'd heard her right. "Did you just accept my proposal?"

"Well, technically, you haven't made one, at least not recently," she said, smiling. "But yes, that's what I was doing. I was agreeing to marry you."

He stood up, gesturing at their half-dressed state. "Even after this fiasco?"

She laughed. "This wasn't a fiasco. This was what finally made me believe we would make it. If we could laugh together when we so desperately wanted to be doing something else, if you could weather my awful moods since the accident and ignore all the times I've turned you down, then what we have has to be real, just the way I always thought it was."

Connor let out a whoop and dove for the phone.

"What on earth are you doing?" she demanded.

"I never let Mom know that little Mick would be staying over," he said, then grinned when Megan apparently answered. "She said yes!" he announced.

Heather could hear Megan's delighted response, and then Mick was on the phone demanding to speak to her. Connor handed her the phone.

"It's about time, young lady," he said enthusiastically. "Welcome to the family!"

"You've made me feel like an O'Brien all along," she told him, misty-eyed by the thought of being a part of this wonderful family forever.

"Well, now it will be official. Why don't the two of you come right over here, so we can get started on the wedding plans?"

Heather smiled at the suggestion. She'd heard that Mick was never one to waste time. "Now might not be the best time," she told him, her gaze on Connor.

Apparently Connor figured out what his father wanted because he took back the phone. "Not tonight," he said pointedly. "See you tomorrow, and thanks for keeping little Mick."

He hung up and turned back to her, his expression surprisingly hesitant. "We're really going to do this? We're going to get married?"

"Unless you're already having second thoughts," she said.

He crawled back into bed beside her and wrapped her in his arms. "Not a chance. This is it for me. I want nights exactly like this for the rest of our lives." He winced, then amended, "Well, maybe not exactly like this."

She snuggled closer, regretting that they couldn't do more. "Me, too."

Connor had been right, after all. Sometimes things became clear only after you got back to basics.

Epilogue

Connor was never sure if Mick had bribed the priest or if Gram had used her powers of persuasion, but he finally agreed to perform the wedding in a far more timely manner than he'd originally insisted was possible. If it had been up to Connor, they could have skipped the whole elaborate church thing, but Bridget had her heart set on it, and, to be honest, he'd seen that Heather wanted it as well. Since he couldn't deny her anything, he'd gone along with the big production.

Now that he was standing in the front of the small church, which Bree and Gram had filled with flowers and decorated with candles, he was glad he hadn't said no. There was something solemn about the moment that made it all feel much more real. He felt hopeful, too, something he hadn't anticipated. And scared senseless, which he had definitely anticipated.

"You okay?" Kevin asked, regarding him worriedly. "You're not going to pass out or bolt, are you?"

"Not a chance," Connor said, his gaze on the back of the church.

When the music began, he watched impatiently as little Mick wobbled his way down the aisle with the rings, Davy and Henry on either side to keep him from getting distracted and taking off with them. Then came Carrie and Caitlyn, looking so grown-up and pleased with themselves in their long satin dresses. Laila and Connie were next as Heather's maids of honor. He noted that Connie's gaze kept straying to Uncle Thomas, who was seated with the ushers.

And then the music swelled and Heather was standing there in a simple, unadorned white satin dress that made her look as willowy and elegant as a model. She quite literally took his breath away, just as she'd been doing since the day they'd met.

So this was why people did this, he thought, awestruck. In a single moment, he was captivated by an image that would stay with him forever. This beautiful woman, the mother of his child, was going to be his wife.

And astonishingly, in that instant, he realized there was nothing the least bit terrifying about it. In fact, nothing had ever felt more right.

Heather had been in a daze for most of the past couple of months. Once she was finally out of the cast and back on her feet, wedding preparations had occupied every spare minute. Bridget and Megan had taken over most of them, organizing the event with the determined precision of some kind of strategic commander in the military. She had only to show up for fittings with the dressmaker and tastings with the caterers and viewings of the flower arrangements Bree had designed. Even at that, it had been a little overwhelming.

She'd fully expected Connor to bolt amid all the craziness, but he hadn't. He'd been steadfast and amazingly upbeat.

Even now, as he waited for her at the front of the church, there wasn't the slightest hint of panic in his eyes. In fact, if anyone was nervous, it was her father, who kept looking at her as if they'd just been introduced.

"I'm still trying to figure out when you went and grew up on me," he said, his eyes damp with tears. "You've turned into a beautiful young woman, Heather. And you've obviously made a good life for yourself here. Connor's a lucky man."

"Thank you," she said, blinking back her own tears. Sensitive to her mother's feelings, she'd been torn about including her father in the wedding, but her mother had been adamant. "He's your father. You should ask him, if you want him here. I'll be fine. And it's past time he met his grandson."

Still, Heather had hesitated. "I don't want you to be uncomfortable."

"I think we can get along for a day or two," her mother said. "We managed it for years."

"Have you told him yet that you're going to be staying on here?" she'd asked her.

Bridget shook her head. "I thought we could get into it after the wedding."

Heather asked one more thing of her mother before she made the call to invite him. "Do you think he'd sing at the wedding?"

"I think he'd be pleased if you asked," her mother said.

And he had been.

Now, though, Charles Donovan ran a finger around

the collar of his tuxedo shirt. "You sure you want me to sing before you say your vows?" he asked nervously. "Mostly I sing down at the pub. Folks there aren't expecting much."

She smiled at his modesty, knowing her mother wouldn't have credited him with the voice of an angel if it weren't true. "I'm a hundred percent certain," she told him.

"And that's the song you want? *When Irish Eyes Are Smiling?*"

She nodded. "With two Irish families, it seems fitting," she told him. "And if this marriage goes the way I intend it to, Connor and I will be smiling together for a very long time."

"Okay, then," her father said.

She drew on his strength as she walked down the aisle. Though she'd been out of her cast and doing physical therapy for a few weeks now, she didn't trust her leg, but looking into Connor's eyes and trusting in her father's steadiness, she practically glided to the front of the church.

Her father put her hand into Connor's, then walked to the side of the altar to stand next to the organist. When he began to sing, his voice soared through the small church. He met Heather's gaze, but then he turned to Bridget and sang the rest of the song to her. There was no question in Heather's mind that it was an entreaty, saying in words he couldn't find on his own, that he wanted to make whatever had gone wrong between them right again.

Hearing that in his voice, seeing the unmistakable love in his eyes, Heather felt doubly blessed. Not only was this her wedding day, but perhaps it would be a fresh start with a new perspective for her parents as well. It was a long shot, but today was definitely a day for dreams to come true.

Driftwood Cottage was bathed in moonlight. Heather and Connor had made the decision to spend their wedding night here, in the house that would be their home. There were still a few final touches to be completed, but Mick had called in extra men to make sure it would be mostly ready for them.

Standing on the porch, Connor looked into Heather's eyes. "We're finally home," he said quietly. "And you look more beautiful than I've ever seen you. What's the old song—something about moonlight becoming you? You look radiant."

"I feel like a bride," she said, a smile on her lips. "Thank you for giving me this moment, for giving me a day like today."

"I should have done it long ago," Connor said. "I don't know what I was thinking."

"I think most people, if they have any sense at all, are a little scared by the idea of marriage, but you had more reasons than most to be afraid."

"Maybe so, but I had you. I knew the kind of person you are. I knew what we had. This decision should have been easy."

"Well, you made it eventually, and we're here now," she said. "Are we going to go inside? I think the wedding night tradition is the one part of all this hoopla that might appeal to you the most."

Connor laughed. "No question about it," he said, inserting the key into the lock and opening the door. He scooped her up and carried her across the threshold, then kicked the door closed behind them. Then, without hesitation, he carried her up the steps and into the master suite.

He'd left the wedding night decor of the room to his sister. Jess had a real romantic streak, and, thanks to the honeymoon suite at her inn, she was an old hand at getting all the touches just right.

Sure enough, there were white rose petals scattered across the bed, which was covered with one of Heather's quilts—a wedding ring pattern, if he wasn't mistaken. A bottle of champagne was chilling in a bucket on a tray with two crystal flutes. There was even a tray of hors d'oeuvres, including chocolate-dipped strawberries. Every surface held an array of candles just waiting to be lit. The cooperative moon spilled its silvery light through the windows.

Heather's eyes sparkled as she looked around. "Connor, it's absolutely beautiful."

"Are you glad you waited to see it?" he asked.

She nodded. "You got every detail exactly right."

"You can thank Jess for all the little wedding night touches."

"I'll definitely do that." She glanced around. "Do you suppose she put my negligee in here?"

Connor grinned. "You won't need it for long, but I believe it's in the bathroom. Why don't we have a glass of champagne first?"

Her gaze held his. "Why don't we?" she agreed in a breathless whisper.

He poured the champagne, then led the way to a loveseat tucked into the nook of the room's large bay window.

When they were seated, he looked into her eyes and saw his soul reflected there.

"We're going to be happy here. I promise you that. I will do everything in my power to make sure you never regret marrying me."

"That's the promise I should be making," she told him. "We're going to make this work, Connor. We're going to beat every depressing divorce statistic and be married for fifty years."

"Longer," he corrected at once. "It's taken me a while to get there, but I do believe that."

And when he leaned in to kiss his bride on this night that would be the start of their journey, he knew with every fiber of his being that they would make it a good one.

* * * * *

Look for MOONLIGHT COVE by Sherryl Woods, the next story in her CHESAPEAKE SHORES series on sale from MIRA Books in May 2011 at your favorite retail outlet.

DISCUSSION GUIDE

1. Connor's distaste for marriage is deeply rooted in his parents' divorce and has been reinforced by his career as an attorney handling bitterly contested divorces. Have you ever known someone whose past experiences have shaped their attitude toward love and marriage? Were they able to overcome the past to find happiness?

2. Connor eventually leaves his Baltimore law firm and returns home to Chesapeake Shores to practice a different kind of law. Why do you think he reached that decision? Who do you think was most responsible for leading him to make the choice to change the direction of his career? Have you ever influenced a friend or spouse's decision to change careers? Under what circumstances?

3. When Connor ultimately recognizes that he can't imagine a life without Heather, she doesn't believe his sudden turnaround. Do you think it's possible to take a fresh look at core values and change so dramatically? Have you ever done so? Why?

4. As Megan O'Brien had felt when leaving Mick, Heather felt she had to leave Connor in order to have the kind of future and family she truly wanted. Megan has admitted that she made such a drastic choice in the hope of getting Mick's attention. The ploy failed. Do you think Heather left for the same

reason? Or was she truly determined to move on to make a new life for herself and her son?

5. Heather had very mixed feelings about being welcomed so warmly into the O'Brien family. She wanted that experience for her son, but it was very difficult for her knowing that she wasn't truly a part of the family and never would be. Have you ever felt that you lost not only a spouse, but a family as well, in a divorce or at the end of a relationship? Were you somehow able to maintain those ties? If so, how did you do it?

6. What role do you think Heather's religious beliefs might have played in her dissatisfaction with her untraditional relationship with Connor? Were those beliefs more important to her mother or to her?

7. Bridget Donovan stayed in her own marriage for years because of her religious beliefs. Do you know anyone who's done that? Or who's stayed for the sake of their children? How difficult has it been? Was it for the best? Or would divorce have been preferable? Why?

8. Connor makes the grand gesture of buying Driftwood Cottage to show Heather how committed he is to their future. Have you ever known anyone who's made a grand gesture to win someone's heart? What did they do?

9. When Connor and Heather try to make love, they find it next to impossible with the cast on her leg

hampering her mobility in bed. In many ways, that moment, when they can laugh at themselves in such an intimate situation, is a turning point in their relationship. How important do you think laughter is in a relationship? Can it bring you closer?

10. It appears likely that there's a budding romance between Mick O'Brien's younger brother, Thomas, and Connie Collins, whose brother is married to Bree O'Brien. How do you think the family is likely to react? Has anyone in your family ever gotten involved with a family friend or in-law? Has it caused problems? What kind?

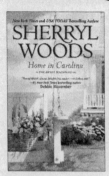
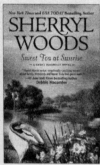

REQUEST YOUR FREE BOOKS!

2 FREE NOVELS
FROM THE ROMANCE COLLECTION
PLUS 2 FREE GIFTS!

YES! Please send me 2 FREE novels from the Romance Collection and my 2 FREE gifts (gifts are worth about $10). After receiving them, if I don't wish to receive any more books, I can return the shipping statement marked "cancel." If I don't cancel, I will receive 4 brand-new novels every month and be billed just $5.74 per book in the U.S. or $6.24 per book in Canada. That's a saving of at least 28% off the cover price. It's quite a bargain! Shipping and handling is just 50¢ per book in the U.S. and 75¢ per book in Canada.* I understand that accepting the 2 free books and gifts places me under no obligation to buy anything. I can always return a shipment and cancel at any time. Even if I never buy another book, the two free books and gifts are mine to keep forever.

194/394 MDN FDC5

Name _____ (PLEASE PRINT)

Address _____ Apt. #

City _____ State/Prov. _____ Zip/Postal Code

Signature (if under 18, a parent or guardian must sign)

Mail to the **Reader Service:**
IN U.S.A.: P.O. Box 1867, Buffalo, NY 14240-1867
IN CANADA: P.O. Box 609, Fort Erie, Ontario L2A 5X3

Not valid for current subscribers to the Romance Collection
or the Romance/Suspense Collection.

**Want to try two free books from another line?
Call 1-800-873-8635 or visit www.ReaderService.com.**

* Terms and prices subject to change without notice. Prices do not include applicable taxes. Sales tax applicable in N.Y. Canadian residents will be charged applicable taxes. Offer not valid in Quebec. This offer is limited to one order per household. All orders subject to credit approval. Credit or debit balances in a customer's account(s) may be offset by any other outstanding balance owed by or to the customer. Please allow 4 to 6 weeks for delivery. Offer available while quantities last.

Your Privacy—The Reader Service is committed to protecting your privacy. Our Privacy Policy is available online at www.ReaderService.com or upon request from the Reader Service.

We make a portion of our mailing list available to reputable third parties that offer products we believe may interest you. If you prefer that we not exchange your name with third parties, or if you wish to clarify or modify your communication preferences, please visit us at www.ReaderService.com/consumerschoice or write to us at Reader Service Preference Service, P.O. Box 9062, Buffalo, NY 14269. Include your complete name and address.

MROM11

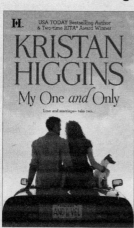

SHERRYL WOODS

32977	ASK ANYONE	___	$7.99 U.S.	___	$9.99 CAN.
32976	ALONG CAME TROUBLE	___	$7.99 U.S.	___	$9.99 CAN.
32975	ABOUT THAT MAN	___	$7.99 U.S.	___	$9.99 CAN.
32962	WELCOME TO SERENITY	___	$7.99 U.S.	___	$9.99 CAN.
32961	SEAVIEW INN	___	$7.99 U.S.	___	$9.99 CAN.
32927	THE BACKUP PLAN	___	$7.99 U.S.	___	$9.99 CAN.
32895	MENDING FENCES	___	$7.99 U.S.	___	$9.99 CAN.
32893	FEELS LIKE FAMILY	___	$7.99 U.S.	___	$9.99 CAN.
32887	STEALING HOME	___	$7.99 U.S.	___	$9.99 CAN.
32852	A CHESAPEAKE SHORES CHRISTMAS	___	$16.95 U.S.	___	$19.95 CAN.
32845	SWEET TEA AT SUNRISE	___	$7.99 U.S.	___	$9.99 CAN.
32814	RETURN TO ROSE COTTAGE	___	$7.99 U.S.	___	$9.99 CAN.
32756	HOME IN CAROLINA	___	$7.99 U.S.	___	$9.99 CAN.
32753	AMAZING GRACIE	___	$7.99 U.S.	___	$9.99 CAN.
32751	HOME AT ROSE COTTAGE	___	$7.99 U.S.	___	$9.99 CAN.
32641	HARBOR LIGHTS	___	$7.99 U.S.	___	$8.99 CAN.
32634	FLOWERS ON MAIN	___	$7.99 U.S.	___	$8.99 CAN.
32626	THE INN AT EAGLE POINT	___	$7.99 U.S.	___	$7.99 CAN.

(limited quantities available)

TOTAL AMOUNT	$	_____
POSTAGE & HANDLING	$	_____
($1.00 for 1 book, 50¢ for each additional)		
APPLICABLE TAXES*	$	_____
TOTAL PAYABLE	$	_____

(check or money order—please do not send cash)

To order, complete this form and send it, along with a check or money order for the total above, payable to MIRA Books, to: **In the U.S.:** 3010 Walden Avenue, P.O. Box 9077, Buffalo, NY 14269-9077; **In Canada:** P.O. Box 636, Fort Erie, Ontario, L2A 5X3.

Name: _____
Address: _____ City: _____
State/Prov.: _____ Zip/Postal Code: _____
Account Number (if applicable): _____

075 CSAS

*New York residents remit applicable sales taxes.
*Canadian residents remit applicable GST and provincial taxes.

MIRA®

www.MIRABooks.com

MSW0411BL